A
FRONTIER
CHRISTMAS

A
FRONTIER
CHRISTMAS

WILLIAM W. JOHNSTONE
with J. A. Johnstone

PINNACLE BOOKS
Kensington Publishing Corp.
www.kensingtonbooks.com

PINNACLE BOOKS are published by

Kensington Publishing Corp.
119 West 40th Street
New York, NY 10018

PUBLISHER's NOTE
Following the death of William W. Johnstone, the Johnstone family is working with a carefully selected writer to organize and complete Mr. Johnstone's outlines and many unfinished manuscripts to create additional novels in all of his series like The Last Gunfighter, Mountain Man, and Eagles, among others. This novel was inspired by Mr. Johnstone's superb storytelling.

All Kensington titles, imprints, and distributed lines are available at special quantity discounts for bulk purchases for sales promotions, premiums, fund-raising, educational, or institutional use. Special book excerpts or customized printings can also be created to fit specific needs. For details, write or phone the office of the Kensington special sales manager: Kensington Publishing Corp., 119 West 40th Street, New York, NY 10018, attn: Special Sales Department; phone 1-800-221-2647.

PINNACLE BOOKS, the Pinnacle logo, and the WWJ steer head logo are Reg. U.S. Pat. & TM Off.

ISBN-13: 978-0-7860-3360-7
ISBN-10: 0-7860-3360-6

First printing: November 2014

10 9 8 7 6 5 4 3 2 1

Printed in the United States of America

First electronic edition: November 2014

ISBN-13: 978-0-7860-3361-4
ISBN-10: 0-7860-3361-4

CHAPTER ONE

Greeley, Colorado

Ralph Walters stood on the depot platform, waiting for the train. He had a long trip in front of him—to Cheyenne by rail, then by stagecoach up to Rawhide Buttes, Wyoming. He was a traveling troubadour, someone who could play the guitar, banjo, fiddle, harmonica, and drum. In one of his acts, he would pass himself off as a one-man band, and play the banjo, harmonica, and drum all at the same time. He was also a skilled magician.

Because entertainment was rare and much appreciated, especially in the small towns, he did a good business.

He was going to Rawhide Buttes to perform for a firemen's benefit show, and for the students in the Rawhide School. Schools didn't pay as much as some of the more adult venues, but he could almost always schedule a school in conjunction with his adult show, and that's what he had done in Rawhide Buttes.

He'd skipped breakfast and lunch because he wasn't

hungry. It was probably a pretty good thing that he still wasn't very hungry. He had awakened with a sore throat and wasn't sure he would be able to swallow, anyway. Reaching up, he wrapped his hand around his throat and thought he felt some swelling there.

"Here she comes!" somebody shouted, and several people moved closer to the track.

Walters remained in place as the big engine came roaring into the station with steam gushing from the drive cylinders and glowing coals dripping from the fire-box. The engineer was leaning on the windowsill of the cab, his jutting chin and hooked nose looking as if they were about to join. Brakes were applied, and the train came to a halt. It sat there with wisps of steam wreathing the drive wheels, the journals and gearboxes popping and snapping as they cooled.

"Board!" the conductor shouted.

Those who were about to make the trip rushed to climb onto the train.

This was old hat to Walters, who had made hundreds of trips on trains as he went from town to town.

The conductor recognized him, and smiled. "Hello, Mr. Walters, riding with us again, I see."

"Yes, but only as far as Cheyenne. There I must take a coach."

"Welcome aboard. I see that your regular seat hasn't been taken."

"Good, thank you." Walters moved down the aisle to the last seat on the left.

With a series of starts and jerks, the train resumed its journey a moment later.

Walters leaned his head back against the seat. He believed he might also be getting a fever.

Sugarloaf Ranch, Colorado

When Smoke Jensen came back from town he had a letter from his friend Duff MacCallister. "Sally, I heard from Duff." Smoke reached for a hot bear claw.

"Don't eat more than one. I'm doing this for the boys in the bunkhouse. What does Duff have to say?"

"I don't know I haven't opened it yet. I thought we would read it together."

Sally smiled. "That was nice of you." She put another tray of dough puffs into the oven.

"How many of those things are you making?"

"We have eight hands spending the entire winter with us, and you know very well that Cal and Pearlie could eat this entire tray by themselves."

Smoke chuckled. "I guess you're right." He opened the envelope and began to read, silently.

"Well, what does he say?"

"He has invited us to come to Chugwater to spend Christmas with him."

"Christmas in Chugwater? That's very nice of him. I wonder why he invited us, though. You would think he would have invited someone like Falcon, or one of the other MacCallisters."

Smoke nodded in agreement. "But he not only invited

us, he invited Matt, too, since he's here to spend the holidays with us."

"Well, be gentle when you turn Duff down. The poor man is so far away from his ancestral home, I'm sure that Christmas is a difficult time for him."

Smoke's eyebrows rose. "Why would I turn him down? I'm the one who hinted that we would be receptive to an invitation in the first place."

"What? Smoke, I thought we were going to New York for Christmas."

"Whatever gave you that idea?"

Sally frowned. "Didn't we make that decision this past summer?"

"You said it had been a long time since you were in New York, and you'd like to go back for a visit sometime. That's not making a decision, that's talking about it. Besides, Matt and I have to be at Fort Russell, Wyoming, in December to sell our horses, so it just seems natural that, since we are going to be up there, anyway, that we drop in on Duff."

"But, Smoke—"

"And didn't you just say that you thought Christmas might be a difficult time for him? Where is your compassion?"

Sally laughed. "I hate it when we are arguing and you use my own words on me."

"Were we just arguing?"

"Of a sort, I suppose."

Smoke smiled then reached for her. "Good. The best part of arguing is making up," he said, pulling her to him.

Big Rock, Colorado

At the moment, Matt Jensen was in Longmont's Saloon, watching a three-card game that Louis Longmont was playing with a traveling gambler named Sherman who had not given a first name.

He had been having an inordinate run of luck since he came to town, so much luck that Longmont was convinced Sherman was helping his odds with a little card manipulation.

Sherman didn't know that Longmont wasn't just a saloon owner. He was also an exceptionally skilled gambler. Practically a magician with cards.

The game they were playing was a simple game, not too unlike the game of finding the pea under the shell. In this case, Sherman had to find the ace after watching Longmont shift the cards around in front of him. Sherman had tried his luck three times, and every time he had lost.

Another patron engaged the saloon owner in conversation. It wasn't idle conversation. It was a setup. The patron was a secret partner, sometimes letting Sherman know by coded signals what cards the mark was holding. In this case, his only purpose was to divert Longmont's attention.

With his opponent's attention shifted, Sherman reached across the table and put a small, barely noticeable, crease on one corner of the ace. Longmont could switch the cards around any way he wanted. Sherman wouldn't even attempt to follow him. He would simply select the card with the creased corner.

"You going to play cards, or are you going to talk all day?" Sherman asked.

Longmont turned back to the table. "Why, I'm going to play cards, Mr. Sherman," Longmont said, smiling easily.

"Only, this time, let's bet some real money," Sherman suggested. He put ten twenty-dollar gold pieces on the table.

"That's a pretty steep bet for a little friendly game like this, isn't it?"

"You own the saloon. Surely you can afford it."

Longmont smiled. "Oh, I can afford it."

As he put his own money on the table matching the bet, Sherman took one last look at the creased card. So far, Longmont hadn't noticed it. How could he? It was so subtle a crease that it was barely discernible, even to Sherman, and he was the one who put it there.

Longmont picked up the three cards and began shuffling them around. Sherman looked over at his partner and nodded. Longmont put the cards down on the table, then began moving them around, in and out, over and under with such lightning speed that the cards were nearly a blur. When he stopped, the three cards lay in front of him, waiting for Sherman to pick the ace.

Smiling confidently, Sherman reached across the table to make his selection . . . then suddenly froze in mid-motion. The smile left his face. His hand hung suspended over the table as he stared at the three cards with a sickly expression on his face.

"Hard to pick out the ace when they all look alike, isn't it, *mon ami*?" Longmont asked.

"Yeah," Sherman said with a weak response. He had been had. Somehow Longmont had not only picked up on the card with the tiny crease, he had duplicated that crease on the other two cards, doing it so perfectly that Sherman had no idea which was the one he had marked.

"Are you going to pick a card or not?"

Sherman turned up a card. It was a queen. "Damn!"

"Maybe this isn't your game," Longmont suggested as he pulled back the money from the center of the table.

"I don't believe the ace is even on the table."

"Oh, it's on the table, all right." Longmont reached for one of the cards.

"Wait a minute. I'll turn it over," Sherman said. "For all I know you have an ace palmed. You can make it appear anywhere you want."

"All right. You turn it over."

Sherman reached for the card Longmont had started for and flipped it over. It was the ace. "Damn," he said again.

"Actually, I can make an ace appear anywhere I want." Longmont picked up a new deck of cards, shuffled them, then spread them all out, facedown, on the table. "Here's the ace of diamonds," he said, turning it up. "The ace of clubs, the ace of hearts, and the ace of spades."

"What? How the hell did you do that?"

"Here are the four kings," Longmont added, pulling them from the spread-out deck. "Here are the queens, and here are the jacks."

"I . . ."

"You have run into someone who was not only able to catch you, but is a hell of a lot better at it than you," Matt said.

The others gathered around the table to watch laughed.

"I tell you what, Mr. Sherman," Longmont said, sliding ten of the twenty-dollar gold pieces back across the table. "Take your money, but leave my saloon and don't come back. When my customers play cards in here, they have a right to expect an honest game."

Sherman stared at the money for a moment, then he reached for it. "A man has to make a living."

"Yes, and most of my customers do that by the sweat of their brow, not by sitting at a table, cheating others."

Sherman nodded.

"And take your partner with you," Longmont added, looking at the man who had attempted to divert his attention earlier. "You can have one last drink, then both of you go."

"Thanks anyway, but we aren't thirsty." With a glance toward his partner, Sherman started toward the door.

"Oh, and *Joyeux Noël*," Longmont called as the two men left.

CHAPTER TWO

Chugwater, Wyoming

When Duff MacCallister rode into town, he was curious at the number of people gathered in the street in front of Fiddlers' Green Saloon. Dismounting, he tied off his horse Sky, then called out to Fred Matthews.

"What's going on, Fred? Why all the people?"

"There's a man standing in front of the apothecary, holding a gun to Damon White's head. He's demanding that a thousand dollars be brought to him within an hour, or he's goin' to kill our druggist."

"At the apothecary, you say?"

"Yes."

"Where is Marshal Craig?"

"He has gone to Cheyenne. He left Johnny Baldwin in charge."

Duff pulled his pistol and stepped out into the street.

"Duff, where are you going?"

"Well, we cannae be losing our druggist now, can we?

And I'm afraid that Mr. Baldwin is too old to have to deal with something like this. I'll be going to talk to the gentlemen who's holding Mr. White. I'll be asking him, nicely, to abandon this project."

"With a gun in your hand?"

"Aye. 'Tis no secret, Fred, that I'm not one of those men who has the talent to quickly extract my firearm. If any shooting is to be done, I'd best have the gun in my hand before it starts."

"I would try and talk you out of it, but I can see that you have already made up your mind."

"Aye, 'tis something I feel I must do."

Holding his pistol down by his side, Duff started toward the apothecary at the far end of the street. As he got closer, he could hear the gunman shouting.

"Bring me the money! One thousand dollars! Bring me the money or this man dies! One thousand dollars!"

All the stores immediately around the apothecary had emptied. No one was on the street close to the gunman and Damon White.

"Bring me the money!" The gunman continued to shout from the wooden porch that extended from the front of the drugstore. He was about to shout something again, when he saw Duff walking toward him. "Who are you? What are you doing here?"

"The name is MacCallister, lad. Duff MacCallister. I'm here because 'tis needin' a bit of cough syrup I am, so I'd be grateful if you'd let the druggist go."

The gunman kept the gun pointed at White's head. "That'll cost you a thousand dollars."

"A thousand dollars, you say." Duff shook his head. "*Och*, isn't that a mite dear, for a wee bit of cough syrup?"

"No. I mean, I'm not going to let this man go until I get a thousand dollars."

"From who?"

"What?"

"Who is it that you expect to give you a thousand dollars?"

"I don't care. Are you dumb? Can't you see I'm holding a gun to this man's head?"

"Aye, that I can see." Duff continued walking until he was at the bottom step.

"You've come far enough. Stop, right there, right now!" the gunman called down to Duff.

"I'll nae be doing that. I told you, 'tis a bit of cough syrup I'm needing."

"If you don't stop right where you are, I'm going to shoot this man."

Duff raised his pistol and pointed it straight at the gunman's head. He was so close that they were separated by less than ten feet. "If you shoot him, I'll shoot you."

"Don't you understand? I'm going to shoot him, if you don't drop that gun!"

"Oh, I'm nae goin' to drop the gun, lad. I'll be needing it, you see, so I can shoot you after you shoot Mr. White." Duff pulled the hammer back and the pistol made a deadly, double clicking sound as the sear was engaged.

For a long moment the two men stood there, a macabre

tableau, Duff holding his pistol pointed directly at the gunman, while the gunman held his pistol to Damon White's head.

The gunman began to sweat, even though the weather was cold. The pupils of his eyes grew large.

"Tell me, lad, don't you think 'tis a bit cold out here?" Duff asked.

The gunman didn't reply.

"If you drop the gun, I can take you down to the jailhouse. I know that they keep the jail warm. Deputy Baldwin is an old man, and old men get cold awfully easily. You could be lying on a bunk in the cell, warm and waiting for your supper.

"Or, we can just carry this out, and you'll wind up in a place a lot warmer than the jail. I'm sure you know what I mean."

The gunman began to shake, then he took the gun away from the druggist's head and pointed it toward the porch. Damon White moved away quickly.

Duff didn't move. "Drop the gun, lad. Drop it, and this whole business will be over."

"You're crazy," the gunman said. "Walking up on me like that. You're crazy."

"Aye, so I've been told."

The man was still holding the pistol in his hand, though the barrel was pointing straight down.

"I'll nae be telling you again to drop the gun."

The gunman opened his hand, and the gun fell to the porch with a loud thump.

"Mr. White, you have a telephone in your establishment, I believe?" Duff asked.

"Y-yes," White said, relief from fear visible on his face.

"Would ye be so kind as to call the marshal's office 'n ask Deputy Baldwin if he would come collect his prisoner?"

"I'd be glad to. And the cough medicine is on the house."

Duff smiled. "'Tis a funny thing. I no longer feel the need for the elixir."

When Duff returned to where he had left his horse, several people applauded him.

"Come into the saloon, Duff, and I'll buy you a drink," someone said.

"I thank you for the offer, Mr. Miller, but I must step into this shop for a few moments," Duff replied, nodding toward the building next door to the saloon. A sign on the front of the building read MEAGAN'S DRESS EMPORIUM.

A bell on the door jingled as Duff stepped inside.

"I'll be with you in a moment," a woman's voice called from the back of the room.

Stepping toward the sound of the voice, Duff saw Meagan Parker on her knees, pinning up the skirt on a dress being worn by Martha Guthrie, wife of the mayor of Chugwater.

"Mrs. Guthrie, 'tis a beautiful picture you make in

that dress. You'll be warming R.W.'s heart, and that's for sure.

Martha, who was a short and rather rotund woman, blushed and giggled at the compliment. "Oh, do you think so?"

"That's exactly what I've been telling her," Meagan said, standing up.

"I'm buying the dress for a Christmas party we'll be giving John, his wife, and our grandchildren," Martha said. "They're coming to town for Christmas."

"Oh, and what a joyous event that will be. I'll have to stop by to say hello," Duff replied.

"Please do."

"All right, Mrs. Guthrie, if you'll go back there and take off the dress, I'll have it finished for you in plenty of time," Meagan said.

"Thank you, dear." Martha took one more look at herself in the mirror. "You do such beautiful work."

Meagan waited until Martha disappeared into the back room, then she kissed Duff. "What brings you here, today?"

"Smoke, Sally, and Matt will be coming to Sky Meadow. I want you to come out for dinner Wednesday night while they are here."

"I'd be glad to." Meagan frowned. "Didn't I see several people gathered in front of the Fiddlers' a few minutes ago? What was that all about, do you know?"

"Aye, 'twas a small disturbance down at the apothecary is all. 'Tis over now."

She examined Duff with a quizzical smile. "Why is it that I think it might have been more than that, and that you had something to do with it?"

"Because you are a woman with a very suspicious heart," Duff said.

"You are aware, are you not, Duff, that there is to be a dance on Christmas Eve?"

"And are you asking me to the dance?" Duff replied with a teasing smile.

"No, you are supposed to ask me."

"Oh. Well then, lass, would you be so kind as to attend the dance with me?"

"Let me think about it," Meagan replied. Then, with a wide smile she continued. "All right, I suppose I can." She was about to kiss Duff again, but at that moment, Martha Guthrie reappeared.

"I left the dress on the table," she said. "How soon will it be ready? I also want to wear it for R.W.'s Christmas dinner for the businessmen of the town."

"Oh, you can pick it up tomorrow," Meagan said.

"Wonderful. Thank you. Mr. MacCallister, please do drop by when John and his family are in town. I know they would love to see you."

"I'll do that," Duff promised.

As soon as Martha left, Duff turned back to Meagan. "I believe you were about to kiss me?"

"I will, but then you must go. I have work to do and, for some reason, I find you distracting."

They kissed again, then Duff turned to leave. "I'll see you at dinner when Smoke and the others arrive."

Elmer Gleason, Duff's foreman, had a most interesting background. He had been a guerilla with Quantrill during the war; had ridden some with Jesse and Frank James after the war; had lived with the Indians for a while, taking an Indian wife; and had gone to sea as an able-bodied seaman, sailing all over the Pacific.

In a way, one could say that Duff had inherited him with the ranch, because when Duff came to develop the land he had filed upon, Elmer was already there.

"They say the place is hainted," R.W. Guthrie had told Duff when he'd first arrived in the territory. He was talking about Little Horse Mine, a worked-out and abandoned gold mine that was on the land Duff had just taken title to.

"Course, I ain't sayin' that I believe in haints, mind you. But that is what they say. Some say it wasn't the Spanish, but injuns, that first found the gold, and they was all kilt off by white men who wanted the gold for themselves. What happened was, after the injuns was all kilt, they became ghosts, and now they haint the mine and kill any white man who comes around tryin' to find the gold. Now, mind, I don't believe none of that. I'm just tellin' you what folks say about it."

As it turned out, the haint Guthrie was speaking of was Elmer Gleason.

Elmer had located a new vein of gold in the mine, and unable to capitalize on it, was living a hand-to-mouth existence in the mine, unshaved and dressed only in skins.

Duff discovered him in the mine, which was on the property Duff had just filed upon. Everything Elmer had taken from it actually belonged to Duff, giving him every right to drive Elmer off, but he didn't. He offered Elmer a one-half partnership in the mine. That partnership had paid off handsomely for both of them.

Elmer had been with Duff from the beginning and was now Duff's foreman and closest friend.

Duff's half of the proceeds from the mine had built Sky Meadow into one of the most productive ranches in Wyoming. His operation was large enough to employ fourteen men.

When Duff returned to the ranch, Elmer was talking to the three other cowboys who had been with him for a very long time. Al Woodward, Case Goodrich, and Brax Walker not only worked for him, but were extremely loyal and top hands, occupying positions of responsibility.

"Get the men out to bust up the ice so's the cows can get to water," Elmer was telling them. "And you'd better send a couple men out to check if any of the beeves have wandered off."

The three men nodded in acquiescence, spoke to Duff a minute, then left to attend to their duties.

"Anything interesting happen in town?" Elmer asked.

"I invited Meagan to come to dinner when Smoke and the others are here."

"Uh-huh. And you talked some feller outta shootin' Damon White, too, is what I heered."

"Where did you hear that?"

"I sent Dooley into town to get some things, and he told me about it when he got back."

"There wasn't much to it," Duff said. "Are you goin' to ask your friend Vi to come to dinner?"

"You mean you don't mind?"

"Why should I mind?"

Elmer smiled. "Well, then, if you don't mind, I'll ride on into town and take care of that."

Duff nodded, then rode on to the barn to get his horse out of the cold.

CHAPTER THREE

Cheyenne, Wyoming

The train had arrived at six o'clock in the morning and the engine sat on the tracks with the boiler making bubbling sounds as the fireman kept up the steam pressure. Smoke, Sally, and Matt stood in the predawn darkness illuminated by the electric lamps that sprouted in profusion all around the depot platform.

The door of the special stock car that Smoke had leased for the trip was opened and a ramp was placed against it. Three horses were led out. As they saw Smoke and the others, they nodded in recognition and apparent relief that they were back among familiar people.

"How long is it going to take us to get there?" Sally asked.

"Five easy hours," Smoke replied. "We'll find some-place to have breakfast, and we won't leave until around nine. That should put us there by two o'clock this afternoon."

Rawhide Buttes, Wyoming

Eighth grade was as high as the school went in Rawhide Buttes. Students who wished to attend high school had to go by boat, seven miles up the Platte River to Hartville. Ralph Walters had given his show at the firemen's benefit, and followed that by performing for all eight grades of the Rawhide Buttes School.

"I apologize for my voice," Walters said to Miss Pauline Foley after the performance.

Miss Foley, the principal of the school, was in her early fifties, about the same age as Walters, and unmarried because the school board required that of its teachers. She reached up to touch her hair and primped a bit. "Why, you have a beautiful voice. The huskiness just added to it. How much longer will you be in town?"

"I don't have another show to do until the seventeenth, and that's in La Bonte," Walters said. "Because I'm feeling a bit under the weather, I may stay here in the hotel and rest for a bit."

"The school board will be having a dinner for the teachers and the parents of all the children on Monday, the eighth. Because the children so enjoyed your visit, I would like to invite you to come as my . . . that is, as guest of the school."

"I appreciate the invitation, Miss Foley . . ."

"Pauline."

"Pauline," Walters repeated. "If I get to feeling any better, I certainly will come."

Leaving the school, he walked four blocks to the Rocky Mountain Hotel, then went up to his room and laid down on the bed. He was feverish, he had a sore throat, and it was becoming increasingly more difficult for him to breathe. He wondered if he should see a doctor.

Sky Meadow Ranch, Wyoming

There was a roaring fire in the fireplace, and the parlor of Duff's house was filled with convivial people. Duff was hosting not only Smoke, Sally, and Matt, but he had invited Meagan Parker, Biff and Rose Johnson, Fred and Bonnie Matthews, and R.W. and Martha Guthrie. Elmer was at the dinner as well, and he had invited Violet Winslow. Known mostly as Vi, she owned Vi's Pies.

"Oh, you should see the beautiful dress Meagan made for me," Martha said to Sally.

"She wanted to wear it tonight," R.W. said, "but I said no. She's going to wear it for the first time at my dinner."

"And that's where you should wear it first," Meagan said.

"Oh, pooh. You're no help," Martha said with a chuckle.

R.W. turned to Smoke. "Mr. Jensen, how long will the three of you be here?"

"We'll be here for Christmas."

"Good! Then you must come to the Christmas dinner I'm giving for the town. It will be next Wednesday."

"I appreciate the offer, Mayor, but we'll be in Fort Russell then," Smoke replied.

"Oh? I thought you were going to spend Christmas with Duff."

"We have to take care of some business at Fort Russell first, but we'll be back here in time to celebrate a Scottish Christmas." Smoke looked over at Duff. "Just how do the Scots celebrate Christmas, anyway?"

"'Tis pretty much like the Christmases you celebrate, I'm thinking. But we'll be having Scottish dishes, such as Twelfth Night Cake," Duff replied.

"And what would be a Twelfth Night Cake?" Matt asked.

"I can tell you," Meagan said. "I got the recipe from a book, and Vi and I made one for practice. It is a very rich fruitcake, almost solid with fruit, almonds, and spices. The ingredients are bound together with plenty of whiskey, then all that is put into a cake tin lined with a rich short pastry and baked."

"It sounds . . . interesting. Sally, maybe you can make some bear claws to sort of go along with it," Matt suggested.

"Nonsense," Sally said. "I'm not going to invade Mrs. Sterling's kitchen."

"I'm sure she would welcome you, Sally," Duff said. "She has no problem with Meagan making the Twelfth Night Cake. Besides, I've had some of your bear claws, and I think they would make a most welcome Christmas addition."

"When are you going to Fort Russell?" Meagan asked.

"We have to be there next Monday," Smoke replied.

"Good. Just so you don't leave before Friday evening. Duff will be playing his pipes in the Christmas concert on that night, and I know he wants to show off for you." Meagan smiled.

"That's not the case, Meagan," Duff complained.

"And weren't you for telling me just the other day that you were thinking that not neither Smoke, nor Sally, nor Matt had ever heard you play, and you'd like to play for them? Or was it a bit tipsy you were, when you were saying such?" Meagan's question almost perfectly imitated Duff's Scottish brogue.

"Sure lass, 'n would you be funnin' with m' accent now?" Duff replied.

The others laughed at their banter.

"We hadn't planned to leave before Saturday anyway, and I would be most pleased to hear you play the bagpipe," Matt said.

"Och, mon. 'Tis nae the bagpipe, 'tis the *pipes*," Duff said.

"All right, the pipes, then. I'll be glad to hear you play them."

"I would love to hear you play them as well," Sally said.

"Before you folks get all excited about this, let me ask you something. Have any of you ever heard the pipes?" Elmer asked.

"No, I can't say that I have. What do they sound like?" Smoke asked.

"You ain't never heard such caterwaulin'. 'Bout the

closest thing I can get to tellin' you what it sounds like, is the cryin' a heifer makes when she gets her legs all hung up in barbed wire."

"Oh?" Duff said, lifting his eyebrow as he stared at Elmer.

"Oh, but it's a real purty caterwaulin'," Elmer said quickly, trying to cover the damage.

Again the others laughed, and they were still laughing as Jarvis Sterling stepped into the parlor. He was a recent émigré from England, and Duff had hired him as his "gentleman's gentleman." Jarvis's wife Angela was Duff's cook. Together, Mr. and Mrs. Sterling ran the house for him.

"Captain MacCallister, Mrs. Sterling wishes me to announce that dinner can now be served to you and your guests."

"Thank you, Jarvis. Meagan?" Duff asked, offering his arm.

Meagan hooked her arm through his, and they led the others into the dining room, where the table was set with gleaming china, sparkling silver, and glistening crystal, all reflecting the light of the overhead chandelier that hung suspended over the middle of a table that was long enough to seat all of them comfortably.

Two days later, much of the town of Chugwater had turned out for the Christmas concert, with music furnished by the First Church of Chugwater choir, the Volunteer

Fire Department Band, and Duff MacCallister, whose name was listed on the program as Captain of the 42nd Foot, Third Battalion of the Royal Highland Regiment of Scots.

The choir sang "O Come, All Ye Faithful," "Hark! the Herald Angels Sing," "The First Noël," and "What Child Is This?" Then Duff stepped in front of the audience. He was wearing the kilt of the Black Watch, complete with a *sgian dubh*, or ceremonial knife, tucked into the right kilt stocking, with only the pommel visible. He was also wearing the Victoria Cross, Great Britain's highest award for bravery. He played "I Know a Rose-tree Springing."

After a few numbers from the Volunteer Fire Department Band, the concert ended with performers and audience singing "Silent Night."

"Oh, it was all so beautiful," Sally said after the concert ended. "And Duff, you were magnificent."

"Why, thank you, Sally. Elmer, if you would see to these good folk, I'll take Meagan home 'n change out of m' kilts."

Smoke started to say, "That's all right, Duff, we can wait while you—"

"Smoke, we'll be going home now," Sally interrupted.

"But there's no need to put him out like—"

"Smoke?" Again, he was interrupted. By a single word and a glare. "Smoke?"

"Oh, uh, yes," Smoke said, finally understanding. "Yes, uh, thank you. We'll just go on home with Elmer."

* * *

"It was nice of them to give us a little time alone," Meagan said as they walked from the theater to her apartment, which was located over her store, Meagan's Dress Emporium. Duff had left his horse in the stable behind the store.

"Aye, after Sally nearly beat him over the head," Duff said.

Meagan laughed. "True, she is most perceptive."

"And 'tis glad I'll be to be out of m' kilts. 'Tis getting a bit chilly."

"Especially considering what you are wearing beneath your kilts, eh, Duff?" Meagan asked with a knowing smile.

"Sure lass, 'n what makes you think you know what's underneath m' kilts?"

"I peeked," she said with a chuckle.

"Did ye now?"

"Aye, 'n 'twas a wondrous thing to behold." Again, she mimicked Duff's accent.

"I dinnae ken about a wee lass that would take a peek under a man's kilts."

"We can talk about it after," Meagan said.

"After what?"

"After," Meagan repeated with a sly smile.

A couple hours later, with a smiling Meagan in bed upstairs in her darkened apartment, Duff stepped into the stable behind her store to saddle his horse for the ride back to his ranch. He was feeling his way through the dark when he heard a voice.

"And would ye be for tellin' me why 'tis ye are waiting, Duff MacCallister? Sure, an' ye should be askin' the young lass to marry you."

"What?" Duff asked in shock, the hair rising on the back of his neck

The voice was that of a woman, and not just any woman. It sounded for all the world like the voice of Skye McGregor.

"Who said that? Where are you?" Duff struck a match, and in the wavering orange glow, examined the inside of the small stable. He saw nothing except his horse, Meagan's horse, and her buggy. There was nobody else there. He let the match burn until it reached his fingers, then quickly blew out the flame and licked the burn, which wasn't severe.

"Did you hear that, Sky?" Duff asked his horse. "Nae, and how could you have heard it, for 'twas in m' own mind the words were spoken."

He led Sky out into the street in front of Meagan's place, mounted, then looked up at the window that he knew was to her bedroom. Though he couldn't see her, he had a very strong feeling that she was looking down at him and made a slight wave, then turned his horse and started out of town at a rapid trot, the hoofbeats echoing back from the dark, mostly empty buildings that lined First Street.

Up in her bedroom, Meagan was standing next to the

window, looking down onto the street. She hadn't told him she would do so, but she wanted to see him one last time before he left. When she saw him wave toward her window, she gasped. Had he seen her?

No, she was sure he had not, for how could he? There was no light in her room and she was standing in absolute darkness. Nevertheless, Duff had glanced up toward her room and waved. Meagan smiled when she realized that he, like her, had wanted one last look . . . even if he saw nothing.

She crawled back into bed, sure she could still feel the warmth of his presence.

Meagan hadn't always lived in the American west. She had arrived in Chugwater less than two years before Duff, having come from Washington, D.C., where her father had been an administrative aide to Senator John Daniel of Virginia. Senator Daniel had been seriously wounded during the Civil War, crippling him, so Meagan's father took on many of the senator's duties.

Senator Daniel had never been married.

"He would make a good husband for you, Meagan," her father had said. "Think of it, you could be the wife of a United States senator."

Meagan had shaken her head. "Papa, he is forty-three years old, and I am but twenty-two."

"You wouldn't have to make dresses for the society women of Washington. You would be one of them."

"I enjoy making dresses, Papa. I'm very good at it, and it pleases me to see women wearing what I have designed."

"Senator Daniel is a wonderful man."

"He is a good man, I will concede that. But I don't love him."

Burt Parker had been increasingly more and more insistent that Meagan marry Senator Daniel, until one day Meagan left her father a note.

Dear Papa,

Please don't be upset that I've decided to go off on my own. If I were a man, I would say I am going to seek my fortune, and you would have no trouble with it. I know that such things are not ordinarily done by women, but as you have told me many times yourself, I am not an ordinary woman.

I love you, Papa, and I will write to you when I am all settled.

Your loving daughter,
Meagan

Taking the one thousand dollars she had saved, Meagan had boarded a train. She'd had no particular destination in mind, but while waiting in the station, she bought a book called *The Williams Pacific Tourist Guide Across the Continent*. It was from that book that she learned about the community of Chugwater.

The Chugwater Valley is 100 miles long. It has been for many years a favorite locality for wintering stock, not only on account of the excellence of the grass and water, but also from the fact that the climate is mild throughout the winter.

In order to get to Chugwater, she would have to leave the train in Cheyenne, then go by coach. When she read about Cheyenne, she almost had second thoughts about her plans.

In such places as North Platte, Julesburg, and Cheyenne, there are gamblers, thieves, prostitutes, murderers—bad men and women of every calling and description under the heavens and from almost every nationality on the globe. When they can prey upon no one else, they prey upon each other. The worst that has ever been written of these characters does not depict the whole truth—they are, in many cases, outlaws from the East who have fled to escape the consequences of crimes committed there. Armed to the very teeth, they often shoot first and speak second.

Meagan had wasted no time in Cheyenne, but went immediately on to Chugwater, where she bought a building for two hundred and fifty dollars, bought material and equipment for another hundred dollars, and started her dressmaking business. She had been so involved with getting her business started that she had no time for men, nor did she meet anyone who interested her until she met Duff MacCallister.

She just wished that she knew, for sure, what future she might have with him.

CHAPTER FOUR

As Duff rode back home, he couldn't get Skye McGregor out of his mind. Or at least, her voice. Had he actually heard her speak to him?

Yes, he had heard it . . . but that may well have been a trick of his mind. The real question was not whether he heard it, but whether she had actually spoken to him. No, that was impossible. Skye had been dead for four years, and not once in that four years had he ever heard her voice before.

"Skye, would you say something to me now, lass?" he asked softly.

There was no response.

"Sure 'n I dinnae think you would be for saying anything to me. So why did you back in the stable? 'Tis marrying Meagan you want, is it?"

Would it be a betrayal of Skye's memory for him to marry Meagan?

That was it, he realized. Almost from the moment he had met Meagan, he had compared her to Skye. He knew what caused him to think he had heard Skye's voice. It was because he was trying to reconcile his love for Skye with his feelings for Meagan.

Pulpit Rock, Colorado

Max Dingo and two other men waited at Pulpit Rock on the stagecoach road between Glen Rock and La Bonte. Dingo, who was their leader, had long, stringy hair hanging down to his shoulders, and a full, unkempt beard. At the moment, he was relieving himself.

"Hey, Dingo, I see the coach comin'," Nitwit Mitt called. His real name was Nat Mitchell, but long ago he had picked up the moniker Nitwit Mitt and accepted the sobriquet without comment.

"All right, boys, let's get ready," Dingo said, buttoning up his trousers.

"How much money you think they're carryin' on that coach?" the third man, Wally Jacobs, asked.

"We won't know till we stop it and find out, will we?" Dingo replied. "Get mounted."

The six-horse team moved at an easy lope, and the wheels of the stage kicked up a billowing trail of dust, a goodly amount of which managed to find its way into the passenger compartment. Otis Boyd, his wife Liz, and their two children, Harry and Kathy, were the only passengers in the coach. Kathy, who was no older than six, began coughing.

Liz Boyd took a handkerchief from her handbag, held

it under the spigot of the water barrel, and wet it. She wrung it out so that it wasn't dripping, then handed it to the little girl. "Here, honey, this will help. Hold it over your mouth and nose. The damp cloth will filter out some of the dust."

Kathy took the handkerchief and did as her mother suggested.

Suddenly there was the sound of gunfire outside, and the coach rumbled to an unscheduled halt.

"What is it?" Liz asked in fear. "Otis, what's going on?"

"I don't know," Otis answered, looking out the window. "It could be nothing, maybe just someone signaling the driver to stop so they can catch a ride."

They heard loud angry voices outside, but couldn't understand what was being said.

Suddenly, a rider appeared just outside the stage. He was wearing a handkerchief tied across the bottom half of his face. "You folks in the coach," he shouted in a loud, gruff voice. "Come on out of there!"

"Oh, Otis!" Liz said in a frightened voice.

Cautiously, Otis opened the door and stepped out onto the ground. He turned and helped his wife down, then the two children.

Liz looked up toward the driver and saw that he was tending to the shotgun guard, whose head was tilted back. His eyes were closed, his face was ashen, and the front of his shirt was soaked with blood.

"Otis, that man has been shot!" Liz cried.

"That he has, lady," one of the two riders said. Both men had the bottom half of their faces covered. "I shot 'im." He held up a canvas bag. "I shot 'im for this here money pouch. And now, I'll be troublin' you folks for whatever money you have."

"What makes you think we've got any money?" Otis asked.

"You're takin' a trip, ain't ya? Folks don't go on a trip, especially what with takin' their whole family with 'em, without havin' some money. Now, you can give it to me yourself, or I'll kill you an' take it off your body. Which is it to be?" The man cocked his pistol and pointed it at Otis.

"Otis, give it to him!" Millie insisted.

"It's all we have to live on until we get settled in my new job," Otis pointed out.

"We'll get by until you are paid. Give him the money!"

"You better listen to your wife, mister."

With a reluctant sigh, Otis took his billfold out and handed it over.

"Come on, Dingo, we got the pouch and the dude's poke. Let's get out of here."

"Dingo?" Otis asked. "Would that be Max Dingo? I've heard of you."

The outlaw sighed and pulled his handkerchief down. "Nitwit, you got one hell of a big mouth, you know that? And you, Mister, you know too damn much." He cocked his pistol.

Thinking he had no other chance, Otis swung out at the outlaw, knocking him down by the surprise of his action. Emboldened by his initial success, he reached down to grab Dingo to administer another blow. From his position on the ground, Dingo raised his pistol and fired. Otis backed away, clutching his stomach. He looked over at his wife with a surprised expression on his face.

"Liz?" he said in a small voice.

"No!" she screamed. "No!" She rushed to her husband, who had fallen to the ground.

"Papa!" Harry cried.

Millie cushioned Otis's head in her lap while he breathed his last gasps.

"Liz, I . . ." His voice drifted off, then he sighed and was still.

"My God!" Liz said, looking up at Dingo, who had regained his feet. "You've killed him!"

"Yeah, I did," Dingo said coldly.

"You've got the money, Mr. Dingo," the driver said. "Please, why don't you just go now, and leave the rest of us alone?"

Dingo looked up at the driver, and the dead shotgun guard, then down at the body of Otis Boyd. He let the hammer down on his pistol, then slipped it into his holster. "Yeah. All right, we'll go. You can call it my Christmas present to you."

Laughing, he climbed onto his horse, which was being held by one of the other two men. "Merry Christmas!" he shouted back over his shoulder.

The driver, Liz, and her two children could hear the demonic laughter as the three men galloped away.

Guthrie Ranch, outside Rawhide Buttes

Suzie Guthrie was in the barn milking a cow when her younger brother Timmy came rushing in. Guess what? I know what I'm getting for Christmas."

"How do you know?" Suzie asked.

"I know, because I heard Mama and Papa talkin' about it. I'm getting a horse. Grandpa is going to give it to me when we go to Chugwater to see him and Grandma for Christmas. It's supposed to be a surprise."

"Then let it be," Suzie said.

"How can it be a surprise if I already know what it is?"

"Well, don't ruin Mama and Papa's surprise by letting on that you know."

Timmy laughed. "That's funny. How can it be a surprise for them, if they already know?"

"It's not a surprise for them, but they want to surprise you. So pretend that you don't know."

"That's silly."

"No, it isn't silly. It's just being nice."

"I know what you're getting, too. Do you want to know?"

"No, I don't want to know."

"Why not?"

Suzie sighed. "I can't expect you to understand. You're still a child."

"I'm twelve years old, only two years younger than you," Timmy said, resolutely.

"Women mature faster than boys."

"You're not a woman. You're just a girl."

Suzie smiled. "And you are my sweet brother." She stood up from the milking stool, then reached down to get the milk pail. "Did you get the stalls mucked out?"

"Yes. I hate mucking stalls. They stink."

Suzie laughed. "And here you're wanting a horse? That means you'll have one more stall to muck out."

"That's different. It'll be my horse. I won't mind it, then."

"I'll remember that when Papa tells you to get busy and you start complaining."

"I'll carry the milk," Timmy said, reaching for the pail.

"Well, that's very nice of you, little brother. Maybe you're growing up after all."

"Hey, where are you going, girl?" a man shouted from the bunkhouse. He had long, unkempt brown hair, and a beak-like nose between narrow, dark eyes.

"We're goin' to the house," Timmy answered.

"Don't answer him, Timmy," Suzie said under her breath.

"Why not?"

"He's . . . not a nice man."

"That's just Sunset. Why do you say that? What did he do?"

"Nothing. Nothing that I want to talk about. Just keep going until we reach the house. Don't talk to him. Don't even look at him."

* * *

Sunset Moss shrugged, then stepped back into the house, joining the other two cowboys. All three were working through the winter for John Guthrie. The Cave brothers, Jesse and T. Bob, were engaged in an intense conversation. Both were redheaded, with red, blotchy skin.

"How much did you say?" T. Bob asked.

"A thousand dollars. He was paid in cash for them last cows he delivered, and he ain't took none of it to the bank yet," Jesse said.

"So what you're sayin' is, they's a thousand dollars cash just lyin' over there in that house." T. Bob pointed toward the Guthrie family house.

"That's right."

"A thousand dollars. How about that? Say, how long would it take us to make that much money?"

"Well, we're drawin' twenty-one dollars and found, per month. At that rate, it would take near four years to make a thousand. But say you was to divide the thousand up into three hundred and thirty-three dollars for each of us, it would still take a year and a half," Jesse said.

"Damn. Is that true?" Sunset asked.

"If Jesse says it's true, it is," T. Bob replied. "Jesse has always been good at cipherin' 'n such."

"I got the milk, Mama," Timmy said, bringing the bucket into the house.

"Well, good for you, Timmy."

Suzie smiled. "Yes, we can always count on Timmy to get the milk."

"Suzie helped," Timmy said.

"Well, that was nice of your sister, wasn't it?" his mother said, smiling knowingly at Suzie. "Dinner's on the table. You two wash up, and get ready."

"Ah, Nora, they don't need to wash up."

"What? John, why would you say such a thing?" Nora asked in a shocked voice.

"Because those breaded pork chops smell awfully good. If the kids don't wash up, they don't eat, which means I can have theirs."

"Yeah? Well you ain't goin' to get my pork chop, 'cause I plan to wash up," Timmy said resolutely.

"You *aren't* going to get mine," Suzie corrected.

"And you ain't goin' to get hers neither," Timmy added.

"Oh," Suzie said with a shudder. "Mama, what am I going to do with him? He goes to school just like I do. Why is it that he hasn't learned anything?"

"Oh honey. I reckon it just depends on what you need to learn," John explained. "He can already ride and rope as well anyone working here. That's the kind of thing that's important to someone who is going to be a rancher."

"You're sure he's going to be a rancher?" Nora asked.

"Of course I'm sure. Why else am I building this ranch, if not to have something to leave to him when I die?"

Nora shuddered. "Oh heavens. Let's not talk about dying, not here, so close to Christmas."

At that moment, the kitchen door opened, and Sunset Moss, Jesse, and T. Bob Cave came into the house. A blast of cold air came in with them.

John looked up in surprise. "Hello, boys. Don't you believe in knocking before you push yourselves into someone's house? I mean, that's not very good manners now, is it?"

Jesse chuckled. "Is it manners you're wantin' Guthrie? Well, I'm afraid we're all out of manners."

"What kind of talk is that to be saying to your employer?"

"Yeah, well, that's just it, Guthrie. You see, we ain't exactly workin' for you no more. We're quittin'. That's what we come in here to tell you."

"It's a hell of a time to be quitting. Christmas is almost here. Have you boys thought this through?" John asked.

"Oh, yeah, we've thought it through, all right."

"Well, you haven't worked a whole month, but being that it's this close to Christmas, I'll give all three of you a full month's pay."

"Nah, that ain't what we want," Jesse said with a twisted smile.

"Well, what do you want?"

"We want that thousand dollars cash you got here," Jesse said.

"What? Are you crazy?"

Jesse drew his gun and pointed at Timmy. "You got two choices. You can either give us that thousand dollars, or I'm goin' to kill the boy."

"John! Give them the money!" Nora cried in desperate fear.

"There's no need for you three to come in here blustering like that," John said. "Why don't you let me just pay you off, and we'll forget all about this.

"You mean you ain't goin' to give us the thousand dollars?" Jesse asked.

"No, I'm not going to give you a thousand dollars."

Jesse pulled the trigger, the gun boomed, and Timmy, with a surprised look on his face, was driven back against the wall by the impact of the bullet.

Nora screamed. "Timmy!"

"Are you crazy?" John shouted in shock and anger.

"The girl's next." Jesse pointed toward Suzie.

"No, wait, wait! I'll give you the money!"

"I thought you might." Jesse smirked.

John started toward the cupboard.

"Just tell us where it is. I don't want to take no chances of you comin' up with a gun from somewhere."

"It's in a gray metal box on the top shelf," John said.

"Get it, T. Bob."

T. Bob Cave walked over to the cupboard, reached up onto the top shelf, and took down the box. He put his hand up there a second time and brought down a pistol. "Would you lookie here. It looks to me like he had a little surprise planned for us."

"Is the money in the box?" Jesse asked.

T. Bob opened the box, then pulled out a packet of bills. "Yeah, it's here!" he said excitedly.

"Well, looks like we're goin' to have us a merry Christmas after all," Jesse said.

"You've got your money, now go," John said. "Go, and leave us to bury our son."

"Jesse, we ain't just goin' to leave, are we?" Sunset reached down to grab himself. "I mean, not afore we have us a little fun. I've had me a hankerin' for the young one for a long time now."

"Sunset's right," Jesse agreed. "Seems a shame to waste this chance. I'll give Sunset the young'un. The mama's good enough for me."

Suddenly, John realized what they were talking about. He grabbed a chair, and raising it over his head, started toward Jesse. "The hell you will!"

Jesse shot him, and John dropped the chair, grabbed the wound over his stomach, then fell.

"John!" Nora shouted.

"I'm first," Jesse said, putting his gun in his holster, then unbuckling his belt as he started toward Nora.

"Run, Suzie, run!" Nora shouted.

Suzie started toward the back door, but Sunset grabbed her, and dragged her back.

"No you don't, missy. Not before me 'n you have us some fun," he said.

Suzie fought back, then Sunset hit her in the face with his fist, and she went down.

Jesse also knocked Nora out, and for the next few

minutes, the only sounds to be heard were the animal-like grunts of pleasure.

When they were finished, Jesse stabbed them both.

"What did you do that for?" Sunset asked.

"They know us by name," Jesse answered. "You want them to tell the law who it is that done this?"

"No, I guess not," Sunset said.

"Let's go."

"Wait." Reaching down, T. Bob removed a brooch from Suzie's torn dress.

"What's that?"

"It's a little silver doodad," T. Bob said.

"Well grab it, and let's go."

CHAPTER FIVE

It was some time before John Guthrie came to. He was lying on the floor in the dining room with a terrible pain in his stomach. He put his hand to his stomach and felt blood.

In a flash, confusion fled and he remembered everything—how the three men who worked for him had come into his house, killed his son, then robbed and shot him.

"Nora? Nora, where are you?"

Slowly and laboriously, John got up, regretting the movement almost immediately. He nearly passed out again, and reached down to grab onto the sideboard. Looking down to steady himself, he saw the bloody bodies of Nora and Suzie. His wife and daughter were naked. "No!" he shouted in agony.

The bleeding started again, and John knew with a certainty that he wasn't going to survive his wound.

Staggering into the study, he managed to sit at the desk, where he took a piece of paper and a pen, and began to write.

Rocky Mountain Hotel, Rawhide Buttes

Ralph Walters pulled a chair up to the window and sat there, looking down onto Center Street. There were no Christmas decorations up yet, and he decided that it was probably too early. He wished some were up, though, something that would break up the cold, bleak view he was seeing.

He put his hand to his throat and felt the swelling. He was sure that it was no more than a case of catarrh and had bought an elixir for it. He looked at the newspaper ad that had prompted him to buy the product.

A Reliable Remedy
ELY'S CREAM BALM
Is quickly absorbed. It cleans,
soothes, heals, and protects
the diseased membrane resulting
from catarrh.

He had rubbed it on his neck and jaws, but it didn't seem to be helping. He had a headache, he was feverish, and he felt weak. It had also been two days since he had eaten anything. Even drinking water made his throat hurt.

Fort Russell, Wyoming

A sergeant major showed Smoke, Matt, and Sally into the commandant's office, then stepped through a door at the back of the room.

Sally looked around the room as she waited. She had an eye for detail and was able to pick out such things as the unit guidons of the 1st Cavalry and the 30th Infantry, the map designating the regiments' areas of responsibility, a picture of President Harrison, a picture of Secretary of War Redfield Proctor, and a picture of the commanding officer of the post, John Stevenson.

A moment later, the sergeant major reappeared. "Gentlemen, you and the lady may enter."

"Thank you, Sergeant Major," Smoke said as he walked Sally to the colonel's office, then followed her in. Matt fell in behind them.

Colonel Stevens had very dark sideburns that came down to join with the moustache over his mouth. He had no chin whiskers. "You have come to sell horses, is that right?"

"Yes. We've been in touch with the War Department," Smoke said. "I have a letter of introduction."

Colonel Stevens smiled. "You don't need it. I've already been contacted by the War Department. It is my understanding that the horses can't be delivered until after Christmas?"

"Yes, sir. The horses are still back in Colorado," Matt said.

For the time being, Pearlie and Cal were looking after

the horses. They actually belonged to Matt, but because he was keeping them on Smoke's ranch, and Smoke's ranch hands had been tending to them, half the profit would belong to Smoke.

Colonel Stevenson started to offer cigars to Smoke and Matt, but he demurred, and glanced over toward Sally. "With your permission, ma'am."

Sally smiled. "Colonel, if the smell of cigar smoke bothered me, I would have expired long ago. Please, feel free to enjoy your smoke."

Colonel Stevenson lit the Jensen men's cigars before he lit his own, then said, "You guarantee that these horses are broken? You know that we get a lot of young soldiers who have never been on a horse before."

"Matt, Pearlie, and Cal spent the last month breaking them," Smoke said.

Stevenson puffed on his cigar for a moment until his head was wreathed in smoke. "All right, the army has authorized me to buy up to one hundred mounts at two hundred dollars per mount. That's twenty thousand dollars." The colonel smiled. "I'd say that's enough money for you to have a happy Christmas."

"I have to agree with you, Colonel," Smoke said.

"I will telegraph the War Department today, I expect to have the final authorization within a week. Can you stick around until then? You and your wife will be my personal guests, and Matt, you can stay in the BOQ. Of course, you understand that the money isn't to change hands until after the horses are delivered, and that won't be until after Christmas."

"True. But the anticipation of it will carry us through Christmas," Matt said.

Colonel Stevenson laughed. "Yes, I suppose it would." He sighed, and shook his head. "It's ironic, isn't it, that I have the authority to spend as much money in one transaction, as I can earn in seven years?"

"Colonel, it has been said, and I believe it, that those who serve in the army do so more from a sense of duty, than money," Smoke said.

Colonel Stevenson nodded. "Ah, yes, duty, honor, country. The motto of West Point is inculcated in the cadets of the Corps, so that it truly does become our watchword. If I served only for money, I would have left the army long ago.

"Will you be here for Christmas? I know that Mrs. Stevenson has become quite fond of your wife, and we would love to entertain you."

Smoke shook his head. "I thank you very much for the invitation, Colonel, but we will be spending Christmas with our friend Duff MacCallister up in Chugwater."

"Duff MacCallister, you say?"

"Yes."

"I have heard much of him. Almost as much as I have heard about you two. What an indomitable three you would be, should anyone challenge you."

Smoke laughed. "This is Christmas, Colonel. I would hope that we face no challenge any more formidable than having to sing Christmas carols."

"Well, as you must remain here for the final authorization, that means there will some post activities you will be able to see and enjoy. So many of these men are far from home, and we like to make their Christmas as pleasant as possible."

"I look forward to it," Smoke said.

"Have either of you ever served in the army?" Stevenson asked.

"My father served during the war," Smoke said. "I've never served."

"My father also served," Matt said. "But I have not."

"Your father? But isn't Smoke your father?" The colonel was confused by the comment.

"No," Matt said, without further explanation.

Guthrie Ranch

Jim Merrick dismounted in front of John Guthrie's house. He was surprised to hear the cow bellowing in pain and knew that it needed to be milked. He knew John well and that didn't make sense. John was a man who took good care of his animals.

Merrick stepped onto the porch, surprised again. The door was standing wide open. What was it doing, standing open, on such a cold day?

He went inside, calling, "John? John? Mrs. Guthrie? Is anyone here?"

As he passed through the dining room, he saw that the table was set for a meal, including food. The pork chops and mashed potatoes were cold, and the bread was stale. It looked as if the table had been set for some time.

Looking toward the kitchen, he saw an arm on the floor. "What the hell?"

Moving quickly into the kitchen, he gasped at what he saw. Mrs. Guthrie and her daughter were lying naked on the floor, their bodies caked with dried blood. The boy was on the floor, too. John was nowhere to be seen. "Where is he? What happened here?"

Merrick looked around and noticed a trail of dried blood on the floor. He followed the trail into the study, and there he saw John slumped across his desk. When he got closer, he saw a sheet of paper on the desk, and he picked it up to read.

To whoever finds our bodies.
We were murdered by three men who
were working for me.

Jesse and T. Bob Cave, and Sunset Moss.

More than likely they'll head toward

That was as far as the note got.

"Oh John. I'm so sorry this happened to you and your family. I'm so sorry." Merrick folded the note over and put it in his pocket. He would take it to town and show it to Marshal Worley. Being just a city marshal, Worley would have no authority, John's ranch being beyond the city limits, but at least he would have some idea as to what needed to be done next.

Merrick started toward the front door, then stopped.

He couldn't leave the bodies of Mrs. Guthrie and her daughter like that. He went into one of the bedrooms, stripped off a couple quilts, and returned to the kitchen, where he covered the nude bodies.

Chugwater

As Duff stepped into the saloon owned by his friend Biff Johnson, he remembered his first visit to Fiddlers' Green. It was shortly after he had filed a homestead claim on his land, on what was now Sky Meadow, and he had come with his kinsman, Falcon MacCallister. The name of the establishment had intrigued him, so he'd asked how the name came to be.

"Tell me, Biff, why do you call this place Fiddlers' Green? Have you fiddlers who play here from time to time?" Duff asked.

"Colonel MacCallister, suppose you tell him about Fiddlers' Green. I know you know what it means."

"Colonel MacCallister?" Falcon looked across the table at Biff for a moment, then he smiled and snapped his fingers. "You are Sergeant Johnson! You were with Custer at Ft. Lincoln!"

Biff smiled and nodded his head. "I knew you would remember it. I was in D troop with Benteen, during the fight."

"No wonder you call this place Fiddlers' Green."

"I still don't know what it means," Duff said.

"It's something the cavalrymen believe," Falcon said. "Anyone who has ever heard the bugle call Boots and

Saddles will, when they die, go to a cool, shady place by a stream of sweet water. There, they will see all the other cavalrymen who have gone before them, and they will greet those who come after them as they await the final judgment. That place is called Fiddlers' Green."

"Do they really believe that?" someone asked.

"Why not?" Falcon replied. "If heaven is whatever you want it to be, who is to say that cavalrymen wouldn't want to be with their own kind?"

"I like the idea," Duff had said.

Biff greeted Duff as he approached the bar. "In town for the mayor's shindig, are you?"

"Aye, that I am," Duff replied. "Will you be going?"

"I'll be there," Biff replied.

The shindig Biff was talking about was an event that R.W. Guthrie held every year during the Christmas season. The dinner, held in the ballroom of the Dunn Hotel, was for the business owners of the town. Although Duff wasn't a business owner from the town, his cattle ranch contributed significantly to the town's economic well-being, so he had been invited. In truth, he would have been there, anyway, because Meagan Parker, who did own a business in town, would have invited him as her guest.

"You'll be going with Meagan, I suppose?"

"Unless I can find another lass who'll go with me," Duff replied.

"Ha! You try that and I would hate to see what

Meagan does to her, to say nothing of what she would do to you!" Biff replied with a laugh.

"Aye, 'tis better I go with Meagan."

"Yeah, I would think so. Do you have time for a scotch before you step over to get her?" Biff asked as he poured a shot of the amber liquid into a glass.

"Aye, and how long does it take to have a nip?" Duff asked, lifting the glass to his lips to toss it down quickly. Wiping his lips with the back of his hand, he threw a wave at Biff and started toward the door.

"I'll see you there," Biff called out to him.

"Did you stop by Fiddlers' Green for a bit of the creature?" Meagan teased when Duff stepped in to her establishment.

"Sure, now, and were you thinkin', lass, that I could face this night without a wee drink?"

"Duff MacAllister! Is it that hard to be with me?"

"What? No, that's not it. I meant—"

"I know what you meant." Meagan laughed. "I was just teasing you. I'm not looking forward to it, either. But R.W. does set great store by these Christmas dinners, and there are some things that we do for people just because they are our friends."

"Aye, that's true, and now 'tis feeling bad, I am, for complaining."

"Come, walk me to the hotel," Meagan invited.

A broad smile spread across Duff's face. "Good idea.

For how can I feel bad if I have the most beautiful lady in all the county on my arm?"

Meagan chuckled. "Are you sure you are Scottish and not Irish? You do have a bit of the blarney in you."

As they walked toward the hotel, they passed under the street lamps and in and out of the bubbles of light that spilled onto the boardwalk. The air was cold and crisp, but the night sky above was filled with glistening stars.

"What a beautiful night," Meagan said, hugging herself as she looked up at the stars. "It's as if God Himself is decorating for Christmas."

A streak of gold flashed across the sky.

"Oh, make a wish!" Meagan said. "All wishes made on shooting stars come true."

"Aye, but only if you can make a wish before the star is gone," Duff replied.

"Oh, pooh. What a joy killer you are. I'm going to make a wish anyway."

"What do you wish?"

"Do you think I'm going to tell you? Wishes never come true if you tell."

"Aye, 'tis what I've heard as well."

"Kiss her."

Duff frowned. "What?"

"I didn't say anything," Meagan said.

"Kiss her," the voice said again. It sounded amazingly like Skye's voice.

"All right, if you think I should."

Meagan stopped walking. "Who are you talking to?"

Duff didn't answer. He took her into a dark space between the leather goods store and the gun shop. There, he kissed her.

"Well," Meagan said, smiling. "I don't know who you were talking to, but I like it."

CHAPTER SIX

Although the hotel had no exterior signs of Christmas on display, inside, there was a big banner on the wall in the ballroom. MERRY CHRISTMAS TO THE BUSINESSMEN OF CHUGWATER, WYOMING

R.W. Guthrie was standing at the door greeting everyone as they arrived. "Duff, Meagan, I'm glad you could come."

"Are you sure that it's all right for me to be here?" Meagan asked.

"What? Of course it's all right. Why would you even ask such a thing?"

Meagan pointed to the sign. Welcome to the business-*men*?"

"Oh, my, I see what you mean. I had Peter Keith paint the sign for me, I should have paid more attention to it. Of course you are welcome, and I hope you find no fault with me for such a dereliction."

"R.W., how can I find fault with my favorite politician?" Meagan asked with a laugh.

R.W. laughed as well. "Duff, does she tease you so?"

"Aye, Mayor, that she does. 'Tis a wonder I can find my way to spend any time with her."

"Duff MacCallister!" Meagan swatted his arm.

R.W. laughed again. "It would seem to me like the two of you are equal adversaries on that front."

"You're pushin' the season a bit, aren't you, R.W.?" Fred Matthews asked, coming in behind Duff and Meagan. "It's three more weeks until Christmas."

"Well now, Fred, I suppose you could say that. But there will be other Christmas celebrations starting pretty soon. I know that some of the businesses and churches are planning events. There's a Christmas dance scheduled, and even some private individuals are holding parties. I thought it would be best to get this out of the way first, being as it's more official than anything else."

"What do you hear from John?" Biff Johnson asked as he walked into the ballroom.

"I got a letter from him just this Monday," R.W. answered. "Ha! Timmy wants a horse so bad that he can't stand it, but John keeps holding him off because he knows I'm giving him one for Christmas. I offered to give it to him already, but John says no, the boy needs to learn patience."

"You know what I think?" Duff asked.

"What's that?"

"I think he already knows he's getting a horse for Christmas. Or at least, he figures to agitate enough make his pa come around."

R.W. laughed. "I'd say you've got him down pretty good, because that is exactly what I think he's doing."

"He's a good lad, and your granddaughter is growing up to be a beautiful young lass."

"That she is, Duff, that she is. And it's a proud grandpa I am."

"How old are your grandkids, R.W.?" Fred asked.

"Timmy is twelve. Suzie, his older sister, is fourteen. And she looks just like her mother, which is a good thing, because Nora is a beautiful woman."

"I'd say John did very well for himself," Fred said.

"Yes, well, I just wished I could have talked him into going into the building supply business with me. I sure would like to have my grandchildren living here in Chugwater."

"You aren't fooling anyone R.W. You just want the extra votes from John and Nora," Fred said.

R.W. laughed good-naturedly with the others. "Well, as you know, women do have the right to vote here in Wyoming, and you never know when you might need another two votes." He looked around. "Looks like everybody's here. Oh, there's Curly Latham. How did I miss him? I'd better go speak to him." R.W. left to greet the town barber, who was quite bald.

Russell Craig stepped through the doorway and chuckled. "Ha! If there's any way to milk another two votes, R.W. will find it. I'm telling you the truth. If he ever decides to run for governor, why, I believe he would win."

"But has he nae been a good mayor? Or have I been

made prejudiced by the fact that he is my good friend?" Duff asked.

"No, don't get me wrong," Craig said. "I think he's been a great mayor. I can say this because, bein' as I am the city marshal, I've had to work with him quite a lot of times, and he's always given me whatever I needed to get the job done."

The mayor returned to the doorway, and as more guests arrived, Duff, Meagan, Biff, and Rose moved on and took their seats at one of the tables. After a few moments, Marshal Craig joined them.

"Who's protecting the town, Marshal?" Biff teased.

"Not to worry, my friends. It's in good hands with my deputies."

As the diners enjoyed the meal, the room was alive with the sounds of dozens of conversations, laughter, and the clink of silverware on china. Duff happened to look up toward the door and saw Titus Gilmore, the telegrapher. The expression on his face was grim.

Duff frowned. "That doesn't look good."

"Oh, Duff," Meagan said, putting her hand on his arm. "He looks like he is bringing bad news to someone."

They watched as Gilmore started toward R.W., then, as if having second thoughts, he changed direction, and walked toward their table.

"Marshal Craig, maybe you'd better handle this." Gilmore handed the message to him.

Craig nodded. "All right, Titus. Thank you."

"I'm sorry. I'm awfully sorry." Turning, Gilmore left quickly.

"That was strange," Marshal Craig said. "I said thank you, and he said he was sorry."

Craig opened the message and read it. "Oh, damn." Closing his eyes, he pinched the bridge of his nose. "Oh, damn."

"What is it, Marshal?" Duff asked.

Craig's only response to the question was to hold out the telegram. Duff took it with some trepidation.

TO MAYOR RW GUTHRIE STOP SON JOHN AND FAMILY
MURDERED STOP BODIES AT RAWHIDE BUTTES
MORTUARY STOP AWAITING INSTRUCTIONS STOP
MARSHAL WORLEY

"Duff?" Meagan asked.

As had been Marshal Craig's response, Duff said nothing, but handed the message to Meagan.

"God in heaven, how awful!" Meagan said after reading the telegram. Almost instantaneously, her eyes welled with tears.

"I don't blame Titus for leaving this with me to deliver," Craig said. "I don't think I ever more fully understood the term, 'let this cup pass from me' as much as I do at this very moment."

"I'll come with you, if you'd like," Duff offered.

Craig shook his head. "No. I appreciate the offer, Duff, but this is something I have to do by myself."

"Marshal, you might want to take him outside before

you tell him," Duff said. "I think he might need a little privacy for such news."

"Yes," Craig agreed. "Good idea, I'll do that."

Duff watched as Marshal Craig walked over to the mayor's table. He was talking to someone, and laughed just as Craig approached. The expression on his face changed from a smile to one of concerned curiosity when he excused himself from the others, then followed Craig toward the door.

"What's up?" asked someone at a nearby table. "Why did the marshal take the mayor outside?"

"What's going on?"

A buzz of concerned, but quiet conversation moved through the room.

A moment later, Marshal Craig came back into the room. He took Mrs. Guthrie by the arm and led her outside, as well.

"Oh, Duff," Meagan said quietly, as she put her hand on his arm again. "What a terrible thing she is about to learn."

The curiosity was palpable as people asked each other for an interpretation of the strange actions.

Marshal Craig returned to the room alone. Under the curious and watchful eyes of all present, he stepped to the lectern from which the mayor was expected to say a few remarks after the dinner. Though nobody as yet knew why, there was a dread certainty that the mayor would not be returning. Marshal Craig held up his hands to call for attention.

"What? Do you mean we're going to have to listen to

both of you make a speech?" someone asked, but his joke died.

Marshal Craig looked at him, not critically, but with a solemn expression on his face. "Ladies and gentlemen, I have some very sad news to report."

All fidgeting stopped as everyone paid very close attention to what the marshal was about to say.

"We have just received word that the mayor's son, John Guthrie, who I think most of you know—he lives near Rawhide Buttes—has, along with his entire family, been murdered."

"What?" Curly Latham shouted. "Russell, that can't be true!"

"I'm afraid it is true," Marshal Craig said. "I would like to ask all of you to bow your heads for a moment of silence. Afterward, those of you who haven't eaten your dinner, and wish to do so, may remain until you have finished. But all other activities are cancelled."

All bowed their heads for a moment of silence until Marshal Craig said, "Amen."

"Marshal Craig, what can we do?" someone called as Craig walked away from the lectern.

"You can pray for the mayor."

"What about the funeral? Don't you think it might be a good idea if we got up a whole group of people who want to go, and all of us go over together?" asked Jason McKnight, one of the partners of McKnight-Keaton Shipping.

"Yes," Marshal Craig said. "I think that would be a very good idea. You think you could organize it?"

"I suppose I could."

"Jason, if you need any help, I'd be glad to do what I can," Fred Matthews said.

"Thanks. We can start right here. Ever'one who thinks they'll be goin' to the funeral, leave your name with me or Fred Matthews."

"Where did the mayor go?" someone asked. "I'd like to tell him how sorry I am."

"He went home with his wife," Marshal Craig said. "He begged to be left alone for the rest of the night."

"Yes, of course. We should leave him alone."

Meagan had not let go of Duff's arm, and she squeezed it tightly. Duff looked at her. She was crying quietly. He put his arm around her and pulled her to him.

"Oh, Duff. This is awful. This is so awful."

"Yes," Duff agreed. "I wonder who did it."

"There's no telling, I suppose."

"Whoever it is, he needs to pay for his crime."

"He will. If not in this world, when he meets God," Meagan said.

"I would like to arrange that meeting for him."

"Duff, what do you mean? That's a job for the law, not for a rancher."

"R.W. is a friend of mine, Meagan. Can you imagine how hurt he is with this happening so close to Christmas? I want the guilty person or persons brought to justice."

"That won't bring his family back, Duff."

"No, but it might bring him some personal satisfaction."

"You're going to do this, aren't you? You are going to go looking for who did it."

"I'm seriously thinking about it," Duff admitted.

"You will go to the funeral, won't you?" Meagan asked.

"Aye, I'll go to the funeral," Duff promised.

"May I have your attention, please?" Fred Matthews called out. "I would like for everyone who plans to attend the funeral to come over here and sign your name. We need as good a count as we can get so we can make all the arrangements."

"Also, let us know if you'll be needing transportation," McKnight added. "And if you have any vehicles you can make available. I can furnish as many freight wagons as we'll need, but it would be a lot nicer if we didn't have to use them."

At the invitation of McKnight and Matthews, several people, including Duff and Meagan, moved over to sign the paper.

CHAPTER SEVEN

Millersburg, Wyoming

It took the Cave brothers and Sunset Moss two days to reach Millersburg from Rawhide Butte, not because the distance was so great, but because they thought it might be best to stay away from any civilization for a while. They soon came to the conclusion that if they were going to stay out of sight, they would need supplies.

"We're goin' to do more 'n just go to the store, though, ain't we?" Sunset asked. "I ain't never had this much money before in m' whole life, 'n I'd like the chance to go into a saloon without worryin' whether I had me the price of another drink or not."

"Me, too," T. Bob said. "We are goin' to go to a saloon, ain't we?"

"Yeah, I don't see why not, long as we get some possibles first," Jesse agreed.

The men stopped at Dunnigan's grocery, where they

bought beans, coffee, flour, sugar, and a slab of cured bacon.

"You boys plannin' on doin' a little prospectin', are you?" Dunnigan asked as he totaled up the purchases.

"What do you mean?" Jesse asked, made suspicious by the question.

"Well, you got enough groceries here to stay out in the field for a month or more. I was just curious is all."

"It ain't none of your business what we're plannin' to do," Jesse said.

Dunnigan chuckled and held up his hand. "You fellas just pay me no never mind. I know how you prospectors are. Let's see, that'll be fourteen cents for five pounds of flour, forty-five cents for five pounds of bacon, thirty-four cents for five pounds of sugar, sixteen cents for five pounds of beans, and thirty cents for two pounds of coffee. All tolled up that comes to—"

"A dollar thirty-nine," Jesse said, speaking up before Dunnigan finished.

"A dollar thirty-nine," the grocer agreed. "Oh, my. Will you boys be out in the mountains come Christmas? Christmas is close, you know."

"We may be," Jesse said as he counted out the money.

"Well, then, let me be the first to wish you a Merry Christmas." Dunnigan wrapped up the purchases and slid them across the counter. "And I appreciate your business."

None of the three men answered as they started toward the door, and Dunnigan shrugged.

"Ernest, who were those men?"

Turning to his wife, he replied, "I've never seen them before in my life, Thelma, but they sure aren't very friendly. I can tell you that."

With their packages stowed away in their saddlebags, the three men stopped at the closest saloon. Cottonwood Saloon was painted in white letters, outlined with black, on the false front of the building.

Stepping up to the bar, they bought a bottle, and each bought a beer, then they found a table. Soiled doves were circulating through the room, teasing the customers to buy drinks. Seeing them, T. Bob caught the eye of one and smiled at her.

"Found something to stir your interest, T. Bob?" Jesse asked as he took a drink of whiskey, then chased it with a drink of beer.

"Yeah, I like that one over there in the yeller dress," T. Bob said, nodding in the girl's direction.

"The one in green is prettier," Sunset said.

"The one in the green dress? Are you crazy?" T. Bob asked. "Look how skinny that 'un is. Why, layin' with her would be like layin' with a board 'n tryin' to poke your nose through a knothole. Besides which, if you'll just notice, she ain't even got no lady pillows."

"Oh, she's got 'em, all right," Sunset said. "I'll admit, they ain't very big, but she's got 'em."

"Not so's you can see 'em," T. Bob said. "Now, you

take that gal in the yeller dress. Do you see that pair on her? They're just right."

"Yeah, well, looks like you're about to get a closer look at 'em, 'cause she's comin' over here now," Sunset said.

The woman in the yellow dress sauntered over to the table. Realizing she had caught the fancy of the three men, she put her hands on the table and leaned forward in front of T. Bob, giving him a good show down the scoop neck of her dress.

"Do you see something you like?" she asked pointedly.

"Yeah, but I ain't seen enough of it yet." T. Bob smiled. "Although, I got me a feelin' you might be willin' to show me. What's your name?"

"The name's Lydia," the girl answered.

"Well, Lydia, how about we go upstairs?"

"It's goin' to cost you," she said.

"How much?"

"Two dollars, unless you want to stay the whole night. Then it'll be five dollars, but we can't take anyone on for an all night until after eleven o'clock."

"Well, what say we do the two dollars now, and if I feel up to it, maybe we'll do an all night at eleven." T. Bob grinned.

"That would cost you another five dollars, not just three more," Lydia informed him.

T. Bob stuck his hand in his pocket and pulled out a large wad of bills. "Well now, little lady, I think I might just have enough money to handle that."

She grinned broadly and put her arm through his. "I think you do as well." She led him to the stairs.

"What about the other two?" she asked as they started up the stairs.

"What about them?"

"Are they just goin' to sit there? Maybe you haven't noticed, but I have several friends who are unengaged at the moment. "

"Is that what you women do? You get business for each other?" T. Bob asked.

"When we can."

"Well, here's the thing, you see. As it so happens, neither one of them two likes women."

"What?" Lydia gasped.

"They just like each other," T. Bob said, laughing at the joke he was playing on Jesse and Sunset.

"Well, I never." She looked back toward the two men, who had no idea of the joke T. Bob had just played on them.

A frustrated T. Bob sat on the edge of the bed. "I don't know what's wrong. I ain't never had that happen before."

"Don't worry about it, hon. Those things happen to men from time to time."

Naked, he began dressing. Once he had his long-handle underwear on, he padded over and took his pants from the back of the chair. The brooch that he had taken from Suzie's body fell out, making a thumping sound as it hit the floor.

"What's that?" Lydia asked as she sat up in bed. The sheet she had been clutching around her fell down, exposing her bare breasts.

"It's just a little doodad that I picked up somewhere." T. Bob held it up.

"Oh, how beautiful!" Lydia said, reaching for it. "Can I see it closer?"

He handed it to her.

"Where did you get this?"

"I, uh, found it."

"This is one of the most beautiful brooches I've ever seen."

"You like it?"

"Yes, I like it."

"I tell you what. You don't never tell nobody what happened here, I mean, uh, you know, that I couldn't, uh . . . preform . . . and I'll give that to you."

"Oh, thank you! I won't say a word about it, I promise."

"Only, don't wear it or anything until after we've left. If Jesse and Sunset see you with it, they'll know I give it to you, 'n they'll likely start askin' questions."

Lydia nodded. "All right. It'll be our secret."

T. Bob was just pulling on his boots when someone started knocking loudly on the door.

"T. Bob, you in there?"

He walked over and jerked the door open. "What are you doin' bangin' on the door like this?"

"We have to go," Jesse said.

"Go? Go where? Why?"

"Come on out of that room and I'll tell you."

T. Bob stepped out into the hallway and closed the door behind him. "What is it?"

"Read this." Jesse shoved a newspaper into his hands.

HEINOUS CRIME

Entire Family Murdered

John Guthrie, his wife Nora, and their two children, Suzie and Timmy, were found murdered in their ranch home five miles north of Rawhide Buttes. Guthrie left a note identifying the killers as Jesse and T. Bob Cave, as well as Sunset Moss.

Their present whereabouts is unknown, but telegraphic messages have been sent to towns throughout the state.

"How the hell could he have left a note?" T. Bob uttered. "He was dead when we left him, wasn't he?"

"I reckon not. Damn, T. Bob, they've got our names. We got to get out of here."

"Where are we goin'?"

"Anyplace but here."

* * *

Fort Russell

The first of the Christmas season observances was being celebrated with much pomp and ceremony. The band played "Patriotic Numbers," according to the program, and the post chaplain and Colonel Stevenson gave long addresses. After that, the cavalry unit presented a "Mounted Drill." Smoke, Sally, and Matt were given positions of honor on the reviewing stand with Colonel and Mrs. Stevenson, and Mr. and Mrs. Joseph Carey. Carey was mayor of the nearby town of Cheyenne. On the grounds, many other civilians were present to watch the mounted cavalrymen perform.

Dressed in his finest uniform, as were all the other soldiers, Captain Charles E. Felker took center stage, giving the commands in a loud and authoritative voice. When the troops took the field, he was mounted on a horse in front of one long line, with all the troopers facing him.

"Column of twos, right!" Felker ordered, his voice rolling across the open area.

In one quick and very precise movement, the troop front formation became a column of twos, facing to the right.

"Guidon post!"

The soldier carrying the pennant galloped from the back of the formation to the front.

"Forward, ho!"

The column started forward with the horses at a rapid trot. Then, two by two, the riders jumped over obstacles.

One file separated from the other and they rode in opposite directions before coming back so that the riders could weave in and out of each other.

The demonstration continued for half an hour, during which the soldiers proceeded at a gallop with sabers drawn, and made more leaps over obstacles. Finally, the troop returned to its original position of troop front where the men and horses were once again in one long line, side by side, facing Captain Felker.

"First Sergeant!" Felker called.

The noncommissioned officer left the formation and rode up to Felker, where he saluted.

Felker returned the salute. "Dismiss the troops, First Sergeant." The captain turned his horse and galloped off the field before the first sergeant gave the order.

Colonel Stevenson and his wife hosted a dinner for Smoke, Sally, and Matt at their home. Dr. Millsaps, the post surgeon, his wife, and his twenty-one-year-old daughter Sue Ellen also attended. The seating arrangement around the table was such that Matt and Sue Ellen were sitting side by side.

Finishing dinner, they heard music from outside and quickly left the table to stand on the porch and listen as they were serenaded by the post singers, who sang not only Christmas carols, but many songs that were the particular favorite of soldiers, such as "I'll Take You Home Again, Kathleen."

Quite cold, they hustled back inside after the impromptu concert. Colonel Stevenson built up the fire and popped corn over the fireplace.

"So, according to Colonel Stevenson, you have come up from Colorado," Dr. Millsaps said to Smoke.

"Yes."

"What have you heard about the outbreak of diphtheria down there?"

Smoke's eyebrows shot up. "Diphtheria? I haven't heard anything about it. Are you saying there is diphtheria in Greeley?"

"I've received information that it is quite rampant in that city."

"Really? We came through Greeley on the train."

"Did any of you leave the train?"

"No."

"Did anyone board the train while it was there?"

"Nobody came aboard, either. Actually, the train didn't even stop there. It just went right on through."

Dr. Millsaps nodded. "That is a very good thing. It means you weren't exposed."

"Doc, can you really get exposed like that? I mean just being around someone who has the disease?" Matt asked.

"Unfortunately, you can. There have been outbreaks where as many as two hundred die in a single town. No stagecoaches are being allowed in or out of Greeley right now. The trains have been ordered to pass directly through, without stopping."

"I thought I read that there was a cure for it now, some sort of anti-toxin," Sally said.

"Yes," Dr. Millsaps replied, looking at Sally with a surprised expression on his face. "How did you know that? There aren't too many doctors who even know that."

"If you knew my wife, you wouldn't be surprised by anything that she knows," Smoke said. "She used to be a schoolteacher, and she reads constantly."

"Well, I'm most impressed with her," Dr. Millsaps said, smiling.

CHAPTER EIGHT

Chugwater

Many of the businesses in Chugwater were shut down so that friends of R.W. Guthrie could make the trip to Rawhide Buttes for the funeral of his son and family. Jason McKnight and Fred Matthews had gathered enough carriages, buggies, coaches, buckboards, and wagons to transport fifty-three people the thirty-one miles. It was a cold and dreary day when the vehicles came together to form a convoy on First Street.

Duff's mount Sky was tied behind the coach in which Duff, Meagan, Elmer, and Vi were riding. Another horse—Sonny—was tied behind R.W.'s coach. It was supposed to have been Timmy's Christmas present.

Jason McKnight, who had appointed himself as wagon master, would make the trip on horseback. After a ride up and down the length of vehicles to make certain that all was in readiness, he returned to the front and let out a yell. "Heah! Wagons, roll!"

"Ha!" Elmer said. "Listen to ole' Jason sing out like that. You'd think he was taking a wagon train across country."

Wrapped as they were in a blanket to keep out the cold, Duff put his arm around Meagan and pulled her close to him. She leaned into him and soon was sleeping peacefully. He stared out at the cold, gray day.

Three hours into what would be a five-hour trip, they stopped for lunch. Buford Hampton said it reminded him of the time he came west with a wagon train, when he was a young man, back in 1855.

Fred came over to talk to Duff. "I'm worried about R.W. and Martha. We can't get them to eat anything. I don't know if either of them have eaten anything at all since they first heard about this."

"It's hard to eat when you're grieving." Duff was speaking from experience, recalling how he had felt after his fiancée Skye was killed back in Scotland.

"I wish you would go talk to the mayor. He sets quite a store by you."

"All right," Duff agreed. "Meagan, would you like to come with me?"

"All right. I don't know if I can say or do anything that will make them feel better, but I'll come with you, if you want me to."

"I do."

They walked up the line of vehicles until they reached the lead coach. R.W. was sitting on a stool behind his coach, staring at the horse he had bought for Timmy.

"It's a beautiful horse, R.W.," Duff said.

"Yes." The one-word response was barely audible.

Duff walked over and squeezed the horse's ear. The horse lowered his head in appreciation.

"R.W., are you a believing man?" Duff asked.

"I thought I was. Until this happened. Now . . . I don't know. All I know is that my son and my grandchildren have been taken from me."

"No, they haven't."

"I know, I know," R.W. said with a dismissive wave of his hand. "I'll see them all in the by-and-by."

"You can see them right now."

"What do you mean?"

Duff leaned back and crossed his arms. "Have you ever heard of a man called Kierkegaard?"

R.W. looked up. "No, who is he?"

"He was a writer and a theologian. He wrote once that when we die, we are kept in God's memory. That's a pretty powerful thing when you stop to think about it. Is there any particular moment with them that you can recall, right now? A moment that gives you pleasure?"

"Yes. The last time they came to visit, we went to Chimney Rock Mountain for a picnic." Despite his grief, R.W. managed a smile. "Timmy scooped up a bunch of tadpoles and started chasing Suzie with them."

"According to Kierkegaard, that moment is in God's memory. That means that all you have to do is think about it, and as you are remembering, John, Nora, Suzie, and Timmy are actually reliving that very moment, right now."

"He hasn't caught her yet," R.W. said. "Timmy's chasing her, but he hasn't caught her."

It didn't escape Duff's notice that R.W. said Timmy "is" chasing her, rather than he "was" chasing her.

Duff smiled, nodded, then turned to walk back to his own coach. Meagan, who had watched the exchange between them without offering any word of her own, followed him.

"Duff?" R.W. called.

The Scotsman turned back toward him.

"Thanks."

Duff nodded again.

"How did you do that?" Meagan asked.

"How did I do what?"

"How did you manage to get a smile from R.W. after what he has been through?"

"I just gave him something positive to think about."

"Do you believe that? I mean that, once someone has died, all you have to do is think about them, and they are there, just on the other side of your thought?"

"Aye, 'tis one of my strongest beliefs," Duff said.

"That is beautiful. I'll have to remember that."

Crowley's Gulch

"Yeah, it's still there," Jesse said, pointing to a small log cabin.

"I'll be damned. I didn't think it would be here," T. Bob said.

"I told you it would be. It's been five years since we

last seen it, but it's well built. It'll more 'n likely be here a hunnert years from now."

"Who owns it?" Sunset asked.

"Don't nobody own it no more," Jesse said. "It was built by a trapper named Crowley fifty years or so ago. That's how come they call it Crowley's Gulch. He's been gone for a long time now, ain't no tellin' how long he's been dead. Anyhow, it's tight against the wind, and even has a fireplace. There's a creek out back for water."

"The creek will be all froze up," Sunset complained.

"We can break out ice and melt it," Jesse said. "We'll hole up here for a while. Let's get moved in."

"How long you plannin' on us stayin' here?" Sunset asked.

"You got someplace else you need to be?" Jesse asked.

"No place in particular, but you may have took notice, there ain't no saloon around here. There ain't no girls, you know the kind I mean, around here, neither. Hell, there ain't even no cafés around here."

"We got bacon, beans, coffee, flour, sugar, and salt. You want more 'n that, we got a whole forest filled with critters we can kill 'n eat. You afraid you're goin' to starve?"

"It ain't that. It's just that what good is it to have money, if you ain't got no place to spend it?"

"You can't spend money if you're dead," Jesse answered. "And right now, what with ever'one knowin' we was the ones that killed the Guthries, there ain't no place we can go for a while, without maybe bein' seen and recognized."

"So, we're just goin' to stay here?"

"Why not? We've got us a house. And anyone who might be comin' lookin' for us is goin' to have to come right through this draw. There ain't no other way in, unless they come over the mountains."

"That's right," T. Bob agreed. He chuckled. "And the only way they can come here like that, is if they're ridin' mountain goats."

"It just don't seem right, us havin' to stay here," Sunset complained.

"Well, Sunset, if you want to go now, go on. Go back to Millersburgh, or to Rawhide Buttes, or Bordeaux. Maybe they haven't heard of you yet."

"And maybe they have. You'll more 'n like get your neck stretched if they have." T. Bob made a fist, then put it beside his neck and made a retching sound in his throat. He let his head flop over to one side and laughed.

"That ain't funny," Sunset grumbled.

"Then I reckon you'd better stay with us for a while longer. Tell you what, come the first big snowstorm— I mean a really big one so's nobody is out lookin' around—we'll leave here, and head south."

"South where?"

"I've always sort of wanted to see Texas," Jesse said.

Sidewinder Gorge, Wyoming

Located in the Laramie Mountains, the gorge was so well concealed by the rocks and ridgelines that guarded its entrance that it couldn't be seen unless someone was specifically looking for it. At the entrance to the canyon was a pinnacle from which someone could keep a watchful eye, thus preventing anyone from approaching without being seen. Down inside the canyon, a fork from the North Fork Laramie River supplied a source of water.

Those were the virtues that had caused Sidewinder Gorge to be selected as an outlaws' hideout. There, too, were built a dozen adobe structures to house the outlaws who had made it their hideout.

Max Dingo, the recognized leader of the group, and Wally Jacobs and Nitwit Mitt arrived after holding up the stagecoach at Pulpit Rock. Their take from that holdup had been a very disappointing one hundred and fifteen dollars.

"Damn. It was hardly worth it," Dingo said in disgust. He was sitting at a table with a woman known as Bad Eye Sal, so called because she had a drooping eyelid. The eyelid was the result of a run-in with a drunken customer when she was a saloon girl down in New Mexico. Two weeks later, she killed the man who had cut her up, then left town. She lived in Sidewinder Gorge, along with twelve men and three other women.

The men paid their way by rustling cattle or holding up stagecoaches and robbing stores. The women paid their way by providing their services to the men.

Bad Eye Sal leaned over the table. "Dingo, I want to leave this place."

"Where would you go if you left?"

"I'd probably go to St. Louis. I have a sister there."

"Does she know you've been whorin'?"

"I expect she does. But I'm her sister, so that won't make any difference."

Dingo grinned. "You're right about that. It won't make any difference, 'cause you ain't goin' nowhere, woman. You ain't leavin' Sidewinder Gorge."

"I promise you, I'll not tell anyone about this place. I'll go far away, where nobody has ever heard of you."

"I told you, you ain't goin' nowhere."

Bad Eye Sal frowned. "You can't keep me here against my will."

"The hell I can't. You belong to me. All four of you belong to me, bought and paid for."

"We might be for your pleasure, but we ain't bought and paid for. What's to keep us from just walkin' out of here?"

"What's to keep you from walkin' out? A bullet in the head ought to do a pretty good job of it," Dingo said with an evil laugh.

Rawhide Buttes

The large convoy made quite a stir when it arrived in town late that afternoon. Marshal Craig had wired ahead to Marshal Worley, advising him as to how many would be arriving, so the citizens of Rawhide Buttes had set up a wagon park to accommodate the wheeled vehicles. Room had been made in the livery stable to receive all the horses.

There was not enough hotel space to provide rooms

for all the arrivals, so the citizens of the town opened up their homes to the visitors. Mark Worley, the town marshal, hosted Duff, while Meagan was hosted by Cora Ensor, who also owned a dress shop.

"It will be a sad Christmas for Rawhide Buttes," Marshal Worley told Duff that evening. "John and his whole family had many friends in town."

"Do you have any leads on where the ones who did it might have gone?" Duff asked.

"I heard that they may have been seen up in Millersburgh, but that don't seem all that likely to me."

"Why not?"

"It's too close to Rawhide Buttes. I'd think they would want to get farther away."

"Perhaps they don't realize that we know they're the ones who did it," Duff suggested.

"I'm sure they know by now. Their names have been in just about every newspaper in the entire state."

"Nevertheless, after the funeral tomorrow, I think I'll ride up to Millersburgh and see if I can get a lead on them."

"I would offer to deputize you," Marshal Worley said, "but I've got no authority up there, so me deputizin' you wouldn't do any good."

"No need," Duff said. "I contacted Sheriff John Martin down in Cheyenne. He is going to send a warrant, by telegram, for me to be sworn in as a deputy sheriff. That will give me the all the authority I need."

* * *

"You have a very nice dress shop here, Cora," Meagan said after Cora had shown her around.

"Nothing like yours," Cora replied.

"Yes, but you're just getting started. It takes a while to get it just the way you want."

"I had counted on Christmas helping me get started this year, but with this business about Mr. Guthrie and his whole family getting killed, I don't know."

"Christmas may be just what people need to help them get through this," Meagan said. "I've got an idea. Suppose after the funeral, I go back home, gather up a lot of dresses, then come back and help you get your store ready for Christmas?"

"You would do that?"

"Sure, I'd be very happy to do it."

"Oh!" Cora said as a wide smile spread across her face. "I would love that! Thank you!"

CHAPTER NINE

Duff stepped into the parlor the next morning wearing the same kilt he'd worn when he performed at the Christmas concert in Chugwater. The same ceremonial knife was tucked into the right kilt stocking with only the pommel visible. The same Victoria Cross was pinned in prominence.

"That's, uh, quite an impressive looking outfit," Worley said.

"R.W. asked me to wear this today to honor his son and family. And to play the pipes," Duff added.

"I expect the church and cemetery will be full today," Worley said.

As predicted, the church was full, with every seat taken and extra chairs brought in. The four closed coffins were lined up, end to end, down the center aisle and draped with palls, black for John and Nora, white for Suzie and Timmy.

The funeral contained eulogies, hymns, and a concluding prayer by the preacher. "Lord, we're sending you a wonderful family, John and Nora Guthrie, and their two children, Suzie and Timmy. Let them know that they were well loved, and will be sorely missed. Amen."

After the service, the coffins were taken out and loaded onto a single wagon, there being only one hearse in town. Sonny, the horse that would have been Timmy's Christmas present, was draped in black and tied on behind the wagon.

The funeral cortege moved slowly down Center Avenue toward the cemetery. Most of the shops were closed; and both sides of the street were lined with people, including even those who weren't present in church for the funeral. As the wagon bearing the coffins passed by, the men removed their hats, and the women bowed their heads.

The day was gray and cold. It began to deliver on the promise of snow, so that by the time they reached the cemetery, the snow started coming down, not as slow-floating flakes, but as small ice crystals. The coffins were set on the ground alongside four open graves. R.W. and his wife took seats in chairs beside the graves, their faces drawn in grief and heartbreak. Nora's parents were deceased, so no one was there to represent her, except R.W. and Martha. They grieved for her as much as they did for John and the children.

The preacher walked over to them, bent down, and spoke so quietly that only they could hear him, then he opened the Bible to read a few words. "I am the resurrection and the life, saith the Lord: he that believeth in me, though he were dead, yet shall he live; and whosoever liveth and believeth in me shall never die. We brought nothing into this world, and it is certain we can carry nothing out. The Lord giveth, and the Lord taketh away; blessed be the name of the Lord."

Closing the Bible, he addressed the gathered mourners. "My brothers and sisters, we are here to say good-bye to John, Nora, Suzie, and Timmy, but in the sure and certain knowledge that the good-bye is only temporary. We will see them again in heaven. Amen."

With that, he nodded toward Duff, who was standing about twenty yards away from the graves. Duff inflated the bag, then began playing "Amazing Grace."

The haunting notes of the melody, made even more so by the unique quality of the pipes, filled the cemetery from front to back, and side to side, moving into and resonating within the souls of all the gathered mourners. Most of the mourners had never heard the pipes played before. As they looked toward the sound of the music, they saw an almost ghostly image of a man wearing a strange-looking outfit that left his legs bare on the frigid day. Despite the unusual sight, music and the moment prevailed, and many present, man and woman alike, shed tears.

Duff walked Meagan to the stagecoach. In one hand, he was carrying a grip that held his Black Watch uniform, and in the other, he was carrying Meagan's luggage. His pipes hung by a strap over his shoulder.

"You played beautifully," Meagan said. "I know that R.W. and Martha appreciated it. As I looked around, I could tell that everyone else did, as well."

"That's the least I could do for the two of them," Duff said. "What I want to do now is find the brigands who did this."

"Do you think you'll be able to find them?" Meagan asked.

"I'm certainly going to try," Duff said.

"I won't even bother to tell you to be careful. You've done this sort of thing more times than I can count. But that doesn't keep me from worrying."

Duff smiled. "'Tis nice to have someone worrying about me."

Meagan smiled at his words. "I probably won't be in Chugwater when you return."

"Oh? And why is that, may I ask?"

"Yes, you can ask. While I was here, I promised Cora Ensor I would come back and help her get her store ready in time for Christmas. That's less than two weeks away, so we're going to have a lot of work to do."

"That's very nice of you."

Meagan smiled again. "It's not a one hundred percent eleemosynary proposition. I'll be supplying most of the dresses she will have for sale."

"Do you have enough for her store, and for your own?"

"I do," Meagan said.

Duff chuckled. "Aye, lass, 'tis quite the businesswoman you are. I've not forgot how you beat me out of half my herd."

"I didn't beat you out, Duff MacCallister. You well know I invested in the cattle when you needed money to get your ranch going."

"Aye, but when I tried to buy the creatures back from you, you wouldn't sell them back. Sure now, lass, and you're not forgetting that?"

"Why should I sell them back? Who knows but that, someday they may all be yours again."

"And how is that to be, I'm asking?"

"Oooh," Meagan said. "You are asking me how it can be that the cattle I now own might be yours again someday, without you having to buy them back? Would you be for telling me, Duff MacAllister, are all Scots as thickheaded as you are?"

Duff laughed. "Sure, lass, and there's been many a man who has tried to break my head open, so, for a man like me, a thick skull can be an advantage." He opened the door to the coach.

As Meagan stepped behind it, she looked around. Determining that the coast was clear, she leaned in and kissed him. "I plan for us to spend Christmas together," she said after the kiss. "Please do keep that in mind."

"I will hold onto that thought." Helping her into the coach, he closed the door, then stepped back to the boot to load the luggage.

Elmer and Vi came up to the coach then.

"Elmer, I was beginning to think you might miss the coach going back," Duff said.

"Not to worry. There's not a thing in this little town to hold my interest," Elmer said.

"Elmer, would you be a friend and take m' luggage back to the house?" Duff asked.

"I will," Elmer replied.

"'Tis a good man you are."

"And don't you forget it," Elmer said with a smile as he helped Vi into the coach, then climbed in behind her. He reached out through the window and took Duff's hand. "Keep the sun in your face, and all the shadows will be behind you."

"Aye, and it may well be that I'll be for needing a wee bit of your Indian wisdom and philosophy, my friend," Duff replied.

"Wagons ho!" Fred Matthews shouted from the front of the convoy.

As the coach began to roll, Elmer waved, and Meagan blew a kiss toward Duff. She stared through the window, keeping Duff in sight for as long as she could.

"Miss Parker, don't you be worryin' none about Duff MacCallister," Elmer said. "I've been around a long time, 'n I ain't never know'd nobody what could handle himself better 'n Duff."

"I know he is quite capable," Megan said. "But it's impossible not to worry a little."

Fort Russell

Smoke and Sally were sitting with the Stevensons on the front porch of the colonel's quarters. It was a cold and clear night, but they were bundled up warmly.

"There is no place in the world I would rather be than right here," Colonel Stevenson said. "And when I say here, I don't necessarily mean Fort Russell. I mean any army post. There is something about a fort at this time of night, just before taps, that is almost spiritual. The men are in their barracks, playing cards, telling stories . . ."

From somewhere they could hear someone singing, accompanied by the strum of a guitar.

"And singing," the colonel continued.

"I would think that the men would be very lonely," Sally suggested.

"No," Colonel Stevens replied. "They aren't lonely. That isn't to say that they don't miss the family they left behind, but they aren't lonely. They're never lonely. They have a new family."

"You're part of their family, aren't you?" Sally asked.

"I like to think that I am."

Mrs. Stevenson laughed. "I'll tell you how much a part of the family he is. Every Christmas since we have been here, he has dressed up as Santa Claus for the children of the post. The first year he suggested that, I told him I thought it might be beneath the dignity of a post commandant, and he said 'dignity be damned,' he was going to do it. Now, I not only go along with it, I'm proud of him for doing it."

"No man is taller than when he stoops to help a child," Sally said.

Mrs. Stevenson beamed. "Oh, what a wonderful thing to say."

"Yes, but I'm quoting someone. That was something Abraham Lincoln said."

"Oh, look, Harris is playing the bugle tonight," Mrs. Stevenson said as a bugler walked toward the salute cannon under the flagpole. "Nobody plays the calls more beautifully."

The salute cannon was glistening in the moonlight as Harris stopped beside it, raised the bugle to his lips, then played it into the pylon-mounted megaphone. The young soldier played the call slowly and stately, holding the higher notes, gradually getting louder, then slowing the tempo as he reached the end, and holding the final, middle C longer than any other note before allowing it to echo back across the quadrangle.

"Man, that has to be Harris," cried a voice coming from one of the barracks.

"I cannot hear that played without getting a lump in my throat," Colonel Stevenson said. "For an old soldier like me, that is mother's milk. Every note resonates in my soul.

"There are words to the song. Would you like to hear them?"

"Yes, please," Sally said.

Colonel Stevenson cleared his throat. "I'm not going to try to sing them, I'll speak them."

> *Day is done, gone the sun*
> *From the lakes, from the hills, from the sky*
> *All is well, safely rest*
> *God is nigh.*

"Colonel, the words couldn't be more eloquent," Sally said.

"It's strange," Smoke said a short time later as he and Sally were going to bed. "I've never served in the army, but as I sat there, listening to the bugle, I could almost feel what the colonel was feeling. I know what he means by the words resonating in his soul."

Sally kissed him. "That's because you have a good soul, Kirby Jensen."

CHAPTER TEN

Millersburgh

Duff didn't get away from Rawhide Buttes until after four o'clock, but it took him just under two hours to make the ten-mile ride. It was already dark by the time he arrived at the small town on the Platte River. A sternwheeler, the *Prima Donna*, was moored alongside the pier with a gangplank stretching from the side of the boat to the bank. He reined in Sky to watch some men rolling beer barrels down from the boat, then loading them onto the back of a wagon. He could see the captain in the lighted wheelhouse, occupying his position of authority with all the dignity due his station.

"Hey, what if one of these barrels was to accidentally break open?" one of the stevedores called out. "You reckon we'd have to drink it all up?"

The other workers laughed at the joke.

As Duff rode on into Millersburgh, he passed several houses, and could smell the aroma of frying chicken.

Somewhere a dog was barking, and at another house, a baby was crying. Riding on into town, he saw that the lamplighter was making his rounds. Most of the businesses were closed, but he headed toward the biggest and most brightly lit building on the street—the Cottonwood Saloon, the first saloon he came to. Stopping in front, he looped Sky's reins around the hitching rail a couple times, then stepped inside.

"What will it be, friend?" the bartender asked when he moved down to stand in front of Duff.

"A decent scotch, if such can be had," Duff replied.

The bartender nodded, stuck a toothpick in his mouth, then turned to pull a bottle down from the wall behind him. He poured a glass and slid it in front of Duff.

Duff lifted it to his nose, took a whiff, then set it back. "This is bourbon, not scotch."

"What difference does it make?"

"It makes a lot of difference to someone who prefers scotch. You keep this, I'll have a beer."

The bartender pulled the cork on the bottle and poured the drink he had put in front of Duff back into the bottle. Then he took down a mug and stepped back to the beer keg.

There was a bar girl standing a few feet down the bar from Duff. Lantern light was kind to her, and her skin glowed soft and golden so that the dissipation of her life didn't show so badly. She managed to look almost as young as her years.

"You are a foreigner?" she asked, smiling at him.

"Aye, lass. 'Tis from Scotland, I am."

"Oh, you are Scotch?"

"Nae, lass, scotch is the drink. Scot is the man."

"Oh, and it's quite a handsome man that you are, too. And I like the way you talk."

The bartender put the beer in front of Duff.

"And would ye be serving the young lass?" Duff asked.

"What will it be, Lydia?"

"My usual," she said as she moved toward Duff. "I thank you for the drink."

Duff recognized the silver brooch she was wearing—a Lion rampant. He had given it to young Suzie Guthrie for her birthday, back in September. He reached out to touch it.

"Do you like my brooch?" the bar girl asked.

"Aye, and would ye be for tellin' me how you acquired it?"

"Someone gave it to me a few days ago."

"Would you take five dollars for it?" he asked.

"Five dollars? You're willing to give me five dollars for this pin? Why?"

"'Tis a Scottish Lion brooch and it reminds me of m' home."

"Sure, mister, if it means that much to you. You can have it for five dollars."

"I thank you, lass." As soon as he had the brooch in his hand, Duff examined the back of it and saw a mark that he knew was there. It was indeed the same pin.

"You said someone gave it to you. Can you tell me anything about the three men?"

Lydia frowned. "How did you know there were three of them?"

"I'm guessing."

"Well, you guessed right," the bartender said. "There was three of 'em. Two of 'em was kind o' redheaded like maybe they was kin, or somethin'. And their skin was sort of blotchy red. The other fella had him a big nose and dark, evil-lookin' eyes."

"Hell, they all had evil-looking eyes, Clyde," Lydia said. "I don't know that I ever heard any of their names, though. But that's not unusual. Most of the men who come to see me don't bother to give their names."

"Their names were Jesse and T. Bob Cave, and Sunset Moss," Duff said.

"T. Bob, yes," Lydia said. "Now that you mention it, I did hear one of them called T. Bob. He's the one who gave me the brooch."

Duff held the brooch out to look at it again. "The man who gave you this took it from the body of a fourteen-year-old girl he had just raped and murdered."

"Oh, Lord. You're talkin' about the Guthrie family down near Rawhide Buttes, aren't you?" the bartender asked. "Yes, I read about that in the paper!"

Lydia shuddered, then handed the five-dollar bill back to Duff. "Here. I can't take money for that. I . . . I can't believe I even wore it."

"I don't suppose you have any idea which way they went from here, do you?" Duff asked.

"No, but I got a good look at their horses as they left,"

the bartender said. "One was ridin' a paint and the other two was on bays."

"One paint and two bays?" Another man had been standing at the end of the bar and, though he had been listening, this was his first comment."

"Yes," the bartender answered.

"Well, hell, mister. I can not only tell you which way they went, I can more'n likely tell you *where* they went."

"How so?" Duff asked.

"On account of 'cause I passed three fellas, two of 'em ridin' bays and one ridin' a paint, just this afternoon as I was comin' into town. Headin' north they was. If they're on the run, they'll more'n likely hole up in Crowley's Gulch."

"Crowley's Gulch?"

"It's about ten miles north of here. It's named after an old trapper that built a cabin there. He's long dead, but the cabin is still there. It's still sound. Hunters use it ever' now 'n then. It'd be my guess that's where they are."

Duff took out two more five-dollar bills and gave one to the bartender, and one to the man who had just given him the information. Then he returned the bill to Lydia.

"No, I told you, I can't accept that," Lydia said, holding her hand palm out.

"You keep it, Lydia," Duff said. "It's not for the brooch, 'tis for the information."

"Oh." She smiled. "Well, in that case."

Duff started toward the door.

"Why, you're not goin' after 'em now, are you, with full dark comin' on?" the bartender asked.

"Aye. I've nae intention of letting the miscreant devils escape justice. And I'll nae be losin' them because I wouldn't go out into the dark."

"I hope you catch them," the bartender said.

"I appreciate your good wishes. And I will catch them," Duff said as he stepped through the door.

"You know what I think?" Lydia asked after Duff left the saloon. Without waiting for a response she answered her own question. "I think he must have known the little girl who was wearing that brooch."

"I wouldn't be surprised," the bartender said.

"I wonder who he is," said the patron who had provided the information.

"I don't know," the bartender replied. "But I wouldn't want to have that man after me."

"But there are three of them, and only one of him," Lydia pointed out.

"Lydia, with a man like that, numbers just don't count."

Although the temperature had been relatively mild when he had left Rawhide Buttes, it had dropped by several degrees, and since leaving Millersburgh, it had turned bitterly cold. Duff pulled the collar up on his wool-lined coat, but he could still feel the biting winter wind that blew in wicked swirls, peppering him with a stinging spray of sand.

"I know, you're cold, Sky. We both are, laddie." Duff had developed the habit of speaking to his horse on long, lonely rides. If anyone asked why he was talking aloud he would explain that it was to reassure the horse. But the truth was there were times when he just wanted to hear a human voice, even if it was his own. And speaking to his horse, he reasoned, was better than talking to himself.

Snow started falling, not drifting down slowly, but swirling about in the cold, biting wind. As it continued to fall, drifts began to gather on the ground, despite being whipped around by the wind. It was getting increasingly difficult to see.

"I know you want to stop, Sky, but consider this, lad. It's just as hard on those raping outlaws we're following as it is on us. And we've the anger in our blood to warm us."

After riding for almost three hours, Duff saw the dark block of what he knew must be Crowley's Gulch in front of him. He considered riding on in, but thought that if the Cave brothers and Moss were there, and he gave himself away, they might be able to escape in the darkness. He decided to wait outside and go in at first light in the morning.

Looking around, he saw a gully that was deeper than his horse was high, and he led Sky down into it. Taking the canvas wrap from around his bedroll, and using rocks to weight it down, he made a cover to stretch over the top of the gully. It reached back just far enough to cover Sky's head.

"Sorry, Sky, this will have to do. I'll take off the saddle and leave the saddle blanket, but I dast not start a fire, lest it be seen."

With such shelter as could be constructed, Duff put his bedroll on the ground, then rolled up in the blankets. His position at the bottom of the gulley kept the wind off, and that made his condition tolerable. He fell into a fitful sleep.

The morning sun rose in a clear sky, and Duff was awakened by the quiet whicker of his horse. He carried a sack of oats with him on such trips, and filled his hat with the grain, fed Sky, then took a handful for his own breakfast. After that, he saddled him, then let the reins hang down. "You stay here, out of sight. I'll call for you when I need you."

Crawling out of the gully, he started toward the buttes. Though he had seen nothing yet, he could smell smoke and knew it had to be the men he was trailing.

"You check the horses, Sunset?" Jesse asked after Moss came back into the little cabin. "They coulda got loose last night. I wouldn't want to be out here on foot."

"They didn't go nowhere." Moss walked over to the fireplace, then, using his hat as a hot pad, took the coffee from the iron grill over the fire, and poured himself a cup. "Are we leavin' here today?"

"No, why should we leave?"

"You said we'd leave if there come up a good snowstorm. Well, one come up."

"Yes, it did," Jesse said. "And it for sure wiped out our tracks so's no one could trail us. A week or two with no trail to speak of and things will die down. Then we'll leave."

"We kilt Guthrie 'n his whole family," T. Bob put in. "There ain't goin' to be no calmin' down."

"True, I didn't mean the folks was goin' to calm down. What I was talkin' about was the comin' after us," Jesse said. "They lose our trail, they get cold, and the next thing you know they'll all be wantin' to go home to have Christmas with their families."

"Christmas." T. Bob punched his left hand with his right. "Damn. I near forgot 'bout that. What do you think we ought to do for Christmas?"

"What do you want to do? Go to church? Go carolin'? Decorate a Christmas tree?" Jesse asked with a snarl. "I swear, sometimes, T. Bob, you can say the damndest things. Are you sure there wasn't somebody else that got into Ma's pants before you was whelped? You sure as hell ain't got none of Pa in you."

"You ought not to say things like that," T. Bob complained.

"Why don't you fry us up some bacon?" Jesse suggested.

"All right," T. Bob agreed sullenly.

"Just bacon? That's a hell of a breakfast, ain't it? You know what I'd like? I'd like some bacon and eggs, and maybe a couple o' biscuits. And some butter and blackberry jam," Sunset said.

"We ain't got none of those things. I reckon if you was in hell, you'd be complainin' that you was wantin' ice water," Jesse said. "I tell you what, Sunset, if you don't want any bacon, don't eat it. Me an' T. Bob will eat your part."

"Didn't say I wasn't goin' to eat it. I was just sayin' what I would like to have."

CHAPTER ELEVEN

Unseen by the men in the cabin, Duff had crawled up onto the roof. He took his hat off and put it over the chimney opening, blocking the smoke from escaping. He held it for a moment, then, when he heard coughing coming from inside, he knew he had accomplished his objective.

Standing, he moved carefully down to the edge of the roof, which was covered with snow—he tried not to slip and slide in the ice—and pulled his pistol.

The three men came rushing out of the cabin, coughing and wheezing.

"What the hell caused that?" one of them asked.

"I caused it," Duff said.

Jesse and the others looked up in surprise. "Who are you?"

"I'm the one who will be taking you three murdering rapists back to Rawhide Buttes to hang."

"The hell you are!" Sunset shouted as he pulled his gun and squeezed off a shot. There was a return shot, and Moss fell back with a hole oozing blood in the middle of his forehead.

"Sunset!" one of the two remaining men shouted.

"If that was Sunset, then you two must be Jesse and T. Bob Cave. Unfasten your gun belts and drop them." Duff kept his gun pointed at them.

"What makes you think we're goin' to do that?" Jesse shouted.

There was another gunshot and the bullet hit the ground right between Jesse's feet, then ricocheted up between his legs and whined out over the open prairie.

"Just so you know I didn't miss, I'll be for taking out your kneecap with this shot," Duff said, aiming at Jesse's knee.

"No, no!" Jesse dropped his gun and raised his hands. "We give up! We give up!"

T. Bob dropped his gun as well.

"That's more like it." Duff tossed down two pair of handcuffs. "Would you lads be so kind as to put these on, for me?"

"Who the hell are you, mister?" Jesse said.

"The name is MacCallister. Duff MacCallister."

"Damn! You're the one kilt all them men down in Chugwater a while back, ain't you?" T. Bob asked.

"Aye, but they needed killing."

"What'd you come after us for? You ain't the law. If you are, I sure don't see no badge." Jesse squinted up at Duff.

Duff held up the Scottish Lion brooch. "This is all the badge I need."

"What's that?"

"It's the brooch one of you gave to a woman named Lydia, back in Millersburgh. That is, after you took it off the body of a fourteen year-old girl named Suzie."

"That ain't true," T. Bob protested.

Duff raised his rifle and fired. Blood, and tiny bits of flesh flew from T. Bob's left earlobe.

"Ow!" T. Bob shouted, lifting his cuffed hands to his ear.

"I don't like lying. Next time either one of you lie to me, I'll take off your entire ear. I know 'tis true, because I'm the one who gave the brooch to the wee lass."

Jesse turned to his brother. "What the hell did you do? You gave that brooch to that saloon gal, didn't you?" he said with an angry growl.

"How was I supposed to know that someone would recognize it?" T. Bob asked.

"You're a damn fool," Jesse said. "And even though you're my brother, I wish you was the one he shot instead of Sunset."

"And which one would you be?" Duff asked, looking at the man who had just spoken. "Are you Jesse or T. Bob?"

"Jesse."

Duff dropped from the edge of the roof and pointed toward the horses that were under the lean-to. "All right, Jesse, suppose you go saddle those three horses and lead them back over here."

"Why do I have to saddle them? Let him do it." Jesse nodded toward his brother.

"You'll do it because you'd rather ride back to Millersburgh than walk back with only one good leg."

Jesse glared at Duff, but without any further remarks, he started toward the lean-to.

Duff whistled. "Sky! Come here, lad!"

Sky came trotting up from the gulley, and Duff mounted, then waited.

Jesse brought the three saddled horses back, and Duff ordered him and T. Bob to drape Moss's body belly down over his horse. After they mounted, he took two ropes and looped them around their necks.

"Hey, what if we fall off?" T. Bob complained. "We could break our necks."

"Aye, 'tis more than likely that would be the case," Duff said. "I'd suggest ye be real careful."

Rawhide Buttes

There were very few citizens in the town of Rawhide Buttes who were even aware that Duff had been in pursuit of the murderers, so when he showed up with two riders in front of him, both of them secured by ropes around their necks, and a third man, belly down over a horse, the townspeople were surprised. Even before Duff reached the jail with his quarry, word spread that the ones who'd murdered the Guthrie family had been caught and were being brought in. The result was that nearly half the town turned out to watch.

"You're goin' to hang!" someone shouted.

"Let's hang 'em now! We don't need no trial!" another called out.

Marshal Worley and Deputy Masters stepped out of the jail, each of them holding double-barreled shotguns.

"There'll be no talk of lynchin' in my town!" Worley said resolutely. "We're goin' to hang these two galoots, but we're goin' to do it legal."

Duff went down to the stable where he boarded Sky and the other three horses.

"I recognize these here horses," the stable owner said, pointing to the horses the rustlers had been riding. "They belong to, that is, they did belong to John Guthrie. I don't know what to do with 'em now."

"I expect Mayor Guthrie will call for them," Duff said.

"All right, I'll keep 'em for him."

"'Tis a good man you are." Duff shook the man's hand.

Leaving the stable, Duff walked down the street to the first saloon he saw. There he saw four cowhands sitting together at one of the tables and another customer standing at the bar, staring at the mug of beer in front of him.

A bar girl smiled and walked over to stand beside him. "Hi. Welcome to the Cowbell Saloon."

"I thank you for the welcome, lass. Bartender, a drink for the young lady, and a scotch for myself."

"No." The girl looked toward the bartender. "I'll pay for my own drink and for his."

Duff laughed at her. "Sure 'n you've got me confused

now, lass. I thought the idea was for the customer to buy you a drink."

"And if he has a second drink, I'll buy it," called one of the cowboys sitting at the table.

"What is this?" the bartender asked. "What's going on here? Why is everyone so anxious to buy this man a drink?"

"Maybe you didn't see, you bein' inside 'n all," another of the cowboys said. "But this here fella just brought in Jesse and T. Bob Cave. They're the men that killed John Guthrie and his family. He brought in Sunset Moss, too, but he was dead."

The bartender smiled. "Then nobody needs to pay for his drinks. They're on the house."

Wally Jacobs was standing at the bar, but when he heard the names, he looked closely at Duff. Then he tossed down his drink and left.

He mounted his horse and rode slowly until he got out of town, then he broke into a gallop. Galloping, walking, and trotting his horse, he covered the nineteen miles to Sidewinder Gorge in less than two hours.

As Jacobs approached the canyon entrance, he stopped, dismounted, and stood with his arms extended out to each side.

Fifteen minutes later, he was in what was serving as a saloon for the outlaw haven. He walked up to Max Dingo. "You said you was lookin' for some more men. Well, I know where we can get a couple more."

"What kind of men are they?" Dingo asked. "I ain't lookin' for just anyone." He was eating his supper of bacon and beans. As a result, his beard was matted with bean juice and grease.

"They're good men, Max. I wouldn't come pitch 'em to you if they wasn't good men. They're both my cousins, 'n I rode with 'em a while down in Colorado."

"All right," Dingo said. "Bring 'em in."

"Well, uh, it ain't exactly goin' to be that easy to bring 'em in."

"What do you mean? You mean you're goin' to have to talk 'em into it? Hell, if you have to do that, I ain't interested in 'em."

"No, it ain't that. They're in jail, 'n they're about to get tried, then more 'n likely, they'll be hung."

"You said they're your cousins. What's their names, 'n what did they do?"

"There names is Jesse 'n T. Bob Cave. And what they done is, they kilt some people," Jacobs said without further elaboration.

"The Cave brothers? Wait a minute, I heard about them. They're the one that killed that rancher 'n his family, ain't they?"

"Yes."

Dingo laughed. "I'll be damned. Yeah, I'd say they more 'n likely will be hung. All right, if they're the kind of men who would do somethin' like that, then they'd more 'n likely be willin' to do about anything I asked of 'em. Also, they'll be glad enough to be free that they'll feel obligated. You think you can bust 'em out of jail?"

"Yes. I'll need two more horses, is all."

"All right. When you goin' to do it?"

"I'll need a couple days to plan things out. The trial's on Monday, and I want to get back for it."

Rocky Mountain Hotel

Ralph Walters should have gone to the doctor when the symptoms first started. It was too late now. He could barely breathe, and he was too weak to even get out of bed. A few minutes earlier, he had called out for help, or at least, had tried to call out, but the only sound that came from his throat was a weak gurgling.

Was he dying? He recalled a conversation he once had with his grandfather. That had been almost fifty years ago.

"Grandpa, what happens when people die?"

"You quit breathing."

"Does it hurt when you are dead?"

His grandpa tapped on the arm of the rocking chair he was sitting in. "Do you think this chair hurts because I'm hitting it?"

Ralph laughed. "That's funny. Chairs can't hurt."

"Neither can dead people."

He had been too young to ask the right questions of his grandfather. What he really wanted to know, but didn't know how to ask, was what happened to a person after they died? At the time of the conversation, he wasn't aware of the concept of a soul. What happened to the soul? He still didn't know the answer, but he was reasonably certain that he was about to find out.

Oddly, he felt no fear, just a sense of wonder and intense curiosity.

You've been dead a long time, Grandpa, but after you're dead I don't reckon time means anything. When you see me, it'll be like you just saw me. Only, I've sure changed since the last time you saw me, so you more 'n likely you won't even recognize me now.

Rawhide Buttes

Duff had remained in town for the trial. After a meal at the City Pig Restaurant, he wandered down to the Lucky Star Saloon. He wasn't there to drink; he was there for the trial. Before noon, charges had been filed against the Cave brothers, and by one o'clock, the Lucky Star was about to be turned into a courtroom, having been chosen because of convenience.

"All right, folks, the bar is closed!" the bartender shouted. "No more liquor can be sold till after the trial!"

Because the bar was closed and the trial was open to the public, many women who had never seen the inside of a saloon went inside to see justice be done.

They had the right to vote, and for a while, they'd also had the right to serve on juries. Although women could still vote, a panel of judges had taken away their right to serve on juries. The fact that they could no longer serve on juries did not lessen their interest in seeing that justice be done, however, especially in a case where a particularly heinous crime had been committed against people that they all knew.

Interest in the trial was so high that all the seats were soon taken up. Because Duff was going to be a witness, he was accorded a reserved seat. The bailiff escorted him to a chair next to Lydia, the girl from the saloon in Millersburgh, from whom Duff had taken the brooch. She, too, would be a witness.

"Hello," she said with a shy smile.

"Hello," Duff replied. "Lydia, isn't it?"

"Yes!" Lydia's s smile broadened because he had remembered her. "I've never done anything like this before." She laughed. "I've been in a saloon, of course. I mean I've never testified in a trial."

"There's nae a thing to it," Duff said reassuringly. "The solicitor will ask you some questions, and you've but to answer them truthfully."

"Solicitor?"

"The lawyer."

"Oh. Well, if all I have to do is answer some questions, I can do that."

CHAPTER TWELVE

Wally Jacobs returned to Rawhide Buttes, leading two saddled horses. He stopped at the livery stable, but had to shout several times before someone finally came out.

"Where is everyone?" he asked, irritated by the delay.

"They're all down at the trial."

"I need to board these horses for a while."

"How long?"

"Just keep 'em 'till I come for 'em."

"Reason I asked, you want to leave the saddles on?"

"No, it'll be at least one day, maybe a couple more." Jacobs signed in, paid one night in advance, then walked on down the street.

He saw a gallows under construction, nearly completed. It was sitting in an open space just beside the jail, visible from the street and from the cell window. "What's that for?" he asked one of the carpenters.

"It's to hang a couple murderin' rapists, that's what it's for," the carpenter replied.

"You mean you've already had the trial?"

"No, they ain't been tried yet. But they're about to be."

"Where is the trial to take place?"

"Down to the Lucky Star Saloon, but it won't do you no good to go there. You won't be able to get a seat. Ever'body in the whole county is wantin' to see them two get what's comin' to 'em."

Jacobs nodded, then continued on down to the Lucky Star. The carpenters were right about the place being crowded. By the time he entered the saloon there were no seats left. That didn't really bother him. He would much rather remain unobtrusively at the back of the saloon, anyway. He could watch everything that was going on without being noticed.

He stepped up the bar. "Gimme a beer."

"No beer."

"You're out of beer? This is a saloon, ain't it? What kind of saloon would run out of beer?"

"We're not out of beer, and this isn't a saloon. Right now, it's a courtroom. The bar is closed till after trial."

At that moment, the deputy sheriff came through a door in the back of the room. "Oyez, oyez, oyez, this here court is about to convene, the honorable Judge Daniel Kirkpatrick presiding. I'll be acting as bailiff. Everybody get up. Bartender, don't you be servin' no liquor of any kind till after the trial is over, these two have been found guilty, and the judge has sentenced 'em to be hung."

"You don't have to be worryin' none about that, Deputy. I closed the bar more 'n an hour ago 'n I ain't served a drop since."

Judge Kirkpatrick was wearing a black robe when he came out of the back room of the saloon and took a seat at his bench, which was the best table in the saloon. It had been placed upon a raised platform that had been built just for this purpose.

He took his glasses off, cleaned the lenses, then put them back on, very deliberately. For a moment, he stared out at the packed room. Finally, he picked up his gavel and pounded it on the table. "Are counselors present for both prosecution and defense?"

"David Tadlock for prosecution, Your Honor," a rather short, gray-headed man said, standing as he responded.

"Robert Rodale for defense, Your Honor." Rodale was a heavyset bald man, with thick glasses.

"Very well, trial may begin. Mr. Prosecutor, opening comments," the judge instructed.

Tadlock walked over to the roped-off area, behind which sat twelve jurors. There had been no voir dire of the jurors beyond ascertaining if all were sober.

He began by reminding the jurors of what outstanding citizens John and Nora Guthrie were. "John was president of the Rawhide Buttes Cattlemen's Association, and Mrs. Guthrie was superintendent of the children's Sunday school. These two men, possessed of souls so evil that it defies description, killed not only Mr. and Mrs. Guthrie, but their two wonderful children.

Because there are ladies present in the gallery, I won't be so graphic as to tell you what perfidious acts they visited upon Nora Guthrie, and her sweet, innocent, fourteen-year-old daughter, Suzie. Needless to say, the evilness of it defies description." He paused for effect, and got the gasps of horror that he wanted from the ladies who were present.

"Prosecution will present irrefutable evidence that the defendants, Jesse and T. Bob Cave, are the guilty parties." Tadlock took his seat.

The court waited an embarrassingly long time for Rodale to give his opening statement.

Judge Kirkpatrick looked over at him. "Mr. Rodale, I will not have this case thrown out on appeal because of inept defense. You will make an opening comment."

Rodale stood, but he didn't approach the jurors. He remained behind the table and looked toward them, with almost a pathetic expression on his face. He started to speak in a halting voice so low only those at the very front of the room heard him.

"Speak up, Rodale, we can't hear you back here!" a man shouted.

Judge Kirkpatrick slammed his gavel against the table. "The next person who shouts out will be removed from my courtroom," he said angrily. "You, Mr. Rodale. Please speak loudly enough that all can hear."

"Yes, Your Honor." Rodale cleared his throat. "I would remind the gentlemen of the jury, that there are no eyewitnesses to the murder, no one we can question as to the validity of their testimony. Without eyewitnesses, it will be impossible for you to find my clients guilty beyond a shadow of a doubt." Rodale sat down.

The first witness for the prosecution was sworn in.

"Tell the court your full name," Tadlock said.

"Jim Merrick."

"Is it true that you are the one who found the bodies?"

"Yes."

"And you found them inside the Guthrie home?"

"Yes."

"What were you doing there?" the prosecutor asked.

"I am vice president of the Rawhide Buttes Cattlemen's Association. I went out to John's ranch to talk about the Christmas dinner the Association was going to have. I saw the back door standing open, which I thought was odd for such a cold day. So I went inside, and that's when I found Mrs. Guthrie and the two children. It was . . . awful."

"Did you see John Guthrie?"

"No, not at that time."

"When did you find Mr. Guthrie?"

"I started searching through the house and found him slumped over his desk. There was blood all over his legs, the chair he was sitting in, and the floor."

"What did you do then?"

"I, uh, covered the bodies of Mrs. Guthrie and the young girl, then I rode back into town as fast as I could and got Marshal Worley."

"Thank you. No further questions. Your witness, Mr. Rodale."

"No questions."

"Witness may step down," Judge Kirkpatrick instructed.

Marshal Worley was the next witness. After a few questions, Tadlock walked over to the evidentiary table and picked up a bloodstained sheet of paper. He showed it to Worley. "Have you ever seen this before?"

"Yes. It's a note, written by John Guthrie."

"Objection," Rodale called. "It is only supposition that Guthrie wrote that note."

"Sustained," the judge ruled.

"Why do you say it was written by John Guthrie?" Tadlock asked the marshal. "Is that what Mr. Merrick told you when he gave it to you?"

"He didn't give me the note. He left it where it was. The first time I saw it, it was on the table under John's hand. Rigor mortis had set in, and he was still clutching the pen."

"And does the note say who attacked him and his family?"

"It does." Worley pointed to the defendant's table. "It says they did it."

Tadlock looked over toward the jury. "In his opening remarks, Mr. Rodale suggested that we have no eyewitness to this murder." He held up the piece of paper. "But this note provides that eyewitness for us, and it is no less than John Guthrie himself." Turning away from Marshal Worley, Tadlock walked back to his seat.

"You may cross, Mr. Rodale," the judge said.

Rodale approached the witness and, for a long moment just stared at him, whether trying to gather his thoughts, or make a point, nobody knew. Finally he spoke. "Marshal Worley, how long have been a city marshal?"

"Three years, here in Rawhide Buttes. I was a deputy sheriff over in Carbon County for a year before that, and, before that, a policeman in St. Louis."

"Then you have certainly been around long enough to understand the term circumstantial evidence, haven't you?"

"Yes, but this—"

"Just answer yes or no, please," Rodale said, interrupting Worley's response. "The truth is, you didn't actually see Mr. Guthrie write that note, did you? It could have been written by Mr. Merrick, couldn't it?"

"What? No, I doubt that."

"You *doubt* it, but you don't know for a fact, do you? Since nobody saw the note as it was being written, no one can state for a fact that Mr. Merrick didn't write it. He was the first one on the scene, was he not? So, it is not impossible to suppose that Merrick, for some reason of his own, could have written that note. The point is, we have no eyewitness, which means we have no one we can question. We have only this note, which prosecution wants us to assume was written by Mr. Guthrie. But in order to do so, we must depend upon circumstantial evidence only."

"I suppose you could say that," Worley said hesitantly.

"No further questions."

Kirkpatrick looked at the prosecutor. "Redirect, Mr. Tadlock."

"Not needed, Your Honor. Mr. Rodale's attempt to portray this note as evidence not in fact is nothing but a defensive ploy, and a weak one at that. Prosecution calls Duff MacCallister."

Duff walked to the front of the room, placed his left hand on a Bible held by the bailiff, and raised his right.

"Do you swear to tell the truth, the whole truth, and nothing but the truth, so help you God?" the bailiff intoned.

"I do."

"Witness may be seated," the judge said.

The prosecutor approached. "You are the one who brought in the two defendants. Is that correct?"

"Aye."

"Objection," Rodale called.

"What is the objection?" Judge Kirkpatrick asked.

"He didn't bring in two men, he brought in three men, one of whom was dead. And MacCallister is the one who killed him."

"Sustained. Counselor will rephrase the question as to the number of men Mr. MacCallister brought in."

"Did you, in fact, bring in three men?" Tadlock asked.

"Aye, three men it was."

"And one, a man name Sunset Moss, was dead when you brought him in?"

"Aye."

"Did you kill him?"

"Aye."

"Why did you kill him?"

"When I attempted to arrest them, Mr. Moss took issue and fired at me. I returned fire. Moss missed. I didn't."

Tadlock returned to the evidence table and picked up the brooch. "Would you tell the court about this, please?"

Duff nodded. "'Tis called a Scottish Lion brooch."

"Do you have some personal connection to the brooch?"

"Aye. I gave it to young Suzie Guthrie for her birthday, last September."

"Did you ever see her wear it?"

"She was wearing it the last time I saw her."

"And is that the last time you saw the brooch?"

"Nae, I saw it being worn by a young lady in Millersburgh."

"And did she tell you where she got it?"

"Objection, that is hearsay."

"I withdraw the question," Tadlock said. "The lady in question will be a witness, and we can get her direct testimony as to how she came by the brooch. Your witness, counselor."

"Mr. MacCallister, did you pursue my clients from a sense of personal outrage?"

"I was outraged by what happened, aye, and who wouldn't be?"

"But nobody else acted on their personal outrage, did they? Only you felt sufficiently driven by revenge to chase them down."

"I can speak for nobody else. But I did chase them down," Duff said.

"And when you found them, your rage over what you think they might have done was enough to cause you to kill Sunset Moss. That is true, isn't it?"

"Nae, 'tisn't true."

"Oh? Didn't you just confess before this court that you shot and killed the gentlemen in question?"

"He was nae gentlemen, and it was nae rage that caused me to shoot him. It was self-defense. He shot at me first."

"But you did feel some satisfaction that he was dead."

It wasn't a question, and Duff felt no need to answer. The two men stared at each other for a moment, then Rodale sat down.

"Mr. MacCallister, is it true that you were deputized by Sheriff Martin so that you had the authority to go after these men?" Tadlock asked from his seated position behind the prosecutor's table.

"Aye, 'tis true."

"Your Honor, permission to approach?" Tadlock asked.

"Both counselors may approach."

As they approached, Tadlock presented a telegram.

"I would like to enter this telegram as evidence. In it, you see that Sheriff Martin did deputize Mr. MacCallister."

"You care to examine, Mr. Rodale?" the judge asked.

Rodale looked at the telegram, then nodded.

"It may be entered as evidence," the judge said.

Tadlock turned and faced the gallery. "And I would like to call my next witness, Mayor R.W. Guthrie."

CHAPTER THIRTEEN

Everyone looked toward the short, stout man with the rather oversized nose as he approached the witness chair. An expression of intense sorrow showed on his face as he was sworn in.

"Mr. Guthrie, I know this is difficult for you, but I show you this brooch, and ask if you have ever seen it before," Tadlock asked.

"Yes, it was given to my granddaughter by Duff MacCallister."

"And did you ever see her wear it?"

"She wore it all the time."

"Thank you, I won't trouble you with any further questions." Tadlock sat down.

"Defense?" Judge Kirkpatrick asked.

"No questions of this witness, Your Honor."

Tadlock stood back up. "Prosecution calls Lydia Smith to the stand."

Lydia, modestly dressed and without makeup, approached nervously. The bailiff swore her in.

"Is Lydia Smith your real name?" Tadlock asked.

"No, sir," she answered.

"What is your real name?"

"Agnes Wood."

"Why are you called Lydia Smith?"

"Girls in my . . . uh . . . profession often use different names."

Tadlock showed her the brooch. "Have you ever seen this brooch before?"

"Yes. Someone gave it to me."

"Is the person who gave it to you present in this room?"

"Yes."

"Would you point him out, please?"

"Him." Lydia pointed to the man sitting at the right end of the table.

"Let it be known that the witness has pointed to T. Bob Cave as the man who gave her the brooch that was taken from young Suzie Guthrie."

"How can we believe this . . . woman . . . when we didn't even know her real name?" Rodale called out.

Angrily, Judge Kirkpatrick banged his gavel on the table. "One more outburst like that, Counselor, and you will be held in contempt!"

"Prosecution rests, Your Honor," Tadlock said.

"Defense, you may make your case now," the judge said.

Rodale stood. "If it please the court, defense calls Jesse Cave."

Jesse was sworn in, then he took the witness chair.

"Did you know John Guthrie?" Rodale asked.

"Yeah, I know'd 'im."

"How so?"

"Me 'n my brother 'n Sunset all worked for Mr. Guthrie."

"When you say Sunset, you are talking about the man MacCallister killed?"

"Yeah."

"How was Mr. Guthrie to work for?"

"He was a good man. He was good to his hands, 'n he paid fair wages."

"Did you, and or your brother, and or Sunset Moss kill John Guthrie and his family?"

"No, we didn't do it," Jesse said.

"Did you know he was dead?"

"Yeah, the three of us was out doin' some work, 'n when we come back to the house, we found Guthrie and his whole family dead."

"Did you see a note that Mr. Guthrie is alleged to have written?"

"No, we didn't see no note."

"Did you notify anyone?"

"No, we didn't tell nobody nothin' 'cause we figured we'd more 'n likely get blamed for it, so we took off runnin'. And, it turns out, we was blamed for it."

Rodale walked over to the table to pick up the brooch. Bringing it back, he showed it to Jesse.

"Have you ever seen this before?"

"Yeah, the little girl used to wear it all the time."

"The witness"—Rodale returned to the prosecutor's

table and referred to his notes—"Miss Wood, says that your brother gave the brooch to her. Is that true?"

Jesse nodded. "Yeah, that's true."

"How did he get it?"

"Why don't you ask him?"

Rodale surrendered his witness to Tadlock, whose attempt to cross-examine went nowhere as Jesse stuck by his claim that they had found the bodies, then ran when they thought they would be blamed for it.

T. Bob also took the stand.

"Did you take the brooch from the little girl?" Rodale asked.

"Yeah, I took it. But she was already dead when I took it."

"Why did you take it?"

"She was nice little girl. I wanted somethin' to remember her by."

"No further questions, Your Honor." Rodale sat down.

Tadlock began his questioning. "Mr. Cave, if you took the brooch to have something to remember her by, why did you give it away—to Miss Wood—within a matter of only a few days?"

"I got to thinkin' that this is a woman's thing, you know? It was embarrassin' to me to keep it, and that's why I give it away."

T. Bob Cave was the last witness, after which the two lawyers gave their closing statements, and the case was remanded to the jury.

* * *

Over in another part of town, at the Rocky Mountain Hotel, Hodge Doolin, the desk clerk, was looking at his registration book. "Mike, when is the last time you seen Mr. Walters?"

"I don't know. Three, maybe four days ago," Mike replied. "He said he wasn't feeling well and I asked if he wanted us to call a doctor for him, but he said no. Why?"

"Well, he paid for several days in advance, but his time is all used up. If he wants to stay any longer, he needs to come down here and either make arrangements to stay longer, or check out."

"You want me to check on him?"

"No, not yet," Doolin said. "He's been a good customer, paid in advance, and he hasn't given us any trouble. Let's give him time to come down on his own. I don't want him to feel like we're rushing him."

"All right. I wonder how the trial is going? I wish I could have been there for it."

"No need to be there," Doolin replied. "I can tell you exactly how it's going."

"Oh?"

"They're going to find both of them guilty, and they're going to hang. Hell, I don't know if you've seen it, but they already have the scaffold built."

"Who hasn't seen it?" Mike replied. "It's standing right out there in front of God and everyone. You think they'll hang 'em before Christmas?"

"I hope so. They took Christmas away from John Guthrie and his family, didn't they?"

* * *

When the jury left the room Wally Jacobs returned to the bar. "Can we buy somethin' to drink now that the jury's gone?"

"Marshal Worley and Deputy Masters says we can't," the bartender replied.

"How long you reckon the jury will be out?" Jim Merrick asked.

"Hell, Jim, you was one of the witnesses in the trial, you ought to know as well as anyone. If you was on the jury, how long would it take you to decide they're guilty?" the bartender asked.

"About five seconds."

"I don't expect it'll take any of 'em much longer than that. I don't see 'em as bein' out all that long."

The bartender's prediction was accurate. The jury deliberated for less than fifteen minutes, then sent word that they had reached a verdict, thus causing the court to be reconvened.

After taking his seat at the "bench," Judge Kirkpatrick took a swallow of something that looked quite a bit like whiskey, adjusted the glasses on the end of his nose, and cleared his throat. "Would the bailiff please bring the prisoners before the bench?"

The bailiff, who was leaning against the bar with his arms folded across his chest, spit a quid of tobacco into the brass spittoon, then leaned over toward the two Cave brothers. "You two get up, and go stand there in front of the judge."

The two men approached the bench.

"Mr. Foreman of the jury, I am informed that you have reached a verdict. Is that correct?" the judge asked.

"That is correct, Your Honor, we have reached a verdict."

"Would you publish that verdict, please?"

"Your Honor, we have found these two sorry, miserable excuses for men guilty," the foreman said.

"You couldn't 'a done nothin' but find 'em guilty," someone shouted from the gallery.

The judge banged his gavel on the table. "Order!" he called. "I will have order in my court." He looked over at the foreman. "So say you all?"

"So say we all," the foreman replied.

The judge took off his glasses and began polishing them as he studied the two men who were standing before him. "T. Bob and Jesse Cave, you two men have been tried by a jury of your peers—"

"Peers hell! They ain't nothin' but a bunch of drunks you rounded up from the saloon," Jesse shouted.

"And you have been found guilty of the crime of murdering John Guthrie, his wife, Nora, his son Timothy, and his daughter, Suzie," the judge said, paying no attention to Jesse's outburst. "Before this court passes sentence, have you anything to say?"

"Yeah," Jesse replied with a snarl. "We kilt 'em. And we raped the women. The little girl was just real good."

"They're evil!" Merrick shouted. "Hang 'em, Judge!"

Judge Kirkpatrick pounded his gavel again and kept pounding it until, finally, order was restored. "Oh, I intend to, Mr. Merrick. Yes, sir, I intend to." He glared at the two men for a long moment, then he cleared his throat.

"T. Bob Cave and Jesse Cave, it is the sentence of this court that on the seventeenth of this month, the two of you are to be hanged by your neck until you have breathed your last."

"Hoorah!" someone in the audience shouted, and again, Judge Kirkpatrick used his gavel to call for order.

"Now would be a good time for you two men to make peace with your Creator," Kirkpatrick said. "Do either of you wish to speak?"

"We're condemned men, right, Judge?" T. Bob asked.

"You are."

"Then I was thinkin', maybe since we're condemned 'n all, you would take some pity on us, and buy us a drink."

Some in the gallery laughed out loud at T. Bob's comment.

"Bartender?"

"Yes, Your Honor?"

"Bring these two men a drink of their choice. Then, you may open the bar again."

"Yes, sir, Your Honor."

"Whiskey!" Jesse called out.

Jacobs joined several others at the bar and bought a beer. Standing at the far end, he drank his beer and stared at the two prisoners until one of them happened to notice him. He held his beer out toward Jesse Cave, then nodded almost imperceptibly.

With just the suggestion of a smile, Jesse returned the nod.

After he and his brother had their drink, the sheriff and his deputy marched them out of the saloon.

"I'll be there come the day of the hangin'," someone shouted. "And I'll watch you both die!"

"Me too!" another put in.

Jesse glared at the men, but said nothing.

"Guilty! They found both of them guilty 'n they're goin' to hang 'em on Wednesday!" a man said, coming into the hotel a few minutes later.

"Hello, Crader," Doolin said. "I was hoping they would be hung before Christmas."

"I plan to be there, bright-eyed and bushy-tailed, to watch both of 'em hang," Crader said.

Jim Merrick and few others followed Crader into the hotel, and all of them started talking about the upcoming hanging. A few minutes later, Judge Kirkpatrick came in to the hotel, and those who were in the lobby rushed over to congratulate him.

"No need to congratulate me, boys. I just did my job," the judge said. He stepped up to the check-in desk. "I've set the seventeenth as the date for the hanging, so I shall require accommodations until then."

"Yes, sir, Judge," Doolin said, checking him in.

"Judge, after you get checked in, come on into the hotel bar and let us buy you a drink," Jim suggested.

"Yeah," Crader said. "We'll toast you good and proper."

"Well, I appreciate that, boys." Kirkpatrick signed in, then went into the hotel bar and restaurant, which was just off the lobby.

"I've never seen so many people takin' on so about some folks that's goin' to get hung," Mike said. "I wonder how many of 'em have ever actually seen someone hung."

"Have you?" Doolin asked.

"Yeah, I seen one once. And it wasn't somethin' I'm in a hurry to see again."

Across town, Dan Hastings, who owned the Rawhide Wagon Freight Company, was having supper with his wife Amelia and their nine-year-old daughter Laura.

"They're goin' to hang 'em both," he said. "They've already got the scaffold built. They didn't testify at the trial exactly what they did to Mrs. Guthrie and her daughter, but Jim Merrick told me personally that—"

"Dan!" Rose said sharply.

"What?"

Rose nodded toward Laura.

"Oh. Oh, yeah. All right. I'll tell you later."

"Laura is going to be an angel in the Christmas play at school," Rose said.

Dan smiled at his daughter. "Why, you don't need a play to make you an angel. You are already my angel."

Laura smiled right back.

"Honey, you haven't eaten any of your supper," Rose said.

"I'm not very hungry, Mama," Laura said.

"But you need to eat something. You have to keep your strength up if you are going to be in the school play."

"It hurts when I eat."

Rose frowned. "What do you mean, it hurts when you eat?"

"My throat hurts when I chew."

"Well, at least eat some mashed potatoes. You don't have to chew mashed potatoes."

"I'm not hungry," Laura complained.

"Try. If you'll just eat the mashed potatoes, we'll go to Miss Ensor's dress shop tomorrow, and buy a dress for you to wear in the play."

"All right," Laura said.

CHAPTER FOURTEEN

Chugwater

Meagan sat in the living room of the apartment over her dress shop, drinking coffee as she looked out over First Street. Since returning home, she had been gathering up the dresses she intended to take back to Rawhide Buttes tomorrow to help Cora get ready for Christmas.

Normally, Christmas was a happy season. The women who came in to buy dresses for themselves and their daughters were always excited. The town of Chugwater had planned to go all out to celebrate. Christmas of 1890 would be the first Christmas since Wyoming became a state, so there were special celebrations scheduled.

But, in light of what had happened to the mayor's family, the question was, would the celebrations go on? R.W. insisted that they would, and even suggested that it would help him and his wife recover from the terrible tragedy that had struck them. But how, Meagan wondered, could someone recover from that?

She took another swallow of her coffee, enjoying the bracing richness of it, lightened with cream and sweetened with sugar, and thought about Duff. Where was he? Somewhere warm and dry? More important, was he somewhere safe?

She had never met anyone like him. Despite his obvious refinement, no cowboy, miner, or mountain man she had ever known was more masculine. Duff was the first to say that he wasn't lightning fast on the draw, but she had seen him make impossible shots, including one that saved her life. An outlaw had been holding her in front of him with a gun pointed to her head, but had made the mistake of barely peeking around her. Meagan heard the whiz of the bullet in flight, and the sound of it striking flesh. Duff had not given a second thought to taking the shot, nor had she been surprised by it.

He was also a humanitarian. She had seen him perform deeds of great compassion in the relatively short time she had known him. She thought of the words of consolation he had given R.W. and Martha, bringing them comfort with the thought that they had to but think of John and his family, and they would actually be reliving that moment.

However, that same man who could be so commiserative when required had set out in pursuit of the men who had murdered the mayor's family. And when he found them, he would show them little pity. But even that, Meagan realized, was an act of kindness for his friend R.W.

Would she and Duff ever get married, she wondered?

She wanted very much for that to happen and hoped that someday it would. But in order for that to happen, he would have to ask her. If he had one failing, it might be that he was unable to discern how deeply she actually felt about him.

She decided then and there if he didn't ask her, she would ask him. The worst that could happen would be that he would turn her down. If he did, it would at least keep her from wasting any more time on a relationship that wasn't going anywhere.

She finished her coffee, then turned away from the window and realized she had drunk coffee just before going to bed. She grimaced. "That's not the smartest thing I've ever done."

She needn't have worried. She was asleep within ten minutes of pulling up the covers and her head hitting the pillow.

On his way back to Chugwater, Duff didn't go by road, but by following the south fork of Antelope Creek. It was dark, and it had gotten much colder.

"Sky, lad, we have been in for some cold rides lately, haven't we?" Duff said, leaning down to pat his horse on its neck. Ahead of him, appearing as if it were an apparition in the gathering gloom, he saw someone coming toward him.

Duff smiled when he recognized him. "Sky, 'tis none other than Elmer Gleason. But what is he doing out here on such a cold night as this?"

He asked his foreman that same question as the two riders closed on each other.

"I knew you'd follow the creek back, seein' as it's shorter than the road, and I thought you might appreciate some hot coffee on a night like this," Elmer said.

"Och, 'tis a good lad ye be, Elmer, 'n I'll fight any man who says otherwise."

Elmer opened a canvas bag, then began pulling out folds of wool until he reached a bottle, which was wrapped round with burlap. He handed the bottle to Duff, who pulled the cork and was rewarded with a curl of aromatic vapor. Holding it under his nose, he could feel the warmth of it.

"Elmer, 'tis a genius ye are. A pure and unadulterated genius." He took a swallow of the coffee, then smiled again as he tasted something that was welcome and familiar. "And would that be a bit o' Mackinlay's that you've added for flavoring?"

"You tell me, Duff. Is there any finer scotch than Mackinlay's?"

"None indeed," Duff replied, taking another swallow.

"Do you plan to share any of that? Or will you be drinkin' it all like the cheap Scotsman you are?" Elmer asked.

"Have a good long pull at it," Duff said, passing the bottle back to Elmer.

Elmer turned the bottle up, drank from it, then handed it back. "We'd best be gettin' on unless you want to stay out here 'n freeze to death."

"Aye, being warm in m' own house 'tis something I've been looking forward to for the whole day."

Upon their arrival at Sky Meadow, a couple of Duff's cowboys came out to meet them. Woodward took hold of Sky, and MacDougal grabbed Elmer's horse.

"You two go on inside and get warm," Woodward said. "We'll take care of your mounts."

"'Tis much obliged I am to ye, Mr. Woodward," Duff said. "I wonder if it's too much to hope for that the Mrs. Sterling has supper ready."

Woodward smiled. "She cooked a big haunch of beef today. Me 'n the others have done et some of it, and I can tell you, it's damn good."

"Elmer, would ye be joining me for supper, lad?"

"I'd be mighty pleased to do so," Elmer said as they walked to the house.

"Mr. MacCallister, it is good to have you home, sir," his cook said. The house was redolent with the aroma of roasted beef.

"Believe me, Mrs. Sterling, it is good to be home."

Unaware that Duff had returned home the night before, Meagan left for Rawhide Buttes the next morning. It was her second trip from Chugwater in as many weeks. By stagecoach, it took just over five hours, but because she was one of only three passengers, the trip was more comfortable than it would have been had the coach been full. She sat next to the window in the rear seat, warmly wrapped in a blanket supplied by the coach company.

Rawhide Buttes

She looked out as the coach rolled into town. GROCERIES AND PROVISIONS, advertised a sign on the first building the coach passed. Next came a hotel, a saloon, an apothecary, another saloon, a leather goods store, and another saloon. The next thing she saw gave her a start. It was a gallows. An announcement was nailed to a post.

At Nine A.M. on December 17,
JESSE and T. BOB CAVE,
the murderers
of *John, Nora, Timothy,* and *Susan Guthrie,*
will be legally hanged on these gallows.
The public is invited.

"Duff got them," she whispered.

"I beg your pardon, dear?" asked the other woman in the coach.

Meagan shook her head. "Nothing. I was just thinking aloud, is all."

The coach stopped at the stagecoach depot.

"Here we are, folks, all safe and sound!" the driver called as he climbed down and opened the door. "Miss Parker, you sure do have a lot of luggage. You want it all delivered to the hotel?"

"No, just this bag." She pointed to one of the four

items of luggage she'd brought with her. "Take the other three to Ensor's Dress Emporium," she instructed, pressing a dollar into his hand. "It's four buildings down, just on the other side of the Rawhide Buttes Bank."

"Yes, ma'am. I'll see that it gets there," the driver replied with a broad smile as he folded the bill and stuck it in his pocket.

It was cold outside without the blanket, but as she had pointed out to the driver, the store was only a short walk from the depot. It wasn't terribly freezing, but she was happy to arrive.

"Oh, do come in out of the cold!" Cora Ensor greeted when Meagan stepped inside a few minutes later. "Did you have a hard trip?"

"No, the ride was smooth, and I was wrapped in a blanket, so it wasn't too bad."

"I can't tell you how much I appreciate you coming all the way up here to help me get my store started."

Meagan took off her coat and hat and hung both of them on a coatrack. "I'm glad to be here. The way I look at it, we are scratching each other's backs. I can make dresses faster than I can sell them down in Chugwater. Your store gives me another outlet."

"And with Christmas coming, I'm sure there will a lot of men wanting to buy something nice for their wives," Cora added.

"And their girlfriends."

"And their girlfriends?" Cora asked. Then she laughed. "Oh, you mean the unmarried men who have girlfriends. For a moment, I thought you meant that some married men might be buying something for their wives and their girlfriends."

"Yes, them, too."

"What? Why, that would be awful!"

Meagan chuckled. "You're just starting your business, Cora. You don't have the luxury of being judgmental. If a man wants to buy a dress for his wife *and* his girlfriend, your job is to sell both dresses to him . . . and keep his secret."

Cora laughed as well. "My, and miss the opportunity for gossip?"

"You have to make up your mind, which do you most want to be? A successful businesswoman, or a gossip?"

"My lips are sealed," Cora said.

"Cora, I predict you will be a wonderful business-woman."

"I would be very happy if I could be only half as successful as you have been, Meagan."

"I'm sure you will be. Did you get the ad placed in the newspaper?"

"Yes, here it is." Cora picked up a copy of the paper from a countertop.

FOR THE HOLIDAYS—
Fine Dresses and Gowns,
Designed and Sewn by
MEAGAN PARKER,
to be found at
ENSOR'S DRESS EMPORIUM.
Good Prices.

"Oh, that's very nice," Meagan said. "But you didn't have to use my name."

"You don't mind that I did, do you?"

"No, not at all. I'm flattered."

Meagan and Cora were unpacking the last of the packages Meagan had brought from Chugwater when the bell on the door jangled. Looking toward the front, they saw a woman and a young girl come into the store.

"Mrs. Hastings," Cora said, smiling at the customer. "How nice to see you."

"I wanted to see how you were coming along with your store. I think it's just wonderful the new things you'll be getting in, just in time for Christmas."

"Yes, I'm hoping I'll do a lot of business in the next few days as people shop for Christmas."

"I'm going to be in the school Christmas play," the little girl said. She coughed.

"That's wonderful," Meagan said.

The little girl coughed again.

"Yes, Laura is going to be an angel," Mrs. Hastings said. "If she isn't too sick, that is. She wasn't feeling too well last night, and she woke up with a terrible cough this morning. She's also been wheezing as she breathes. I don't know what's wrong with her."

"You must get better, Laura," Cora said. "I certainly wouldn't want you to miss being in the play."

"The reason I'm here," Mrs. Hastings said, "is that I

want to buy an angel's costume for Laura. I know it's almost too late for that but—"

"It isn't too late at all," Meagan said. "I would be happy to make one for her."

When it was obvious that Mrs. Hastings had no idea who Meagan was, Cora introduced her. "This is Meagan Parker. She is a dressmaker who has her own shop in Chugwater. She has made most of the dresses I'll be featuring in my shop."

"Oh, how wonderful," Mrs. Hastings said. "Isn't that wonderful, Laura?"

"Yes, ma'am. Mama, my throat hurts."

"Then we need to get you back home. It looks like a storm is coming, and I don't think it will do you good to be out in it, what with a cold coming on."

CHAPTER FIFTEEN

"Isn't she a darling little girl?" Cora asked Meagan after Mrs. Hastings and Laura were gone.

"Yes, but I'm a little worried about her. I hope Mrs. Hastings takes her to a doctor."

"Why bother? Everyone knows there's nothing you can do about a cold, except just ride it out."

"If that's what it is," Meagan said.

"Why do you say that? Do you think it might be something other than a cold?"

"I don't know," Meagan admitted. "Maybe not. But the sore throat, the wheezing, the way her voice sounded. That is a little worrisome, as if it might be something more than just a cold."

"Well, if it gets worse, I assure you that Mrs. Hastings will see the doctor. She is a very good mother, and she dotes on that child."

"I'm sure she does. Please don't think I'm casting aspersions on her."

"I make no such assumptions. I know you're just concerned." Changing the subject, Cora pointed to one of the dresses Meagan had brought with her. "You said a few minutes ago that I should attach a bow to the bodice. What color would you suggest?"

"Oh, I would say red," Meagan replied with a broad smile. "The color will be in accordance with the season."

"Will you be spending Christmas here in Rawhide Buttes?" Cora asked, as she went through a box of colorful ribbon bows.

"No, I'll be returning to Chugwater a few days before Christmas. We have a Christmas dance every year, and I don't want to miss it."

"You don't want to miss the dance? Or you don't want to miss someone who will be at the dance?" Cora asked with a knowing grin.

"Well, if you must know, I don't want to miss someone who will be at the dance."

"Aha! I knew it!" Cora said. "It's Mr. MacCallister, isn't it? I know you were together while you were here for the funeral. They said he was here for the trial, too, but I didn't attend the trial. I've heard of him. I think everyone in Wyoming has heard of him. He is quite the hero, but what is he like?"

"I'm not sure I know how to answer that," Meagan said. "He's a Scotsman—charming, imperious, and uncompromising."

"I would say that you answered it fairly well," Cora said. "He's more than just a friend, isn't he?"

"Yes," Meagan said without going into any more detail.

"Well, would you let me buy you lunch?" Cora asked.

"Yes, I would appreciate that."

The dining room at the Rocky Mountain Hotel was very well appointed. The tables were covered with white tablecloths and the crystal and silver gleamed from the gaslights in the large, glass globes that hung from the ceiling.

The two young women were greeted when they arrived at the dining room. "Hello, Cora. Your table is ready for you and your guest."

"Thank you, May Ellen. This is Miss Meagan Parker. She is the wonderfully talented dressmaker who will be supplying my shop with a whole line of new dresses."

"How wonderful!" May Ellen said, and led them to a table.

They sat, they ordered, then as they waited for their meal they talked about Cora's dress shop.

"If you get very successful, and I know you will, I won't be able to supply you with enough dresses to keep you going," Meagan said. "You're going to have to hire a full-time seamstress."

"I know. I've already spoken to a lady here about coming to work for me. I intend to make your dresses the top of the line."

"Has she agreed?"

When Cora nodded, Meagan continued. "Before I return, I'll help you decorate your store for Christmas."

"Oh, I just love Christmas, don't you?"

"Yes, I do . . . though this Christmas will be quite melancholy back in Chugwater."

"Oh, yes, of course. You are talking about Mayor Guthrie, aren't you? What a terrible tragedy it was to lose an entire family like that. At least the men who did it have been caught, and will pay a just punishment."

"Yes, I saw the sign as I came into town. I knew that once Duff started after them, they would be caught."

"It seems like it just come on to her," a man at the next table was saying. "First it was Billy; he started coughin' and wheezin' and havin' a hard time breathin'. Now it's his mama."

"It's goin' around," said the other man at the table. "I hear Booker is took down with it too. An' he's got a awful fever. Al Peterson said his wife is sick with it."

"What does the doctor say about them?"

"I don't know. I ain't a' heered. What's he say about your wife and boy?"

"I ain't sent for him yet, but I aim to if they ain't neither one of 'em any better by tomorrow."

Cora looked at Meagan and frowned. "That sounds like what Laura Hastings has."

"Yes, it does. And it doesn't sound good."

"I'm sure it's no more than a few cases of catarrh," Cora said. "That seems to be quite a common illness during the winter. I'm sure Laura will be over it by Christmas."

In another part of town, Dr. George Poindexter was examining Laura Hastings. He gave her a glass of water. "Take a sip of this."

"I'm not thirsty."

"You don't have to take but one sip."

Laura took a drink of water, then winced as she swallowed.

"Does it hurt to swallow?" he asked.

"Yes sir."

He put his fingers to both sides of her throat and felt that the lymph nodes were swollen. "Open your mouth and say 'ahh' for me, would you, honey?"

"Ahh." Laura said. Her voice was hoarse, and she was wheezing with every breath she took.

He looked up at Mrs. Hastings. "Has her nose been running?"

"Yes, it has."

"I want you to keep her home from school over the next few days. And don't let anyone get around her."

"How can I not let anyone get around her? I have to be around her. I'm her mother."

"Of course," Dr. Poindexter said. "That doesn't apply to you, anyway. You've already been exposed. I mean, don't let anyone else around her."

"Exposed? What do you mean, exposed?"

"I'm not sure that it means anything, yet. We'll just have to wait and see."

"I have to go to school," Laura said. "I'm in the Christmas play."

The doctor put his hand on her shoulder. "Well, we have a few more days until Christmas. Let's just see how this plays out, shall we?"

Later that same evening, Deputy Jason Masters stepped up to the cell occupied by the Cave brothers. "Do you boys see this here?" He held up something for their inspection. "This here is a calendar. Today is Monday, December fifteenth. Christmas is Thursday, December twenty-fifth. That means there's only ten more days till Christmas.

"When you two was kids, did you get excited, countin' off the days till Christmas? I know I did. What do you say we count off the days together? Today is the fifteenth, tomorrow is the sixteenth . . . this is fun, ain't it? Where did we stop? Oh, yeah, next day is the seventeenth and . . . uh . . . wait a minute. Somethin' is s'posed to happen on the seventeenth, ain't it? What is it? Oh yeah, I know. You two boys is goin' to get your necks stretched come the seventeenth, ain't you? And guess what, that's just two days from now." Masters laughed.

"Oh, have you looked out the window? From your cell, you've got a real good view of the gallows that was built just for you. Ain't nobody else ever been hung on it. That ought to make you feel real proud. I've talked to

Mr. Dysart, the photographer. He's going to get a picture of the two of you hangin' there. It's goin' to make you boys real famous.

"Some folks, when they get hung, why their tongue sticks out like this." Masters stuck his tongue out and made a sound deep in his throat, like someone strangling.

"I hope you two boys do that. It'll make a real good picture, seein' you with your tongues all stuck out like that."

Jesse and T. Bob glared at him, but made no response.

As the deputy walked away from the cell, still chuckling, T. Bob climbed up onto the bunk and looked through the barred window. "He's right, Jesse, they've done got the gallows built already."

"Get down from there and quit lookin' at it," Jesse said. "That won't do nothin' but drive you crazy."

"They're goin' to do it, Jesse. They're goin' to hang us," T. Bob said.

"They ain't hung us yet."

"But they're goin' to. There ain't no way we're goin' to get out of this."

"I told you, get down from there and quit lookin' at it," Jesse said again.

"I can't help but look at it. It's just outside the window."

Jesse clenched his teeth. "Then don't look through the window."

* * *

In the wee hours of the seventeenth, Wally Jacobs lit a candle to push away the darkness inside the livery stable. Following the bubble of light, he found his horse and the two horses Dingo had given him. He saddled them, then led them out quietly, across the street and down the alley until he reached the back of the jail-house. There, he tied the horses off.

One of the horses whickered, and Jacobs looked around quickly to make certain nobody was observing him.

Inside the jailhouse, Deputy Jason Masters was dozing at his desk when something awakened him. Opening his eyes, he glanced around the nearly dark room, illuminated only dimly by the low flame of a kerosene lantern. It was very cold outside, but a pot-bellied, coal-burning stove was keeping the room warm. A blue-steel pot of coffee sat on the stove, perfuming the room with its rich aroma.

Outside the small building the wind moaned, rattling the shutters and whistling through the cracks.

He looked toward the clock on the wall, its pendulum moving back and forth in a measured *tick-tock*. According to the clock, it was three-thirty in the morning. He stood up, rubbed his eyes, stretched, then walked over to the stove to pour himself a cup of coffee.

Holding the coffee, he stepped over to the jail cell to

look inside. The two brothers were wide awake, sitting on their bunks.

Masters took a slurping drink of his coffee. "Can't you fellas sleep any?"

"No," Jesse growled.

"Oh I get it. You're excited about Christmas, aren't you? Yes, it'll be here in a couple days and . . . oh, no, wait. Doggone it." Masters snapped his fingers. "Come to think of it, you won't be here for Christmas, will you? You're goin' to hang in another"—he looked toward the clock—"five and a half hours. Well, I'll tell you what. Come Christmas Day, I'll step into the saloon and have a drink for you two boys. How will that be? Merry Christmas," he said with a malevolent chuckle.

Masters turned away from the cell, the grin still on his face. He was startled by the sight of someone standing by his desk. "Who the hell are you? How'd you get in here?"

"The name is Wally Jacobs, and I've come to visit your prisoners."

"Are you crazy? It's three-thirty in the morning. There's no visiting at three-thirty in the morning."

"Deputy?" Jesse called.

"Now, what the hell do you want?" Masters asked, turning back toward the jail cell. Both prisoners were standing just on other side of the bars, and they were grinning broadly.

"Is that any way to treat our cousin?" Jesse asked.

"Your cousin?" Masters replied, a look of concern on

his face. At that moment, he felt a hand clasp over his mouth, while another hand flashed quickly across his neck. There was a stinging sensation, then a wetness at his collar.

Jacobs let go of him and stepped back. Masters dropped his coffee, felt his legs turn to rubber, then he fell to the floor. Putting his hand to his throat, he pulled it away and looked in horror at the blood on his fingers. He screamed, but the scream was in his head only. His windpipe had been cut, and he could make no sound.

As he was losing consciousness, he saw Jacobs opening the cell door.

The two men hurried out, and T. Bob stepped over to look down at the fallen deputy. "Now who won't be celebrating Christmas?" He sneered.

"The horses are saddled, and in the alley behind the jail," Jacobs said. "Let's get out of here."

"We ain't goin' nowhere yet," Jesse said. "We got other business to take care of."

"What business?" Jacobs asked.

"That judge that sentenced us, Kirkpatrick, has come back to town to witness the hangin'. I heard Masters and Worley talkin' about it. He's stayin' in the hotel. We're goin' to pay him a visit."

"We ain't got time for that," Jacobs objected.

"Yeah, we do," Jesse said. "We're goin' to take time for it."

They grabbed the horses and moved through the alley, tying them off behind the hotel, then went inside the front. The lobby was dark, except for one kerosene lantern burning dimly on the desk. As the desk clerk snored loudly, they checked the registration book.

"He's in Two-Twelve," Jesse whispered.

Taking the spare key to the room, the three men left the desk clerk undisturbed, and moved quickly and quietly up to the second floor. They walked down the carpeted hallway until they found the door. Slowly, Jesse unlocked the door, then pushed it open.

The steady, rhythmic breathing told them that the judge was sleeping soundly.

Jacobs took out his knife.

"Wait," Jesse said. "I want him to know he's about to die."

Jesse put on the judge's shoulder. "Wake up. Wake up."

The judge snorted, then opened his eyes. "What is it? Who is there?"

"You don't recognize us?" Jesse asked. "You're the one that sentenced us to hang, and you don't even recognize us?"

"You!" the judge gasped.

Wally's knife flashed across Kirkpatrick's throat.

His eyes opened wide in shock, then he fell back down onto the pillow.

"Let's get out of here," T. Bob said.

"Not yet," Jesse said.

"What do you mean, not yet? What's left?"

"We're takin' him down to the gallows and we're goin' to hang him there."

T. Bob frowned. "You mean carry him through the lobby?"

"No. We'll push him through the window and out into the alley."

CHAPTER SIXTEEN

One of the carpenters who had built the gallows walked into Kathy's Diner during the breakfast hour. In a highly agitated state, he looked around till he spotted Marshal Worley. "Marshal, you'd better get down to the gallows fast."

"What happened? Pete, don't tell me they collapsed during the night."

"No sir, it ain't that. It's somethin' worse. It's somethin' much worse. You'd better get on down there, right now."

"Kathy, I'll get you later," Marshal Worley called as he followed Pete toward the front door.

"No problem, Marshal," she called back.

The marshal hurried alongside Pete. "Now what is it, Pete?"

"You'll see."

Even before they reached the jail, Worley saw scores of people gathered in the street in front of the building, but he couldn't see the gallows. They had been built in between the jailhouse and the blacksmith shop, which was next door. And the crowd was growing as more people started running toward the scene.

He quickened his gait. Arriving at the crowd, he started pushing the people aside. "Make way. Let me through!" he ordered.

When he got to where he could see the gallows he stopped, gasping in shock and anger. Two bodies were hanging from the gallows—his deputy, Jason Masters, and Judge Daniel Kirkpatrick.

The newspaper put out an EXTRA edition that hit the streets before nine o'clock.

PRISONERS ESCAPE JAIL

Shocking Scene on Main Street

This morning Judge Daniel Kirkpatrick and Deputy Jason Masters were found dead, suspended from the gallows that had been constructed for the legal execution of T. Bob and Jesse Cave.

After cutting the bodies down, Marshal Worley checked the jail, where he discovered that the cell door was open and the Cave brothers were missing. The two had been sentenced to hang for the brutal slaying of John Guthrie, as well as Mr. Guthrie's wife, son, and daughter.

It is the marshal's belief that the prisoners had assistance in escaping, as it seems quite unlikely they could have opened the jail cell door by themselves.

"Oh, my!" Cora said when the newspaper was delivered.

"What is it?" Meagan asked.

"Those men who murdered Nora Guthrie and her whole family have escaped. And not only that, they murdered poor Deputy Masters and Judge Kirkpatrick."

"Oh, that is awful," Meagan said.

"It's also frightening."

"I see no reason to be frightened of them. It would extremely foolish of them to come back to Rawhide Buttes."

Cora nodded. "Yes, now that you mention it, I think it would be foolish of them. I shan't let them spoil my Christmas." She set the newspaper down. "Tell me, Meagan, do you think it is too early to decorate the store for Christmas?"

"No, I don't think it is too early at all," Meagan said. "After all, Christmas is only a week away. Besides, I'll be going back in another day or two, so if I'm going to help with the decorations, we must get started right away."

Sidewinder Gorge

Late that afternoon, Jacobs and the Cave brothers rode into the entrance of the gorge. Jacobs dismounted and stood with his arms extended out to each side for a moment. They saw a puff of smoke, followed by the sound of a gunshot.

"What the hell? They're shooting at us!" T. Bob hollered, frightened.

"Hold on," Jacobs said.

Two more puffs of smoke were followed by two more gunshots.

"That's the signal," Wally said as he remounted. "We can go in, now."

Inside the canyon, Max Dingo sat at a table in the outlaw saloon. He was told that three riders were coming in.

"Who are they?" he asked.

"It's Wally and the Cave brothers," Nitwit Mitt said.

"Good, good. He got 'em, I see. Bring 'em to me as soon they get here."

Fifteen minutes later, the three men were standing in front of Dingo.

"Here they are," Nitwit said.

"How much money do you two boys have?" Dingo asked, looking at Jesse and T. Bob.

"We don't have no money at all. We was in jail, and what money we did have was took from us," Jesse said.

"I sort of thought as much," Dingo replied. "Tell me, just how do you expect to pay for your time while you are here?"

"What do you mean, pay for our time while we're

here? Who should we pay? And why should we have to pay to be here?" Jesse asked indignantly.

"Why, you should pay me, of course. And as to why, it's simple. As long as you are inside this canyon, you are safe. Nobody from the law knows about it, and even if they did know, they couldn't get in. You're as safe here as you would be inside a fort. Don't you think that's worth something?"

"Well, I—"

Dingo held up his hand to stop him. "Are you hungry? We got beans, ham, bread. You're welcome to any food we have as long as you are here."

"Thanks!" Jesse grinned.

Dingo smirked. "That comes with the rent you'll be payin' for stayin' here."

"Where are we s'posed to get the money that we're to pay you with?" T. Bob asked.

"Well, boys, I expect you'll get it the way ever'one else in here does. You'll find a job to do, you'll do it, then you'll give me one third of whatever you make."

"One third?" Jesse exclaimed, spittle coming out with the shouted word.

Dingo turned and looked at Jacobs. "Wally, didn't you explain things to these boys?"

"I haven't had time to explain it all, yet. Anyway, I figured that more 'n likely, you'd do a better job of tellin' 'em how things work here."

"How things work, yes indeed," Dingo said. "Jesse, T. Bob, I have to tell you that I don't understand why you two are bellyachin' about this. If we hadn't arranged to break you out of jail, by now you'd both be crow bait."

Jesse shrugged. "So what's next? Do we go out and look for something that will make some money for us?"

"You'll stay here, eating my beans and staying out of trouble, until I find something for you to do."

"What if we don't want to stay here?" T. Bob asked. "What if we just moved on right now, and took our chances?"

"Where are you going to go? More to the point, how are you going to get there?" Dingo hadn't moved from the table.

"What do you mean, how are we goin' to get there? I reckon we'll just ride out on the same horses we rode in on," T. Bob said.

"Not on my horses, you ain't."

T. Bob was confused. "Your horses?"

"Tell me, boys, are those the same horses you was ridin' when you was caught?" Dingo asked.

Jesse thought a minute. "No, they're different from the ones we had."

"Where did you get the horses?"

"They was out back of the jail when Wally broke us—" Jesse stopped and stared at Dingo for a long moment. "They're your horses, ain't they?"

Dingo smiled. "That's right. I told Wally that he could *borrow* them so you two would have some way to get here once you escaped. If you stay here, you'll be needin' a way to get around. Especially if you are going to find some way of making money for me."

Jesse looked at T. Bob, then back to Dingo. "So what you're sayin' is, we can keep the horses, and we can stay here and eat the food, but we'll be workin' for you. Is that right?"

Dingo smiled broadly. "You're right, Wally. These boys is pretty smart, after all."

Chugwater

It was beginning to show signs of the season. Volunteers were wrapping greenery and red ribbons around the lampposts, and the merchants were beginning to decorate their establishments. Only the R.W. Guthrie Building and Supply Company was not joining the other merchants. It was still draped in black bunting.

Duff rode into town to pick up the mail. Seeing a letter from Meagan, he smiled and took it with him over to Fiddlers' Green to read.

Biff greeted him heartily. "Duff, Rose made haggis, neeps, and tatties for lunch today. I can't stand the stuff, but I know you like it, so there's some back in the kitchen, keeping warm for you."

"Ye do know, don't ye, Biff, that the only reason I call ye m' friend, is because you had the good sense to marry a Scottish lass?"

"So you tell me. Have a table in the back there. I'll bring your meal and a dram."

As he waited for the meal, he opened and read Meagan's letter.

Dear Duff,

By now, I'm sure you have heard that Jesse and T. Bob Cave have escaped. In doing so, they murdered poor Deputy Masters and Judge Kirkwood. They hung the bodies on the very gallows from which they were scheduled to hang.

Marshal Worley says that he has contacted Sheriff Martin in Cheyenne, and Martin will raise a large body of deputies to go in pursuit, which means you will not have to. I hope that you don't, for I would worry about you. I have never known of anyone as evil as these men appear to be.

On a happier note, I am nearly finished with my task here, and Cora's store is all ready for Christmas. I shall be returning home in two more days, in time for the Christmas Eve dance.

> *Love,*
> *Your Meagan*

Biff brought the plate and the Scotch. "From Meagan?" he asked, indicating the letter.

"Aye."

"Does she say when she'll be back?"

"Before Christmas, she says."

"Are you plannin' on marryin' that girl?" Before Duff could reply, Biff held out his hand. "I know. It's none of my business. But I'm talkin' to you as a friend, not just your friend, but as a friend to both of you. I know you have strong feelings for her, and she's certainly made no secret of how she feels about you. So, if you don't plan on marryin' her, the only right thing to do is to let her know how things are."

Duff was silent for a long moment, drumming his fingers on the table.

Biff cleared his throat. "I'm sorry if I made you angry, Duff, for that wasn't my intention. I just felt that—"

Duff held his hand up to stop Biff in mid-sentence. "Ye haven't made me angry, lad, for there is truth in what you say. But there is Skye."

"Skye is dead, Duff."

"Aye, but there is still so much of her in my heart that I dinnae know if it would be fair to Meagan."

"Duff, Skye loved you. Do you think she wouldn't want you to be happy?"

"There is much to what you say," Duff replied.

"You're damn right there is. Look, I know I just spoke out of turn, but it's like I said. You are a good friend. If you were my brother, I wouldn't be talking to you any different than I am now. I've got to get back to the bar. You just think about what I said."

Duff nodded. "Aye. I'll think about it." He watched Biff walk away, recalling Skye, in memories that were sweet . . . and painful.

Ian McGregor owned the White Horse Pub in Donuun in Argyllshire, Scotland. His daughter Skye was a buxom lass with long red hair, flashing blue eyes, and a friendly smile. She and Duff were soon to be married, their banns already posted on the church door.

"Skye, would you step outside with me for a moment?" Duff asked.

"Ian, best you keep an eye on them," one of the customers said. "Else they'll be outside sparking."

Skye blushed prettily as the others laughed at the jibe. Duff took her hand in his and walked outside with her.

"Only four more weeks until we are wed," Skye said. "I can hardly wait."

"No need to wait. We can go into Glasgow and be married on the morrow," Duff suggested.

"Duff MacCallister, sure and m' mother has waited my whole life to give me a fine church wedding now, and you would deny that to her?"

Duff chuckled. "Don't worry, Skye. There is no way in the world I would start my married life by getting on the bad side of my mother-in-law. If you want to wait, then I will wait with you."

"What do you mean, you will wait with me?" Skye asked. "And what else would you be doing, Duff MacCallister? Would you be finding a willing young lass to wait with you?"

"I don't know such a willing lass," Duff replied. "Do you? For truly, it would be an interesting experiment."

"Oh, you!" Skye said, hitting Duff on the shoulder.

He laughed, then pulled Skye to him. "You are the only willing lass I want."

"I should hope so."

Duff bent down to kiss her waiting lips.

"I told you, Ian! Here they are, sparking in the dark!"
a customer shouted.

With a good-natured laugh, Duff and Skye parted.

That was the sweet memory, but Duff couldn't have
the sweet without the painful. Unbidden, that recollec-
tion sneaked in, as well.

Duff and Skye were halfway to the office of Sheriff
Somerled when they saw him and three of his deputies
coming toward them. Chief Deputy Rad Malcolm was
one of the men with him.

"Sheriff," Duff called. "I was coming to see you."

"Shoot him!" Sheriff Somerled shouted.

"No, Sheriff!" Skye shouted, jumping between Duff
and the sheriff.

The sheriff and all three deputies opened fire. The
flame patterns of their pistols lit up the night. The sound
of gunfire roared like thunder.

"Oh!" As Skye spun around toward Duff, he saw a
growing spread of crimson on her chest. She fell to the
road and, even as the sheriff and his deputies continued
to shoot, he managed to pull her off the road and
through the shrubbery.

"Skye!" Duff shouted, his voice racked with pain and
horror at what he was seeing. "Skye!"

She lifted her hand to his face, put her fingers against
his jaw, and smiled. "Och, 'twould have been such a

*lovely wedding." She drew another gasping breath, then
her arm fell and her head turned to one side. Her eyes,
though still open, were already clouded with death.*

"No!" Duff shouted. "No!"

Duff subsequently exacted a terrible revenge from
those who had killed Skye, but that hadn't brought her
back, and as he'd told Biff, the memory of her still
burned in his heart. In truth, Meagan occupied just as
much of his heart as did Skye. Would it be fair to
Meagan to have to share him in such a way?

But Biff was right. Duff was going to have to make a
decision soon. He was either going to have to commit to
Meagan, or let her go.

CHAPTER SEVENTEEN

Sky Meadow Ranch

As Smoke, Matt, and Sally rode up to the ranch house, they were met by Duff and Elmer.

"Welcome back," Duff said. "How was your trip to Fort Russell?"

"It was most successful." Matt dismounted with a broad smile on his face. "So successful that we have come bearing gifts."

"Come on. Let's get in out of the cold," Duff invited."

"Smoke, you and Matt take in the packages," Sally said.

"I'll help," Elmer offered, motioning to a nearby cowboy to take care of the horses.

Once inside, the packages were set on the table, with Smoke pointing out which ones were for Elmer, as well as Jarvis and Angela Sterling.

"And you say this one is mine?" Elmer asked, pointing to one of the gaily wrapped boxes.

"It is indeed," Sally said.

"Thank, you." With a big smile, he picked up his package and started to pick at the bow. "Let's just see what's in here."

"No, you don't! You put that down, now!" Sally cried.

"What?" Elmer replied, shocked by the outburst. "Well, look here. Didn't you just say this 'n was mine?"

Sally put her hands on her hips. "I did. But these are to be put under the Christmas tree, and they can't be opened until Christmas morning."

"What Christmas tree?" Elmer asked. "We ain't got no Christmas tree."

"Then I suggest you get one."

"Yes, ma'am," Elmer replied with a smile.

"Elmer, you just learned in one minute what it took me ten years to learn," Smoke said. "When Sally speaks, it's the law."

Duff and the others laughed.

"Speakin' of law," Elmer said, "Duff done a little lawin' of his own while you all was gone, what with him chasin' down 'n bringin' in the bastards who murdered the mayor's family." Then, realizing what he had said in front of Sally, he apologized. "Oh, I beg your pardon, ma'am. Please excuse the language."

Sally frowned. "Never mind that. What do you mean, murdered the mayor's family?"

"You haven't heard? It's been in all the papers." Elmer told what had happened to R.W. Guthrie's son, daughter-in-law, and their children.

"Oh, that poor man," Sally said. "I know how proud he was of his son and grandchildren."

Smoke turned to Duff. "And you brought them in, did you?"

"Aye. It was three men, Sunset Moss, and Jesse and T. Bob Cave. I'm afraid that I had to kill Sunset Moss. He left me no choice."

"Good for you. You saved the county the price of a rope," Smoke said.

"That's a little gauche, isn't it, Smoke?" Sally asked.

"Didn't you just agree with Elmer when he called them bastards?" Smoke replied. "Are you saying Moss didn't deserve to die for what he done?"

"For what he *did*, not for what he *done*." Sally, ever the teacher, corrected Smoke's grammar. She smiled. "And yes, he deserved to die."

Rawhide Buttes

In the Rocky Mountain Hotel, Hodge Doolin was examining his registration book. He saw that Ralph Walters was now three days past due on paying his room rent.

"Mike, I know I said I wasn't going to say anything to him, but how about running upstairs to Mr. Walter's room? He's three days late. Ask him to please stop by the desk and settle his account. Also, to let us know if he is going to be with us any longer."

"All right." Mike left the check-in desk and started up the wide, foot-worn stairs that led up to the second floor.

He heard a loud burst of laughter coming from the bar and shook his head.

Reaching the second floor, he walked down the long, rose-carpeted hallway until he reached the last room on the left. He knocked on the door. "Mr. Walters?"

No answer.

He knocked again. "Mr. Walters, are you in there?" He still didn't get an answer and wondered if Walters had already left, but didn't tell anyone. He tried the door, but it was locked. "Mr. Walters?" he called again.

When he didn't get an answer the third time, he took out his skeleton key, inserted it in the keyhole, then turned it. He pushed the door open about a quarter of the way, then called out again. He didn't want to take a chance on getting shot.

"Mr. Walters?" Still getting no answer, he stepped into the room. Walters was lying on the bed, his neck swollen as large as his head. His mouth and eyes were open . . . and his skin had a bluish tint.

"Lord in heaven!" Mike gasped.

Turning away from the bed, Mike shut the door and locked it, then hurried down the stairs. Doolin was entering numbers in his account ledger.

"He's dead," Mike said in a quiet voice.

Doolin looked up. "Who's dead?"

"Mr. Walters, the feller you sent me up to see. He's lyin' there in his bed, dead as a doornail."

"You mean somebody murdered him? Damn. We'd better get the marshal."

"No, I don't think nobody kilt him. He just died. Only

I tell you the truth, Hodge, he's the damndest lookin' corpse I done ever seen."

"All right, don't say anything about it to anyone else in the hotel. Just go down to the mortuary and get Tom Welch."

Dr. Poindexter adjusted the electric lamp in his office as he read the article in the *Boston Medical and Surgical Journal*.

Diphtheria is a serious bacterial infection usually affecting the mucous membranes of the nose and throat. It typically causes a sore throat, fever, swollen glands, and weakness. The most telling sign is a sheet of thick, gray material covering the back of the throat.

Symptoms are a sore throat and hoarseness, painful swallowing, swollen glands, difficulty in aspirating, discharge of the nose, fever, and chills.

Dr. Poindexter quit reading, then he bowed his head, and pinched the bridge of his nose. "My God," he said quietly.

"Doc! Doc! You in here?"

Dr. Poindexter looked up to see Carl and Edith Lester come in. Carl, who owned a saddle and leather shop, was carrying his son in his arms. Danny was gasping for breath.

"Doc! You've got to do something for m' boy!" Lester said in a near panic. "He can't breathe!"

"Put him on the table," Dr. Poindexter said, pointing to the examining table. "Jenny, I'm going to need a scalpel and a hollow tube."

Jenny, who was not only his nurse but also his wife, provided the scalpel, then went back for the hollow tube. He began feeling around on the boy's neck until he found the Adam's apple, or larynx, then just below that, the cricoid. That's where he put the point of the scalpel.

"Hold on here, Doc. Are you goin' to cut my boy's throat?" Lester asked angrily.

"That's exactly what I'm going to do, unless you want him to die," Dr. Poindexter said. "He's got to have air, and his windpipe is closing down."

He made a horizontal cut about half an inch long and half an inch deep, exposing the cricothyroid membrane, which he also cut. Into the hole, he inserted the hollow tube that Jenny had provided him. "Breathe, Danny, breathe!" Dr. Poindexter said.

"He isn't breathing." Jenny leaned over and put her lips around the end of the hollow tube.

"What is she doing?" Lester asked, still in a high state of agitation. He started to reach for Jenny, but Dr. Poindexter pulled him back.

"Mrs. Lester, if you want your son to survive, keep your husband away from him."

"Carl, I'm sure they know what they are doing," Mrs. Lester said. Her words did seem to have a calming effect on her husband.

Jenny blew softly into the tube, took another breath, then blew again, then again.

"George, I feel his breath," she said after a moment. "He's breathing!" she added excitedly.

"Thank God," Dr. Poindexter said. "Good job, Jenny."

"Will he be all right now?" Lester asked anxiously.

"I can't promise you that," Dr. Poindexter said. "I can only say that he isn't going to die immediately. What I have to do now is get the mucus membrane from his larynx."

"How are you going to do that?"

"Look, Mr. Lester, I know you are concerned. But please, just let me do what must be done, then I'll explain it all later."

"All right. I'm sorry. Just do whatever has to be done, Doc. Don't pay me no never mind. The thing is, I'm just awful worried."

"I understand, and you have every right to be worried, because Danny's condition is quite serious. But I promise you, I'll do everything that I can. Jenny, I'll need a solution of three parts water to one part hydrochloric acid. Would you prepare that for me, please?"

"Do you want it in a bowl, or an aspirator?"

"A bowl."

As Jenny prepared the solution, Dr. Poindexter opened a drawer and removed a feather. When the solution was mixed, Jenny came over to stand by Danny, and held the glass bowl containing the acid and water solution. Dr. Poindexter dipped the end of the feather into the acid, removed the tube he had inserted into Danny's neck, and sticking the feather into the open hole, began twirling it around. He did that for a few seconds, then picked up a long rubber hose and stuck one end of it into the opening in the boy's throat. He began sucking at the other end. After a moment, he removed the end of the hose from the boy's throat and blew through the hose, expelling a combination of blood and yellowish pus.

After several such applications, he introduced a solution of carbolic acid into the nostrils.

Danny immediately sneezed and coughed.

"What are you doing to him?" Lester asked angrily.

"Mr. Lester, please," Jenny said calmly, putting her hand gently on Lester's shoulder. "Let the doctor do his job."

"Carl, if you can't watch this, go outside," Mrs. Lester ordered.

"You mean you can watch it?" Lester asked.

"Yes, if it helps my child, I can watch it."

Lester glared at Dr. Poindexter for a moment longer, then pointedly turned on his heel and left the room.

"Close the wound on his neck," Dr. Poindexter ordered. "Let's see where we are."

Jenny put a bandage around the boy's neck, closing up the tracheotomy wound. She bent down very close to him. After a moment, she raised up. "He's breathing on his own, now," she said, a big smile spreading across her face.

"Good." Dr. Poindexter brushed a fall of hair back from his forehead, leaving a smear of blood.

Quickly, Jenny got a damp cloth and wiped the blood away.

"He's breathing on his own? Does that mean he's cured?" Mrs. Lester asked.

"No, but it means we have a start. Mrs. Lester, I'm going to give you a solution that you should use to swab out his throat once every hour. Also, put him in bed in a room where you can open the window to allow outside air to enter."

"But, Doctor, it is so cold!" Mrs. Lester complained.

"Yes, it is, so keep him well wrapped up in blankets. But it is very important that he gets fresh air."

"All right."

"Call Carl back in. You can take Danny home now."

Mrs. Lester stepped to the door of the examining room and called out, "Carl, you can come in now."

"How is he?" Carl asked, hurrying back into the examining room."

"He has a chance," Dr. Poindexter said. "I've given Mrs. Lester instructions on what needs to be done. Also, and this is very important. Go straight home from here, and once you get home, don't leave the house again until I tell you that you can. Don't leave and don't let anyone come visit you."

"What do you mean, don't let anyone visit us? We're planning a Christmas dinner for all our friends," Mrs. Lester objected.

"You're going to have to cancel it."

"I can't stay away from work," Carl said. "I have projects that need to be completed."

"Your customers will just have to understand. I'm putting you and your entire family on quarantine."

Carl didn't understand. "Quarantine? What does that mean?"

"It means you can't go see anyone, and nobody can come to see you."

"What about goin' to the store for groceries?"

"No, you can't do that."

"Hell, what if we run out of food?"

"How long can you go with what you have now?" The doctor looked at Mrs. Lester.

"Three or four days," she replied.

"In three days, I'll bring you some more groceries."

"How come you can come see us if nobody else can?" Lester asked.

"Because I'm a doctor, and it's my job to take such a chance."

"Doc, maybe you don't know it, but Christmas is comin'. What right you got to treat us like this?"

Dr. Poindexter took a deep breath. "You're right, it is nearly Christmas." He spoke quietly, using Lester's first name. "Carl, Do you think I would treat you like this if I didn't absolutely have to?"

"All right. Whatever you say, Doc," Lester said in acquiescence.

"Mr. Lester, Danny has diphtheria."

"Oh, God in heaven! Diphtheria?" Edith Lester put her hand to her mouth. "That means he's going to die!"

"Not necessarily," Dr. Poindexter said. "We may have gotten to it in time. If you do what I tell you to do, there's a chance we can save him."

"All right. I can understand why we need to keep Danny away from ever' body, but why can't I go to work?" Lester kept asking questions.

"The reason you have to be quarantined is because you and your wife have been exposed to diphtheria. You may not come down with it . . . and chances are you won't, or you would already be showing symptoms. But, whether you show symptoms or not, you can still be a carrier. Do you want to infect the rest of the town?"

"No, I reckon not," Lester said sheepishly.

"Then please, do what I say. Now, take Danny home, and take care of him."

"Come on, Carl. Let's do what the doctor says, please," Edith said.

Lester nodded. "All right. I'll do what you say, Doc, but please don't let him die. Just don't let him die."

"I'm going to do what I can for him, Mr. Lester."

After the Lesters left, Dr. Poindexter sat at his desk, smoking his cigar and staring off into space.

"George, are we going to have an epidemic of diphtheria?" Jenny asked.

Dr. Poindexter sighed and ran his hand through his thinning, gray hair. "First there was Laura Hastings, and now Danny Lester. I'm afraid we just might be heading in that direction."

"Oh, George, surely not!"

"Maybe I'm jumping to conclusions here, but everything I've seen so far certainly makes me think that might be the case."

CHAPTER EIGHTEEN

With the Lesters gone and the immediate crisis temporarily dealt with, Dr. Poindexter continued to research all he could find about diphtheria.

At the moment, he was reading the article on diphtheria in the *Boston Medical and Surgical Journal*. When he came to what he was looking for, he smiled. "Jenny, listen to this. 'In 1883, a Swiss-German pathologist identified and described the bacterium that causes diphtheria. A year later, German bacteriologist Friedrich Loeffler developed an antitoxin, which has proved effective in treating the disease.'"

"What does that mean, exactly?" Jenny asked.

"It means that if I can get hold of enough of this antitoxin, I can treat this before it takes over the whole town."

"Where are you going to find it?"

"Ahh, I'm afraid you've got me there, darlin'," Dr. Poindexter said. "I'm going to have to send a telegram off, asking for help."

"Do you think it's wise to let people know that we may have diphtheria? Might it not spread a panic?"

"Yes, it could well do that. Another problem is that I may wind up having to put the entire town on quarantine, and if word gets out too quickly, I fear people will panic and start leaving town. That could spread the disease over the entire state, causing an even bigger disaster."

"How are you going to send off a telegram without letting the telegrapher know? If he finds out something like that, the whole town will know within an hour."

"I just won't use the word diphtheria. At least, not in the way that he would recognize it." Dr. Poindexter stood and grabbed his coat. Leaving his office, he walked down to the telegraph office, where he wrote out a telegram.

POSSIBLE OUTBREAK OF CORYNEBACTERIUM STOP
REQUEST IMMEDIATE SUPPLY OF ANTITOXIN SERUM
SUFFICIENT TO TREAT INFECTED STOP NUMBER
COULD REACH HIGH AS ONE HUNDRED STOP
DR. GEORGE POINDEXTER STOP RAWHIDE BUTTES

"Please send this to the chief surgeon at the United Medical Center in Cheyenne," Dr. Poindexter said, handing the message to the telegrapher, Howard McGill.

He read it. "What is this cory . . . coryne . . . ?"

"Corynebacterium," the doctor said, pronouncing the word for him. "It's a type of respiratory ailment."

"And this here serum will take care of it?"

"Well, Howard, it will if we send for it instead of standing here talking about it."

McGill chuckled. "All right, Doc, I understand. I'll get it sent off right away."

When Dr. Poindexter returned from sending the telegram, he found Tom Welch, the town mortician, had arrived in his office.

"Hello, Tom. What can I do for you?"

"Doc, I just got a man in that I think you'd better come have a look at."

Dr. Poindexter chuckled dryly. "Well, Tom, if you've got him, it's probably a little late for me to be looking at him, isn't it?"

"Yeah, well, that ain't why I'm wantin' you to see him. It's the way he looks that I think you ought to see."

"All right. I'll come down to your place and have a look."

The undertaker's business was between the lumberyard and the hardware store, a convenient location because Welch not only embalmed the bodies, he also made the coffins. For that, he needed material from both his neighboring business establishments.

The body was that of a male who appeared to be in his early fifties. His neck was swollen to the size of his head. He was naked, and several large lesions were visible on both legs. His mouth was open as if he had been gasping for breath as he died

Dr. Poindexter leaned over to look into his mouth and

saw several deep necrotic ulcers present on the tongue and the inner surface of the cheeks. The back of his throat was covered with a thick gray membrane. He straightened and asked, "Who is this man?"

"According to Hodge Doolin, his name is Ralph Walters," Welch said.

"Doolin? From the hotel?"

"Yes, that's where this man was staying. Hodge said that after nobody had seen him for a couple days, he sent Mike up to check on him, and found him dead in his room."

"Has his family been notified?"

"As far I know, he has no family here. I haven't been able to find anyone who knows anything about him. I'm going to have to get him declared indigent so I can bury him."

"So he was just passing through town?"

"From what I've gathered. Hodge said he was sort of a traveling troubadour who went from town to town playing music and entertaining with stories."

"Did he do a show here?"

"I don't know," Welch said. "So, what about it, Doc? What killed this fella?"

"Diphtheria," Dr. Poindexter said.

"Diphtheria? Damn, have I been exposed?"

"Probably not, but when you are finished with him, wash your hands thoroughly, and use a lot of soap."

Leaving the mortuary, Poindexter walked two blocks to the Rocky Mountain Hotel. Hodge Doolin was watching as Mike and a volunteer were hanging a large banner on the wall above the fireplace. ROCKY MOUNTAIN HOTEL WISHES MERRY CHRISTMAS TO ALL.

"Joe, lift your end about an inch," Doolin directed.

Joe complied.

"About another inch."

Again the banner was moved.

"No, that's too much. Come back down."

"Well, make up your mind, Hodge. We ain't exactly buildin' a house here, you know. All we're doin' is hangin' a sign," Mike said.

"Yes, but we may as well do it right," Doolin insisted. "All right, you've got it now. Put in the tacks."

As the two men secured the sign, Doolin turned away, then saw Poindexter standing there. "Hello, Doc, what can I do for you?"

"I just left the mortuary,"

"Ah, yes, Mr. Walters. Damn. He must 'a been dead for two or three days. I ain't never seen a body that had a neck all swolled up like that."

"Had he complained about not feeling well?"

"A couple days ago he asked for an extra blanket, said he was cold, but hell, that wasn't nothin'. This time of year lots of folks want extra blankets. He did say that his throat was sore. I asked 'im if he wanted me to call a doctor, but he said he didn't want one. I should 'a called you anyhow, I reckon. But I never figured he'd up and die on us like that."

"Tom Welch said he didn't have any family here."

"None that nobody knows anything about. He just got here last week."

"Why was he in Rawhide Buttes, do you know?"

"I think he come here to entertain the kids in school," the hotel clerk said.

"And did he?"

"That I can't tell you. You'll have to ask Miss Foley."

"Yes, Mr. Walters was here," the teacher said.

"What was he like?" Dr. Poindexter asked.

"Well, I found him to be quite a nice man. He even asked me out, but of course, I told him that wouldn't be possible," Miss Foley said, smiling as she reached up to touch her hair. "He was very entertaining, though I think he would have been even more so, if had had been able to sing."

"He didn't sing?"

"No, he said he was having trouble with his voice. You could tell just by listening to him. His voice was rather hoarse, though it carried well enough that he was able to keep the children entertained with his stories. Oh, and such marvelous stories they were, too. He told one about a Chris, the Christmas Bird who would eat flowers, then turn the color of the flowers he consumed. And he illustrated it by drawing pictures on the blackboard with colored chalk. The children were very entertained."

Keeping his voice matter-of-fact, the doctor inquired, "Were Danny Lester and Laura Hastings present for his performance?"

"They were both here. As I recall, there were no children absent on that day, although both Danny and Laura have been absent since that day. I do hope Laura is back in time for our Christmas pageant. Oh. Even though you have no children in school, you are invited. The entire town is invited to see the children perform. They have been working so hard to prepare for it.

"How are you feeling, Miss Foley?"

"What do you mean, how am I feeling?"

"I mean, have you had any spells of dizziness? Is your throat sore?" Dr. Poindexter reached out to put the back of his hand on Miss Foley's forehead. "Have you had any fever?"

"No, I feel just fine. Why are you asking?"

"I'm asking because you were exposed to Mr. Walters."

"What about Mr. Walters? Has he taken ill?" she wondered.

"I'm afraid he has died," Dr. Poindexter replied.

"Died? Oh, heavens!" Miss Foley gasped, putting her hand to her chest. "Oh, how tragic. The children enjoyed him so."

"I'm sure they did."

"Dr. Poindexter, do you think I might be taken ill?"

"From Mr. Walters? Probably not, you were exposed to him long enough ago that if you were going to be ill, the symptoms would be presenting by now."

"Oh. Well, that is good to know. The children have been working so hard on their play, I would hate to be the cause of it not being done."

Dr. Poindexter started to tell her that there would be no play, regardless of whether she was ill or not, but he decided against it. "Yes, well, I thank you very much for the information, Miss Foley."

"You're quite welcome, though I'm sorry it had to do with such a sad bit of news. Do tell Mrs. Poindexter hello, for me, won't you?"

"Yes, thank you, I will."

Having returned to the office, Dr. Poindexter went straight to his desk, opened the bottom drawer, and pulled out a bottle of whiskey. He poured himself a drink that filled half a water glass.

Jenny looked up from what she was doing. "George! What are you doing, drinking in the middle of the day?"

He did not take the glass from his lips until he had drunk the entire thing. Then he wiped his mouth with back of his hand. "I have found where it started, Jenny. I know where the cases of diphtheria are coming from."

"Where did it start?"

"It was brought here by man named Ralph Walters."

She shook her head. "That's not a name I recognize."

"You wouldn't. He just came to town a few days ago. You know why?"

"Why?"

"He was here to entertain the children at school. He already had the disease when he arrived."

"Where is he now?"

Dr. Poindexter's heart was heavy. "At the mortuary. He's dead, but before he died, he exposed every child in town. And those children have exposed their parents, and those parents may have exposed others." Dr. Poindexter

"What are you going to do?"

"I don't know. God help me, I don't know."

"Doc! Dr. Poindexter!" someone shouted from outside.

Jenny stepped up to the window. "It's Mr. Sinclair. He's carrying Helen."

The doctor walked over to open the door as Sinclair came rushing in, holding a little girl in his arms.

"Doc, it's my daughter! She's stopped breathin'! Do something! Please, do something!"

Dr. Poindexter could tell by looking at the little girl's face that there was nothing he could do. She had already died.

Sky Meadow Ranch

Ahead of him, Duff could see the snowcapped, purple mountains. To the observer, it was a Christmas scene as could be portrayed by Currier and Ives, a lone rider on a horse, leaving a trail in the snow behind him. The house before him had gleaming windows and displayed a green wreath with a red bow. From the chimney, a curl of white smoke climbed into a bright, blue sky.

After stabling Sky, Duff walked to the house, stomping the snow off his boots on the back porch before he went inside. He could smell the aroma of cinnamon and sugar and knew that Mrs. Sterling was doing everything she could to make Christmas a gala event. Stepping into the kitchen, he saw Mrs. Sterling wasn't working alone, for Sally was just as busy.

"Where are Smoke and Matt?" he asked, pouring himself a cup of coffee.

"They've gone out to find a Christmas tree," Sally said.

"Tree? Why do we need a tree? We already have a Christmas wreath hanging in the front window."

"Don't be such a Scrooge," Sally said. "You need more than a wreath. You also need a tree."

Stomping noises came from the back door and they rushed from the kitchen. Smoke and Matt had brought the tree into the house. Mrs. Sterling suggested that it should be placed in the parlor, and the men set it up there.

She and Sally returned to the kitchen to put it to rights and soon joined the men in the parlor. Decorations had been pulled out and they began decorating the tree.

"I wish Meagan could be here helping us," Sally said. "I'm looking forward to seeing her again. But, this close to Christmas, I'm sure she is very busy with her dress emporium, getting ready for the holidays."

"She is busy, but not with her shop," Duff said. "She went back to Rawhide Buttes to help a friend get her store ready for Christmas."

"That's very nice of her. She will be back before Christmas, though, won't she?"

"She plans to be."

"There's a dance Christmas Eve," Elmer said. "You

had better believe that Miss Parker won't be missing that."

"A dance on Christmas Eve? How nice," Sally said. "Is everyone invited?"

"I really don't know," Duff said. "But you are invited. Whether 'tis an open dance or nae, the three of ye will be m' guests."

The next morning dawned clear. Duff stood at the window in the front parlor, drinking a cup of coffee as he looked out over the field of snow glistening brightly in the morning sun.

"Good morning," Smoke said, coming into the room behind him.

"Have you got coffee?" Duff asked.

"Just poured myself a cup."

"Where are the others?"

"Matt spent the night in the bunkhouse, and hasn't come in yet. Sally is in the kitchen with Mrs. Sterling."

Duff frowned. "Why did Matt stay in the bunkhouse?"

"He was playing cards with Al, Case, and Brax last night. He said he didn't want to come in late and wake everyone up."

"Here he comes now," Duff said, looking out the window again.

Matt and Elmer were coming toward the house, leaving behind a track of black holes made by their footfalls in the white snow.

A moment later, the two men began stamping their feet on the front porch, so as not to track snow into the house.

"They'll be wanting coffee." Duff walked back into the dining room to pour a second cup for himself and one for Elmer. Smoke followed him and poured a cup for Matt. When the two men came in, they were greeted with hot coffee.

"Thank you," Elmer said, accepting the cup, then taking a swallow. "I tell you what, it might have faired off, but it sure as hell didn't get no warmer. I hate cold weather. I truly do."

"Elmer, you've been all over the world," Duff said. "I'm sure that in your travels you've been to places that don't get cold."

"Pago Pago. It never gets cold there. And the women wear no tops," he added with a broad smile.

Duff raised his mug in the manner of a salute. "There you go. Why didn't you stay there?"

"The only way I could 'a stayed was iffen I had jumped ship," Elmer said. "The island is too small for a person to hide out for long. I've always thought I might like to go back someday, though. You know what? Once you 'n Miss Parker get married, you ought to take a trip there. That would be a real nice place for you to go to."

"Be ye nae so quick to get me married, Elmer," Duff said. "I told you last night, dinnae ye be rushing me.

Elmer laughed. "Yeah, I know you keep puttin' it off. But you ain't foolin' no one, Duff MacCallister. You 'n Miss Parker will be gettin' married before you know it."

"We'll see. Listen, how about having someone hitch up the sleigh for me? I told Smoke and Matt I'd take them into town this morning."

"Will you be visiting our friend Biff at Fiddlers' Green?"

"Aye, 'twould be the only decent thing to do. Sure 'n Biff would be upset if we didn't call on him now, wouldn't he?"

"We?"

"I expect you'll be goin' along as well."

Elmer grinned. "I thought you'd never ask."

"You'll be seeing Mrs. Winslow?"

"I never pass up the opportunity to have a piece of pie."

"A piece of pie. Right," Duff said with a broad smile.

Vi Winslow was a widow. She and Elmer Gleason had been "keeping company," as Meagan described it.

CHAPTER NINETEEN

Chugwater

The sleigh glided smoothly and swiftly through the snow, and the trip into town had been accomplished rather quickly. Duff took care of some business at the Chugwater Bank and Trust, then they stopped by Vi's Pies for a cup of coffee and a piece of pie.

"When will Meagan get back from Rawhide Buttes, have you heard?" Vi asked Duff.

"'Tis my understanding she'll be back a few days before Christmas."

"Good, then she'll be here in plenty of time for the dance," Vi said.

"What dance?" Elmer asked innocently.

"What dance?" Vi reached out and pulled the piece of pie away from him. "Elmer Gleason, if you don't know about the Christmas dance, you can just find yourself another place to have pie."

Duff, Smoke, and Matt looked at each other and grinned.

"Oh, *that* dance," Elmer said. "Sure I know about *that* dance, for haven't I asked you to go with me?"

"You have not."

"Then I'll be askin' you now."

Vi smiled and slid the pie back to him. "Why, I would be happy to go with you, Mr. Gleason."

Leaving Vi's Pies, the four men walked down the street to Fiddlers' Green.

"Hello, Duff, Elmer. Good to see that you could make it out on a day like today," Biff Johnson said by way of greeting.

"It's a good day for sleighing," Elmer replied.

"Biff, I'll be wanting ye to say hello to m' friends Smoke 'n Matt Jensen," Duff said.

"Any friend of Duff MacCallister is a friend of mine. Brothers, be you?" Biff asked.

"Of a sort," Smoke replied

Suddenly, Biff got a knowing look on his face and put his hand to his forehead. "Glory be! Smoke and Matt Jensen? Sure 'n I've heard of the two of you. Why, you two men are famous. And here you are in my saloon."

"And a very nice saloon it is," Smoke said graciously.

"Would you boys be wanting a dram? Or do you think it's a bit too early yet?" Biff asked.

"Och, mon, tis already five p.m. at the White Horse

pub in Donuun in Argyllshire," Duff said, speaking of his hometown back in Scotland.

"Then it is plenty late enough," Biff replied, smiling as he poured scotch into a glass. "I know that Elmer will have a beer. What about you two?" He held the bottle up by way of questioning Smoke and Matt.

"Beer will be fine," Smoke answered for both of them.

Before drawing the beers, Biff slid the glass across the bar to Duff, and Duff lifted it. "To all the lads who are waiting at Fiddlers' Green," he proposed.

"No matter the color of the uniform," Elmer added.

Sidewinder Gorge

Jesse, T. Bob, and Jacobs were standing at the bar— a few boards stretched between barrels—in what passed for a saloon. It served beer and whiskey, though the cost per drink was three times what it cost on the outside. When Jesse had complained about it, he was told that he and his brother were free to leave, but reminded that they couldn't take the horses with them.

"You boys seem to have made yourselves to home, eatin' my food, stayin' under my roof," Dingo said. "And right now, you're drinkin' my beer."

"Yeah, well, I see that you're keepin' a careful tab on what we're drinkin'," Jesse said. "I expect you'll be collectin' your money as soon as we get some."

"You expect right. And that brings up a good point. Just when are you goin' to do somethin' to earn your keep?"

"Like what?" Jesse asked.

"Like findin' some way to bring in some money."

"Do you have something in mind?" Jesse asked.

"Rob a store, hold up a stagecoach. I don't care what you do. But if you're goin' to stay here, you have to do somethin'. I didn't take you to raise."

"Max, what about Duff MacCallister?" Nitwit Mitt asked.

Jesse looked at Nitwit. "What about 'im?"

"I understand he's the one who hunted you boys down," Dingo said.

"Yeah, he's the one done it, all right." T. Bob put in his two cents' worth.

"Then I take it that you two don't hold him in very high regard?"

Jesse snorted. "You take it right."

"It could be that these here boys might be just the ones to take care of the job you been wantin' done," Nitwit pointed out to Dingo.

The outlaw leader nodded slowly. "Yeah." He took a few more minutes, then agreed. "Yeah, you might be right."

"We might be the ones to take care of what?" T. Bob asked.

"Killin' MacCallister," Dingo said.

"Wait a minute. That's what you want? You want us to kill MacCallister?"

"Is there somethin' wrong with that? You would like to see him dead, wouldn't you?"

"You're damn right there's somethin' wrong with

that," Jesse said. "We'd like to see him dead, but I sure as hell ain't got no plans in mind to go after 'im."

"Why not?" Dingo asked. "If you are, you sure got my blessin'."

"Your blessin' ain't enough. Like the feller here said, me an' T. Bob has already done tangled with him once, 'n I don't aim to run across him again if I can help it."

"What if you was to get paid to take care of 'im?" Dingo asked. "Not only get paid, but if I let you keep the horses and stay here without havin' to pay anything?"

Jesse wasn't sure about that offer. "Why do you want him kilt?"

"I'm not the only one. A lot of people want him dead," Dingo said.

"Yeah, but there ain't nobody else ever actually offered to pay someone to have him kilt. Leastwise, not as far as I know. Why do you want him kilt?"

"Because he killed my brother, Johnny Taylor."

"Taylor? I thought your name was Dingo."

"We had different fathers. Ma just made up names for us, seein' as neither one of us ever actual seen our old man. And truth to tell, I don't think she even knew who it was that spawned either one of us, seein' as she was a saloon gal and sometimes laid with half a dozen men a night."

Jesse considered that information. "How much are you willin' to pay?"

"One hunnert dollars."

"That ain't much for goin' after a man like Duff MacCallister," T. Bob complained.

"It is when you consider that I'll let you keep your horses, and eat and stay here for free."

"What good is horses to a dead man? I've seen MacCallister shoot. No, sir, I intend to stay as far away from him as I can," T. Bob said.

"Do you think, for one moment, that MacCallister ain't goin' to be comin' after you again?" Dingo asked. "You boys killed the son of the mayor of Chugwater. Not only the son, but his wife and children. MacCallister tracked you down once. He'll do it again. Trust me, you are goin' to have to deal with him one way or the other."

"He's right, T. Bob," Jacobs said. "He had a personal stake in what you men done, which is why he come after you in the first place. Soon as he learns you've escaped, he's going to be comin' after you again."

"With someone like that, two to one ain't that good of odds." Jesse looked at Jacobs. "Would you come with us?"

Jacobs looked over at Dingo. "Make it a hunnert and fifty dollars. If you do, I'll join 'em, and that'll give us fifty dollars apiece."

Dingo combed his fingers through his beard, pulling out bits of food. He examined his fingertips for a moment, then flipped them away. "All right. I'll go a hunnert 'n fifty."

Jacobs looked at the other two for a moment, seeking their approval. They nodded. "Okay. You've got a deal."

"You think you boys can do it?" Dingo asked. "Somebody like MacCallister takes a lot of killin'."

Jacobs removed the makings and rolled himself a

cigarette. "That's all right. Me an' these two boys has done a lot of killin'."

"When will you do it?" Dingo asked.

"Soon as we get the money."

Dingo shook his head back and forth a couple times. "You ain't goin' to get the money till the job is done."

Jacobs smiled. "Far as I'm concerned, you can figure he's as good as dead right now."

"Good as, don't mean he's dead," Dingo said.

"He will be," Jacobs promised.

"Oh, and we ain't got no money 'tall," Jesse complained. "Like you said, we been eatin' your food and drinkin' on the tab here for a couple days. If we leave here to try 'n pull a job, or go take care of MacCallister, it's goin' to be damn hard, seein' as we ain't got so much as a penny to our name."

"I tell you what. I'll give twenty-five dollars apiece, now. That should hold you over until you can find a job to do. There's money to be made if you'll just do it."

"But one-third of whatever we steal goes to you, right?"

Dingo smiled. "Yes, but look at it this way. Two-thirds of the money goes to you."

"He's right, Jesse. If two-thirds of the money goes to us, that's more 'n we got now," Jacobs explained.

"All right," Jesse agreed. "Let's go find some money."

Sky Meadow Ranch

Duff, Smoke, Sally, and Matt were having breakfast at the kitchen table.

"Matt, what in the world is that you are eating?" Duff asked as he spread jam onto his toast.

"Gravy and biscuits," Matt replied. "Don't tell you've never eaten it."

"I have never eaten such a concoction, and it looks awful. I'm amazed that Mrs. Sterling even knows how to prepare . . . gravy."

"I guess I'm guilty of that," Sally said. "I asked Mrs. Sterling if she would mind if I fixed breakfast, and she graciously consented to letting me share the kitchen with her this morning."

Duff shuddered. "I hope you dinnae try to teach her how to make it."

Sally laughed. "I didn't."

"Duff, Sally came up with what I think is a pretty good idea this morning," Smoke said.

"What's the idea?"

Smoke grinned at his wife. "I'll let her tell you."

She jumped right in. "I'd like to go to Rawhide Buttes. I can help Meagan and her friend get her store ready, and we can be back in Chugwater in plenty of time for Christmas."

"And Matt and I would like to go, too," Smoke said. "Matt has been there before, but I've never seen the place. It's always fun to go to someplace new."

Duff laughed. "You do know that Rawhide Buttes is nothing like Denver. It isn't even like Chugwater. 'Tis a small place."

"Does it have a hotel and a place to eat?" Smoke questioned.

"Aye, that it does. And even a couple acceptable pubs."

Smoke grinned. "Then it's worth seeing. What do you say? Would you like to go up with us?"

"You go on, and tell Meagan I'll be along soon. I've a few more things to take of here before I can leave."

"Is it something Matt and I could help you with? If so, we could stay and go when you do."

Duff shook his head. "No, you go on. I'll have Mrs. Sterling pack a lunch for you to have along the way."

"Great!" Smoke said.

Sidewinder Gorge

"I've got me an idea how we can come up with a little money of our own," Jacobs said.

"When you say money of our own, does that mean that you got an idea that don't have nothin' to do with sharin' ever' dime we get with Dingo?" Jesse asked.

"We'll have to give him some money, but he don't need to know how much we got in the first place."

"Yeah," Jesse said. "Yeah, that might work. What's your idea?"

"A bank over in Sweetwater."

"Sweetwater? Jesse nodded. "Yeah, I know Sweetwater. I ain't never been there, but I've heard of it."

"I been there. It's a little flyspeck of a town," Jacobs offered. "They ain't got no law 'cept for a sheriff who's so old he can't barely get around. That bank's just beggin' to be robbed."

"How big is the town?" Jesse asked.

"I don't know. A hunnert fifty, maybe two hunnert people."

Jesse frowned. "That's all? How much money you reckon could be in *that* bank?"

"I doubt there's over four or five hunnert dollars in the bank. But that's the beauty of it, don't you see? If there ain't a whole lot of money in the bank, then they're not goin' to be expectin' anyone to rob it. Hell, they'll prob'ly pee in their pants when we go in. It'll be like takin' candy from a baby."

T. Bob had been idling nearby, listening to their conversation. "Yeah, but if they don't have no more 'n five hunnert dollars, is it worth it?"

"Let's see now. If I'm doin' my cipherin' right, five hunnert dollars split three ways would be a little over a hunnert 'n fifty dollars apiece. And you've got how much money, now? Twenty-five?"

Jesse laughed. "Looks to me like he's got you there, little brother. All right, Wally, let's go rob us a bank."

CHAPTER TWENTY

Sweetwater, Wyoming

The town was small, just as Wally had said, but the board sidewalks were full of men and women, farmers and ranchers, looking in the windows of the shops, hurrying to and fro.

"What the hell?" Jesse was not happy. "I thought you said they wasn't no more 'n a couple hunnert people here. There's that many out on the street."

"Must be because of Christmas," Jacobs said. "Anyhow, there ain't hardly none of 'em wearin' guns, so they ain't nothin' to worry about. Let's do it and be done."

"Wait a minute, wait a minute." Jesse said, holding up his hand. "Let's not be in such a hurry. What do you say we ride up 'n down the street once just to have us a good look-see?"

"Yeah, that's probably a pretty good idea," Jacobs agreed.

"T. Bob, you take the left side. Count everybody you see carryin' a gun. Wally, you check the folks that's mounted. I'll take the right."

The three men rode slowly down the entire length of the town, then they turned their horses and rode back.

"I didn't see nobody that was armed," T. Bob said.

"I seen only one on my side, but I'd be willin' to bet he ain't never fired it at nothin' more dangerous than a tin can," Jesse said.

Jacobs smiled. "Well then, what do you say we make us a little withdrawal? T. Bob, you stay outside with the horses."

They rode to the bank and dismounted. T. Bob held the reins of all three horses with his left hand, while in his right he held his pistol, though he kept it low and out of sight.

As soon as Jacobs and Jesse were inside, they pulled their pistols.

"All right, people. I don't reckon I have to tell you what this is," Jacobs shouted, waving his gun around.

"God in heaven! It's a holdup!" someone cried.

"Nah, we're just collecting for Christmas," Jesse said. "You, teller. Empty out your bank drawer and put all the money in a bag!"

Nervously, the teller began to comply, emptying his drawer in just a few seconds. He handed the bag to Jacobs, who'd kept his gun pointed on him.

"Damn. Lookie here!" Jacobs held the bag high. "Whoowee! There's two, maybe three thousand dollars here."

"Let's take it and be gone!" Jesse shouted.

"You'll take nothin'!" a customer suddenly shouted.

Jacobs swung his gun toward the customer, who was also armed. The customer fired first, but missed. The outlaw returned fire and didn't miss. Jesse fired toward the teller's window, and his bullet shattered the shaded glass around the teller cages. Another customer in the bank fired and Jesse returned fire, killing him.

"Let's get the hell out of here!" Jacobs shouted.

The townspeople outside the bank heard the shots and realized at once what was going on.

"The bank!" someone shouted. "They're robbin' the bank!"

"Jesse, Wally!" T. Bob shouted. "Get out of there! Fast!"

One of the armed townspeople ran toward the bank with his pistol drawn. T. Bob shot him. Seeing one of their own shot down, the townspeople began screaming and running for cover.

Clutching the canvas bag in his left hand, Jacobs backed out through the door. Jesse followed, firing back into the bank. T. Bob, who was already mounted, passed the reins over to them.

"Let's get out of here!" he shouted to the other two.

Across the street, a young store clerk, no more than a boy, came running out of the store wearing his apron and carrying a broom in one hand and a rifle in the other. He dropped the broom, raised the rifle, and fired at the three robbers. His bullet hit Jacobs in the head, killing him instantly. He fell from the horse with the money sack still in his hand.

"They got Wally!" T. Bob shouted, throwing his leg over to dismount.

"What are you doing? Keep going!" Jesse yelled.

"But the money!"

"To hell with the money!" Jesse's voice was pitched high in fright.

"We can't just leave it!"

"You stay if you want. I'm gettin' the hell out of here!"

Seeing that Jesse didn't intend to stop, T. Bob remained mounted, and the two brothers started away from the bank at a gallop.

Several others were armed, and bullets began flying. One of the bullets killed Jesse's horse. Even as he was going down, Jesse leaped from the saddle and ran toward the nearest hitch rail. Spooked by the gunfire, several horses tied there reared and pulled against their restraints. Jesse untied the closest horse and jumped on, then galloped down the street after T. Bob, who hadn't stopped to wait for him.

By the time the sheriff got the townspeople organized and mounted, the bank robbers had opened up a lead of two miles. The pursuit was ineffective at best, and after a fruitless gallop of no more than fifteen minutes, the posse decided that since the would-be robbers had not gotten away with the money, they would do better to go back to town to bury the dead.

Sidewinder Gorge

Tim Adler walked into the main house, pushing Bad Eye Sal in front of him. "Look who I found trying to leave."

Dingo, who had been drinking a beer, put down his glass and looked at Bad Eye Sal with an evil smile on his face. "I thought we had talked about this."

"Max, please, let me go. You've got no right to keep me here if I don't want to stay."

Dingo stepped up to her and, with a vicious back-hand, knocked her to the floor. "Get back into your room. I'll deal with you later. If you try and leave again, I'll kill you."

"Ha!" Adler said. "She tried to tell me she was goin' to town to get somethin' for you, but I know'd she was lyin'."

"Thanks for bringing her back," Dingo said as he picked up his beer.

"Listen, I heard you was goin' to give Jacobs 'n them Cave brothers fifty dollars apiece if they can kill MacCallister. Is that true?"

"Yeah."

"They ain't goin' to get the job done."

Dingo took a swallow of his beer, then studied Adler over the rim of the glass. "Why do you say that?"

"MacCallister is too good for them."

"There's three of them, only one of MacCallister."

"From what I heard they was three to one before, too. Only MacCallister kilt one of 'em, and brung the other two in. I'm tellin' you, they ain't goin' to get the job done for you."

"Are you goin' to tell me that you can?"

"Me, Jed Depro, Aaron Pollard, and Merlin Morris can. That is, if you'll give us the same amount of money you're givin' them."

Dingo raised an eyebrow. "A hundred and fifty dollars?"

"They's four of us," Adler said.

"So?"

"You're givin' them fifty dollars apiece. That's what we want."

"What makes you think you can do it, if they can't?"

"We can do it 'cause we're smarter. And that's what it's goin' to take. It's goin' to take someone who is smart."

Dingo nodded. "All right. I'll give you fifty dollars apiece if you kill MacCallister."

Adler smiled. "You got yourself a deal!"

"You don't get the money until after the job is done," Dingo said.

Adler ran his hand across the short, black stubbles on his cheek. "All right," he said after a moment's pause. "All right. We'll do it."

* * *

"I ain't never seen this here MacCallister feller. What does he look like?" Pollard asked when Adler told the others about the deal he had made.

"I don't know. I ain't never seen 'im neither," Adler replied.

"Well, if there ain't none of us what's ever seen 'im, how are we goin' to find 'im?"

"They say he's a big 'un, 'n from what I've heard about 'im, he spends some time in Chugwater. So that's where we'll be headed," Adler replied.

"Chugwater? I been there a couple of times," Depro said. "That's near a day's ride from here."

"We'll start out first thing in the mornin'," Adler suggested.

"They got a saloon there, do they?" Morris asked.

Adler frowned. "You ever been anywhere, where there ain't no saloon?"

"No."

"Then it's more 'n likely they got one in Chugwater."

"They do have one there," Depro said.

"Then that's where we'll start."

"What about Wally 'n them two brothers? If they get there first, they'll be the ones gettin' the money."

Adler smiled. "More 'n likely they'll be lookin' for some store or somethin' somewhere to get a little money before they start lookin' for MacCallister. But it don't matter none if they do get there first."

"What do you mean, it don't matter? What if they kill him before we do?" Morris asked.

"Like I said, it don't matter none. If they kill 'im first, all it means is that they'll be doin' the job for us. But they won't be gettin' no money."

"Are you sayin' you don't think Dingo will actually pay once MacCallister is kilt?" Depro asked.

"Oh yeah, he'll pay all right. He just won't pay them, 'cause they'll be dead," Adler replied with a broad smile.

Dingo stepped outside the house to meet Jesse and T. Bob as they rode up. "Where's Wally?" he asked as the two men dismounted.

"He's dead."

"Dead? What happened?"

"He was kilt while we was robbin' a bank over in Sweetwater," T. Bob said.

Dingo smiled. "You robbed a bank, did you? Well, that's just real good of you boys. How much money did you get?" He showed absolutely no concern over the news that Wally Jacobs, supposedly one of his friends, had just been killed.

"We didn't get none," T. Bob said.

"How can you rob a bank and not get no money?" Dingo asked.

"We got money all right. We got what looked like a couple thousand," Jesse explained. "Wally, he was carryin' the money sack when we come out of the bank, and as we was ridin' out of town, he got hisself shot in the head. He went down and the money sack went down with him."

"And you didn't pick it up?"

"They was more bullets flyin' aroun' than ants at a picnic," Jesse said. "Believe me, that wasn't no place to be. Me 'n T. Bob barely got out alive as it was."

"What happened to the horse Wally was mounted on?" Dingo asked quietly.

"What happened to his horse? I don't know. It run off, I suppose. Why do you care about his horse?"

"It wasn't his horse. It was mine, same as the horses you boys is ridin'. Seems to me like you boys didn't do nothin' but get a man kilt and a horse run off for nothin'."

"We got a horse kilt, too," T. Bob said. "The horse Jesse was ridin' got shot from underneath 'im just as we was ridin' out."

"How did you get here, then?"

"I stoled another horse," Jesse said with a proud smile, pointing the mount he had been on.

Dingo looked at the horse for the first time. "Yeah, I see that it's a different horse. Get rid of him."

"What do you mean get rid of him? He's a good horse," Jesse said. "Oh, I know what it is. You don't like it that I got m' own horse now."

"That ain't it," Dingo said. "I just don't want no stoled horses around here. When one of 'em gets loose, they most of the time go back to whoever owns 'em, and that could lead folks back here."

Jesse couldn't believe what he was hearing. "You say get rid of it. Get rid of it how?"

"Shoot it," Dingo said.

"The hell you say. I'm not going to shoot my—"

Dingo interrupted Jesse in mid-comment by pulling his pistol and shooting the horse. The horse, with a whicker, fell where it stood, then lay on the ground kicking.

"That was a hell of a thing for you to do! What made you shoot an innocent horse like that?" Jesse asked.

"You're a strange one, you are," Dingo said. "You kilt a whole family, includin' kids, and you're concerned about a horse? A horse that ain't even yours?"

"Yeah," Jesse said. "Yeah, I guess I see what you mean."

"Finish it off," Dingo ordered.

Jesse pulled his pistol and pointed it at the horse's head, then pulled the trigger. "Seems a damn shame, though. How are me 'n m' brother goin' to kill MacCallister iffen I don't have a horse?"

"I'll get you another horse, which means you'll owe me for two of 'em. But for now, you don't worry none about killin' MacCallister. I've got that took care of."

Jesse smiled. "You mean the sumbitch has been kilt?"

"Not yet, but I've got four good men out to do the job."

Chugwater

Four men stepped into Fiddlers' Green, then went straight to one of the two potbellied stoves that were glowing red from the coal fire inside. They stood with their hands extended out into the bubble of heat that surrounded the stove.

"Are you fellas wantin' anything to drink, or are you just comin' in to get warm?" Biff asked. "Which, don't get me wrong, I'd be a miserable sort if I didn't let someone warm themselves on a cold day like this."

"Whiskey," one of the men said.

"For all four of you?"

"Yeah. Bring it over to that table." Adler pointed to the corner table.

Biff poured the drinks, then put them on a tray and nodded at a young woman who was standing next to a cowboy at the bar. "Molly, take these drinks over to the gentlemen, will you?"

"Sure thing." She took the drinks over to the table just as the men were taking their seats.

"Tell me, girl, does a fella by the name of Duff MacCallister ever come in here?" Adler asked.

"Oh yes. He comes in often. He and Biff are great friends," Molly answered.

"Who is Biff?"

"He's the man standing behind the bar. He owns the place. Anything else I can do for you?"

"Yeah, you can go away and leave us alone. We've got some palaverin' to do."

"I'll be glad to oblige," Molly replied with a practiced smile. Turning, she walked back to the bar.

"Fifty dollars apiece," Adler said. "And all we got to do is kill one man."

"From what I hear, he's not that easy a man to kill," Pollard said.

"How hard can it be if there's four of us, and only one of him?"

"How will we know who he is?" Morris asked. "There ain't none of us ever seen 'im."

"If he comes in here, I expect we'll know soon enough," Adler said.

CHAPTER TWENTY-ONE

Duff rode along with the Jensens as far as Chugwater. "Just stay on this road. Once you cross the Platte River, you can follow Rawhide Runnel on in to the settlement."

"What's a runnel?" Matt asked.

"'Tis naught but a watercourse, a small stream."

"You mean a creek?" Matt asked.

"Aye, a creek."

"Well, why didn't you say so?"

Sally laughed. "Duff, I love the way you use the language."

He grinned at her. "You'll not forget to tell Meagan that I'll be up in a couple more days?"

"I will personally tell her," Sally said.

"Come on. We'll never get there if we don't start," Smoke said, urging the other two on.

Duff watched them ride away, then headed for Fiddlers' Green.

Tying Sky off at the hitching rail in front, he went inside. The saloon was comfortably warm, heated by the stove that sat on an iron pad in the middle of the floor. He saw two people sitting at the table nearest the piano . . . a young cowboy whose face Duff recognized, but whose name he couldn't recall, and Molly, the only bar girl who was working.

"Hello, Duff. Good to see you," Biff greeted from behind the bar as a big man stepped into the saloon.

"Hello, Biff."

"Have Smoke and Matt returned from Fort Russell yet?"

"Aye, but they've left again, this time to go to Rawhide Buttes."

At the corner table, a different conversation was going on.

"Did you hear that?" Depro asked. "The bartender called him Duff. Ain't that what Dingo said was MacCallister's first name?"

"That's it, all right," Adler said.

"What do we do now?" Pollard asked.

"For now, we'll just keep an eye on him."

At the bar, Duff removed his coat and gloves.

"I'll have a—"

"As if I didn't know what you would have." Biff laughed. He was already pouring scotch into a glass.

"Hello, Mr. MacCallister," the young bar girl greeted him.

Duff smiled, and held his glass out toward the two. "Biff, how about a bit o' the creature for Molly and the young lad who is occupying her time?"

"Why, thank you, Mr. MacCallister," the cowboy said.

"Be ye findin' work, lad?"

"No, sir. None to speak of, what with it being winter. A little part-time here 'n there, is all."

"What's your name?"

"It's Nicholson, sir. Bob Nicholson."

"Well, Mr. Nicholson, 'tis not good that a man be without employment during the Christmas season. If ye be of a mind to, come out to Sky Meadow with me, and I'll present you to m' foreman, Mr. Gleason. I believe we can accommodate a willing worker. You are a willing worker, are you not?"

"Yes, sir! I'm a very willing worker," Nicholson said. "And thank you, sir! Thank you very much!"

"I don't care what anyone says, Duff, I think you're a good man," Biff said as he poured drinks for Molly and Nicholson.

"I thank ye kindly for your endorsement," Duff said.

"Mr. MacCallister, uh, the truth is, I don't have a horse," Nicholson said.

"Well, that doesn't matter all that much. After we leave here, we'll stop by Merrill's Livery and rent one for you to ride out to the ranch. Once you're there, Elmer will fix you up with a mount, 'n ye can bring the rented animal back."

Nicholson flashed a big smile. "That's just real decent of you, Mr. MacCallister."

"It's just common sense, lad," Duff replied. "I can't have someone workin' for me if he dinnae have a horse, now can I?"

"No, sir, I reckon not," Nicholson said.

Adler slapped the table. "That's it."

"What's it?" Morris asked, confused by Adler's comment.

"They're goin' to the livery stable to get a horse. That's where we'll wait for 'im."

"We ain't goin' to call 'em out or anythin' are we?" Pollard asked. "The reason I ask is, I don't think fifty dollars is enough to actually have to face someone down."

"No, we ain't goin' to call the sumbitch out. We're just goin' to shoot 'im," Adler said.

Adler and the other three men walked down the street to the livery stable. A cold wind was blowing and it had begun to snow. When they stepped into the livery stable they were out of the wind, but not out of the cold. An odor hung in the air.

"Damn, it stinks in here," Pollard said. "Ain't nobody ever heard of mucking out the stalls?"

"He prob'ly thinks it's too cold. That's why he's all cooped up in the office there, sittin' by the stove," Adler said.

"What are we goin' to do about him?" Morris asked.

"We ain't goin' to do nothin'. Hell, he don't even know we're here. Come on. Let's climb up into the loft and get us a place to wait."

"Adler, there's goin' to be two of 'em," Pollard said. "What'll we do about that?"

"If the other fella starts runnin' when the shootin'

starts, we won't do nothin' about it. But if he sticks around, we'll shoot him, too."

"We ain't gettin' paid to kill him," Pollard said.

Adler giggled. "We'll throw him in as a bonus."

When they reached the loft, they saw that the gable door was closed.

"Get the door open," Adler said.

"Soon as we open it that cold wind is goin' to start blowin' snow in on us," Morris said.

"You know any other way we're goin' to be able to shoot 'im if we don't open the door?

"No, I'm just sayin' is all."

In Fiddlers' Green, Duff turned down a second scotch, choosing a cup of coffee instead.

"Mr. MacCallister, what have you heard from Miss Parker?" Molly asked. "Do you know when she'll be back?"

"Before Christmas, I'm told," Duff said.

"Well, I for one will be glad when she returns. I want to buy a new dress for myself for Christmas."

"I expect Duff will be just as glad to see her return as you," Biff said. "Isn't that right, Duff?"

"I've nae intention of waiting till the lass returns," Duff said. "I'll be goin' to Rawhide Buttes myself in a couple days."

"Tell her that the missus and I say hello," Biff said.

At that moment, Marshal Craig stepped into the

saloon. Closing the door behind him, he stood just inside for a moment as he shivered then began brushing away the snow. "Brr, it's colder 'n hell out there."

Molly laughed. "Doesn't seem to me like it would have to be very cold to be colder than hell. At least, not from what I've heard of the place."

Marshal Craig laughed as well. "You may have a point there." He stepped up to the bar. "Biff, do you suppose I could have a cup of coffee with a bit o' sweetener, if you get my drift?"

"I think I can accommodate you," Biff replied.

"I just got some new Wanted posters in," Craig said. "There was a bank robbery up in Sweetwater a few days ago."

"A bank robbery, you say?" Biff replied as he poured a little whiskey into the marshal's cup of coffee.

"Yes, well, actually, it was more like an attempted bank robbery. Turns out that as they were leaving, one of the bank robbers was shot and killed. He was the one carrying the money, so the other two didn't get away with anything."

"Anyone else killed?" Duff asked.

"Yeah, two more, I'm afraid. Both innocent citizens of the town," the marshal replied.

"Och, 'tis a shame at any time when such perfidious behavior can take the lives of the innocent, but especially at this time of year. There'll be some sad Christmases with their families, I'm thinking."

"I'm thinking so as well," Marshal Craig said. "And get this, Duff. Guess who the bank robbers were?"

"I wouldn't know where to start guessing."

"Yeah, you would, if you thought about it. It was Jesse and T. Bob Cave. A couple people recognized them."

"I'll be. Would it be one of them who was killed?"

"No such luck. They both got away. It was a man named Wally Jacobs who was killed."

Duff frowned. "I don't believe I've heard of him."

"No reason you should have. I don't think he ever quite got around to makin' a name for himself."

"So Jesse and T. Bob got away, did they? It would be a foine Christmas if those two blaggards would wind up being caught in the next few days."

"It would be at that," Craig agreed.

"How is R.W. getting along, Marshal?" Biff asked. "I haven't seen much of him since the funeral."

"It's a sad time for him and Nora. You know what he's been doing? He's been spending a lot of time just starin' at that horse he bought for his grandson. It's a pitiful thing to see."

"Aye, I can understand. I'm more than just a bit familiar with grief." Duff finished his drink, then looked over at Nicholson. "Lad, would ye be up to tellin' Molly good-bye now, so you can come out to the ranch with me?"

"Yes, sir!" Nicholson said happily.

* * *

"Damn. It's so cold layin' here in this open door like this that I can't hardly feel my fingers," Morris said.

"Blow on 'em," Pollard suggested.

"Blow on 'em? What the hell is that supposed to do?"

"Quiet, here they come," Adler said.

"I wish we'da brought our rifles along," Morris said. "If we had rifles, we could shoot 'em both from here."

"It woulda looked a little suspicious with four of us walkin' down the middle of the street carryin' rifles, wouldn't it?" Adler asked.

"That's rather strange," Duff said.

"What's rather strange?"

"The door to the loft of the livery stable is open. Walt normally keeps that door closed to keep out as much of the cold air as possible."

"Maybe he's cleaning out the loft," Nicholson suggested.

"I suppose that's possible," Duff agreed, then saw a sudden flash of light in the hayloft and knew he was seeing a muzzle flash even before he heard the gun report and the singing whine of a bullet frying the air between the two of them.

"Get down!" he ordered.

"Mr. MacCallister, I don't have a gun!"

"Get over there behind the corner!" Duff shouted, even as he was pulling his pistol and moving to his left.

At least three more shots were fired and all three

bullets hit the ground, then ricocheted away with a loud whine.

Duff didn't know if there were four shooters, or one shooter who shot multiple times. That question was answered when he saw simultaneous muzzle flashes. He couldn't actually see his assailants as they were in the dark shadows of the loft, but fired twice into the dark maw, just to keep their heads down until he could improve his position.

He ran to the watering trough closest to the livery stable, then dived behind it. Two more shots were fired from the loft, and both hit the watering trough. *Thock thock.*

Duff looked back across the street, and satisfied himself that Nicholson was in no immediate danger. When he looked back toward the livery, he saw Walt Merrill standing there, drawn from his office by the gunshots.

"Walt, get back!" Duff shouted, waving toward him.

Walt looked at him in curiosity, but made no effort to move.

Duff fired at the ground close to Walt, startling him. "Get back!" he shouted again, waving and pointing toward Walt's office.

Finally, Walt understood what Duff was shouting about and turned and ran back inside, slamming the door to the little room behind him.

Another shot came from the loft, and Duff was ready. Aiming just to the right of where the flame pattern had appeared, he squeezed the trigger.

A body tumbled through the open loft door, hitting hard and raising dust where it fell onto the street below.

"Damn it!" a voice shouted from within the livery. "He got Pollard!"

Duff could hear the water gurgling through the bullet holes in the water trough, even as he got up and ran toward the door of the livery. He shot two more times to keep the assailants back. When he reached the big, open, double doors, he ran on through to the inside.

"Where'd he go? Morris, do you see him?" the voice cried.

"I think he come inside."

"I know he come inside, you dumb idiot. My question is where is he? Depro! Do you see him?"

"No."

Duff moved quietly through the barn, looking up at the hayloft just overhead. Suddenly, he felt little pieces of hay falling on him and he stopped, realizing that someone had to be right over him. Then he heard a quiet shuffling of feet. He fired twice, straight up, and heard a groan and a loud *thump*.

"Adler, he got Depro! We got to get out of here!"

"And would ye be for tellin' me just how ye plan to do that?" Duff asked. "There's only two ways down. You can jump, or you come down the ladder. Either way you try, I'll kill you, unless you throw down your guns first."

"Let's do it, Adler," Morris said. "I don't mind killin' someone for fifty dollars, but I'll be damned if I'm willin' to get kilt for that."

"All right, MacCallister. We'll be comin' down the ladder," Adler said.

Though Duff had not seen any of them, he had heard the names called and now recognized them by the sound of their voices. "Come to the edge and drop your guns down—holsters, belts, and all," he ordered.

A moment later, the pistol belts with the guns in the holsters were dropped down. Then two men climbed down.

"What happens now?" Adler asked.

"I hope you boys didn't have any plans for Christmas," Duff said. "For you'll be spending it in jail."

"It won't be the first time I've spent Christmas behind bars," Morris said.

Duff chuckled. "Sure now, and I'm not surprised by that."

Marshal Craig put the two men in a cell, locked the door, and turned to Duff. "They're all yours."

"Lads, I heard you say that you were being paid fifty dollars to kill me. Would ye be for tellin' me who it was that would make such an offer?"

"Why should we tell you?" Adler asked.

"Were you paid in advance?"

"No."

"Then why wouldn't you tell me? You'll nae be hanging, you dinnae kill anyone. If you weren't paid, what do you owe the man who got two of your friends killed for nothing?"

"He's right, Adler. We don't owe Dingo nothin'," Morris said.

"Dingo? Would that be Max Dingo?" Marshal Craig asked.

"You got a big mouth, Morris," Adler said.

"Tell me, lad, what kind of pie do you like?" Duff asked Morris.

"Apple pie. Why do you ask?"

"I'll see to it that you get a piece of pie for telling me who wanted me killed."

"He's right," Adler said. "It was Max Dingo. And I like cherry pie."

"Do you know where I might find this gentleman?"

"I know where he is," Marshal Craig said. "Or at least, I've heard where he is. They say he is holed up somewhere in the Laramie Range. Nobody's ever tried to find 'em, and truth to tell, it would near 'bout be suicide to even try, seein' as how he has a regular fort there."

"That's right," Adler said. "He's got at least ten men with him there. You'd be a fool to go after 'im."

"I thank you for the information," Duff said as he turned away from the cell.

"Hey, what about our pie?" Morris called.

"I'll bring it to you," Duff promised.

CHAPTER TWENTY-TWO

Sky Meadow Ranch

"So, you had a little excitement on the way here, did you?" Elmer asked Bob Nicholson as he started to show the newly hired hand around the ranch.

"Wasn't on the way here. Happened before we even left town," Nicholson answered. "Four men jumped Mr. MacCallister. And he wound up killin' two of 'em, and takin' the other two to jail. I swear, I ain't never seen nothin' like that."

"Yes, well, four to one wasn't very fair, I'll admit," Elmer said.

"I guess so. But them odds didn't seem to bother Mr. MacCallister none."

Elmer chuckled. "No, you misunderstand what I'm sayin', boy. I don't mean four to one wasn't fair to Duff. I mean, it wasn't fair to the four poor souls who were dumb enough to try 'n take him on."

"You mean he's done stuff like this before?"

"I'll just say this. I've rode with Quantrill and Jesse James, I've sailed the seven seas, and I've lived with the Injuns, so there ain't much in this world I can truly say that bedazzles me. But Duff MacCallister is someone who does."

"I know 'bout the shoot-out in Chugwater, when eight men had come to kill him, and he kilt all eight of 'em," Nicholson said. "I think ever'body has heard about that."[1]

"Yes, well, Biff Johnson got one of 'em. Duff will be the first one to tell you that."

Though Elmer didn't mention it, there were actually nine, not eight, who had come to kill Duff, and it was Elmer who'd killed Angus Somerled, the leader of the group, when Somerled had the drop on Duff and was just about to pull the trigger.

"Come on, let me show you the finest ranch in all of Wyoming," Elmer said proudly.

Duff MacCallister's Sky Meadow Ranch had not grown haphazardly, but was the result of very careful planning. The most prominent building was the main house, called "The Big House" by the men who worked there. Also on the grounds were a barn, a machine shed, a smokehouse, and an icehouse. Several other buildings included a bunkhouse, a kitchen and mess hall, and another private dwelling.

A long, low building with a porch that ran the full length of the structure, the bunkhouse had a bay area in the middle with six bunks on either side. Four coal-burning

---

1. *MacCallister: Eagles Legacy*

stoves, two on either side, did an adequate job of keeping the occupants warm, even on the coldest winter days, because the bunkhouse was well insulated. One end was a bit better furnished than the rest. It housed the bunks of Al Woodward, Case Martin, and Brax Walker, the three men, other than Elmer, who had been with Duff the longest. It was their longevity, rather than any sense of superior position, that improved their area. They had been there long enough to acquire a few additional items to make them more comfortable.

Next to the bunkhouse was Elmer's house, which had a living room and a bedroom. Next to his house was the kitchen and mess hall. The cook had a private room just off the kitchen.

"We run nothin' but Black Angus cattle here," Elmer explained as he showed Bob Nicholson around. "That's the first thing Duff done once he got his ranch started. They was some other ranchers that kinda laughed at 'im, but you better believe there ain't none of that's alaughin' at 'im now. The Black Angus bring in anywheres from 30 to 40 percent more 'n Herefords."

"Yes, sir. I heard Mr. MacCallister was the one that got Black Angus started here in Russell County."

"That he did. He knew all about 'em 'cause that's what he raised back in Scotland. And it ain't just here that he's got 'em started. They's ranches all over the West that's raisin' Black Angus now, 'cause of Duff."

"You like workin' for him, don't you?" Nicholson asked.

"I don't work *for* him, son, I work *with* him," Elmer said, emphasizing the words to stress the difference.

"I ain't known him all that long on account of he ain't actual been here for very long. But in that short 'o time, why I reckon I'd have to say he's the best friend I've ever had. I know he's the best man I've ever known."

Nicholson made no response, because no response was expected.

"All right. I've showed you near 'bout ever'thing there is to show." Elmer pointed back toward the bunkhouse. "There's three empty bunks in there. You can tell which ones they are on account of the mattresses are rolled up. Just choose one, unroll your mattress, and make yourself to home."

"When do we start work?"

Elmer chuckled. "I'm glad to see you're concerned about it. We don't do all that much work in the wintertime, 'cept maybe haul hay out to the animals now 'n then when the snow is so iced over that the beeves can't get to their graze. Most of the time in the winter we just sort of look for things to be done. And from now till after Christmas, we'll more 'n likely not be doin' nothin' at all 'cept maybe lie around and sleep, or play cards, or some such. Truth is, I don't know why Duff even hired you. We sure don't need nobody else. Most ranchers start layin' off in the winter."

"I know. That's how come I don't have any work. Mr. Tadlock paid off all his men but about three or four. I don't know why Mr. MacCallister hired me, either. He just asked me if I was workin', and I told him no I wasn't."

"Well, there's your answer then. He seen you was out

of work and just wanted to help, is all. I reckon that's it. Come on, let's go into the mess hall and get a cup of coffee. Hell, Cookie might have even made some doughnuts."

Elmer led Nicholson into the mess hall redolent with the aroma of coffee and something recently baked.

"Jones, you old belly robber, can a couple hard-working men get a cup of coffee?" Elmer called.

Jones, who was the cook for the ranch hands, stepped into the dining room. He was a small man, with white hair and wrinkled skin. "You show me a couple hard-working men and I might oblige them."

Elmer chuckled. "Well, you've got me there, pardner. In weather like this, I don't reckon we do that much hard work. But you know yourself that when the time comes, we work hard. So how about the coffee?"

"All right, all right. I hate to hear a grown man beg. Go ahead. Get yourselves some coffee if you want."

"What are you bakin' that smells so good?"

"It ain't none of your business," Jones replied. He used a wooden spoon to spear through the holes of a couple doughnuts and held them out toward Elmer and Nicholson. "They're hot."

Elmer reached out to grab one, then he jerked his hand back. "Damn, they're hot!"

"Didn't I just say that?" Jones let the two doughnuts slide off onto a table.

"Does Mr. MacCallister eat out here with the men?" Nicholson asked.

"No, he has his own cook, Mrs. Sterling. You think he

wants to trust eating food that's been cooked by an ex-con like Jones?" Elmer reached again for one of the doughnuts and was able to pick it up. He took a bite.

"How is it?" Jones asked.

"I've had better," Elmer said nonchalantly.

"Where? On one of those mysterious islands you're always talkin' about?"

"Nah. In Australia it was. Lamingtons. That's a cake with a chocolate icin'. There ain't nothin' nowhere in the world can touch that."

"Gimme back that doughnut, you inconsiderate old man," Jones said, reaching for it.

"Except maybe your doughnuts," Elmer said, jerking it back before Jones could grab it.

"Mr. Gleason called you an ex-con," Nicholson said. "Is that true?"

Jones squinted at Nicholson. "What if it is?"

"Nothin'. I was just wonderin' if it was true or if he was just teasin'."

"It's true," Elmer said. "Tell 'im what you was in for, Jones."

"Murder," Jones said.

"Murder?" Nicholson repeated.

"Yeah. I was cookin' at a ranch down in Texas. One of the cowboys got too curious about me, so I kilt him."

Nicholson was beginning to be made a little uneasy by Jones's stare.

"You want to know how I kilt him?" Jones asked.

"Sure . . . I guess." Nicholson was beginning to wish he had never brought up the subject.

"I kilt him with a poison doughnut."

"Ahh!" Nicholson gasped, dropping the doughnut.

Jones and Elmer both laughed.

"Boy, you're just too damn easy to tease," Elmer said. "You'd better watch that, or the rest of boys will be on you like a duck on a june bug."

"I . . . I see what you mean," Nicholson said, joining in the laughter. "My pa always did say I was too wet behind the ears." He reached down to pick up the doughnut he'd dropped.

"Here," Jones said, taking the doughnut. "I'll get you another 'n. Anyone who can laugh at himself is all right in my book."

"Thanks," Nicholson said. "I think I'm goin' to like it here."

Rawhide Buttes

Smoke, Sally, and Matt arrived in town in mid-afternoon. People were walking up and down the boardwalks, exchanging greetings. Some were hanging Christmas decorations in store windows.

"This is what Christmas is all about," Matt said. "Small towns where everyone knows each other, wishing each other Merry Christmas."

"You sound like Charles Dickens," Sally said.

"Who?"

"He wrote the story *A Christmas Carol*. You could say it's about a small-town Christmas."

"I've never heard of it."

"How can you not have heard of it?"

"Because he ain't like me," Smoke said. "He ain't very educated."

"Ohhh!!" Sally said, shuddering. "Sometimes I forget that you like to say things like that on purpose, just to irritate me."

Smoke laughed.

"'Boy, do you know whether they've sold the prize turkey that was hanging up there—not the little prize turkey, the big one?'" Matt said, mimicking an English accent as he quoted from the novel.

"You are both impossible!" Sally said, but she, too, joined in the laughter.

"That looks like the best hotel in town," Smoke said, pointing to the biggest building on the street.

"It looks to me as if it is the only hotel in town," Sally replied.

"Then, by definition, doesn't that make it the best hotel in town?"

Laughing, the three tied off their horses in front of the hotel, then went inside, where Smoke got two rooms for them, signing the register as Kirby Jensen.

"I see you have a dining room," Smoke said.

"Yes, sir, Mister . . ." Doolin paused to examine the registration book, "Jensen. And many think it is the best place to eat in town."

"Good."

"Smoke, as soon as we've put our stuff in our room, I'm going to go find Meagan," Sally said.

"All right."

"Smoke?" Doolin asked. "See here, are you Smoke Jensen?"

"Yes."

A huge smile spread across Doolin's face. "My oh my." He extended his hand across the counter. "I have heard much about you, sir. May I say that it is a pleasure to have you as a guest in our hotel?"

"Thank you." Such effusive reactions to his name no longer embarrassed Smoke, simply because they happened so often. Long ago, he had taken Sally's advice to accept graciously the accolades bestowed on him.

"Sir," Sally started.

"Please, it's Hodge. Hodge Doolin."

"Mr. Doolin, could you tell me how to find Cora Ensor's Dress Shop?"

"Indeed I can. You just go out the front door, turn left, walk two blocks, and you'll find it right on the corner. There is a sign painted on the front window."

"Thank you," Sally replied with an affable smile.

Meagan looked up when the bell over the door jingled. For just a moment, she was surprised at who she saw coming into the store. "Sally?"

"Hello, Meagan."

"What in the world are you doing here in Rawhide Buttes?"

"I came to help you and your friend get ready for Christmas. I think Duff is getting a little anxious that maybe you won't make it back in time."

"Ha. I'd like to think that." Meagan noticed that Cora was looking on with a curious smile on her face.

"Cora, this is my friend, Sally Jensen. Sally, this is Cora Ensor."

The two exchanged greetings, then Sally said, "I'm serious. I'm here to work. So what can I do?"

"Right now, we're trying to think of something to promote Christmas in the store," Meagan said. "So any ideas or suggestions you might have would be most welcome."

CHAPTER TWENTY-THREE

Even the Cottonwood Saloon was ready for Christmas. Six green, red-bowed wreaths were placed over all of the *O*s in the saloon's name, which was painted across the false front.

It was pleasantly warm inside the saloon as Smoke and Matt stepped up to the bar.

"What'll it be, gents?" the bartender asked.

"A whiskey for warmth, and a beer for taste," Smoke said.

"I'll have the same," Matt added.

"What do you mean, no?" asked a man's loud, gruff voice. "Look, sister, you ain't nothin' special. I'm not askin' you to go upstairs with me, I'm tellin' you to. You don't have no choice as to whether to say yes or no. If I decide to take you upstairs with me, you'll damn well go."

"You may think so, but I still have the right to say who I will and who I will not do business with."

242   *William W. Johnstone*

"Carol, do you have a problem there?" the bartender asked.

"It's not anything I can't handle, Nate, thanks," Carol said resolutely. She looked back at the man who was harassing her. "I told you no, and that's the end of it."

Suddenly and unexpectedly, the man slapped Carol in the face, hitting her so hard she fell to the floor with blood streaming from her nose and mouth.

"Conroy, get out of my saloon, now!" Nate bent over, but a pistol suddenly appeared in Conroy's hand.

"Uh-uh," Conroy said. "You bring that scattergun up from under the bar, now. And you'd better be holding it by the end of the barrel, or I'll shoot you dead where you stand."

"Conroy, you got no right doin' this," said one of the other customers.

"You want some of this?" Conroy asked.

"No, but . . ."

"Then stay out of it. Nate, let me see that scattergun now.

Carefully, Nate picked up the double-barreled shotgun, holding it as Conroy had suggested, by the muzzle end, and lay it on the top of the bar.

Conroy holstered his pistol, reached over to retrieve the gun, broke it down, and extracted the two shells from the breech. Then, leaning the empty gun against the bar, he turned his attention back to Carol, who was still lying on the floor. "Get up. Get up and come upstairs with me. I ain't goin' to ask you again."

"Good. I'm glad you aren't going to ask her again,"

Matt said. Pulling out a clean handkerchief, he handed it to Carol, then helped her up.

"What's it to you?" Conroy asked.

"Since the young lady doesn't want to go with you, I thought perhaps she would go upstairs with me," Matt said.

Carol looked at the man who had come to her assistance. Her face was creased with a smile of recognition. "Hello, Matt. It's been a long time. When was it?"

"Almost a year ago," Matt said.

"I'd be happy to go upstairs with you."

"Well, now." Conroy smiled, but there was no humor in his smile. "What are you trying to do, make me jealous?"

"Go away, Conroy." Carol dabbed at her nose, then pulled the handkerchief away to examine the blood. "Even saloon girls can make a choice and I choose him."

"Nate, do you have a clean towel back there?" Matt asked.

"Y-yes, sir, I do," Nate said, stuttering in his nervousness.

"Hand it to me, would you?"

Conroy put his hand on his pistol. "There better be nothin' but a cloth in your hand when it comes back up."

Nate pulled a clean white cloth from under the bar and handed it to Matt. Matt poured whiskey on it, then handed it to Carol. "Hold this on the cut on your lip," he suggested.

"Mister, you're just gettin' a little too personal with my girl," Conroy said.

"I'm not your girl, Conroy, and I never have been," Carol said.

"Are you goin' to stand there and say you ain't never took me up to your room?"

"One time," Carol said. "And I got a black eye for no reason. I don't have to do anything with someone who would do that, and I won't."

"You like to hit women, do you?" Matt asked.

"What's it to you?"

"Anyone who would hit a woman isn't much of a man."

"You know what, mister? I've had about a belly full of you. I see that you are wearing a gun. How about we settle this now?"

"You're wanting to draw on me, are you?" Matt asked.

Again, Conroy smiled a tight, cruel, and confident, smile. "Yeah, I am."

The others in the saloon moved to get out of the way, but Smoke very pointedly stepped up behind Matt and, reaching down for the whiskey bottle, poured himself another shot.

"Mister, are you crazy?" Conroy asked. "What are you doing standing right in the way, like that? Can't you see that me 'n him is about to start shootin' here?"

"Just him," Smoke said.

"What?"

"You said 'me and him.' Of course, I know that you meant to say, 'he and I,' as in the two of you. But it won't be the two of you, it'll just be him. You won't even get your shot off."

"All right. Get your fool ass kilt. It's your own doin'," Conroy said.

Conroy didn't call his move. He made a lightning draw, but by the time his pistol had cleared the holster, Matt's gun was already in his hand, and a little finger of flame erupted from the end of the barrel.

Matt's bullet hit Conroy in the middle of his chest, and he died with an expression of shock and disbelief on his face.

Conroy wasn't the only one shocked. People in town had seen him in action before, and were convinced that it was unlikely he would ever encounter anyone who could beat him in a fair draw. And it could be said that this wasn't even a fair draw. Conroy had gone for his gun without a word of warning.

It didn't take longer than five minutes for Marshal Worley to come pushing through the front door with pistol in hand. Seeing Conroy lying on the floor, the marshal lowered his pistol. "I'll be damned. I see Conroy finally ran into someone faster 'n he was. Was it a fair fight?"

Everyone began to talk and shout at once.

"Hold it, hold it! How 'm I supposed to understand you if you're all talkin' at the same time?" He looked toward Carol, and saw her bruised and bloodied face. "I got a feelin' you're involved in this."

"Only as an innocent bystander," Matt said.

"Who are you?" Marshal Worley asked.

"I'm the one who killed Conroy."

Worley smirked. "I sort of figured that. I mean, what's your name?"

"Jensen. Matt Jensen."

"I'll be damned. I've heard of you, Mr. Jensen. Would you like to tell me what happened?"

"He drew on me, and I shot him," Matt said.

"There has to be more to it than that."

"Conroy started beating up on Carol," Nate said. "When Mr. Jensen here stepped in, real nice like, Conroy started on him. Next thing you know, without so much as a how do you do, Conroy went for his gun. Lightning fast he was, and I figured he was about to put another notch on his gun handle. But Mr. Jensen was even faster. Conroy never got off so much as one shot."

"Is that pretty much what all of you say?" Marshal Worley asked the others.

"Yeah," half a dozen responded.

Worley put his pistol away, took off his hat, and ran his hand through his hair. He looked back at Carol. "You all right, girl?"

"Yes, I'm fine, thank you."

"There ain't goin' to be no charges," Worley said. "Conroy needed killin', and that's all there is to it."

"Drinks are on the house, boys!" Nate shouted, and there was a rush to the bar.

Carol took a step toward Matt. "Thank you. I don't know what I would have done if you hadn't come along."

"I'm glad I happened to be here," Matt said. "Oh, let

me introduce my friend. Smoke, this is Carol . . . I don't know her last name."

"Oh honey, girls like me don't have last names, you know that," Carol said with a smile.

"Carol, this is Smoke Jensen."

"Is he your brother?"

Smoke chuckled. "Thanks for not asking if I'm his father."

"In a manner of speaking, he is my brother." It was a strange way of responding to Carol's question, but Matt offered no further explanation, nor did she pursue the subject.

"Open your mouth," Dr. Poindexter said.

Barney Sadler complied. He was the first adult Dr. Poindexter had seen with the disease.

Using a tongue depressor, the doctor examined Sadler's throat, and saw that it was covered with white mucus. It was presenting itself exactly like diphtheria. "When did you first notice the symptoms?"

"The what?" Sadler replied, his voice weak and raspy.

"When did you first start getting sick?"

"About five days ago."

"Have you been around any schoolchildren?"

"No, I ain't been around no schoolkids or any other kind of kids. I don't have no kids. Hell, Doc, you know that."

"Have you been around anyone who has been around schoolkids?"

"Why do you keep asking that question? What does that have to do with anything?"

"Please answer my questions, Mr. Sadler. Believe me, they are important."

"Well, like I said I ain't been around . . . no, wait. I helped Rufus McCoy build some things that's goin' to be used at school. Seems they're plannin' on havin' a play, and Rufus wanted me to help him build a manger and a stable and such. He's around kids all the time, seein' as he works as a janitor and handyman at the school."

"Thank you for the information."

"I still don't know why it's so all-fired important about whether or not I been around anyone who's been around schoolkids."

Poindexter picked up a rubber-ball atomizer. "I'm going to spray this into your throat now, and it's going to burn."

"Wait a minute. Didn't I tell you my throat was already hurtin'? Why do you want to do somethin' that's goin' to make it hurt even more?

"I'm sorry, Mr. Sadler. It has to be done."

Sally stood with her hands on her hips as she looked around Cora's store. "Yes," she said, nodding her head. "Yes, that's what we'll do."

"What's what we'll do? What are you talking

about?" At the moment, Cora was putting a dress on a mannequin.

"I have an idea," Sally said. "I think we should do a special display for Christmas."

"Well, that's what we are doing, isn't it? I mean all the dresses we are displaying are for Christmas. Though, in truth, any dress in the store can be bought for Christmas."

"No, I'm thinking more than that. I mean, let's do something artistic, something that will make people smile, something that will have them telling others about it so that they will want to come in to see it as well."

"Oh, I see what you are saying," Cora said. "You want to put up a Christmas tree."

"No," Meagan said, shaking her head. "I think Sally has something else in mind."

"A Christmas tree, yes, but let's not stop there."

"Oh, you mean like bunting and greenery and such?" Cora looked around the inside of her store. "I suppose we can, but with all the colorful dresses and bolts of cloth that we have in here, wouldn't a few more ribbons just get lost?"

"How good are you at drawing?" Sally asked.

"I suppose it depends on what I need to draw."

"Faces."

"Faces?"

"On paper bags," Sally said. "We're going to draw lots of faces on lots of paper bags."

"Whose faces are we going to draw?"

"Nobody's in particular. Just faces of women and

children. Then we are going to fill the sacks so that they look like people's heads, and we're going to give them hair made of yarn."

Cora laughed. "I don't have an idea in the world what you are thinking about, but I already like it."

"You'll like it even more once we get it finished," Sally promised.

"Whatever it is," Cora replied.

"I think I know what you are talking about when you want to do a display," Meagan said. "And Sally is right, Cora, you will like it even more once we are finished."

CHAPTER TWENTY-FOUR

"I don't have any choice, Jenny," Dr. Poindexter said after he sent Sadler back home with instructions not to leave his house, and not to come into contact with anyone. "I'm going to have to apply a city-wide quarantine. This whole town is in danger and I'm going to shut it down."

"Can you do that?"

"If you mean do I have the authority, to tell the truth, I don't know whether I have the authority to do something like that or not. But I'm going to assume that I do. I don't see as I have any other option."

Leaving his office, Dr. Poindexter walked down the street to the jail. He stood out in front of the building for a moment, watching as the scaffold was being torn down. Because the scaffold had been used not to execute the two men who killed the Guthrie family but to display the bodies of the deputy sheriff and the circuit judge, the town had declared that it should be removed as quickly as possible.

Dr. Poindexter dreaded what he was going to have to do, but it was something that he knew had to be done. Squaring his shoulders with determination, he pushed open the door and stepped into Mark Worley's office.

The marshal was sitting at his desk, filling out forms. He looked up. "If you're here about Conroy, he won't need you," Marshal Worley said.

"Conroy?"

"Bud Conroy. He just got himself shot over in the Cottonwood. But he was dead by the time I got there, so there's no need for a doctor. Who called you, anyway?"

"Nobody called me. I don't know anything about anyone getting shot."

"You don't? Well then, what brings you here?"

"Marshal, are you aware of the corpse that Tom Welch got from the Rocky Mountain Hotel?"

"Yeah, I seen him. Damndest looking corpse I ever saw. That's why I told Tom to have you take a look at him."

"I saw him. We've got trouble, Marshal. We've got major trouble."

"We've got trouble? What do you mean? Are you fixin' to tell me that you think the fella was murdered? I mean, I admit it looked a little strange, the way his neck was all swollen up like it was. But I didn't think he'd been murdered."

"It wasn't murder. It would be better if it had been murder. That way, the rest of the town wouldn't be affected."

"Now you're losin' me, Doc. How is the rest of the

town affected by findin' that fella dead in his hotel room? Especially if he wasn't murdered."

"The rest of the town is affected because I have to ask you to put the entire town on quarantine. I don't want anybody to be able to come in, and I don't want you to let anyone leave."

"What?" Marshal Worley shouted. "Doc, what the hell are you talking about? Why would you want to close down the town like that?"

"Diphtheria, Marshal. I've treated three cases, and young Helen Sinclair has died with the disease."

"Where did this diphtheria come from?" Worley asked. "How did it get started in our town?"

"It started with Ralph Walters, the corpse that came from the hotel. Evidently he was a traveling entertainer of some sort. He exposed the children in school, and they are exposing everyone else. It's going to spread, and it's going to spread fast. The best we can do is keep it contained."

"Oh, Lord. If it come from him, the kids in school wasn't the only ones that he was around. He done a show for the firemen's benefit. There must have been forty or fifty that was there. I was there." Worley took a quick breath. "Damn! Does that mean I have it?"

"How long ago was the show?"

"It was a little over a week ago."

"Then the chances are you don't have it. You would have been showing symptoms, by now."

"Well, isn't there something you can do about it?

I mean, yeah, you say shut down the whole town, but what about the ones that's already got it?"

"I've sent to Cheyenne for an antitoxin serum. It depends on whether they have any, and if so, if they have enough that they can send some to us."

"How soon do you need the town shut down?"

"Right away. Oh, and Marshal, here comes the hard part. We're going to have to close any place where people gather. That means school, saloons, and stores."

"We can't do that, Doc. It's Christmas! I know for a fact the school has a play planned. The merchants have all made special plans for the Christmas season, and the people will want to be buying Christmas presents and the like. And the saloons? Why, if we close the saloons, there will likely be a riot in the streets. Hell, you know that as well as anyone!"

"Marshal, we don't have any choice. We have to act, and we have to act fast. I just pray that it's not already too late. The sad truth is, if we don't close all these places, we are going to start having a lot of bodies to bury. Now which would you rather have? Would you rather have a few disgruntled people? Or would you rather have people start dying on you?"

Marshal Worley sighed, and ran his hand through his hair. "Is it really that bad?"

"Yes, I'm afraid it really is that bad. Like you said, it's Christmas. Do you think I would come here to suggest this if I didn't think it absolutely necessary?"

"You do realize, don't you, that it's going to take an army of deputies to get this done?"

"I know it is going to be a difficult task."

"That's easy for you to say, Doc. All you have to do is tell me to do it. I'm the one that has to get it done."

"True. But it isn't easy to treat diphtheria patients, either, and I expect they'll be piling up on me pretty soon."

"Oh," Marshal Worley said. "Damn, Doc, you're right. I had no business bellyachin' about how hard it's goin' to be for me. Neither me nor any of my deputies will have it as hard as you. I'm sorry I mouthed off like that."

"No apology needed, Marshal. Just do what you can to help me keep this under control."

"You got it," Marshal Worley said. "I guess I'd better start rounding them up. Oh, what about the church? Are you saying I have to close the church as well?"

Dr. Poindexter stroked his cheek for a moment before he replied. "We're probably going to need the church."

"That's what I was thinking. I expect a lot of people will be wanting to come to church to pray."

"Yes, that, too," Dr. Poindexter said, though he didn't expand on his rather strange answer.

Cora and Meagan soon saw what Sally had in mind when they started drawing faces on the paper sacks. Clothing the dress forms, they stuffed the long sleeves of the dresses so that they became arms, then placed the paper sack heads on them. The result was several lifelike figures, both adult and child, gathered around a well-decorated Christmas tree.

"Oh, it looks as if they are having a Christmas party!" Cora said.

"I just know this is the most beautiful Christmas display in the whole town," Meagan replied as she added another gaily wrapped package under the tree.

"It is all because of you," Cora said to Sally.

"Nonsense. We did it together," Sally said.

"This is going to be the best Christmas I have ever had," Cora said, her voice bubbling over with enthusiasm. "I haven't been this excited about Christmas since I was a little girl."

"It makes me anxious to get back home," Meagan said. "Thanks to Sally's idea, I'll do the same thing in my store."

"Oh! How unthinking of me!" Cora said. "Here, I've taken all your time to help me get ready, at the expense of your own store."

Meagan smiled. "Not to worry, Cora. Your store is just getting started. You need something like this to attract attention. My store has been going for a few years. I don't need to introduce anyone to it. They already know that it is there. And it won't take me too long to decorate it, once I get back home.

A tinkling bell on the front door announced a visitor, and with smiles on their faces, they turned to welcome the caller, or, in this case, callers. It was Smoke and Matt.

"It looks like we came to the right place," Smoke said.

Sally introduced Smoke and Matt to Cora.

"This looks interesting," Smoke said, pointing to the display the three women were putting together.

"Well, it's all thanks to Sally," Cora said. "She came up with the idea. I can hardly wait until members of the Downtown Merchants Association see it. They will be pea green with envy."

Another man came into the store then.

"My," Cora said. "I don't believe I've ever had this many men in my store at the same time. Welcome, Deputy Collins. Are you looking for a Christmas present for a lady friend?"

"No ma'am. I wish I was. I hate to do this to you, Miss Ensor," Collins said with a troubled expression. "But I ain't got no choice. We're havin' to do it to ever' business in town."

"Do what?" Cora asked, the expression on her face mirroring her confusion at the strange comment.

Collins handed her a sheet of paper. "I'm sorry," he said again.

BY ORDER OF DR. POINDEXTER,
QUARANTINE
HAS BEEN DECLARED IN RAWHIDE BUTTES.
All places of business are hereby CLOSED.
Nobody will be allowed to enter or leave town
until the QUARANTINE has been lifted.

Cora frowned. "What? You can't close my business! What are you talking about?"

"What is it?" Meagan asked.

"Look at this!" Cora handed Meagan the piece of paper.

"What?" Meagan asked with a gasp as she read the paper. She looked up at the man who had delivered it. "You can't close Cora's business. It's nearly Christmas!"

"It ain't just Miss Ensor's business, ma'am. Ever' business in town is being closed," Collins said.

"Wait a minute," Smoke said. "According to this, we can't even go back home."

"It ain't me," the deputy said. "All I'm doin' is helpin' to spread the word. From what I understand, it's Doc Poindexter doin' it."

"Surely the doctor can't do this by himself. He is being backed by the marshal, is he not?" Cora asked.

"Well, yes, ma'am, I reckon his is, seein' as it was the marshal what give me these here papers to pass out to all the stores and such."

"Is the marshal in his office now?" Meagan asked.

"Yes, ma'am, he is."

Meagan folded up the sheet of paper that had the announcement. "We'll just see about this. I can't stay here over Christmas. I have to get back home."

"Yes, ma'am, but even if you decide to go, I don't know how you're goin' to get it done. There won't be no stagecoaches or even freight wagons runnin'. And the marshal plans to have a deputy posted on all the roads, stoppin' anyone from comin' in, and keepin' ever' one that's in the town now from leavin'."

* * *

Meagan, accompanied by Sally, Smoke, and Matt, stepped into the marshal's office a few minutes later.

Marshal Worley had the cylinder out of his pistol and was using a rod to poke a small cloth wad through the barrel. He looked toward Smoke and Matt. "Are you two here about the shootin' in the saloon? I told you, there wouldn't be any charges. Ever' one there says it was self-defense."

"What shooting?" Sally asked, looking toward Smoke. "Were you involved in a shooting?"

"It wasn't Smoke, Sally. I was the one," Matt said.

"And neither of you were going to mention it?"

"I was going to tell you about it later," Smoke said. "To tell you the truth, a dress shop didn't seem the place to discuss it. Especially as you were all sort of excited about the Christmas decorations."

"I guess you're right," Sally agreed.

"If you ain't here about the shootin', why are you here?"

"This is why we are here," Meagan said, showing the marshal the paper Collins had delivered to Cora Ensor. "What is the meaning of this?"

"Just like it says, Miss Parker. The whole town is under quarantine."

"But why would you do such a thing? Do you have any idea how much money all the businesses have invested in getting ready for Christmas? You can't just shut the town down like this! Don't you understand that some of the businesses could wind up going bankrupt?"

"You'll have to go plead your case with the doc," Marshal Worley said.

"The doctor? What does he have to do with it?"

"He's the one that established the quarantine. All I'm doin' is enforcin' it."

"Doctor Poindexter, I don't understand why we can't go home," Meagan said. She and Sally had gone there as soon as they left the marshal's office.

"Diphtheria is a terrible disease, Miss Parker. Surely you understand that we can't take a chance on spreading it to other towns."

"Diphtheria?"

"Yes, ma'am, diphtheria. We have an outbreak in this town, and I'm trying to keep it from getting any worse."

"But neither one of us are sick. I would think you would want everyone who isn't sick to get out of danger," Meagan said, taking in Sally with a wave of her hand.

"You don't know whether you are sick or not. You were in contact with young Laura Hastings, were you not?"

"Yes."

"That means you have been exposed. Some contract the disease, but present no symptoms at all. But even though they are not affected by the disease, they are still carriers and can infect others. You might already have infected this young woman."

"But you don't understand. It's Christmas. I have obligations back home. And forget about me. What about your own citizens? Don't you realize that if they aren't able to do business during the Christmas season some of them could go bankrupt?"

Dr. Poindexter pinched the bridge of his nose. "Do you think I wanted to do something like this at Christmas? Everyone has obligations. Including me. And my biggest obligation is to prevent, if at all possible, an epidemic of diphtheria.

"Now, which is worse, Miss Parker? Would you prefer several businesses go broke, or several men, women, and children die of diphtheria?"

"Diphtheria?" Meagan asked in a quiet voice. "Are you saying we have an epidemic of diphtheria?"

"Yes, ma'am, or so it appears."

"The little Hastings girl? Oh, my God, has she died?"

"No, but a little girl named Helen Sinclair has died. And a man named Ralph Walters. And others are sick."

"Oh, I . . . I didn't know that. Yes, of course, if that is the case, I can see that you have no choice."

Meagan recalled the visit of young Laura Hasting to Cora's store, as well as the conversation she'd overheard in the dining room of the hotel. Even then, she'd begun to have a rather disquieting feeling that some sort of illness was going around.

CHAPTER TWENTY-FIVE

"Diphtheria?" Smoke said, when Sally returned to the hotel to tell him what she had found out at the doctor's office."

"Yes. Evidently two have already died. Smoke, I feel like such a fool going there to complain the way I did."

"You aren't a fool. On the contrary, it would have been foolish not to follow up on this. You know what I think?"

"What?"

"I think Matt and I should go back to see Marshal Worley."

Sally chuckled. "Didn't you once say never apologize, that it makes you look weak?"

"Oh, I don't plan to apologize."

Marshal Worley was standing in front of his office, leaning on the post that supported the overhanging roof, when Smoke and Matt approached.

"Did you speak to the doc?" Worley asked.

"No, but Sally did," Smoke said. "Marshal, we were wondering . . ."

"I can't do it, Smoke," Worley said, shaking his head. "I can't let you folks leave, and keep ever'one else here. How would that look?"

Smoke smiled. "It would look like you're playing favorites. but that's not what I was about to say."

"Oh? What was it?"

"It's going to take some effort to enforce this quarantine. If you think you could use us, Matt and I would be happy to volunteer as deputies."

"You would do that?" Marshal Worley asked, surprised and obviously pleased by the offer.

"Yes. That is, if you want us."

"Yes, absolutely I want you! That would take a lot of the worry from me. I don't know how to thank you, Smoke."

There was only one church in town, and its pastor, the Reverend Nathaniel Sharkey, was Presbyterian by affiliation. Despite his denomination, he conducted his services in an ecumenical way so as to accommodate every citizen in town, regardless of their religious background.

Sharkey was working on his Christmas Eve service in his office with the door open when he happened to look up and see Dr. Poindexter come in through the front of the church. He found that a little strange, for while

Poindexter was a regular attendee of the Sunday services, he had never come to church in the middle of the week.

Sharkey stood, assuming that Poindexter was coming to see him, but the doctor walked down to the front of the church, then kneeled before the altar. The pastor stepped out of his office, but not wanting to interrupt the doctor at his prayer, he stood there quietly as Dr. Poindexter remained on his knees.

Not until Dr. Poindexter stood up, did Reverend Sharkey approach him.

"Good afternoon, Doctor."

"Reverend."

"Won't you come into my office and have a cup of coffee? I'm working on my Christmas Eve sermon, but I'm due a break. I would love it if you drink some coffee with me."

"Thanks, I believe I will," Dr. Poindexter said, following the preacher back into his office.

A small wood-burning stove sat in the corner, doing a good job of keeping the office warm. Reverend Sharkey used an old purificator cloth as a hot pad and lifted the blue metal coffeepot off the stove, then poured two cups. "You look troubled, George," he said as he handed one of the cups to the doctor.

"I'm afraid there won't be a service on Christmas Eve, or Christmas Day," Dr. Poindexter said.

"What? Why of course there will be a church service. Why would you even suggest such a thing?"

"Reverend, we are facing an epidemic of diphtheria."

Reverend Sharkey's eyes widened. "We have a diphtheria epidemic?"

"We are on the verge of one, yes."

"Oh, my. I hadn't heard. I can see why you came to the Lord in prayer."

"I'm going to need more than the Lord. I'm also going to need the Lord's house."

"What do you mean?"

"As you know, Reverend, we don't have a hospital in town. If someone needs extra care, I generally keep them in my office for a few days. I have a room in the back just for that. But I'm afraid we may wind up with fifty, sixty, maybe even a hundred patients. I simply don't have room for that many patients, and I can't be running from house to house to tend to them. I'm going to need a place to keep them."

"In other words, you want to turn the church into a hospital," Reverend Sharkey said.

"Yes," Dr. Poindexter replied. "Reverend, I know this is asking a lot of you, and if you don't want to . . ."

"Of course I will do it," Reverend Sharkey replied. "I don't know what we will do for beds, or even sheets and blankets. But I'm perfectly willing to let the church be used as a hospital."

"We can use the pews as beds. I hope we can convince people to bring any extra sheets and blankets they may have to you. They will have to donate them, because after they have been exposed to the diphtheria germ, it will be necessary to burn them."

"If you give me some instruction on what to do, I'll be glad to help you tend to them."

"I can't ask you to do that. You'll be exposing yourself to the disease."

"Aren't you exposing yourself?"

"It's my job to tend to people. I'm a doctor."

"And it's my job to tend to souls. I'm a pastor. I will be here with you, Doctor."

Dr. Poindexter smiled, and reached out to put his hand on Sharkey's shoulder. "You're a good man, Reverend."

Sharkey's smile was grim. "I'll start around town now, gathering up as many sheets and blankets as I can."

Chugwater

Early in the afternoon, Duff stepped into Fiddlers' Green, where he saw that there was a lively card game in progress at one of the tables. It was crowded with brightly colored poker chips and empty beer mugs.

One of the players threw his cards on the table in disgust, then stood up. "I've had it, boys. This is the unluckiest chair I've ever sat in. I ain't drawed a winnin' hand at all."

Jason McKnight laid down his cards and glanced over toward the bar. "Duff, come on over and join us. We have an empty chair here, if you're feelin' lucky."

Duff tossed the rest of his drink down, then wiped the

back of his hand across his mouth. "I'd be glad to. Who's been the winner so far?"

"That'd be Doc Presnell, here," Jason said. "You'd better watch out for him. He's got a lucky streak going this afternoon."

"Lucky my hind clavicle," Dr. Presnell said. "It's just that I know how to cheat without getting caught."

Such a comment in a game among strangers might be a dangerous thing to say but where all were friends, it merely brought the laugh it was meant to bring.

Duff bought forty-five dollars' worth of chips and stacked them up in front of him. Cards were dealt, the game was played, and he won the first hand.

"Better watch it, Doc," Jason said. "Duff's got him a lucky streak coming. I can feel it in my nose."

"Ha. He can feel it in his nose," said one of the other players. "Tell me, Doc, you being a doctor 'n all, have you ever he'erd of such a thing?"

"Well, with a nose that big, I wouldn't doubt it," Dr. Presnell said, and the others around the table laughed.

"What do you hear from Miss Parker?" Stan Hardegree asked. He owned a ranch just north of Chugwater. "The reason I ask is I haven't bought a Christmas present for my wife yet, and Miss Parker is real good at helpin' choose something."

"She'll be back before Christmas," Duff said as he picked up the dealt cards for the second hand.

"Good," Hardegree said as he examined his hand.

"Hah! And I might just win enough money with this hand to pay for it, too."

"Most people wait until a few hands are dealt before they start trying to run a bluff. Stan starts as soon as he picks up the cards," McKnight said.

The game continued for several hands. Duff was winning a little more than he was losing, but he wasn't the big winner. Neither was Doc. Apparently, Duff's play changed the dynamics to the point that everyone seemed to be winning a bit more.

Duff happened to look up toward the door just as Marshal Craig came into the saloon.

Seeing Duff at the table, Craig went over.

"Hello, Russell," Duff greeted with a smile.

"I just received a telegram from Rawhide Buttes with some disturbing news," Craig said.

Duff's smile faded. "Meagan is in Rawhide Buttes."

"Yes, I know."

Duff felt a sense of concern. "Marshal, don't tell me something has happened to her."

"No, not that I know of. At least, not yet."

"What do you mean, not yet? What is this about?"

"Diphtheria, that's what it's about. According to the telegram I just received, the entire town of Rawhide Buttes is under quarantine. No one is allowed into town, and no one can leave."

"Will the quarantine last through Christmas?" Duff asked.

"I don't know. I just know that the stagecoach won't be running until further notice."

"Then I'm going to get her," Duff said, standing.

Marshal Craig put his hand gently on Duff's shoulder. "Duff, didn't you hear what I said? Nobody can enter the town. Nobody can leave the town, either. Not until this is over. Marshal Worley has the entire town shut down."

"Can he do that, Russell?"

Marshal Craig nodded. "Yes. He can do that."

"Can we send telegrams?"

"Yes, I don't see why you couldn't do that."

Duff looked at the other players sitting around the table. They had been following the conversation closely. "Gentlemen, I'll be taking m' leave of ye. I've enjoyed the game."

He gathered up the poker chips, about sixty dollars' worth, and took them over to Biff. "Hold on to these for me, would you, Biff? I'm going down to the telegraph office."

"You'll be sending a message to Meagan, will you?"

"Aye, and one to Smoke as well."

"Tell her the whole town will be thinkin' about her, and we'll be keepin' her in our prayers."

"I will," Duff promised.

It took him only a couple minutes to go from the saloon to the Western Union office. He pulled the door open and walked inside.

Titus Gilmore stepped up to the counter. "Hello, Duff. Need to send a telegram?"

"Yes, to Rawhide Buttes."

Gilmore had just picked up his pencil, but he glanced up at Duff. "Rawhide Buttes? I just got a telegram from there about half an hour ago."

"About diphtheria," Duff said.

"Yes. How did you hear so fast?"

"Russell Craig told me about it. That's why I need to send a telegram. Megan Parker is there. So are Smoke Jensen and my other houseguests. As a matter of fact, I'll be wanting to send a telegram to Smoke as well."

"All right," Gilmore said. "Who first? Miss Parker?"

"Yes."

"I'm ready," Gilmore said, holding the pencil over a tablet. He wrote out what Duff wanted on the telegram.

HEARD ABOUT DIPHTHERIA EPIDEMIC STOP ALL HERE
SEND LOVE AND PRAYERS STOP WILL COME SOON AS
I CAN LOVE DUFF.

Gilmore counted the words. "That will be four dollars and twenty cents. Ready for the next one?"

Duff nodded and told him what to write to Smoke.

AM AWARE OF YOUR SITUATION STOP LOOK AFTER
MEAGAN AND STAY SAFE STOP DUFF.

"That one will be two dollars and eighty cents," Gilmore said.

"Please get them sent right away," Duff said, proffering the payment.

"You can stay right here and watch. Before you leave the door, it'll be there."

From the *Chugwater Defender:*

Diphtheria Outbreak

Word has reached this newspaper that an outbreak of diphtheria has struck the town of Rawhide Buttes. The entire town has been shut down, with schools and businesses closed. Stagecoach and freight traffic into and out of town has been suspended and Marshal Worley has posted guards on all the roads to enforce that edict.

Dr. Poindexter has sent a request to Cheyenne for the antitoxin serum that has, in recent years, proven to be effective in treating diphtheria. It is believed that if a sufficient supply of serum can be acquired in time, that it can cure the afflicted and prevent many deaths.

It is understood that the serum is available and will be dispatched immediately.

The next day a second article appeared. A follow-up piece, informing the readers on the status of the diphtheria antitoxin serum.

Diphtheria Antitoxin Will Pass Through Chugwater Tomorrow

MEDICINE ON THE WAY
TO RAWHIDE BUTTES

The residents of Rawhide Buttes are facing the prospect of a most dismal Yuletide due to the dreadful outbreak of diphtheria. As reported in an earlier edition of the Defender, Dr. Poindexter has declared a quarantine in an attempt to isolate the disease.

But, God willing, a Christmas miracle may be in store for the beleaguered citizens of the stricken city. One hundred lifesaving vials of diphtheria antitoxin are on their way to Rawhide Buttes. Were the messenger to be carrying gold, the shipment would not be more valuable.

Rawhide Buttes

Smoke was standing at the west end of the road that came from Millersburgh. Matt was standing at the other end. Their job was to prevent anyone from entering or leaving town. It wasn't that they had to prevent people from coming into town. All they had to do was explain that the town was dealing with an epidemic of diphtheria, and people were more than willing to turn around.

It was much more difficult to deal with the people

who wanted to leave. Often entire families were traveling in wagons loaded with all their possessions.

"You got no right to keep us here," one man was saying. He and his wife were plainly dressed, wearing overcoats against the cold. Two small children were in the wagon behind their parents, looking at Smoke with confused and frightened expressions on their faces.

"What is your name, sir? Smoke asked.

"My name is Bailey, Ron Bailey. I'm a decent citizen and I've never been in no trouble in m' whole life. Like I say, you can't keep us here. I've got a wife and kids to look after."

"Where are you planning to go?"

"To Millersburgh," Bailey said

"Do you have family there?"

"No, but that don't matter."

"Mr. Bailey, look at it this way," Smoke said. "Word of the diphtheria epidemic has already gotten out. Like as not, the people of Millersburgh have already set up a roadblock outside of town. Once they learn you are from Rawhide Buttes, they aren't going to let you in."

"The man's right, Ron," Bailey's wife said. "If they don't let us in, what will we do then? I've no intention of spending Christmas in a wagon because they won't let us come into town."

"So you would rather stay here, and take a chance on one of us gettin' the diphtheria, or maybe our young'uns?" Bailey asked.

"Mr. Bailey, if none of you have the disease now and if you just stay in your home until the danger is passed, chances are you'll all be all right. The doctor has sent for some medicine that will cure the disease in those that already have it. That will stop it from spreading any further."

"Ron, let's go back. How bad can it be if we just stay home?"

"All right," Bailey said reluctantly. He slapped the reins over the backs of his team, and the horses started to turn the wagon.

"I appreciate it, Mr. Bailey," Smoke said. "You're doing the right thing."

He stood in the middle of the road, watching the wagon go back into the town. He hated doing it, but knew he had done the right thing. Not only to prevent any possible spread of the disease, but because he was sure no other town was going to allow anyone from Rawhide Buttes to come into their town.

CHAPTER TWENTY-SIX

Sidewinder Gorge

Max Dingo had an arrangement with Moe Dunaway, the owner of a small store halfway between Hartville and Rawhide Buttes, to provide Dingo and Sidewinder Gorge with provisions from liquor to food, ammunition, and newspapers.

The newspapers weren't merely for idle curiosity. An up-to-date source of news was vital to someone like Dingo. Through the accounts in the paper, he could ascertain if anyone was looking for him or any of his men. It also provided him with windows of opportunity. As he read the story about the shipment of diphtheria antitoxin, he realized that it was just such a window.

"Ha!" Dingo said. "Boys, we just got a Christmas present."

"What's that?" Jesse Cave asked.

Dingle held out the newspaper and struck it with the

back of his hand. "Rawhide Buttes is having a diphtheria epidemic. And that's going to make us rich."

"How is it going to make us rich?"

"You'll see."

Rawhide Buttes

"My throat hurts," Cora said. "Oh, Meagan, what if I am coming down with diphtheria?"

"It may just be a case of catarrh," Meagan said. "Don't get worried yet. Let's go see the doctor."

"How? We're supposed to stay inside. We're under quarantine, remember?"

"I don't think that's for someone who needs to see the doctor. Come on. I'll go with you."

When the two women reached the doctor's office, they saw a sign on the front door. DR. POINDEXTER HAS RELOCATED TO THE CHURCH.

"Oh, my," Meagan said. "The situation must be bad if the doctor has to spend all his time in church now."

Reaching the church a few minutes later, they were surprised by the number of people they saw around it. When they stepped inside, they saw at least a dozen people stretched out on the pews. They were greeted by Reverend Sharkey.

"Good morning, ladies. What seems to be the problem?"

"What's going on? Why are all these people here?" Cora asked.

"The church has been turned into a hospital," Reverend Sharkey said. "Do either of you need to see the doctor?"

"Cora does."

"Sore throat? Difficulty in swallowing?" Reverend Sharkey asked.

"Yes," Cora replied. Her voice was growing hoarse.

Reverend Sharkey nodded. "All right. Have a seat over there. The doctor will come see you as soon as he can."

As they waited for the doctor, Meagan looked out over the nave, where she counted at least seven children and five adults, all patients. Dr. Poindexter and one woman were being kept busy, attending to them.

"That's Jenny Poindexter," Cora pointed out. "She is the doctor's wife and nurse."

"They are really busy," Meagan said. "It looks like they could use help."

"Who would do such a thing, though?" Cora asked. "Wouldn't anyone who came to help be exposing themselves to diphtheria? Which reminds me, why don't you leave now, and go back to the shop before you catch it, too?"

"What do you mean, too?"

"I've got it," Cora said. "I know it, and you know it."

Meagan didn't reply. She was pretty sure that Cora was right.

Their fears were confirmed a few minutes later when Dr. Poindexter found the time to come over and make an examination.

"Is there anything you can do for it?" Meagan asked.

"Right now, I'm afraid that all we can do is treat it symptomatically," he said.

"What does that mean?" Cora asked.

"It means your throat is going to swell shut so that you can't breathe. I can fix it so that you will be able to breathe, but that does nothing to cure the disease."

"Is there no cure?" Meagan asked.

"Yes, there is an antitoxin that will cure it. I've sent for it, but in the meantime, all I can do is keep as many alive as I can until it gets here."

"How do you do that?"

"That depends on how far along it is. If the disease has advanced to the point that the throat is swollen shut, I have to do a tracheotomy and an intubation. That means I have to cut a hole in their throat so they can breathe. If we catch it early enough, we can treat the throat with a solution that will dissolve the covering of mucus membrane." Dr. Poindexter smiled at Cora. "Fortunately in your case, Miss Ensor, we seem to have caught it early enough. I'll go prepare the solution."

A moment later, Dr. Poindexter returned with an atomizer.

"Are you going to spray me with perfume?" Cora asked with a smile.

Dr. Poindexter returned the smile. "I'm glad to see that you still have your sense of humor. But yes, this is very much like a perfume atomizer. I'm going to spray the solution into your throat. I warn you, it is a mixture of water and acid, so it is going to be painful. But it must be done."

"All right," Cora said, closing her eyes and preparing herself.

"Doctor! We need a tracheotomy now!" Jenny called.

Dr. Poindexter handed the atomizer to Meagan. "Here, my dear. You can do this. Spray until it is all gone. And Miss Ensor, I encourage you to cough as often and as hard as you can. You need to clear the mucus from building up in your throat."

Even before Dr. Poindexter left, Meagan began spraying the mixture into Cora's throat. Almost immediately, Cora began to cough.

By the time the solution was exhausted, Cora had coughed up a good deal of yellow pus. She was breathing a bit easier when Dr. Poindexter returned.

"Good, good," he said, looking at the cloth into which Cora had coughed. "You seem to have gotten rid of a lot of it."

"Doc!" someone called, coming in through the front door of the church. "It's my wife! She can't breathe!"

As Dr. Poindexter left to tend to the new arrival, Reverend Sharkey came over to speak with Meagan and Cora.

"Miss Ensor, I've got a place for you over here. Unfortunately, we have run out of sheets and blankets."

"Oh, do I have to stay? Can't I go back home?"

"I'm afraid not. You'll have to have your throat treated again in a couple hours."

"Cora, I'll go back to your place and get you a sheet and blanket," Meagan offered.

"I suggest you get the oldest you can find," Reverend Sharkey said. "They will have to be burned after this."

"Get the ones off my bed," Cora said. "You've been my guest, so I gave you the newest."

"All right."

There was nobody on the street, and all the stores were empty as Megan hurried back to the dress shop. They had left the front door unlocked, and when Meagan went inside, she saw Sally working with one of the figures in the Christmas display.

"Sally?"

"I didn't feel like staying in the hotel room. Smoke is helping the marshal, and I was all alone. I thought I would come down here and spend some time with you and Cora, but when I found you gone I decided to work on the display." Sally looked around the store. "You and Cora have done such a wonderful job, it's a shame nobody is going to be able to enjoy it."

"Cora is sick," Meagan said. "She has diphtheria."

"Oh, Meagan, no. Where is she?"

"She's at the church. Dr. Poindexter has turned the church into a hospital. Oh, Sally, you should see it. It is filling up very quickly. I'm here to get some bedsheets, then I'm going back. I'm going to help the doctor."

"What a wonderful idea. I wonder if he would take my help as well."

"I'm sure he would. Right now, he is overwhelmed, with so many patients and only he, his wife, and Reverend Sharkey to tend to them."

When Meagan and Sally returned to the church a few minutes later, they found Cora lying on one of the pews. She appeared to be sleeping, though she was shivering from cold. Quickly, Meagan covered her, then put a pillow under her head.

"Thanks," Cora murmured.

Even more people were in the converted hospital than there had been when Meaghan left to retrieve the sheet and blanket. Dr. Poindexter was doing another tracheotomy.

"Miss Parker," Reverend Sharkey said. "Dr. Poindexter asked if you would mind staying around for a while and helping out."

"Of course I don't mind," Meagan said. "What does he want me to do?"

"He said that you did a good job in applying the spray mixture to Miss Ensor's throat, that perhaps you could do that with others."

"All right. Where do I get the mixture?"

"Mrs. Poindexter will keep you supplied. All you'll have to do is administer the spray."

"I would like to help, as well," Sally said.

Dr. Poindexter overheard. He finished the surgery and joined the women. "Yes, of course I can use you. But I hope you understand that you will be exposing yourself to the sickness. I can't promise you that you won't come down with the disease."

"I'll be no more exposed than you, your wife, the reverend, or Meagan," Sally said.

"The difference is, they have already been exposed in one way or another," Dr. Poindexter said. "You haven't."

Sally smiled. "I have now."

Dr. Poindexter nodded, then grunted what might have been a laugh. "Yeah, I suppose you have."

"So, what would you have me do?"

"Mostly just mix the acid and water solutions. Mrs. Poindexter will show you how. And spray the applications into the throats of the people as it is needed," Dr. Poindexter said. "Meagan, you've already done this once. You can show her what to do the first time."

"All right," Meagan said.

"Doctor, come quickly!" Reverend Sharkey called. "Mrs. Abernathy has stopped breathing!"

"Jenny, bring the tools. I may have to do a tracheal intubation," Dr. Poindexter said. "Meagan, you and . . ." he paused, looking for a name.

"Sally."

"Sally, come with me. You two may as well see what a tracheal intubation is, so that if I need your assistance in one of these procedures, you will at least have some idea of what is going on."

Meagan and Sally hurried after the doctor, who walked quickly to the other side of the church. Reverend Sharkey was standing there, holding the hand of a middle-aged woman stretched out on the pew. Jenny arrived at about the same time, carrying a tray on which there were several items, one of which was a scalpel.

Dr. Poindexter picked up the scalpel and made in incision in Mrs. Abernathy's neck. Sally and Meagan watched the procedure, including the part where some of the mucus was sucked out.

Meagan felt herself growing very light-headed, and stumbled back a few steps before Sally caught her.

"Are you all right?"

"Yes," Meagan said weakly. "I just got a little dizzy, is all."

"Sit down and put your head between your knees," Dr. Poindexter ordered, and Meagan followed his directions.

"I'll get you a drink of water," Sally offered. Moving to the water barrel that was set up at the back of the church, she hesitated, wondering if the couple of drinking cups handy had been used by those who had already been stricken with the disease.

Reverend Sharkey came to her assistance. "Here, let me show you something." He took a clean sheet of paper and folded it into a triangle. Then, after four more folds, he opened it up, forming a perfect cup. That done, he held the cup under the spigot, filled it with water, then handed it to Sally. "Here you go, my dear."

"Oh, what a marvelous thing to know," Sally said with a broad smile.

"I learned this during the three years I was a missionary to China," Sharkey said. "The Chinese are very particular about using community drinking vessels. The only way I could get them to take communion was by providing them with individual cups."

Sally took the water back to Meagan, who looked very pale.

"I don't blame you for getting a little dizzy there. I was getting a bit woozy myself, watching."

"That isn't it." Meagan took the water, drank, then felt

the pain in her throat. "Sally, I'm coming down with diphtheria."

Cheyenne

"There are one hundred vials of the serum," Dr. Taylor said to Deputy Sheriff Gib Crabtree. "Take the buggy. It is seventy-five miles to Rawhide Buttes. I've arranged for you to change teams at Goodwin's Ranch, Davis Ranch, Little Bear, Chugwater, Blue Elder, and Bordeaux. That's every ten miles. You should be able to maintain a steady, ten-mile-per-hour speed, which means you should be to Rawhide Buttes inside of eight hours."

"Unless I'm held up by weather," Crabtree said.

"I talked to the stagecoach driver this morning. He said that as of yesterday the roads were clear. And Chugwater and Bordeaux both say there is no snow. I don't foresee any difficulty from the weather. Stop by Lambert's Restaurant before you leave. Norman has fried a chicken to take with you. You can take a bottle of whiskey to help keep you warm and keep up your strength, but don't get drunk."

"I won't."

When Crabtree came out of Lambert's a few minutes later, he was surprised to see thirty or forty people gathered around the buggy.

"This is a good thing you're doin', Deputy," said David Friedman, owner of Friedman's Clothing. "I tell you what. When you get back, stop by the store and pick you out a shirt. It'll be on the house."

"And all the beer you can drink for a week," added the owner of one of the saloons.

Several other businessmen made similar offers. Someone was holding a sign. GOD SPEED YOU ON YOUR MISSION, DEPUTY CRABTREE.

Crabtree thanked everyone, climbed into the buggy, and lashed the back of his team, leaving town at a gallop.

Rawhide Buttes

"Is that better?" Sally asked after she finished spraying the acid mixture into Meagan's throat.

"Oh!" Meagan replied. "Oh, my, that hurts!"

"I'm sure it does, but it is necessary to keep your throat open, so you can breathe. I'm sorry to have to do it."

Despite the pain, Meagan managed a smile. "Now I know what I was doing to all the people I treated."

"You were keeping them alive."

"Christmas," Meagan said.

"What?"

"I had such plans for Christmas. Now, there won't be a Christmas."

"Of course there will be a Christmas," Sally said. "We may have to have it a little later, after everyone is cured, but I promise you, we will have a Christmas."

"Sally, why don't you go to your hotel room and just stay there? Cora has the disease, I have it. There's no sense in you coming down with it, as well."

"And what good would that do? I'm already exposed to it. What if I went to the hotel, caught the disease, and nobody knew about it? At least here, I'm already in the hospital."

Meagan laughed. "Yes, I guess if you look at it that way, I'm lucky that I was here."

"Absolutely," Sally said, laughing with her.

"What in heaven's name are you two finding to laugh about?" Cora asked in a hoarse voice.

"*Joie de vivre*," Sally said.

"What?"

"Joy of life," Meagan translated.

"What we have left of it," Cora said, then all three laughed at the black humor.

CHAPTER TWENTY-SEVEN

Chugwater

Everyone in town knew about the diphtheria in Rawhide Buttes, and they knew about the antitoxin that was being taken to Rawhide Buttes as fast as was humanly possible. The sheriff at Cheyenne had sent a telegram to Walt Merrill, asking him to have a fast team ready to attach to the buggy when it came through. The telegram had also provided an estimated time of arrival.

Because of that, nearly every citizen in Chugwater was out on the street to witness the arrival and departure of what was being called a "race for mercy."

Duff and Marshal Craig were standing in front of Merrill's Livery about five minutes before the time the courier was expected.

"You're sure that's your best team, Walt?" Duff asked, looking at the two horses that Johnny and Abe, Walt's two assistants, had brought out front. "I've got a vested interest in this, you know."

"What do you mean?" Walt asked.

"Meagan Parker is up in Rawhide Buttes," Marshal Craig said.

"Oh, yes, well, I can see why you might be concerned. But you don't need to worry about this team. I doubt there's any faster horses anywhere in the entire state." Walt walked over to the team already in harness to pat the perfectly matched pair on their necks. "You are goin' to do us proud, aren't you, boys?"

As if he could understand the question, one of the horses whickered and nodded his head.

"Here he comes!" someone shouted

Looking down South Chugwater Road, Duff saw a rooster tail of dust. Then the buggy appeared out of the dust, and he saw the driver leaning forward in the seat, urging his team into a gallop. Despite the cold weather, the team was lathered with sweat from their exertion. Duff was sure they hadn't been at full gallop since Little Bear, some ten miles south, but they were making an impression as they arrived.

"Heah! Heah!" the driver called, shouting partly for the entertainment of the gathered crowd. The calls certainly weren't needed to spur the team on.

"Johnny?" Walt Merrell called.

"Yes, sir?"

"Soon as we get his team disconnected, you take those horses for a cool-down walk, then rub 'em down good, you hear me? Make sure they have water and oats. They've earned it. Me 'n Abe will connect the new team."

"Yes, sir," the sixteen-year-old said.

"Whoa! Whoa!" the driver called as he applied the brakes, causing the back wheels of the buggy to slide until it came to a halt.

"Hurrah for you!" someone shouted to the driver.

"Deputy Crabtree, I'm Marshal Craig. Welcome to Chugwater."

"You got the word to have a fresh team ready for me?" Crabtree asked.

"We've got them, and I'll have them connected within five minutes," Walt said.

"Thanks," Crabtree said. "I, uh . . ."

"The necessary is around back," Walt said.

Hopping down, Crabtree hurried to the back of the barn. When he came back the team was connected.

"We have some coffee for you, Deputy," Marshal Craig said. "Cream and sugar? Or black?"

"Black," Crabtree said.

Marshal Craig smiled. "Spoken like a true lawman. I'll hand it to you when you're in your seat."

"Thanks." Crabtree climbed into the buggy, then reached for the cup.

"Clear the way!" Marshal Craig called to the others.

With a loud shout and the crack of a whip, the buggy left, going north on First Street, which at the end of town turned to Ty Basin Road.

Duff and the others watched until all that could be seen was the billowing cloud of dust that rose up behind the buggy. Then he walked back to Fiddlers' Green.

"Did you watch the courier drive off?" Biff asked as he poured a glass of scotch.

"Aye, that I did," Duff said. "And 'tis hoping I am that the medicine does the job, for 'twould be a sad Christmas for those ailing, as well as their families."

"And friends," Biff added.

"Aye. And friends."

"I wonder what time he'll get there."

"The marshal says they expect him there by four o'clock this afternoon."

"That'll be a fast trip," Biff said.

Duff nodded. "Aye, but with fresh horses every ten miles, and keeping them at a rapid pace, he'll be going like lightning."

Rawhide Buttes

With each passing hour, more people were brought in to the improvised hospital, filling all the pews in the nave and transept, and even laid out on the floor in the chancel area. The question on everyone's lips was, "When will the medicine get here?"

"We just got a telegraph report," Marshal Worley said. "The medicine has passed through Chugwater, and it is a little ahead of schedule."

"It will be good when it gets here," Dr. Poindexter said, speaking quietly to those helping him. "But I'm afraid it will be too late for some."

"Do what you can, Doctor," Reverend Sharkey said. "Just do what you can."

"I have two patients who are in extremis." Dr. Poindexter pointed to the pew that had been set aside for the most severe.

One of the patients he was talking about was Marie Mason. Even though they had told her husband, Nick, that he was putting himself at risk by staying here with her, he refused to leave her side, and was sitting on the floor beside her, holding her hand. He hadn't moved in the four hours since he brought her to the church.

Dr. Poindexter went over to check on her, but as soon as he approached her, he realized that she was dead. Reaching down, he closed her eyes, which had glazed over with death.

With one hand, Mason was holding his wife's hand. His head was bowed, and his other hand covered his eyes. He had neither moved nor given any indication that he even knew Dr. Poindexter was standing beside him.

"Mr. Mason," Dr. Poindexter said quietly.

"You don't have to tell me, Doc," Mason replied without looking up. "I know that she is dead. I felt it the moment life left her body. It was as if her soul paused just long enough to tell me good-bye."

"I'm sorry. I am so very sorry."

"The medicine isn't here yet, is it?"

"No."

"Even if it had arrived, it wouldn't have done Marie any good, would it?"

Dr. Poindexter shook his head. "I'm afraid not," he admitted. "The disease worked very quickly."

"Ask the pastor to stop by for a moment, would you?"

"Yes, of course."

From her position on the opposite side of the church, Sally saw Dr. Poindexter talking to the pastor, then she saw Reverend Sharkey start toward the pew where the critically ill had been placed. She knew that meant one of the patients had died, but she withheld any comment. She didn't want to upset Meagan or Cora.

Another died early that afternoon. The victim was a young boy. Funerals were prohibited because of the quarantine, and there wouldn't have been a place to hold them anyway, as the church was being used for a hospital. But, as he had for Marie Mason, Reverend Sharkey said a prayer over the boy, then the deceased were taken from the church.

Every patient in the makeshift hospital saw the two bodies being removed, and though no one said anything, Sally couldn't help thinking that they were all wondering who would be next.

A wagon had been summoned from the undertaker, and it backed up to the front of the church. There were two open coffins in the back of the wagon and the bodies, without being embalmed, were put into the pine boxes, then the lids closed over them.

Tom Welch had hired half a dozen men to dig graves. At least ten were already open in anticipation of their use. The mourners were told to select any grave, and were given the choice of closing the graves themselves or leaving them open, in which case the gravediggers would close them.

Marie Nelson and the twelve-year-old boy were buried at approximately the same time, but in two different areas of the cemetery. Nick Mason was the only one at the burial of his wife Marie. Reverend Sharkey went there first to say a few words over the coffin that lay beside the six-foot-deep hole.

"We commit our sister Marie to the ground, earth to earth, ashes to ashes, dust to dust, looking for the general resurrection in the last day, and the life of the world to come through our Lord."

"Thank you, Pastor," Nick said.

Reverend Sharkey nodded, put his hand on Nick's shoulder for just a moment, then started across the cemetery to where the boy was to be buried.

"We had a long time together, Marie. Fifty-three years," Nick said, speaking quietly after the parson left. "Our only child, Hazel, died when she was two years old, and we never were able to have any more. You've missed her for fifty years, but I reckon you're holdin' her in your arms now. If you don't mind, I'll be speakin' to you ever' night in my prayers. I reckon you'll be able to hear me. In the meantime, ole' girl, just find you someplace comfortable so you can sit and wait for me. I'll be there soon as I can."

Nick couldn't leave the coffin, a plain pine box, lying by the grave to be buried later. He couldn't just leave her lying out like that, so he tied ropes around each end of the coffin, then let it down into the grave himself. After withdrawing the ropes, he started shoveling dirt into the hole. It was as if the sound of the dirt falling on the coffin drove nails into his heart. He couldn't stop the tears from running down his face.

* * *

Unlike Nick Mason's lonely vigil over his wife's grave, a few more people stood at the boy's interment—his parents and two sisters. The grandparents, who also lived in Rawhide Buttes, wanted to come, but the family had talked them out of it.

"You're older," Red Lattimore had said to his mother and father. "It just makes sense that if you're older, you're more likely to catch the disease. Even if you don't catch the diphtheria, it can't be good for you to be standin' out in the cold. We'll take care of buryin' Leonard our ownselves."

Reverend Sharkey spoke the same words over the boy's coffin that he had said over Marie Mason. Then he stood by as the family lowered young Leonard into his eternal resting place.

Confluence of the Blue Elder and Cherry Creeks

Crabtree changed horses at Blue Elder Ranch, and with a fresh team, started out on his next leg. He had gone about five miles when he saw a barricade of tree limbs lying across the road in front of him.

"Whoa! Whoa!" he called, pulling the team to a stop.

The horses had been running at a very rapid clip, and were made uncomfortable by the stop. They whickered and twitched as Crabtree sat, looking at the barricade.

At first, he thought the blockage was caused by accident, but as he studied it more closely, he noticed the ax cuts, and realized the tree had been chopped down. He also saw the track in the sand indicating it had been dragged from where it was cut and purposely laid across the road. He got down from the buggy, then stepped up to examine the roadblock.

"Who would do something like this, and why?" he asked aloud.

"We did it." Two men appeared from behind a boulder. Both were carrying pistols. "Because we wanted to stop you.

"Why would you do such a fool thing?" Crabtree asked. "What do you want to stop me for? I'm not carrying any money."

"Oh, yes, you are. You're carryin' twenty thousand dollars."

"What? You're crazy! What do you mean I'm carrying twenty thousand dollars? Why, I don't have but five dollars! If you want five dollars to drag this tree out of my way, it's yours." Crabtree reached into his pocket for the five-dollar bill.

"Keep your money," one of the men said. "We don't want it."

"Well then, what do you want?"

"You're carryin' some medicine, ain't you? Some medicine for Rawhide Buttes?"

"Yes, I am."

"That's what we want."

"Are you crazy? There's folks that are dependin' on that medicine. Now, I'm goin' to ask you to move that

out of the way so I can get on with it. Don't you understand? There's folks goin' to die if they don't get this
medicine."

The man laughed. "What do you think about that,
Jesse? There's folks in Rawhide Buttes who are goin' to
die if they don't get this here medicine."

"Well then, we'd better get it to them, don't you think,
T. Bob?" Jesse replied. He reached into the buggy and
picked up the bag that contained the medicine. "After
they pay us."

"After they pay you?" Crabtree said. "What are you
talking about? What do you mean, after they pay you?"

"I mean you're goin' to leave the medicine with us,
then you're goin' to keep on with your trip. And when
you get to Rawhide Buttes, you tell the good folks there
that if they want this medicine, they're goin' to have to
pay for it."

"Pay how much?"

"Like I said, twenty thousand dollars."

"You're crazy. This medicine already belongs to them.
They ain't goin' to pay you twenty thousand dollars.
They can't. Rawhide Buttes is a small town. How are
they goin' to come up with that much money?"

"I reckon they'll find a way, if they don't want all
those folks dyin'," Jesse said. "Now, get on with you."

Crabtree didn't move, and Jesse pulled the hammer
back on his pistol. "Get on with it, or I'll shoot you dead
right here, and find some other way to get the message
to 'em."

Crabtree glared at him for a moment. "I can't go nowhere till that tree limb is moved out of the road."

Jesse eased the hammer down on his pistol, then smiled. "Get it pulled out of the way, T. Bob."

The outlaw stepped around behind the boulder, then reappeared a moment later, mounted on a horse. One end of a rope was looped around the saddle horn, the other end tied to the tree limb. The horse pulled it out of the way.

"Now get!" Jesse said

Crabtree climbed into the buggy and snapped the whip over the team, starting them out at a gallop.

Sidewinder Gorge

"Twenty thousand dollars?" Max Dingo asked, spittle flying from his mouth. "I told you to ask for ten! Ten thousand they would pay without a second thought. Twenty thousand? They're going to balk at that."

"Let 'em balk," Jesse said. "In the end, they'll wind up payin' it. What other choice do they have? Anyway, what's the problem? I thought you wanted as much money as we can get."

"That's just it," Dingo said. "I want as much as we can get. We can't get twenty thousand dollars. We could get ten, and they would have hurried to get the money to us. Now they are going to start figuring out how not to give us twenty thousand."

"Like I said, they ain't go no choice," Jesse said. "If they want the medicine, they'll pay us. Besides, there are quite a few of us who'll be getting a part of the take here, and twenty thousand goes a lot farther than ten thousand. You get a third of ever'thing. A third of twenty thousand dollars is sixty-six hunnert dollars."

Dingo smiled. "Yeah. Yeah, that's right, ain't it? I wouldn't have asked for that much, but what is done is done."

"So, what do you think we should do now?" Jesse asked.

"We'll give 'em a little time to fret about it, and to need the medicine even more than they need it now, then we'll get in touch with them, and tell them where to take the twenty thousand. By that time, they'll be more 'n ready to deal with us."

"That ain't right," Bad Eye Sal said after Jesse and T. Bob left.

"What ain't right?"

"Keepin' that medicine away from folks that need it. They's probably lots of kids needin' that medicine."

"What the hell does a gal like you care about kids?" Dingo asked.

"I have a kid."

"You do? You ain't never told me 'bout no kid you have. How come I ain't never seen it?"

"Do you think I want her knowing that she has someone like me for a mama?"

"A girl, huh? How old is she?"

"She's fourteen."

"Ha! She's just the right age. Didn't you tell me you

started *workin'*"—he sneered at the word—"when you was fourteen? Where is she now?"

"That's somethin' you'll never know, Dingo," Bad Eye Sal said resolutely.

"You don't have to tell me. I know where she is. She's in St. Louis, ain't she? That's why you been so all-fired anxious to leave. You're wantin' to go to St. Louis on account of that's where your daughter is. Well, I'll tell you what. After all this is over, why don't me 'n you just go to St. Louis together? We'll get your daughter 'n bring her back here. You'd like that, wouldn't you?"

"I don't ever want you anywhere around my daughter," Bad Eye Sal said.

Dingo laughed. "You'll change your mind. One of these days you'll be beggin' me to bring your daughter here."

Uva, Wyoming

Nearly everyone in town had turned out to greet Gib Crabtree and cheer him on. A fresh team waited for him, but to the surprise of all, he didn't go to the livery stable, stopping instead in front of the marshal's office.

"Why are you stopping here, Deputy?" Marshal Wiggins asked, stepping out of his office. "The fresh team is down at the livery."

"I've been robbed, Marshal," Crabtree said, setting the brake on the buggy and climbing down.

"Robbed? Someone robbed you? Why, how much did they get?"

"They got everything. They took the medicine. All of it."

"Who did it? Where did it happen?"

"It was at Blue Elder and Cherry Creeks," Crabtree said. "Two men done it. I don't have an idea in hell who they was, but they called each other Jesse, an' somethin' like Peebob."

"Peebob? Could it have been T. Bob?"

"T. Bob. Yes." Crabtree nodded.

"I'll be damned. It was Jesse and T. Bob Cave, and I'll tell you now, no two sorrier outlaws have ever lived. But why would they want the medicine?"

"For money," Crabtree replied. "They want twenty thousand dollars, then they said they'll give the medicine back."

"From who?"

"They want it from the folks in Rawhide Buttes. That's where the sickness is."

"Rawhide ain't got many more people than we do. I don't know if they even have that much money."

"Well, whether they do or not, they need to be told about it," Crabtree said. "Where's the telegraph office?"

"It's just down to the corner, on this same side of the street," Marshal Wiggins said, pointing.

"I'd better get the message off."

CHAPTER TWENTY-EIGHT

Rawhide Buttes

Dr. Poindexter was standing at the back of the church with Jenny, Sally, and Reverend Sharkey. They were all enjoying a cup of coffee Sharkey had made a few minutes earlier.

At the moment, twenty-three patients were laid out on the pews of the church, including Meagan Parker and Cora Ensor. Three more had died and had been taken by Tom Welch to the mortuary.

"I think the ones we have right now are stable," Dr. Poindexter said. "If we can keep their throats cleaned out, I believe they'll be able to hold on until the medicine gets here."

"How long will that be?" Sally asked.

"I'm told that it could be here before four o'clock. By the way, Mrs. Jensen, if you ever decided you would like to, I believe you would make a wonderful nurse."

Sally smiled. "I appreciate the compliment. But I've

been watching your wife. I'm afraid that I don't have the skill, the patience, or the compassion to be a nurse."

"Nonsense. I've been watching you. You are doing a great job."

At that moment, Howard McGill came into the church and walked over to them. He had a worried expression on his face.

"What is it, Howard?" Dr. Poindexter asked. "Do we have more patients?"

"No, I'm afraid it's much worse than that, Doc. I just got this telegram from Deputy Crabtree. He sent it from Uva."

"Crabtree? Isn't he the one who is bringing the medicine?"

"Yes, sir, only he doesn't have it anymore."

"What?" Dr. Poindexter asked, speaking the word so loudly that it reverberated throughout the church. "What do you mean, he doesn't have it? Don't tell me he lost it, somehow!"

"Maybe you better read this."

"Read it aloud, George," Jenny suggested.

Poindexter read it through silently, then he closed his eyes and pinched the bridge of his nose. He handed it to Reverend Sharkey. "You read it, Reverend," he said quietly.

Sharkey cleared his throat, then read aloud. "'Jesse and T. Bob Cave took medicine from me. They demand twenty thousand dollars be paid before they release it. Crabtree.'"

"Twenty thousand dollars?" Jenny Poindexter exclaimed. "Are they crazy? I doubt there's that much money in the entire town!"

"What kind of evil person would do something like that?" Howard McGill asked.

"Mr. McGill, I agree with you." Reverend Sharkey said. "It does take someone incredibly evil to do something like this, and the Cave brothers have already shown, by their earlier perfidious actions, to be a perfect fit for that mold."

"How are we goin' to raise twenty thousand dollars?" McGill asked. "I think Mrs. Poindexter is right. I don't think there's that much money in the whole town."

"I don't know, but we're goin' to have to try," Dr. Poindexter said. "I just have no idea where to start."

"Why not start at the bank with Joel Montgomery?" Reverend Sharkey asked.

"Smoke and I can come up with five thousand dollars," Sally said. "But it's in the bank in Colorado."

"Come with me, Mrs. Jensen," Dr. Poindexter said. "We'll see Mr. Montgomery together."

"No," Reverend Sharkey said. "You're needed here, George. I'll go see him."

"Reverend, tell him I can come up with five thousand," Meagan said in a hoarse voice, having overheard the conversation. "It's in the bank at Chugwater."

"Reverend, it would be better to get Smoke to go with you," Sally said. "Smoke can be very persuasive."

"I'll get Marshal Worley to go with us as well,"

* * *

Smoke was leaning against the hitching rail to which his horse, Seven, was tied when he saw Marshal Worley and Reverend Sharkey coming toward him. At first, he thought nothing of it, then he remembered that the church had been turned into a hospital, and that Sally was working there. For a moment, he felt some anxiousness, wondering if Sally had come down with the disease.

"Sally?" he asked as the two men approached him.

It was a part of his profession that Reverend Sharkey was a very insightful man, and he perceived Smoke's apprehension at once. "Mrs. Jensen is working very hard, and has been quite a blessing to us all," Reverend Sharkey said quickly, putting Smoke's fear at ease. "She has gotten into the scheme of things very quickly. I don't know what we would do without her."

"That's Sally all right," Smoke said with a proud smile. "Give her any situation where she thinks she would be more of a help than a hindrance and she will pitch in."

"The reason we are here, Mr. Jensen, is because she wanted me to ask you to go to the bank with us."

"Go to the bank?" Smoke's concern was replaced with curiosity.

"Perhaps you should read this telegram we received," Marshal Worley suggested.

Smoke read the telegram, then shook his head. "Duff told me about Jesse and T. Bob Cave. They are the ones who murdered the Guthrie family, aren't they?"

"Yes. And my deputy and Judge Kirkpatrick," Marshal Worley said.

"Sometimes the evil of man knows no boundaries," Reverend Sharkey added.

"So, you are wanting to go to the bank to raise money to pay the extortion money, right?" Smoke asked.

"At this point, I don't see that we have any choice," Reverend Sharkey said. "Your wife has generously pledged five thousand, and so has Meagan Parker. That leaves only ten thousand dollars to raise. I'm sure that Joel Montgomery can help us raise it.

"Joel Montgomery?"

"He's our banker."

"All right," Smoke said. "I'll go talk to the banker with you."

Joel Montgomery was quite tall, silver-haired, and very dignified-looking. He read the telegram then stroked his chin. "Are you sure you want to do this?"

"Do we have enough money in this town?" Marshal Worley asked.

"This bank has total assets of ninety-six thousand, seven hundred and fifty-four dollars. But that money belongs to the depositors. I can authorize loans to qualified borrowers, and indeed it is the interest received from such loans that allows the bank to stay in business. But even if we turned everything over to them, there is no guarantee that we would get the medicine."

"We have to try, don't we, Joel?" Reverend Sharkey said.

"You have to raise only half of it," Smoke said.

"Between Miss Parker and my wife and I, we have pledged ten thousand dollars."

Montgomery shook his head. "No, the bank would still have to raise all the money. Most money transactions from bank to bank are by wire as a promissory on the actual species transfer. As long as that ten thousand dollars remains in other banks, it will do nothing to increase the availability of funds here."

"Well, what are we going to do about it, Joel?" Reverend Sharkey asked. "We have to have that medicine. According to Dr. Poindexter, nothing he has done is curative. All he has been able to do is deal with the symptoms on a temporary basis. If we don't get that medicine, an awful lot of people are going to die."

"Maybe we can negotiate with them, explain that we just don't have that much money readily available," Montgomery suggested.

"How are we going to negotiate with them?" Reverend Sharkey asked. "We don't know where they are."

"They are going to have to get in touch with us again, in order to give us instructions on how to deliver the money," Marshal Worley said. "Perhaps we can get a lead on them then."

"We don't have to wait," Smoke said.

"What do you mean, we don't have to wait?" Marshal Worley asked. "What else can we do?"

"We can send a telegram to Duff MacCallister."

"Isn't he the person who brought those men in the first time?"

"He is indeed," Marshal Worley said with a broad

smile. "And Smoke Jensen is absolutely correct. If there is anyone on the outside who can help us right now, Duff MacCallister would be the one. Go ahead, Mr. Jensen. Get in touch with him."

"All right," Smoke said.

"I'll come with you, just to let Howard know that this is official."

There was a sign on the front door of the Western Union office.

Closed due to Quarantine,
By order of Marshal Worley.
Howard McGill, *Telegrapher.*

Marshal Worley knocked on the front door, but there was no answer. He knocked louder.

"Can't you see the sign? We're closed!" a voice called from within.

"Howard, it's the marshal!" Worley shouted. "Let me in!"

Through the door window a moment later, they saw the telegrapher approaching. He pulled the door open, then stepped back to let the marshal and Smoke in. "Are we off quarantine?"

"Not yet. But we need to send a telegram."

"It's because of the one we got a while ago saying that the medicine has been stolen, isn't it?"

"Yes," Marshal Worley said.

"All right. What's the message?"

Smoke wrote the message and handed it to him. "This telegram is to go to Duff MacCallister at Sky Meadow Ranch in Chugwater, Wyoming."

"Mr. Jensen, am I mistaken in assuming that there might be a particular relationship between Mr. MacCallister and Miss Parker?" Reverend Sharkey asked.

"No, you aren't mistaken. The two are very close. Why do you ask?"

"You might inform him that Miss Parker has been stricken with the disease. Such knowledge might spur him to greater effort."

"Meagan is sick? Why didn't you tell me earlier? How bad is it?"

"Dr. Poindexter seems to think that all his remaining patients are stable for the moment. Depending, of course, upon the timely arrival of the medicine."

"You're right. Duff should be told," Smoke said. "I'll add it to the message, but only because he should know. That won't be necessary to get him to help us."

Sky Meadow Ranch

Duff knew from experience that winter feeding was the biggest source of financial loss in a ranch operation. It was often what would make or break the ranch as a business, so it required very careful management with an eye to absolutely no waste.

He, Elmer, Woodward, Martin, Walker, and the new man Nicholson were riding on the range. Several patches of snow remained on the ground from the last snowfall, but the cover was thin enough that the animals could find their own graze if they were out of the shadows of the mountains.

"We must push the creatures back to where the snow is thin enough that they can get to the graze," Duff said as they found cattle standing in the shadows.

The six men went about their task, herding the animals out of the shadows with shouts and by rushing toward them. It took a couple hours, but by the time the sun was low in the western horizon, a wide, white field was filled with thousands of black-coated cattle. Quickly, the cattle learned why they were there, and they began scraping and grazing.

"This will keep them until we get another heavy snowfall," Elmer said.

"Aye, but from the looks of the sky, I expect that will be sooner than we want," Duff said. "I'm thinking 'tis going to be a white Christmas, for sure. And to think that when I was a wee lad, the thought of a white Christmas always brought me joy."

"We're sure close to Christmas now," Elmer said. "I sure don't want to miss the dance."

"Ha! You had better not miss it," Woodward said. "If you do, you'll be payin' for your pies at Vi's Pies just like the rest of us."

"You mean Mr. Gleason doesn't pay for his pie?" asked Nicholson.

"Why do you think he's took up with the lady in the first place?" Martin teased. "It's just so he can get his pie free."

Walker turned his attention back to the direction they

were headed. "Say, isn't that one of the boys that delivers telegrams for Western Union?"

"Aye," Duff said.

"I don't like telegrams," Elmer said. "They most always bring bad news."

"Maybe 'tis good news," Duff suggested. "The antitoxin serum should be in Rawhide Buttes by now. Perhaps it's a telegram from Meagan saying that the quarantine has been lifted, and she'll be comin' home in time for Christmas."

"Well, now," Elmer said. "And wouldn't that be a good Christmas present for you?"

Duff put his horse Sky to a gallop, quickly closing the distance between himself and the telegram delivery boy.

"Lad, I'm Duff MacCallister. Have you a telegram for me?" he asked, pulling up as he reached the young rider.

"Yes, sir," the boy said. "The lady in the house said you would be out here."

"I've no coins with me at the moment, but if you'll ride back to the house with me—" Duff started to say.

"There's no need," the boy interrupted. "The lady in the house gave me a quarter, sir."

Duff smiled. "I thought she probably had. 'Tis an honest lad you are for acknowledging it." He took the telegram and as he read it, the smile left his face.

MEAGAN STRICKEN BUT STABLE STOP CAVE
BROTHERS STOLE MEDICINE FROM COURIER STOP
DEMANDING TWENTY THOUSAND DOLLARS FOR
RELEASE STOP DO WHAT YOU CAN STOP SMOKE

Rawhide Buttes

Meagan didn't know what awakened her. She lay on the front pew, fighting the dizziness and straining to breathe. She had a headache and a sore throat and felt disconnected from reality. It was dark in the church, the only light a small electric lamp that glowed in the narthex.

She closed her eyes for a few moments, hoping to go back to sleep, but sleep wouldn't come. When she opened them again, a soft shimmering glow appeared between her and the ambo, and she wondered if another lamp had been turned on. As she stared at the glow, she realized it wasn't just a light but a woman with long red hair and flashing blue eyes. The glow came from the gleaming white gown the woman was wearing.

"Are you really there?" Meagan asked.

"Aye, lass, 'tis really here I be, 'n 'tis a Blythe Yule an a Guid Hogmanay I would be wishin' to ye," the woman said, speaking in a thick Scottish brogue.

"Who are you?"

"If ye be givin' it some thought, Meagan, ye'll ken my name, I'm thinkin'."

"No," Meagan said. "It can't be. It isn't possible. I am seeing Skye McGregor, and yet, I know that I am not seeing you."

"Things seen are temporal. Things not seen are eternal."

"Can others see you?"

"Nae, lass, 'tis nae for others that I am here."

"Why are you here?"

"I dinnae want ye to lose faith, Meagan. Duff will be here for ye, an' all will be foine."

"Meagan? Meagan, do you need something?" Sally asked.

Meagan saw Sally coming toward her, then, looking back toward the front of the church she saw only darkness. The glowing presence was gone.

"No, I'm fine."

"Are you sure you don't need anything? You were talking."

"Was I? I must have been dreaming." *Was I dreaming?*

CHAPTER TWENTY-NINE

Cheyenne

Duff had come to Cheyenne to see Sheriff Martin, but learned that the sheriff was with Governor Barber. According to the ornate grandfather's clock, he had been waiting in the reception area of the governor's office for nearly half an hour. To help control his building anger, he studied the office.

On one wall was a calendar with every day dutifully marked off. Above the month sheet was a full-color Currier and Ives print of two night trains racing out of Washington, DC, sparks flying from the stacks, and every window in every car shining brightly. It was a dramatic, if unrealistic representation. Just below the calendar was a radiator providing heat for the room, even as wisps of steam drifted up from the air vent, and a puddle of condensed water lay on the floor. To the right of the radiator was the door that led to Governor Barber's private office.

"Please," Duff said to the bookish-looking man in an ill-fitting brown suit who was the governor's private secretary. "My business with the sheriff is quite urgent."

"I doubt, sir, that your business can be more important than the governor's business."

"The sheriff is with the governor, is he not?"

"Yes."

"I must speak with him."

"As you said yourself, sir, the sheriff is with the governor. You may wait here until the meeting has ended."

"Be ye daft, mon? Do ye nae understand the term *urgent*? Hundreds of lives are at risk," Duff said. "Now laddie, if ye don't tell the governor this very minute that I'm here to speak with him, I'll be for laying ye out on this very floor, 'n letting my ownself in through that door."

"Very well, sir, but it is you who will have to deal with the governor's ire," the private secretary said, huffing to show his displeasure with the interloper. He went into Governor Barber's private office, but it was Sheriff Martin who came back out.

"Duff, what are you doing out here? Why didn't you just come on in?" he invited.

"You'll have to ask that rather supercilious gentleman why I was so detained," Duff said, nodding toward the governor's secretary as he came back out of the office.

"I was just doing my job, sir," the secretary said.

"Mr. Patrick said you mentioned something about hundreds of lives?"

"Aye, the ones in Rawhide Buttes."

"Then you know that Jesse and T. Bob Cave stole the serum."

"Aye, I know that the serum was stolen, 'n I know that it was those two black hearts who did the deed."

"Come on in. I was just telling the governor about it."

Governor Barber had a round face and a handlebar moustache. He was standing as Duff came into the room.

"Mr. MacCallister, I'm sorry you weren't granted immediate entry. I'm afraid that Mr. Patrick can be a bit overzealous at times."

"Aye, but 'tis water under the bridge, now." Duff addressed Sheriff Martin. "You said that you are aware that the scoundrels who took the serum were the Cave brothers?"

"Yes. Deputy Crabtree heard them address each other by their Christian names. He didn't hear their last name, but how many Jesse and T. Bob's can there be?"

"Then you know that I have dealt with them before."

"Yes."

"I want you to appoint me deputy sheriff again."

"I'll be glad to," Sheriff Martin said.

"Wait a minute, Sheriff," Governor Barber said.

For a moment, Duff feared that the governor was going to raise some opposition to him being appointed as deputy, but that fear evaporated when the governor spoke again.

"Mr. MacCallister, suppose I appointed you as a special deputy to the office of the governor with police authority all over the state? That way you would not be limited by county jurisdiction."

"I would be much obliged for such an appointment," Duff said.

"Sheriff Martin, would you be a witness, sir?"

"I would be honored," Sheriff Martin said.

"Raise your right hand."

Duff raised his right hand, and repeated the oath as spoken by the governor. "I, Duff MacCallister, do solemnly swear that I will support the Constitution of the United States, and the Constitution and laws of the State of Wyoming, that I will bear true faith and allegiance to the same, and defend them against enemies, foreign and domestic, and that I will faithfully and impartially discharge the duties of a peace officer to the best of my ability, so help me God."

Governor Barber smiled. "Deputy MacCallister, you are now authorized to perform your duty anywhere within the boundaries of the state of Wyoming."

"Thank you, sir," Duff said. "Now, with the permission of both of you gentlemen, I'll be about m' duty."

Sky Meadow Ranch

"You're worried about Meagan, aren't you?" It was rare that Elmer used Meagan's Christian name, but he spoke it in a way that communicated his concern, not only for Meagan but also for Duff.

"Aye. The blaggards have stolen the very medicine needed to make her well, Elmer. And I'll nae stand by and watch it happen."

"I'd like to go with you."

"I appreciate the offer, Elmer, but 'tis nae your fight. I've brought in those two before 'n I'll do it again. I won't promise they'll be brought in alive this time."

"There's more than two of 'em."

"From what I've heard there's but Jesse and T. Bob Cave."

"More 'n likely Max Dingo is part of it. If he's a part of it, there'll be ten or twelve of 'em. And I know where they are hidin'."

Duff looked up in surprise. "And how would ye be knowin' that, Elmer, I ask you?"

"Duff, I've never kept it secret from you that I once rode the outlaw trail, have I?"

"Nae, lad, you've been truthful about it from the beginning."

"Like I say, I know where you might want to start lookin' for the lowlifes that done this."

"You know where they are?"

"I can't say as I know for sure 'n certain. But I do have a real good idea as to where they might be. There is a secret place where outlaws on the run sometimes congregate. Truth be told, I've spent some time there my ownself, and I ain't never before told nobody about it on account of I always sort of felt like it wouldn't be a very righteous thing for me to do. I mean, turnin' on folks that once took me in. Do you understand that?"

"I understand honor, Elmer, even if it is among thieves."

"Yeah, well, when somebody steals medicine that's meant for innocent folks, includin' women and children, then in my mind they don't deserve no more honor. I'd say that, more 'n likely, you might find 'em in a place called Sidewinder Gorge."

"Sidewinder Gorge? Where would that place be? In all the time I've been here, I've never heard of it."

"Ain't nobody never heard of it, 'ceptin' them folks that has to hide out there. What you do is, you follow the Laramie River west till it forks. The north fork leads into the Laramie Mountains. There's a canyon there that you can't see from outside, but you can see sort of a big rock stickin' up, kinda like a—what do you call it? An oblick?

"Obelisk?"

"Yeah, one of them. But here's the thing . . . they near always have someone on top of that oblick, and he can see you long before you'll ever see him. So if you're plannin' on gettin' in there, you're goin' to have to be real careful and sneaky as all hell."

"Elmer, I thank you for the information."

"Like I say, there's liable to be ten or twelve of 'em," Elmer said. "An' bein' inside like they are, it ain't goin' to be easy to get to 'em."

"We'll do whatever it takes," Duff said.

Rawhide Buttes

Once again, Marshal Worley came to the north end of town to speak with Smoke. Again, the expression on Smoke's face indicated some worry about Sally.

"Your wife is fine," Marshal Worley said, speaking quickly to alleviate Smoke's concern.

"Thanks for telling me. That's comforting."

"I'll tell you the truth. I don't know how she can be, though. I mean, what with the way she's right in the middle of ever'thing. She gets right in the face of those who are sick, squirting into the patient's throats that potion Dr. Poindexter's wife makes up. We need that medicine."

"Have we heard anything from the people who stole the medicine?" Smoke asked. "Have they contacted us to tell us where to take the money?"

"No, we haven't heard from them. But we have heard this, which is why I came out here to see you. I thought you might be interested in this telegram we just got from Duff MacCallister." Worley showed the message to Smoke.

BELIEVE STOLEN MEDICINE IN SIDEWINDER GORGE
STOP NEED HELP STOP BRING MATT STOP MEET IN
UVA EARLIEST CONVENIENCE STOP DUFF

Smoke looked up toward Marshal Worley. "Did you read this?"

"Yes."

"If Duff needs help, I'm going, quarantine or no. And I'm going to ask you not to try and stop me."

"I've no intention of trying to stop you," Marshal Worley said. "I've spoken with Dr. Poindexter. Under the circumstances, he's willing to lift the quarantine on you and Matt."

"Thanks," Smoke said.

Uva

It began snowing as Smoke and Matt rode from Rawhide Buttes to Uva, the snow falling so hard that it was difficult for the rider behind to see the rider ahead. They took turns leading, so that sometimes Smoke's horse Seven would have to break the path, and sometimes Matt's horse Spirit would. The snow slowed their journey, their path marked by a long, black line behind them.

It was growing dark when they rode into town. Despite it being just past sundown, there were people everywhere, walking up and down the boardwalks, riding up and down the street in buggies, surreys, buckboards, and even wagons. In addition, Uva was alive with lights shining from restaurants, saloons, and businesses that were staying open late to allow customers to shop for Christmas. Already the town had been decorated with green boughs, and the windows of the shops were hung with red-bowed wreaths.

"It sure looks different," Matt said. "This town is all lit up. Rawhide Buttes is dark as the inside of a mine."

"Yep, a quarantine will do that to a town," Smoke said.

"Where do you think we'll find Duff?"

"Where do you think he's most likely to buy a drink of scotch?"

Matt chuckled. "Probably not at a leather goods store. Wait, isn't that his horse over there?" He pointed to the hitching rail in front of the Sunset Saloon.

"I do believe it is," Smoke replied.

The two men rode over to the hitching rail where, even if they hadn't recognized Sky, they would have recognized the brand—the letters *SM* enclosed in a circle.

Tying off Seven and Spirit alongside Duff's horse, Smoke and Matt stepped into the saloon. Although some of the larger towns had electricity, Uva did not. The illumination came from glowing kerosene lanterns, attached to four wagon wheels that hung from the ceiling. The lanterns did a fairly efficient job of pushing away the darkness, though the light was somewhat dimmed by the billowing clouds of tobacco smoke from pipes, cigars, and cigarettes.

"There he is," Matt said, pointing to Duff, who was sitting alone at a table near the piano. At the moment, the scarred and cigar-burned piano was quiet.

"Go join him. I'll bring the drinks," Smoke said as he headed toward the bar.

A moment later, Smoke came to the table carrying two beers and a scotch.

"I hope the scotch here meets with your approval," Smoke said as he put the shot glass on the table in front of Duff. "It isn't Mackinlay's."

"Nae lad, that it is not. But for the moment, it will do."

"He was asking about Meagan," Matt said.

"I knew you would be wanting to know about her, so I spoke with Dr. Poindexter just before we left," Smoke said. "He said her condition hasn't worsened . . . but neither has it gotten any better. She's going to need that antitoxin before she can fully recover."

"The medicine that was stolen," Duff said.

"Yes."

"How many others are ill with the disease?"

"When we left this afternoon, there were twenty-three in the hospital, including Meagan. There may be at least that many more sick in their own homes."

"Hospital?"

"Actually it's the church. They've turned that into a hospital," Smoke explained.

"What about the woman Meagan stayed to help? Cora Ensor," Duff asked.

Smoke nodded. "She's sick as well. I imagine Meagan caught the disease from her. I just hope Sally doesn't catch it. She's in the hospital twenty-four hours a day, now, helping out."

"Oh, Smoke, forgive me. I hadn't even thought of Sally."

"They say that God watches over fools, babes, and drunks. I will add and the virtuous," Smoke said. "It comforts me, and makes me believe that Sally will be all right."

"Have ye heard anything from the vandals that took the medicine?" Duff asked.

"Nothing except what they told the courier who was bringing the medicine to us. They told him they wanted twenty thousand dollars, but so far they've not shared with us how we are to deliver the money."

"Are there plans to deliver the money?"

"Meagan has put up five thousand dollars, and I've offered another five thousand. I think the banker can raise the remaining ten thousand, but it's as I said, we have no idea how the money is to be delivered."

"It won't be delivered at all," Duff said. "We're going to find the evil men who did this and take the medicine from them."

A loud burst of laughter came from a table on the far side of the room, and both Smoke and Matt glanced toward the sound.

"Isn't that—" Matt started to say, but Duff stuck his hand out and laid it on Matt's arm, stopping him in mid-sentence.

"Yes, but don't call attention to it," Duff said.

The man Matt had noticed was Elmer, who was sitting at the table with several others, entertaining them with some tall tale. Again, the men laughed out loud.

"Elmer is gathering information for us," Duff said. "Have you eaten?"

"No," Matt replied.

"Nor have I. Let us avail ourselves of whatever viand might be available here."

Over a supper of beans, bacon, and biscuits, the three men discussed what lay before them.

"I need to tell you right away that you should disabuse yourself of any idea that Jesse and T. Bob Cave are the only two men involved. There may be as many as ten."

"You said in your telegram that they were in a place called Sidewinder Gorge," Smoke said. "But Marshal Worley has lived here for over twenty years, and he said he's never heard of it."

"That's all right. Elmer has," Duff said.

CHAPTER THIRTY

After their supper, the three men left the saloon to go to the hotel where Duff had taken a room.

"I took one room because I don't plan for us to stay here tonight," Duff explained. "The room is so we can have a place to meet and plan our operation."

They were sitting in the room when Elmer arrived. He smiled at Smoke and Matt, and reached out to shake their hands. "I saw you two fellers when you came into the saloon, but I thought it might be best not to let on that I had an idea as to who either one of you was."

"How was your spy mission?" Duff asked.

"Spy mission?" Elmer smiled. "Yeah, I guess you could call it a spy mission. Well, sir, if you was to ask me, and I reckon you just did, I'd say it was successful. Least wise, I gathered up a lot of information."

"All right. We're listening."

"I'm going to need me a pencil and some paper so's I can draw all this out for you," Elmer said.

"Draw what out?" Smoke asked.

"Why, I'm goin' to draw out where at you can find the outlaws that took the medicine."

Duff supplied the paper and Elmer began filling it with lines and shapes.

"Now, the hideout is—"

"Hideout?" Smoke asked.

"Yeah, it's where outlaws has hid for ten, maybe fifteen years," Elmer said. "Like I was sayin', the hideout itself is about twenty-five, maybe thirty miles, from here, an' you can find it by followin' the Laramie River due west, till you get to the fork. The North Fork runs into the canyon, but it passes under some rocks, so if someone was lookin' at if from the outside, why, they'd never know that it continued on under them rocks, then come up on the other side."

As Elmer was explaining the setup, he was also illustrating it. "This here is the only way in. It's so narrow that people goin' in on horseback has to go single file. And this here oblick—"

"This what?" Matt asked.

"Obelisk," Duff said.

"Yeah, well, what it is, is a tall skinny rock. And Dingo keeps somebody on top of that rock all the time, to keep a lookout. So there ain't no one goin' to be able to get in there, without Dingo knowin' about it. And even if you could get in, why, they's places all over where they can stand and hold off an army."

"How many are inside?" Duff asked.

"Accordin' to them boys I was talkin' to back in the

saloon, they's at least ten inside, 'n maybe as many as twelve. And that ain't countin' the saloon gals."

"The saloon gals?" Duff asked. "You mean there are women inside?"

"They was only two when I was there. Now there could be three or four."

"Will they be part of the defense?" Smoke asked. "What I mean is, will they be armed and shooting at us?"

"I ain't goin' to say for sure that they won't be shootin' at us, but more 'n likely they won't be. Like I said, they ain't nothin' but saloon girls. They ain't really outlaws," Elmer explained.

He continued with his map. "This here is the main buildin', an' more 'n likely, this is where at we're goin' to find the medicine. This here same buildin' is where Dingo stays all the time, an' it's where ever'one comes to eat. Also, when they're plannin' out somethin' they're goin' to be doin', this here buildin' is where they do it. You can't miss it, bein' as it's the biggest buildin' in the whole place. I'd say it's about thirty foot long 'n maybe ten foot wide. I can't swear to it 'cause it's been near five years since I was in the place, but near as I can remember, they's no more than two, maybe three more buildin's."

"What are they made of?" Matt asked.

"Logs, chinked with mud."

"Thank you, Elmer. In all my time in the military, I have never received a more thorough briefing." Duff paused for a moment, then chuckled dryly. "Nor one that presented a greater challenge."

"You said according to the ones you were talking to back in the saloon," Smoke said. "Are they part of the entourage?"

"Are they what?"

"Are they part of the people who live inside the outlaw fort?"

"Nah, they don't live there. But some of 'em goes in 'n out to deliver whiskey and possibles 'n sech."

"How do they get in?"

"They's a signal they give so's the feller that's on guard will let 'em pass."

"Do you know the signal?"

"I know what it was when I was there. But they change it around."

"Makes sense," Smoke said.

"It don't matter none. I know how to get us in so as they won't see us."

"How is that? I thought you said that a guard posted on the obelisk could see anyone trying to come in," Duff said.

Elmer smiled. "If we come up on it while it's dark, stay on the east side of the fork, 'n cling real close to the rocks, even on the brightest moon, there will be so many shadows that you can get all the way up the rocks themselves without bein' seen. And once you're on top of the rocks, why, they'll block you from anyone aseein' you."

"Elmer, I don't care what the others say about you," Duff teased. "I think you're a good man."

"Duff, seein' as we're goin' to be some outnumbered once the fightin' starts, I was wonderin' if you might like an idea I've got. It was somethin' me 'n some of the boys I fought with done back durin' the war."

"What's that?" Duff asked.

"I stopped by the hardware store to get these," Elmer said, taking a couple boxes of brass tacks from a sack. He emptied the tacks onto the bed, then emptied a box of .44 cartridges alongside.

"What you do is, you stick these here tacks into the end of the bullets. That'll make 'em so that when one of 'em hits flesh, they'll leave big holes, sometimes blow off an arm, or shatter a leg bone. That takes the fight out of 'em just real fast."

Elmer demonstrated by pressing the brass tacks into the soft lead noses of the bullets. The heads of the tacks were about a third of an inch across and the nail part sunk into the lead better than half an inch.

"What this does is, the brass head will go on inside the body, while the lead flies apart in all directions. It also makes a near miss near 'bout as deadly, 'cause if one of the bullets hits a rock wall, why, it'll splinter out into lots of pieces that'll still do the damage."

"Ordinarily, Elmer, I would disdain such a tactic," Duff said. "But these black-hearted evil monsters are trying to ransom medicine that would cure my Meagan and dozens of other innocent people. So I say we do it."

For the next several minutes, the four men worked at

modifying the ammunition. These bullets, they decided, would be used in their rifles . . . all of them .44 caliber Winchesters. They didn't do anything to the bullets in their pistols.

After they finished, they decided to leave and travel through the night until they reached their objective. After all, they couldn't get lost. As Elmer had explained, all they had to do was follow the Laramie River.

Once they reached the fork in the river, Elmer suggested that they stay there until just before dawn. "We got us damn near a full moon tonight. Best to wait until just before dawn. By then, the moon will be below the Laramie Mountains and won't be shinin' down so bright. We can use them shadows I was talkin' about to sneak in."

When they bedded down, the sky was clear. Not only was there a nearly full moon, the night was filled with bright stars. They went to sleep quickly, aided by the fact that they were all tired from the long distances they had traveled during the day.

As they slept, a front moved in from the northwest, and their slumber was visited by an unusually heavy fall of snow. The snow came down softly, silently, from the night sky, so that it was quite a surprise when they awoke the next morning to find themselves nearly buried in snow.

"Damn!" Elmer said.

"What's wrong?" Matt asked.

"This snow! I can sneak us in . . . but come daylight there will be tracks on the ground that the lookout can see. He'll not only be able to see that we was here, why, he'll even see where it was that we went."

"It can't be helped," Duff said. "We've got to go in. We have to get that medicine to Rawhide Buttes."

"You know, don't you, Duff, that when they see that we've come in, they'll get ready for us. They'll put ever'body in all these positions they done got ready for such a thing. Why, it'll be like the four of us tryin' to attack a fort."

"Not four of us, just me," Duff said. "I'll nae be askin' anyone else to go in with me."

"Now that's a hell of a thing for you to say to me, Duff. I thought me 'n you was friends," Elmer said. "Why would you say you don't want me with you?"

"I'm just saying that—"

"I know what you was just sayin'," Elmer said, interrupting Duff's response. "Smoke, what do you 'n Matt think about him sayin' he didn't want us to go in with him?"

Smoke chuckled. "Hell, Elmer, with that thick brogue of his, I don't listen to him half the time, anyway."

Duff laughed. "All right, 'twould appear that 'tis a bunch of dunderheaded addle brains I've surrounded myself with. But then a fool attracts fools, I suppose. 'Tis welcome I'll be for the company."

"Elmer, I've something important to ask you," Matt said.

"Oh? And what would that be, sonny?"

"Come Christmas, do you think you could talk your friend Vi into giving me a free piece of pie?"

"Matt, I'll personally see to it that she gives you a whole pie. Any kind you want."

"That would be apple," Matt said.

"All right, men, let's go," Duff said.

Saddling their horses, they followed Elmer through the darkness toward Sidewinder Gorge.

Rawhide Buttes

When Meagan opened her eyes, she again saw the woman with long red hair, flashing blue eyes, and a gleaming white gown. She knew it wasn't a mere illusion. She knew she was seeing Skye, and was fairly certain she knew why.

"Have you come for me?" Meagan asked. "Is it my time?"

"Nae, Meagan, I've not come to take you, but to warn you. The young lass Laura Hastings needs help quickly. She can't breathe, and no one is near."

"Laura?"

"Aye. You'll find the doctor in the narthex, drinking coffee. You must hurry."

"I'm not sure I can even walk," Meagan said.

"You can walk."

Meagan got up from the pew, amazed that the dizziness and the weakness seemed to have passed. She moved quickly through the center aisle, and saw Dr. Poindexter standing there, drinking coffee. "Doctor?"

Dr. Poindexter looked at her in surprise. "Miss Parker,

what are you doing up? You need as much rest as you can get."

"It's the young Hastings girl," Meagan said. "You must go to her quickly! She's struggling for breath."

Dr. Poindexter set the coffee cup down, and started into the nave. "Jenny! Mrs. Jensen! It's the Hastings girl! Hurry! We'll be doing a trach!"

Laura was on the right side of the church, lying in the second pew from the back, near the wall. Dr. Poindexter moved to her quickly, passing the other patients, who were asleep.

Jenny arrived then with scalpel and a hollow tube. Sally came behind her, carrying the mixture of acid and water.

"Is she still alive?" Jenny asked anxiously.

"Yes, but she is struggling." Working quickly, Dr. Poindexter made a small cut in the throat, then inserted the hose. With the hose inserted, he blew gently into the tube, supplying much-needed air.

"You do this," he said to Jenny, who began blowing softly into the tube.

While Jenny provided breath for Laura, Dr. Poindexter began scraping the mucus buildup from her throat. After about five minutes of work, Laura began breathing normally.

"George, she's breathing on her own," Jenny said.

Dr. Poindexter nodded, then stood and looked down at her. "How in the world did she know?"

"How did who know what?"

"Miss Parker," Dr. Poindexter said. "She is on the

very front pew on the other side of the church, yet she is the one who came to tell me that Laura was struggling to breathe."

"She came to tell you? That's impossible," Sally said. "I was just with Meagan no more than half an hour ago. She didn't even have the strength to sit up."

"Well, she's right back there. You can ask her your—" Dr. Poindexter paused in mid-sentence and looked back toward the narthex. "Where is she?"

Sally backed out of the pew and looked toward the front door of the church. She saw Megan lying on the floor." "Doctor! Jenny! It's Meagan!" she said as she hurried toward the collapsed woman.

Because she was already in the center aisle, Sally was the first one to reach Meagan, and she knelt on the floor beside her. "Meagan! Meagan! Are you all right?"

Meagan opened her eyes and looked up into Sally's face. "Yes. Why are you asking me if I'm all right?"

Sally chuckled in relief. "Because you are lying on the floor."

Meagan looked around. "What in the world am I doing here? How did I get here?"

By then Dr. Poindexter had arrived as well. "You came to tell me about the little Hastings girl."

"Oh! What about her? Please don't tell me she has died."

"She hasn't, thanks to you."

"Thanks to me? What did I do?"

"Miss Parker, are you telling me you don't remember coming back here to tell me that Laura wasn't breathing?"

"No, I don't have any memory whatever of coming back here. Besides, how would I know that?"

"That's a very good question," Dr. Poindexter replied. "How would you know that?"

"I'm confused," Megan said.

"Yes, aren't we all? Mrs. Jensen, would you help my wife get Miss Parker back to her bed? Or at least, what is passing for a bed."

"Yes," Sally said.

With Sally on one side and Jenny on the other, the two women got Meagan back to her feet and started toward the front of the church.

"Meagan, you don't remember anything about coming back here to tell the doctor about the little girl?" Sally asked.

"The last thing I remember is you talking to me a while ago. I have no idea how I got here. I don't even remember getting up from the pew."

In fact, Meagan did remember seeing Skye, and leaving the pew to take the warning. But she knew if she explained it, they would think that her illness had affected her brain.

She wasn't too sure that it hadn't.

CHAPTER THIRTY-ONE

Sidewinder Gorge

Just as Elmer had promised, the shadows were there and the four men were able to move through the darkness. For the moment, the very snow that would give away their tracks also deadened the sound of the hoofbeats so that they were not only unseen, they were also unheard as they approached.

Once they reached the base of the hill, Elmer assured them they were out of the line of sight from anyone who might be standing the lookout position on top of the pinnacle. Staying close to the stone wall, they continued on through the narrow pass until they were inside.

They ground-hobbled their horses in a natural pocket that would keep their mounts safe from any shooting that might take place.

Duff cocked his rifle, then moved out of the shelter provided by the rocks. He had a view of an open expanse of white undisturbed snow. Across the open area he saw four buildings, one considerably larger than the other three. From the chimney on the largest of the four buildings, a rope of black smoke climbed into the sky, turning quickly from the dove gray of dawn to the bright blue of a crisp, winter day.

Duff also saw a stable, which was about three quarters of the way across the open area. If he and the others could get there without being seen, he was pretty sure that he would have a clear view and a commanding position, not only of the main building, but of the other three, as well. However, there was no way they would be able get there without leaving a trail through the snow, one that would lead directly to them and give away their position.

"Lads," he said. "If we can get to the stable, we'll have a tenable position," he said.

"We'll be leavin' tracks behind us," Elmer said.

"It cannae be helped. We cannae do anything from here. The medicine is here and I don't intend for us to leave without it. We've come too far to give up."

"We're with you, Duff," Smoke said, his voice calm and reassuring.

"All right. Let's go," Duff said, starting toward the stable.

They were halfway there when Duff heard a voice from behind.

"Move quickly, Duff, for soon someone will be stepping out of the main building, 'n you'll not be wanting to be caught out here, will you?"

"Skye?"

"Run, Duff. Run to the corner of the stable!"

There was an urgency to the voice, spurring Duff into doing exactly as the voice warned. "Run!" he urged. "Someone is about to come out of the house."

None of the others questioned how Duff might know such a thing, and broke into a run behind him. The running was difficult. The snow was nearly knee deep, meaning that it not only made footing difficult and slippery, its very depth also impeded their progress.

Finally, they reached the stable and moved behind it so that they were out of sight of anyone who might step out from the house. Someone did, and stepping no more twenty feet from the back of the house, he began urinating.

"Damn. That's Nitwit Mitt," Elmer said quietly.

"A friend of yours?" Duff asked.

"Hardly a friend. I never could prove it, but I think he killed a woman friend of mine."

"How did you know he was about to come out?" Matt asked.

"It was just a lucky guess," Duff replied.

"Hey, fellers! Don't eat the yeller snow!" Nitwit Mitt called out. Cackling with glee, he followed the deep rut he had made in the snow back into the house.

"Your friend Nitwit Mitt must be half blind," Matt said. "How could he not have seen the trail we just left?"

"Yeah, we're lucky. I guess he had to pee so bad that he wasn't paying any attention," Smoke suggested.

"I reckon so, but I don't see how . . ." As he was speaking, Matt looked back in the direction from which he had just come, and gasped. "What? That isn't possible!"

"What is it?" Duff asked.

"Look!" Matt pointed toward the snow. It lay behind them in an unbroken pristine whiteness! But, how could that be?

Duff looked back at the snow. Though he had heard her voice before, for the first time Skye appeared before him. "Did you do that?"

"What do you mean, did I do it?" Matt asked. "How could I do something like that?"

"I'm not talking to you. I'm talking to her," Duff said, pointing to the glowing image of Skye.

"Talking to who?"

"I'm talking to her," Duff said again, pointing to Skye once more. "Do you not see her?"

"Good Lord, Duff, have you gone daft on us? There's nobody there," Smoke said.

"Never mind," Duff said. "'Tis time to call the blaggards out."

The four men took positions in the stable. Smoke and Elmer climbed up to the hayloft, while Duff and Matt remained on the ground.

"Dingo!" Duff called. "Dingo, you and all your men come out with your hands in the air!"

"What? Who the hell is calling me?" Dingo shouted back from inside the house."

"They're in the stable! I see them!" another voice said.

Duff saw a window go up and the barrel of a rifle

protrude through the opening. He didn't wait for the outlaw to shoot. His round crashed through the window, then he heard a scream.

"My arm! My arm! That bullet took off half my arm!"

From the hayloft, Smoke saw somebody kneeling at another window. Whoever it was had a rifle, and Smoke snapped off a shot toward him. The man tumbled forward, crashing through the window and lying facedown and motionless on the front porch.

Two men came running out of the back of the big house, starting toward one of the smaller houses.

"I'll take the one in the lead, you take the next one," Duff said, raising his rifle to his shoulder. Both Duff and Matt fired at about the same time. Duff's was a head shot, and even from that distance Duff could see blood and brain detritus spurting, fan-like, from the outlaw's head. The man Matt shot grabbed his stomach, then fell forward, flipping over onto his back before he hit the ground.

Nitwit Mitt got a shot off from the front door of the house, but before either Duff or Matt could respond, they heard Elmer shout from the loft above them. "Don't nobody shoot him! That nitwit is mine!"

Elmer took Nat Mitchell, alias Nitwit Mitt, out with one shot, the doctored bullet causing a huge wound in his chest.

Duff saw T. Bob drop down out of a window on the side of the house and try to crawl away. Matt saw him as well, and aimed.

"No, Matt. This one is personal." Duff shot T. Bob,

and saw a pool of blood turn the snow red. The outlaw stopped moving.

"You kilt my brother!" Jesse yelled. In his anger, he ran from the front door toward the stable, firing his pistol. Duff lay down his rifle and stepped out of the stable, holding his arm crooked upward at the elbow with his pistol in his hand. Then, as if fighting a duel, he presented his side to the charging outlaw.

Jesse continued to fire away as he charged toward Duff, and one shot was so close that Duff could hear the pop of the bullet as it passed within an inch of his ear. He returned fire, one shot. One shot was all that was needed. Jesse tumbled forward, where he lay facedown in the snow.

Four more men came running out of the house then, all four shooting and screaming curses at the top of their voices. It wasn't necessary for Duff to assign targets. The selection seemed to come naturally, and after an exchange of fire, all four men went down.

"Dingo! Dingo!" someone called from inside the house. From the sound of the voice, Duff knew that it was the first one he'd shot, the man who had been hit in the arm. "Dingo, me 'n you is the only ones left! They's only the two of us now!"

"Shut up, you fool!" another voice called.

"I'm goin' out!" the first man called. "I'm givin' myself up!"

Shortly after that exchange, someone stepped out onto the front porch. He was holding one dangling bloody arm with his other hand. "I give up! Don't shoot, don't shoot! I can't put my hands in the air!"

"Come on. We'll nae be shooting ye," Duff said

The man started across the open area between the house and the livery.

Duff, who was still standing outside, held his fire.

Suddenly there was a shot from within the house, and the man who was giving himself up fell forward.

"Sure 'n 'twas not very smart of you, now, was it, Dingo? You're the only one left."

"I'm comin' out," Dingo called from within the house. "Don't shoot."

"All right. Come out. But if your hands aren't in the air when you step through that door, you'll be shot."

The door opened and Dingo, following Duff's orders, walked out into the front of the building. Amazingly, he was smiling. "I expect you boys have come for the medicine."

"Aye, 'n we'll be takin' it now," Duff said.

"Hello, Dingo," Elmer said.

When Dingo saw Elmer, he laughed. "Elmer Gleason. Well, I'll be damned. I thought you was no longer ridin' the outlaw trail. Decided to go out on your own, did you? I know why you're here now. You boys are plannin' on takin' the medicine, then gettin' the twenty thousand dollars for yourself."

"Where is the medicine?" Elmer asked, not bothering to correct Dingo's assumption."

"I'll tell you what," Dingo said. "I was in for one third

of this, but seein' as you boys sort of have the upper hand now, I'll make a trade with you for one fifth."

Suddenly, another shot came from the house, and Dingo, with a shocked expression on his face, fell face-down into the snow. There was a bleeding hole in his back.

Duff pointed his pistol toward the front door of the house. "I'll be asking ye to come out now, with your hands up!" he called.

A woman came out, holding a pistol in her hand.

"Drop the gun, lass," Duff ordered.

"He had nothing to trade," the woman said as she dropped the pistol.

"Sal," Elmer said. "You're still here? I thought you had left, long ago."

"I wanted to," Bad Eye Sal said. "I tried, but he wouldn't let me go."

"What did you mean when you said Dingo has nothing to trade?"

"He doesn't have the medicine," Sal said. "I do."

EPILOGUE

Rawhide Buttes

With the quarantine lifted, and the afflicted cured, businesses had reopened, and everyone agreed that the decorations in Cora's shop were the best. Even the men of the town came around to see the figures displayed around the Christmas tree.

On the morning of December 25, the entire town was gathered at the school, which was presenting its Christmas play.

Laura Hastings, wearing the angel costume Meagan had designed and sold, appeared to speak her lines. "Fear not: for, behold, I bring you good tidings of great joy, which shall be to all people. For unto you is born this day in the city of David a Saviour, which is Christ the Lord. And this shall be a sign unto you; Ye shall find the babe wrapped in swaddling clothes, lying in a manger."

After delivering her lines, Laura made a quick bow,

then withdrew to give the others the opportunity to play their roles.

The rest of the play continued without a hitch, then Miss Foley thanked everyone for coming and invited them to have cake, coffee, and cookies supplied by the parents of the schoolchildren.

"You're not upset with me for missing the dance?" Duff asked, after they took a piece of cake and a cup of coffee over to one of the tables that had been set up.

Meagan smiled. "Duff, how can I be upset with you? If you hadn't brought the medicine in time, I wouldn't even be here now." She took in the others with a wave of her hand. "A lot of these people wouldn't be here now."

"But ye are aware, lass, that 'twas not just me. Elmer, Smoke, and Matt were there, too."

"Yes, and we can't forget Sally. She was there with all of us for the whole time. It's a wonder she didn't come down with the illness herself."

Laura came walking over to them. "Mama told me to tell you thank you for making my costume. But she didn't really have to tell me to do that. I was going to do it anyway."

"Well, you are very welcome, sweetheart," Meagan replied. "And don't you look beautiful in it?"

"Thank you," Laura said, beaming under the comment. She began looking around the room as if trying to find someone. "I wonder where she is? I thought she would be here for the Christmas play."

"Who are you looking for, honey? Are you looking

for Miss Ensor? She's here. She's right over there talking to Miss Foley," Meagan said.

"No, not her. I'm talking about the lady who came to help me when I was really sick and couldn't breathe. She said she would find you, and you would tell the doctor."

"What did the lady look like?" Meagan asked.

"She was a very pretty lady. You know what I think? I think she was a angel. I mean a real angel, not just someone pretending to be an angel like me."

"You know what I think?" Meagan replied.

"I know," Laura said. "You think I'm silly."

"No, I don't think that at all. I think you really did see an angel, with gleaming red hair, shining blue eyes, and a glowing silk gown."

"You saw her, too, didn't you?" Laura said excitedly. "You're right. She did have red hair!"

"Yes, I saw her."

"I'm going to tell Mama that you saw her, too." Laura hurried back across the room to find her mother.

For the entire time Meagan and Laura were talking, Duff said nothing, but he did squeeze Meagan's hand.

"I know you think I just told her that I had seen her angel to make her feel good," Meagan said.

"No, I don't think that at all. I think you did see Skye."

"Skye? Wait a minute. Duff, are you telling me that you saw her, too?"

Duff smiled. "It would appear that Skye has had a very busy Christmas.

Turn the page for an exciting preview!

THE GREATEST WESTERN WRITERS OF THE 21ST CENTURY

William Johnstone and J. A. Johnstone have created a brilliant new series: a saga of two men—one a gunfighter, the other a Yankee lawman—building a future in the West's most dangerous territory.

WELCOME TO HANGTREE, TEXAS— THE MOST DANGEROUS PLACE IN THE WORLD

In 1866, the border between the U.S. and Mexico is a hotbed of gunrunners, mercenaries, and the Emperor of Mexico's spies, saboteurs, and double agents. Additionally, West Texas is plagued by Comanche warriors. Into this mix ride two massive gangs of the meanest, most kill-happy bunch of bloodthirsty ravagers to ever draw a breath.

Sam Heller and Johnny Cross have got the marauders in their sights, but they aren't ready for the slaughter and destruction the raiders unleash on Hangtree County. Suddenly the good guys in Hangtree are dangerously outnumbered. Sam and Johnny turn to cunning, pitting one gang against the other. And what that won't do, a liberated army howitzer just might, as the border explodes into an all-out white-hot civil war.

SAVAGE TEXAS: REBEL YELL by William W. Johnstone *with J. A. Johnstone*

On sale now, wherever books are sold!

GONE TO TEXAS
—Note posted on property abandoned
by those who left Dixie
for points west after the War

CHAPTER ONE

"Trust! That's the heart and soul of the gunrunner's trade," Honest Bob Longford said. His statement was subject to doubt, if the reaction of his listeners was any gauge.

Sully bridled, stiffening as if insulted. Hunchbacked Hump Colway sneered, muttering under his breath. Lank looked surprised. Fitch choked on his whiskey. He was drinking from a brown bottle, head tilted back, throat working as he guzzled.

Honest Bob's remark sank in, throwing Fitch off his rhythm. Fitch coughed and sputtered. The whiskey was raw, pungent. It went down the wrong pipe, burning like fire.

Fitch's head felt like it was exploding. Brown liquid spewed from his mouth and nostrils. He staggered, wheezing, gasping, eyes tearing. He was careful not to drop the bottle, though.

Some of the outlaw gang laughed at him.

Fitch would have cursed them, but he lacked the

breath. He sat down hard in the dirt, still mindful to hold the bottle upright.

"You made me choke on my redeye, Bob," Fitch said, wiping tears from his eyes.

"Reckon his remarks was a bit hard for you to swallow, eh, Fitch?" Half-Shot said slyly, working the needle.

"I'm gonna have a little fun with Fitch," Lank said, nudging Half-Shot in the ribs with an elbow. "Watch this."

"Uh-oh," Hump Colway said.

Lank went to Fitch and snatched the bottle from him. "Gimme that before you waste any more, hombre."

"Hey! Gimme that back," Fitch wheezed.

Lank raised the bottle to his mouth and started drinking.

Fitch struggled to his feet. "Gimme that, you! I ain't playing—" He lurched toward Lank, groping for the bottle.

Lank warded off Fitch's fumbling attempts with his free hand.

"Don't be like that," Fitch growled

"Better break this up before it gets out of hand." But Hump made no move to interfere. He knew better.

Fitch lunged, grabbing for the bottle. Lank side-stepped, evading. Fitch stumbled. He nearly fell but recovered

Lank upturned the bottle. He gulped, gurgling and draining the last of the whiskey.

Fitch crouched, breathing hard. "I'm ain't funning, damn you."

"Give him the bottle," Hump said.

Lank lowered the bottle, his face red and flushed. "Sure. Catch!" He tossed the bottle underhand at Fitch.

Moving with surprising speed, Fitch grabbed it out of the air. He held it upside down, a last scant few drops dribbling from the bottle. "Empty!"

Lank's shrug said, *What of it?*

"You drunk it all to spite me," Fitch accused.

"I drunk it because I was thirsty," Lank said. "Besides, you had enough—"

Fitch threw the bottle at him. Lank dodged in time to keep from getting hit in the head.

Fitch charged, barreling into him and knocking him off balance. He launched a looping roundhouse right, slamming Lank's jaw with an audible thud. Lank went down, taking a pratfall.

Some of the outlaw gang laughed, mainly those standing where Lank couldn't see them. He was a bad man to cross. They all were.

Lank sat up, dazed. Fitch stood ready, fists upraised.

"You hit me!" Lank said wonderingly, rubbing the side of his swollen jaw. His eyes shone with a wild light. He grabbed for his gun.

"Don't!" somebody cried, but it was too late. It was always too late.

Fitch drew first, firing before Lank's gun cleared the holster. He pumped a couple quick shots into Lank.

The reports were loud in the oven-like air, the smell of burnt gunpowder heavy.

"Damn!" Half-Shot whispered, awed.

A hush came over the gang.

Lank flopped back down in the dirt, raising a small cloud of dust. His chest was shattered by three bullet holes. Blood pooled from them, so dark it was more brown than red, soaking his shirtfront.

His eyes were open, unseeing. He looked puzzled, abstracted, as if trying to work some complicated sum in his head. His right leg kicked a couple times and then was still.

"That tears it," Honest Bob said. "He's done."

"Ya reckon?" Sully said sarcastically, because he was that kind of hombre. Never an encouraging word.

Fred Sullivan was his real name. Sullen Fred Sullivan, they called him. Sully.

Fitch stood still, motionless, a line of gun smoke curling from the barrel of the gun in his fist. He shook his head as if trying to clear it.

He turned, facing the rest of the gang. The gun turned with him, pointing at the outlaws but not at anyone in particular. Those in his line of fire were careful to keep their hands away from their guns and avoid making sudden moves. Or any moves at all.

"You all seed it. Lank went for his gun first . . ."

"We saw it, Fitch. Now put down the gun before anybody else gets hurt," Honest Bob said.

Drunk though he was, Fitch couldn't help but see the humor in the sweet talk. He giggled. "Hurt? Hell, he's daid!"

"Easy does it," said a voice behind Fitch. "You don't

want to kill nobody else. You don't want to get killed yourself."

It was the voice of Sefton, standing with a gun to Fitch's head. Fitch's eyes widened when he felt the muzzle of the gun against the back of his skull.

"Nothing personal, Fitch, but I surely will blow your head clean off if you don't drop that gun. And I mean right now," Sefton said calmly. He could afford to be calm—he had the drop on Fitch.

Fitch swallowed hard, letting the gun slip from his fingers. It fell into the soft sandy soil without going off.

Sefton swung the gun barrel hard against Fitch's head. It hit with a *thunk*.

Fitch staggered, going wobbly in the knees. He stayed on his feet, though. Sefton hit him harder, frowning. Fitch went down. Sefton's frown smoothed out.

Bending down, Sefton picked up Fitch's gun. "He did enough damage with this already. Too much."

"Hang on to that gun. Fitch is gonna want it later," Honest Bob cautioned.

"So what? Who gives a damn what he wants?"

"We're gonna need every gun we've got when the Comanches show. Drunk or sober, Fitch can shoot."

"He sure proved that!" Half-Shot said.

"We'd be in a fine fix if them savages showed now," Honest Bob added. "They'd sure 'nuff catch us with our pants down!"

That struck home with the others, because it was true. They looked around, scanning for Comanches, finding none. But that didn't mean they weren't somewhere near, hiding.

A couple outlaws stood over Lank, eyeing him. Honest Bob went down on one knee beside the body for a closer look.

"Dead?" somebody asked casually.

"Dead as they come," Honest Bob said.

A harsh metallic smell of fresh-spilled blood came off the corpse. The bullet holes in Lank's chest were closely spaced together.

"Nice target grouping," Honest Bob murmured admiringly.

"I said that boy could shoot!" Half-Shot cackled.

"Yeah, if he gets any better, we won't have any men left," Sully said sourly.

"Can't say I cared too much for Lank. He was always trying to get at a fellow, like a burr under the saddle." Half-Shot said.

"Him and you both," Hump Colway cracked.

Half-Shot gave him a dirty look, but Hump ignored it.

"Lank won't play no more of his sly tricks," Half-Shot mused.

"He tried them on the wrong man this time, that's for sure," Hump agreed.

Honest Bob rose, brushing dust off the knees of his pants. "Got to get that body out of sight. Can't let the Comanches see that. Dead white man's liable to give them ideas."

"They don't need to see Lank for that. They already got plenty of ideas on that score," Sully said.

"Some of you men get some shovels and bury him," Honest Bob ordered. He was the leader of the gang, at least out on the plains where the day's mission was concerned.

Hump Colway drifted away, making himself scarce, a habit of his when hard work was involved.

Honest Bob's beady-eyed gaze fell on Half-Shot and Sully. Although there were plenty of men in the gang, they were the nearest to hand. And their gun-handling skills were only fair to middling compared to some of the others, an important consideration.

"Get to it, you two," Honest Bob snapped. "Don't plant him near the water or the horses."

Half-Shot and Sully stayed in place, not moving.

"What's the problem? You deaf or something?" Honest Bob demanded.

Half-Shot held his hat in his hands, turning it around by the brim, fidgeting. "It's too damn hot for any grave digging," he said at last. Sully nodded in sullen agreement.

Honest Bob thought it over and decided not to push it. There'd already been one senseless killing. "What do you suggest?" he asked, throwing it back to them, trying in vain to keep the harshness out of his voice.

"Dump him behind some rocks out of sight," Sully said.

Half-Shot looked like he was thinking it over. "That'll do for a start, but pile some rocks on top of him so wild animals can't get at him."

"Want to hold services over him, too?"

"Hell, Sully, that's the least we can do. After all, Lank was one of us."

"Didn't you just get done saying you didn't like him?"

"Haul him out of sight and pile some rocks on him," Honest Bob said. "Get two more men to help you out. Tell them I said so."

That seemed reasonable. Half-Shot and Sully dragooned two of the gang's smaller fry, lesser even than they, into helping. Each took hold of a limb by ankle or wrist, lifted Lank off the ground, and lugged him a stone's throw away, behind some boulders.

There was no shortage of boulders at the secret meeting place under the cliffs on the Texas plains. Numerous rockfalls and landslides had peeled off from the scarp. The burial detail picked up rocks from the ground, covering up Lank.

Fitch lay sprawled flat on the ground, stunned, groaning. Honest Bob and Sefton carried him to the wagon and rolled him under it, out of the sun. Half-Shot joined them. They stood for a moment looking down at Fitch, who lay twitching and breathing heavily through his mouth.

They turned, looking east across the wide open plains. Sefton pushed back his hat brim, wiping the sweat from his forehead on his shirtsleeve.

"What was that you was saying before about trust, Bob?" Half-Shot asked slyly, starting up. He was a needler. He liked to pick at people if he thought he could get away with it. He was not unlike Lank on that score.

"Something about trust and gunrunning, I do believe?" he pressed.

Honest Bob cut him a sharp side glance but then condescended to reply. "I was about to make some remarks on that subject, now that you mention it."

"Looks like your proposition got shot down along with Lank."

"How so?"

"Lord knows Lank wasn't the easiest person in the world to get along with, but he and Fitch seemed to get on all right. Yet Fitch burned him down quick as winking!"

Sefton spat. "What choice did he have? Lank was reaching. What the hell!"

Half-Shot flinched, fearing he might have irked Sefton. He wasn't one you wanted to rile. He was moody, unpredictable. He stalked off, to Half-Shot's evident relief.

Honest Bob caught the play, chuckling. The other's momentary fright put him in a good mood. "Fitch gunning Lank proves my point."

"Which is?" Half-Shot asked.

"Trust *is* the basis of the gunrunner's trade."

"You're loco, Bob," Sully said, walking up. "What a damn fool thing to say!"

"What's got you in an uproar, Sull?" Honest Bob asked mildly. "It sure ain't Lank getting killed. You never had any use for him."

"Lank was an idjit, pulling a damn-fool stunt like that on Fitch. But at least Fitch had a skinful of hooch," Sully said, spitting out words like a snapping turtle going after live bait. "What's your excuse?"

Greatly amused, Honest Bob gave Half-Shot a wink that only he could see.

"Trust?" Sully said. "*Trust*? Maybe you forget who we're dealing with!"

"I ain't forgetting nothing, Sull."

"Comanches, that's who! Them red devils would cut all our throats given half a chance, and you talk about *trust*!" Sully went on, warming to his theme. "Never mind about them heathens, though. Take a look closer to home. Look at Fitch killing Lank over a bottle of rotgut whiskey . . . and not even a full bottle, neither! Trust? Hell, we don't even trust each other!"

"Speak for yourself. Personally, I trust all the boys. Trust them with my life. Otherwise, I wouldn't be here now." Honest Bob smiled.

"Sometimes you talk like a politician," Sully sneered.

"There's no call for that kind of abuse," Honest Bob said sharply.

"That was out of line, I admit," Sully said, backing down.

"See that it don't happen again."

"Sorry."

Two more of the gang, Melbourne and Chait, drifted over to see what all the jawing was about, as did Santa Fe Comancheros Felipe Mercurio and his pistolero bodyguard Rio.

Honest Bob was mindful that he was drawing an

audience and began playing to them. "You know what your trouble is, Sully?"

"I'm sure you're gonna to tell me, Bob."

"You're a man of little faith. Me, I trust the Comanches!"

That provoked a lot of loud protests from the others, dirty laughs, groans, eye-rolling expressions of disgust.

Honest Bob held up his hands to quell the noise. "Let me explain, let me explain. You'll all admit that the Comanche wants guns. That's plain to see. We wouldn't be here if it wasn't true. Them red rascals want guns and ammunition. Want them bad. And that's good, by Heaven, because we've got them!"

"Damn straight," somebody shouted.

"I'm talking about the real goods here, the quality. We ain't foisting no castoffs on our Indian friends—no rusty out-of-date smoothbore muskets, no pieces with broke firing pins, jammed actions, and bent barrels. No, sir." Honest Bob went on. "We got new guns . . . and like-new guns," he conceded. "Like new I said. Barely used, in good condition. We got long guns and carbines, famous name brands like Winchester, Sharps, and Henry! Repeaters! Repeating rifles! We've got them.

"Why, most of the cavalry out West ain't even outfitted with repeating rifles yet! Mostly, they've got outdated single-shot jobs."

"They got repeaters at Fort Pardee," Chait said pointedly.

"Sure, and look at all the trouble they had getting them," Honest Bob countered. "Their first shipment was hijacked out from under their noses before they ever took delivery. They had a devil of a time getting them back."*

"They got 'em now," Chait pressed, his buddy Melbourne at his side, urging him on. They were a pair of professional guns, gunslicks hired for the protection their skills could bring.

They weren't beholden to Honest Bob or any of his Hog Ranch crowd. Like the man said, they didn't give a damn whether school kept or not, and they didn't care who knew it.

"Look at all the trouble they have holding onto them! Troopers are always deserting, going over the hill with a repeater and a good horse," Honest Bob said. "But never mind about them Fort Pardee blue bellies nohow. They're at less than half-strength and stretched mighty thin, too.

"From what I've heard tell, they ain't gonna be a problem for much longer," he added darkly in an aside. Those who knew what he meant didn't react to it.

"Here's my point. When it comes to guns, Mr. Comanche can't get a better gun nowhere," Honest Bob went on quickly.

He noticed Mercurio standing nearby, listening intently. "Now before I go on, let's give credit where credit is due. Fact is, we wouldn't have these fine guns if not for Señor Mercurio here and our good friends in Santa Fe."

---

*See *Savage Texas*.

Mercurio was a stocky middle-aged man with thick black hair and a bushy mustache. He was a member of the Santa Fe Ring, longest established and most powerful Comancheros in the territory. He nodded, acknowledging the other's words.

"To continue," Honest Bob said, "here's a question. What do Comanches like more than guns?"

The outlaws shouted various answers.

"Horses!"

"Horse stealing!"

"Women!"

"White women!"

"No, no, amigos," Rio said, standing at Mercurio's elbow. He was Mexican American, one of a group of Hispanics associated with the Hog Ranch gang. Rio was a dangerous man. "What does the Comanche love best of all? *Killing*."

"That's it! Killing is what those heathens love best!" Sully cried. "They'd like nothing better than to take our scalps."

"If they could," Melbourne said meaningfully, patting his holstered gun to show what he meant. He fancied himself quite the gunman.

Honest Bob nodded agreement. "That's it! Eagle Feather and his bucks would like nothing better than roasting any and all of us over a slow fire. Sure, they'd kill us if they could, but not before putting us through an almighty hard time first. Never mind that that would kill off the best source of guns they've got or will ever have.

"Or take our late friend Lank. Now you just don't go stealing a man's redeye. Everybody knows that. It ain't done. But Lank couldn't help himself. He just naturally liked getting folks riled up. That was his nature.

"That's the bedrock truth of my calculations. *People are gonna do anything you can't stop them from doing.* I trust in that and act accordingly. I trust the Comanches to kill us if we don't outgun them and outsmart them

"That's why I say trust is the basis of our business," Honest Bob concluded.

"I don't know about that, Bob, but there is one thing that you've proved beyond a shadow of a doubt."

"What's that, Half-Shot?"

"That you sure 'nuff like the sound of your own voice!"

Half-Shot's crack got a laugh from some of the men.

"Of that there can be no doubt," Honest Bob said, laughing along with the others to show that he was a good sport. He wasn't, not really. But he could fake it when he had to. It was all part of being a leader of men, he told himself

The group started to break up into smaller knots, going about their chores.

"Keep your eyes open and your guns handy, boys. Eagle Feather will be along directly," was Honest Bob's parting comment.

Sully didn't much care for company, not even his own. Still, he wanted to be off by himself. Not too far off, though. It wasn't safe. Comanches were beyond masters at taking stragglers and making them disappear.

Sully's path took him past a freight wagon nestled at the foot of a cliff. It was the wagon under which Fitch lay in a moaning stupor.

The gun wagon.

Guns and ammunition were in wooden crates in the hopper. The wagon team had been unyoked and corralled with the rest of the horses to prevent the Comanches from stampeding a harnessed team and running away with the wagon and its precious cargo of firearms.

Ricketts sat up on the front box seat, pale-eyed and swarthy with bristly beard stubble like steel wool. He flicked the edge of a thumbnail against the phosphorus-coated tip of a wooden matchstick. A lucifer type incandescent match, self-igniting. The tip sputtered, hissing into flame.

Sully recoiled, thunderstruck. "The hell you doing, Ricketts?"

"What does it look like?" Ricketts asked mildly.

"Like you're fixing to get yourself blowed up and me along with you!"

Ricketts waved away his concern. "I'm lighting my cigar, Sully, ya danged fool." He spoke as if talking to a child, a slow child.

The hot plains air was very still in the lee of the cliff. Ricketts had no need to cup a hand around the flame to protect it. He held the fire to the tip of a fresh cigar clenched between his teeth and puffed away, setting the cigar alight.

"Don't you know not to play with matches around gunpowder?" Sully demanded. "You'll blast us all sky-high!"

"I know what I'm doing," Ricketts said chuckling. "That's why they got me playing nursemaid to this here gun wagon and its combustible insurance policy."

The "insurance" was a desperate last resort against Comanche treachery. In the wagon behind the seat stood a big keg of gunpowder lashed in place, a length of quick-burning fuse cord coiling out of a hole in the barrel lid.

Ricketts's job was to light the fuse to blow up the wagon and its contents if the Comanches tried a cross and jumped the gunrunners.

"Quit your fussing, Sully. Danged if I'm gonna lay off cigars just cause you're fussing like an old woman." Ricketts touched a fingertip to the match. It was cold. He broke the matchstick in two, tossing the fragments at Sully. Sully scuttled away, cursing.

Ricketts laughed. But he stopped laughing when he glimpsed a dust cloud in the east.

The site was on a flat. Ricketts was raised up higher than the others by virtue of being perched up on the wagon box seat. "Hey! Hey, you all. Looky there!" he shouted, rising up, pointing at the dust cloud in the distance. "It's *them*! Here they come!"

The outlaws turned to see what Ricketts was pointing at, studying on the dust cloud some miles away. It wasn't much. Just a thin brown smudge floating in the air a few degrees above the horizon. A dirty fingerprint on the rim of the upside-down, yellow-white bowl of sky.

The gunrunners were stung into action. They scrambled, grabbing up rifles and gathering closer together. There was a lot of peering, craning, and neck-stretching. A couple men climbed up on boulders to improve their vantage point.

They looked . . . and wondered.

"Is it them?"

"Don't look like much."

"Don't take much to kick up dust out there."

Honest Bob moved among them. "Look sharp, boys, and step lively. The scalp you save may be your own. Or even better, mine."

They were gunrunners and Comancheros—Honest Bob and Sully, Mercurio and Rio, Fitch, Hump, Half-Shot, and all the rest. They numbered a baker's dozen in all, unlucky thirteen, a gang of whites and Mexicans who sold guns and ammunition to the Comanches. A dangerous trade.

They were gathered in the barren wastelands of the North Central Texas plains on a hot afternoon in the fall of 1866 for a meeting with a Comanche raiding party.

The War Between the States had been over for a year and a half. Yet that titanic conflict between North and South was but a brief moment in time compared to the centuries-long struggle for the frontier.

The War for the West was an epic clash between

Indians and Caucasians for dominance of that part of the planet.

Paramount among all mounted Plains Indian tribes were the Comanches. They were Lords of the Great Plains, masters of a vast prairie expanse in the center of the American heartland bounded on the east by the Mississippi River and the west by the Rocky Mountains.

The Comanche broke the back of the Spaniards' northward thrust out of Mexico, limiting their Great Plains holdings to a few scattered fortress towns—Santa Fe, San Antonio, and a handful of others.

Next came the Anglos, English-speaking Texas settlers the Comanches called *Tejanos*. An irksome folk, they were numerous and land-hungry.

For long years, tribesmen kept the Texans bottled up east of the ninety-eighth meridian, a longitudinal line running north-south through such settlements as Dallas and San Antonio. They tormented the Tejanos with relentless raids of rape, robbery, torture, and murder. The ninety-eighth parallel marked the limiting line of westward American expansionism.

Yet the Texans were stubborn. Worse from the Comanche point of view, the Texans were adaptable. Slowly but surely, they learned the ways of making war on horseback, Indian style. The frontier conflict, always fought with bitterness and cruelty on both sides, was fast becoming a war of extermination.

Then came secession and the war between the Union and the Confederacy. Frontier expansion was halted for the duration. The whites were so busy trying to kill each other that their war against the Indians was neglected.

The War was finally over and American westward migration was once more in full flood, greater than ever. Comanches once more felt the pressure as hordes of returning whites nibbled locust-like westward, crowding past the ninety-eighth parallel to the hundredth parallel.

Longitude 100 degrees west now marked the frontier. It was the dividing line between civilization and wilderness.

Part of the line ran north-south through Hangtree County, Texas.

The gunrunners' meeting place was some fifty miles west of the line, where the bounds of Hangtree County blurred with the beginnings of the Llano Estacado. The Llano, "Staked Plains" to the Spaniards, was a vast wilderness misnamed by some early American mapmaker as "The Great American Desert."

It wasn't, not really. Subsequent events would soon prove the contrary. But its endless expanse of emptiness sprawling under the big sky tended to have an unnerving effect on travelers. There was a sense that here was the rim of the abyss, the edge of darkness.

The Llano was prairie flatland, hundreds of square miles in area. It had water and grass enough to support the buffalo in all their teeming masses. In time, it would prove equally capable of supporting great cattle herds and then the great land rush would be on.

But not yet. Not while the Comanche still held sway over the region.

The meeting place was set at Bison Creek under Boneyard Bench.

The Llano, though flat, was not without distinctive landforms—cuts, rises, folds, rock spurs, outcroppings, ridges, hills, and more.

The Bench was a limestone plateau rising out of the flat, a shelf-like scarp whose eastern edge featured a sharp twenty-five-foot drop. Its eastern face of cliffs ran north-south for dozens of miles.

A solid, impenetrable wall, there were no gaps and passes. Riders went around it. On a horse, there was no way to climb the cliffs. They formed a giant wall or bench set amid the flat.

Gravity is a useful thing. The Comanche set it to work by stampeding buffalo herds eastward across the plateau and over the edge, causing them to fall to their deaths. Descending to the flat, the braves would harvest the carcasses.

Long years of such practices had littered the foot of the cliffs with the skeletal remains of hundreds, if not thousands, of buffalo. Heaps and mounds of clean-picked bones glared whitely under the midday sun where the gunrunners waited.

Thus the name given to the site by whites—Boneyard Bench.

Cracks in the cliffs held springs, which issued streams of water. Buffalo routinely drank their fill during wanderings.

The largest such watercourse was Bison Creek. It was

an ideal spot for those wishing to conduct their business far from prying eyes. It was well-watered. Sheer, unscalable cliffs shielded against attack from the west. Rockslides, boulders, and fans provided plenty of cover.

The gunrunners were massed in a shallow basin at the foot of the cliffs south of Bison Creek.

A cleft in the cliffs served as a makeshift corral, its open end roped off. Guards were posted to keep watch over it.

Comanches were passionate horse thieves. If they could steal the gunrunners' horses, they would, and damn the consequences!

The unhorsed gun wagon stood in the center of the basin. Men were grouped around it in a half-circle facing east, the cliffs protecting its rear from the west. The gang was well-armed with repeating long guns and six-guns.

The Comanches appeared not in the east where the dust cloud had first been sighted but in the south near the cliffs.

"Looky there!" Half-Shot cried, indicating a second dust cloud to the south. It showed near the cliffs several miles away, much closer than the dust to the east.

The south cloud moved north toward them while the east cloud stayed where it was. Strong sunlight streamed down from overhead, gilding the southern dust plume. At its base rode a knot of mounted men, ten in number. They came on at a steady walk.

"That's them all right," Melbourne said. "Dirty stinking redskins!"

"They're not so bad," Hump Colway said.

"The hell you say!"

"Not as bad as some white folks. At least they don't try to rub my hump for luck."

"Is that lucky?" Chait asked, genuinely curious.

"Not for them," the hunchback said. "The last few who tried, I shot them to pieces. Lucky for me, though," he added. "Must be."

"How do you figure?"

"I'm still here," Hump said.

"Is that so great?" Melbourne said, snickering.

"To me it is. Beats being dead," the hunchback said.

The Comanche riders narrowed the distance, closing on Bison Creek hollow.

"Huh! They don't look like much," Sully said, disdainful.

"Reckon you don't look like much to them," Hump said. "You don't look like much to me."

Sully knew better than to mess with Hump and kept his mouth shut. He was worried about the Comanches, not Hump's slighting remark.

The Comanche riders were short stocky men riding small scruffy horses. But they were killers, horseback warriors. The horses were Indian ponies born of a long line of wild mustangs with endurance far beyond their more domesticated cousins.

The braves were Quesada, most aloof of all Comanche tribes, making made their home deep in the Llano. They generally shunned not only whites and their works but their fellow red men as well. Their standoffishness served them well, protecting them from catching the whites' diseases such as smallpox.

Somewhere in the Llano's trackless wastes lay their homeland, its whereabouts unknown to whites. It was hidden somewhere in the expanse but where, no living white man could say.

The brave at the point sported a lone feather rising vertically from the back of his head, held in place by a headband. He was Eagle Feather, leader of the band. He raised a hand, signaling a halt. The Comanches reined in, watchful and waiting.

Honest Bob motioned for them to advance and they rode in.

The braves showed wide faces, high cheekbones, dark watchful eyes. Thick, greasy, shoulder-length black hair was worn loose or in braids. Most of them wore white men's shirts—plaid or patterned, open and unbuttoned—and knee-high moccasin boots. Some wore breeches, others loincloths.

A few bows and arrows, war hatchets, and a lance or two were seen among them, but were far outnumbered by firearms. Firearms were the weapon of choice. Some were armed with long guns, rifles, and carbines. A few had six-guns tucked into their belts.

The gunrunners were wary, restive.

"Easy, boys, easy," Honest Bob said. "This ain't the first time we've been to the fair. Don't get trigger-happy and we'll get through this fine just like we've done before." He readied himself to start forward. "Stand ready, Ricketts!" he called.

"I'm ready!" Ricketts sat perched on the wagon's box seat puffing a cigar. His hand was closed around a line of fuse cord, its end curling out the top of his fist.

Honest Bob gave him a two-fingered half-salute. He turned, facing the Comanches. "Sefton, you come with me. I'm gonna meet Eagle Feather halfway."

"All right, Bob." Sefton was a fast draw and a cool-nerved customer.

"You men cover us," Honest Bob told some of the others.

"Right!"

Honest Bob and Sefton started forward. Honest Bob was empty-handed, carrying no rifle. He wore twinned belt guns and could get at them fast if he had to.

Sefton held a rifle cradled against his chest, muzzle pointed skyward. He could get it into action quick enough. That went double for the six-gun holstered at his side. Others were faster—Melbourne and Chait, for sure—but Sefton had better judgment.

The Comanches sat their horses, watching the duo approach. The braves were motionless, stock-still. Mask-like faces were cut deep with hard lines. They were stoics with good poker faces.

Their horses were well-trained, but the nearness of Bison Creek water made them restless. Their long faces and snouts were powdered with dust. No doubt they'd been ridden a long way between waterings.

Honest Bob halted a few man-lengths from the Co-manches, Sefton stopping alongside him. Honest Bob held up his right hand palm out in the I-come-in-peace gesture. "Howdy, Eagle Feather!"

Eagle Feather nodded, some of his men grunting as if to themselves, the lines in their faces deepening into scowls.

That was all right with Honest Bob. He didn't give a damn if they liked him or not. Not that there was much chance of them liking any white man unless he was on the business end of a scalping knife. But they liked the guns he sold well enough, and that was what counted.

"You got guns, Honest Bob?" Eagle Feather asked. He always called the gun dealer by his full moniker of "Honest Bob," whether in mockery or not was known only to himself. Comanches held little faith in the honesty of whites, period.

"Got gold?" Honest Bob countered.

"Ugh." Eagle Feather nodded. *Yes.*

"You can see the wagon for yourself. We're ready for business, so let's get to it." Honest Bob indicated the dust cloud in the east. "Your friends out there can come in, too. We're not afraid. We'll give them a warm welcome."

"You trade horses for guns?" Eagle Feather asked, thrusting his hatchet-faced head forward. "They good horses. Fast, strong."

Honest Bob shook his head no. "You know my policy, Eagle Feather. I only trade for gold or cash money. Gold, silver, or jewelry."

"Eagle Feather know. We catch plenty horses, by damn! Good horses!"

Stolen horses, Honest Bob knew. Presumably the

eastern dust cloud was made by them and the braves tending them. Maybe. Or maybe it was the rest of a war party standing by waiting for the signal to attack.

"Eagle Feather tell braves stand off. Honest Bob no want horses," the Comanche said, indicating the eastern dust cloud.

"That's the way of it," Honest Bob said.

"When you go, we water horses here at Bison Creek, yes."

"When we go, you can do what you damn well please for all I care."

"No want horses, good horses?" Eagle Feather pressed.

"No stolen horses, thanks," Honest Bob said, shaking his head. "I don't want to hang."

"You look good that way, by damn!" Eagle Feather's eyes gleamed and the corners of his wide mouth quirked upward in grim amusement. A rare show of emotion for him.

"You'd like to see me hang, wouldn't you, Eagle Feather," Honest Bob said. It was not a question.

"Eagle Feather want see all gunrunners hang,"

"Then who'd sell you guns?"

"Always greedy white men sell Comanches guns."

"Not good guns like I got."

"Mebbe so, Honest Bob. Mebbe so. Eagle Feather want all Comancheros hang. You cheats."

"That ain't so, Eagle Feather. You know that. I never cheated you."

"You cheat but not so bad as other white men," Eagle Feather grudgingly allowed.

"The truth of it is, you'd like to see all white folks hang," Honest Bob said, grinning.

"Mebbe so, mebbe so."

"Well, let's get to business." Honest Bob turned and walked away, Sefton following.

The Comanches came afterward, walking their horses at a slow pace.

CHAPTER TWO

"The gang's all here," Sam Heller said to himself. "Gunrunners, Comanches—and me. The uninvited guest." He was in a covert, a kind of shooting blind. A sharpshooter's nest.

It was in a cleft at the top of the rock walls of the eastern face of the bench overlooking Bison Creek. A V-shaped crack dropped vertically from the edge of the cliff. It was six feet wide and ten feet long, tapering downward.

It was five feet wide up on the cliff top, forming a kind of cup-shaped hollow or basin. The cup was roomy enough for Sam to curl inside. Its floor consisted of loose rocks and dirt, which filled the cleft from its base to cup. Scrub brush, weeds, and vines grew from the surface of the dirt at the top of the cup.

The cliff top rim was thick with brush. Shrubs and bushes covered Sam, screening him from view of any of those below who might casually glance upward at the scarp.

Excerpt from REBEL YELL 377

It was a tight fit in the sharpshooter's nest, sharing it as he did with his rifle and supplies. Sam lay on his side in the nest, legs together and bent at the knees. He propped himself up on an elbow.

He was a big man, six foot four, 210 pounds, full-grown, and in the prime of life. He wanted to stay that way, a condition that would require some deft maneuvering and more than a little bit of luck in the next twenty-four hours or so. He had yellow hair and a same-colored beard, looking like a blond Viking. He hailed from Minnesota but had spent most of his youth in the West. A committed Unionist, he had fought for the North throughout the war.

Sam wore a dark, battered slouch hat, buckskin vest, brown denims, and moccasin boots. The boots were knee-high and worn under the denims. Beside him in the nest was a knapsack and canteen.

He was armed with a Winchester rifle, a .36 Navy Colt worn on his left hip in a cross-belly draw, and a bowie-style Green River knife sheathed on his right side. Twin bandoliers crossed chest and shoulders, their loops holding rifle cartridges.

The rifle was one of the new Winchester 1866 models, Sam's piece having been one of the first to come off the production line. It was one of the most effective and up-to-date weapons on the frontier—in the world, for that matter.

A keen-eyed viewer would have noticed that the rifle displayed several unique modifications. Special socket rings and fittings showed at the front stock and butt. Sam had chopped the rifle, sawing off most of the barrel and butt stock to create a mule's leg, as sawed-off repeating rifles were popularly called. It was generally worn in a custom-made holster on Sam's right hip, though not at the moment.

Sam was a born outdoorsman, and his trade required him to spend a good amount of time on narrow streets and in crowded saloons, gambling dens, meeting halls, cafés, and such in frontier towns and settlements. Easier to sport a mule's leg in those places than tote a long rifle.

It could be put into action quicker, too, a vital attribute in deadly encounters where a matter of split seconds might spell the difference between life and death. He could unlimber the mule's-leg faster than most triggermen could shuck a handgun from a holster.

There were times, though, when a man preferred to work at a distance rather than up close. For such times, a long gun was necessary.

Thus the special fittings on the mule's leg, allowing different-length barrels to be attached to the muzzle, with similar arrangements at the rear allowing for the add-on of wooden stocks in place of the standard curved pistol-grip handle. The piece had all the modifications as Sam lay curved in the hollow, awaiting the moment of truth.

He'd waited a long time, weeks of solitary prowls through plains, badlands, and back trails, searching for signs that would lead to his quarry. He was a special agent with a presidential warrant. His mission was to break up the gangs supplying weapons to the Comanches of the Texas frontier.

The hundredth meridian *was* the Texas frontier, so Sam had set up his base of operations in the town of Hangtree in Hangtree County. What began as a mission had become a quest. He'd seen what the Comanches could do when it came to turning the frontier into a living hell.

There were many Comancheros of the rank-and-file variety, foot soldiers of the gunrunners' trade, who dealt directly with the Indians. They were renegades, enemies of humanity, and Sam killed them when he could.

But they weren't his real target. He was after the big fish, not the small fry. He wanted the ones at the top of the pyramid, the ringleaders, the organizers who supplied the contraband in bulk.

A long dark trail had led him to Bison Creek under Boneyard Bench. Honest Bob Longford and the rest of the bunch were far from unknown to Sam Heller. He'd long been aware they were Comancheros, part of the Hog Ranch outfit.

The Hog Ranch was a low dive, a deadfall that lay near Fort Pardee. It was a thieves' den, a magnet for saddle tramps, drifters, and outlaws. It featured cheap whiskey, saloon girls, and gambling. It was a great favorite with the cavalry troopers of the fort, despite having been posted off-limits by their commanding officer.

Sam had had his eye on the Hog Ranch for some time, but it was only in the last few weeks that his suspicions had taken shape regarding the expedition to the Llano. He had trailed the gunrunners to Bison Creek, always keeping out of sight.

Under Boneyard Bench, Honest Bob's bunch had tied in with the next rung of the ladder, Felipe Mercurio, who would lead to the Comanchero bigs. With his sidemen, he had supplied Honest Bob with a wagonload of weapons. Mercurio was the Santa Fe Ring's man. The Ring were known Comancheros, biggest in the territory.

Mercurio's presence was the first link to directly tie the Ring to gunrunning on the Llano. He and his men had met Honest Bob and company at the creek the previous day at dusk, delivering the wagon full of guns. They'd stayed the night, sitting around the campfire with the Hog Ranch crew, eating and drinking while Sam made cheerless camp hidden on the cliff top above.

He guessed they were sticking close to the site until the Comanches took possession of the weapons. Maybe Mercurio wanted to make sure the transaction was completed in full and Honest Bob didn't make off with some of the guns to resell them on his own. Mercurio might also be dogging Honest Bob for his share of the proceeds.

Whatever the reason, Sam meant to find out. He was no lawman, though he could have been called a law enforcer in the loosest sense of the term. He was a man on a mission, authorized by the highest law in the land, the President of the United States.

He was not bound by the rules of evidence and legal protocol. He didn't have to prove a case against his quarry in court or even bring them back alive. In fact, it was often preferable to leave as many dead as a warning to others.

He was a troubleshooter, and it was his job to shoot trouble

It had been a long hard hunt. As he watched the negotiations below him, he thought back to the past few days.

Alone, he had dogged Honest Bob's crew from the Hog Ranch to the Llano, trailing them just at the edge of vision, following them into the badlands. Their southwesterly course took them toward Boneyard Bench.

Sam knew the way. In the months since first arriving in Hangtree County, he'd ridden trail in the territory, crisscrossing it a number of times. He wished to live, so he'd learned where the water was. The twenty-five miles of the bench's eastern front was the source of three different dependable watercourses. Bison Creek was the most abundant of the three.

Sam guessed the gunrunners would make for it. Breaking off direct pursuit, he detoured northwest, taking a course that would bring him to the north end of the bench. He knew there was no way through the scarp, only around it. He rounded the gentle slope where the north edge of the bench joined the flat and rode up on top of the plateau, heading south.

The landscape was all earth tones—a dust-muted blur of grays, yellows, and browns—speckled here and there with patches of dark green. On the plains, the winds blew mostly from the west, sometimes from the north. They could whip up a hellbender of a gale, but the air was hot and still, though from time to time, a welcome breath of a breeze lifted. It barely stirred up a scrum of dust, whipping it a few inches above the ground for several dozen yards, only to let it fall, exhausted.

The plateau summit was flat tableland that came to an abrupt end in the east. Sam was careful to ride far enough into the interior to avoid skylining in the east and being spotted by anyone in the Boneyard. In the other three directions it showed empty plains as far as the eye could see. If Comanche raiders spied him, he would be in a tight spot. There was nowhere to hide, not when once seen.

What seemed unyielding monotony of landscape proved to present a variety of terrain. Seemingly featureless plains were broken by rises and dips, rocks, trees, and brush.

The prairie unrolled as Sam rode south. If he'd guessed wrong, if Honest Bob had altered his southwesterly course toward the bench for points unknown, Sam would have lost him. It was highly unlikely that he could pick up the gunrunners' trail again.

But if he was right, if Honest Bob planned to set up shop somewhere in the Boneyard, the detour could save Sam many hours of hard riding. The Boneyard offered water and cover, things generally unavailable farther out on the plains.

High overhead, black V shapes circled. Vultures searching for carrion.

Several hours later, a ring of green brush took shape in the distance. It bordered a shallow basin about eight feet wide and three feet deep. A waterhole. A small spring lay beneath the basin, filling it with several inches of muddy brown water.

Sam halted, stepping down from the saddle. Small game trails arrowed in and out of the basin rim, indicating that local wildlife drank from the spring.

Good. That means the water isn't poisoned, he thought. Sometimes waterholes were contaminated by trace elements of corrosive minerals.

Sam cupped a hand, scooping out some water and tasting it. It was not warm but hot from the sun, brackish and muddy. It tasted good to him, whose water supply was so tightly rationed.

He filled his canteens, then let Dusty, his horse, drink. The animal was a gray Steel Dust, part mustang, short and scrappy. After watering the horse, Sam let it browse on the greenery ringing the waterhole, then he saddled up and moved on, reaching what he judged to be the midpoint of the plateau. Ahead lay a small cone-shaped hill, looking like an overgrown ant mound. A stand of thin straggly trees grew at its base. The cone was a landmark, a signpost pointing to Bison Creek below.

Sam halted at the mound about a hundred yards away from the cliff edge. He stepped down and tied the horse's reins to a tree branch.

Tree? Little more than scrub brush, really, but no less welcome for all of that. A man without a horse on the plains was for all intents and purposes a dead man. That's why horse theft was a capital crime on the frontier. Stealing a man's horse was pretty much the same as condemning him to death. The frontier was no country for a man afoot.

Dusty began nibbling on the green leaves. He wasn't the type of horse who ran away. He'd stay in place when his reins were free with their ends dangling on the ground. But Sam wasn't a man to leave things to chance. No telling when the unexpected would rear its ugly head and let chaos loose.

Sam heard noise—voices, shouts, horses neighing, movement. The sounds made his skin tingle, quivering like a struck drumhead.

He prowled the edge of the cliff, screened by thick bushes. The rim was not a straight line, solid and unbroken, but was saw-toothed with seams and fissures. One in particular looked promising, a V-shaped vertical cut topped by a dirt-filled hollow cup.

Nearing the edge, Sam ducked down and lay flat on the ground. He crawled to the cliff's edge, staying low. He parted the brush, looking down.

Rock walls dropped straight down to the flat twenty-five feet below.

Yes, gunrunners were making camp at Bison Creek.

A cut in the cliff wall below had been pressed into service as a makeshift corral. Sticks and branches were used for a palisade type fence and gate. A thin trickling vein of Bison Creek ran through it. There was green grass for grazing. Two guards were posted outside the gate, armed with repeating rifles.

There was not much work to be done by the gun-runners. Their tasks were finished and they busied themselves with eating, drinking, smoking, and loafing.

Sometimes a trick of the air currents brought a taste of tobacco smoke to Sam's nostrils. He thought of his own tobacco pouch and sighed. No smoking now, not for him. He couldn't risk having the smoke seen by the foe.

He sternly put the thought of it out of his mind, but the craving kept sneaking back.

He had a hat to keep the sun off his bare head, a canteen full of water, and beef jerky to chew. Nothing for him to do but watch and wait.

Late afternoon shadows were falling and the sun was lowering in the west when the next round of newcomers arrived.

Felipe Mercurio and the Comancheros rode in with the gun wagon. Two men sat up front on the box seat. Five men rode escort alongside. Honest Bob's bunch acted glad to see them.

Sam knew the man in the passenger seat beside the wagon driver. Mercurio was a well-known figure along the owlhoot trail on both sides of the Rio Grande. A killer, slaver, dealer in contraband, he was henchman to Quatro Matanzas, driving wheel of the Santa Fe Ring.

That was a surprise. Sam hadn't known the Ring reached so far east.

While Mercurio and Honest Bob conferred, the

newcomers squared away their mounts in the corral. The gun wagon was placed at the foot of the cliff. Half-Shot showed the new arrivals to the cooking pots so they could chow down and drink up, not necessarily in that order.

Sam's empty stomach rumbled. No hot meal for him. He dared not risk lighting a fire. He used his blade to cut off a chunk of beef jerky, jammed it between his jaws, and went to work on it. Strong white teeth slowly ground it to pulp. It had to be chewed slowly if he wanted to keep those teeth intact and unbroken. He washed it down with sips of muddy water from his canteen.

One of many such cheerless meals he'd had on the trail, but that was how he managed to stay alive.

The sun set, a cool breeze whipping a snaky line of dust eastward. Venus twinkled low in the west, stars brightening in a blackening sky.

Sam rose, shaking out the kinks of knotted muscles from his long vigil. He went to his horse, stroking its muzzle. He took some dried parched corn from his saddlebag and munched it, washing it down with several mouthfuls of water. He made camp nearby, a simple camp with no fire. He spread his bedroll on the ground and used his saddle for a pillow. He lay on his back and went to sleep with the Navy Colt in his hand under the blanket.

Sam awoke sometime during the night. He sat up, blankets falling around his waist, Navy Colt held steady in his hand. What woke him? Natural body rhythms or something afoot in the night? He looked around, eyes accustomed to the dark. Dusty stirred nearby, aware he was up.

A half moon hung in the sky. Fitful night breezes rose out of the west and northwest. Somewhere out on the plateau a coyote howled, a lonesome sound that never failed to send a chill along Sam's spine.

It sent the same reaction, but for different reasons. Was it a coyote? Or a Comanche imitating a coyote, signaling to his fellows, maybe giving the signal to move in for the final assault?

The night cries were not repeated. Sam sank back down, pulling the blankets up, and went back to sleep, gun in hand.

When he woke again, the sky was lightening in the east. He stretched, then got up. "Going to be a big day!"

It was a cold cheerless breakfast he fixed for himself. No coffee. A fire was needed to make coffee. He consoled himself with a slug of whiskey gulped from a pocket flask he carried.

"For medicinal purposes only," he told himself. It was no time to go on a tear, but a drink wouldn't do him any harm. Might do a bit of good.

He took a generous swallow of the stuff, a line of fire plunging down his throat, blossoming into welcome heat in his belly. Welcome recompense for his dog's breakfast of pemmican and parched corn washed down with tepid murky water.

Another belt of the whizz would sure go down good,

but he capped the flask and put it away. Only half-joking, he said, "Satan, get thee gone . . ."

It was light enough for him to get about his business, so he picked his way along the cliff rim, returning to the spot he had chosen for his sharpshooter's nest. The brush screened him from those on the flat below. Through spaces in the foliage, he could spy on the gun-runners' camp without being seen.

Sam set to work shaping up his shooting platform and readying his weapon. It was a good feeling, knowing the showdown was nigh.

He'd been on the trail for days . . . weeks. Weeks of burning days and chilly nights. Even the steadiest nerves became taut and worn from relentless stress.

However long the wait, he could stand it, especially with the end in sight. The nearness of his quarry was a tonic.

It was more than a bit provocative, that nearness. He had to fight the urge to start lining up the gunrunners in his sights and opening up on them, burning them down. He was seized with an almost overwhelming desire to get an early start on the cleanup but fought it down.

The long day wore on. Sam told himself he should have known that the Comanches would wait till the last before showing.

They did it deliberately, of course. It was a stalling tactic designed to prey on the nerves of the gunrunners, wearing them down. Comanches were always looking to maximize their advantage at the expense of their foes—

or friends; the role could change in a moment according to want and whim. If they saw an edge they'd take it; if not, they'd make it.

Sam readied. "The gang's all here," he muttered again.

CHAPTER THREE

Tension was thick among the gunrunners. They lacked the Comanches' mask of stolid indifference and were no good at hiding their emotions. Inside their heads, fear and anxiety warred with greed.

It wasn't that the Comanches didn't give a damn whether they lived or died. They did. In a shooting scrape, they were careful not to risk themselves pointlessly. They were known for breaking off attacks they thought they couldn't win, showing that they valued their lives no less than the whites.

The numbers between the two groups seemed about even, with the gunrunners having a slight advantage.

That was not so good for the whites perhaps, since each Comanche warrior reckoned himself to be the match of two or three *taibohs*—whites. It was how the Comanches saw themselves.

Was it true? That remained to be seen. But that

confidence bordering on arrogance might give them an edge.

Grouped in a loose semicircle whose ends were anchored to the cliffs, the gunrunners had their backs to the rock walls and stood between the Comanches, the corralled horses, and the gun wagon. The outlaws' postures were stiff with tension, most of them sharp, angular. A few affected nonchalance and might even have meant it. But in the main, no matter how calm and uncaring a man looked on the outside, it was hard to remain cool and unruffled in the presence of hostiles whose fondest wish was to hang them head down over a small fire . . . just for starters.

The gunrunners were heavily armed. Rifles were held pointed down or away from the braves. Not too far away, though.

Sam recognized the band's Quesada markings. They knew something of him, too, or would have had they known of his shadowy presence, for the Comanches well knew of the one they called *El Solitario*, the lone rider with the long gun who dogged their war parties, killing them from a distance.

El Solitario who rides alone. The Man with the Devil Gun.

Comanche braves were born hunters, successful predators in a hard and unforgiving environment. It was rare that the hunter became the hunted, rarer still when the hunted were the Comanches themselves. But in recent moons, their bravest and boldest had fallen victim to the Taiboh with the long gun.

Whoever he was, El Solitario threw a wide loop, roaming most of Comancheria deep into the panhandle country between the Arkansas and Red rivers. He prowled west into New Mexico, south to the Rio Grande, even venturing into the remote vastness of the western Llano wilderness they proudly claimed for their own.

As they saw it, the phantom killer struck without warning, not for gain or plunder, which they could understand, but simply for the killing. They could understand that, for they often fought merely for prestige and glory, but it was not a trait they generally attributed to white men. El Solitario opened fire on warriors in camp or on the trail day and night, and when he struck, bodies piled up.

More than one campfire conclave had concluded in blood and slaughter as the unseen rifleman lurked in the darkness beyond the flickering circle of firelight. But of the nearness of Man With the Devil Gun lurking on the cliff top above, Quesada braves and outlaw gunrunners alike were blissfully unaware.

Wiry and long-limbed, Eagle Feather was at the fore leading his braves to the gun wagon. He was sided by henchman Han-Tay, his second in command. Han-Tay was deeper in the chest, thicker in the arms. The notorious Maldito rode abreast of but apart from the other two in the leading wave.

"Maldito? That little fellow?" Gunslick Melbourne scoffed. "He ain't big enough to carry that name considering all I've heard about him. What a killer he's s'posed to be—"

"He lives up to his rep," Hump Colway said curtly.

Maldito was short even for a Comanche, almost dwarfish, being some inches short of five feet tall. His upper body development was powerful, impressive.

"Look at the size of them arms, them hands," Half-Shot marveled. "Strangler's hands if ever I seen them. He gets them hands on you, he could tear your head off without half-trying!"

"Well he ain't gonna get a hand on me. I'll shoot him first," Melbourne said. "Now what do you think of that?"

Maldito's head was wider than it was long. A triangle of muscle descended from ears to his shoulders, making it look like he had no neck. His eyes seemed on the verge of popping from their sockets. They were the fierce rolling eyes of a wild horse. The rest of his visage was stony, blank-faced.

The band of braves were loosely bunched together, except for a rider or two bringing up the rear. Among them was Barbero, the scalp hunter. The reins of his horse were decorated with scalps of all types and colors.

"Looky there! One of them scalps come off a yellow-headed woman," Half-Shot husked breathlessly.

"A couple look like they come off kids. They're smaller," Sully said.

"Seeing that makes my blood boil," Melbourne

muttered. "It ain't right. He's flaunting it. Might as well be waving it in our faces!"

"That's why he does it," Hump said matter-of-factly.

Chait's elbow nudged Melbourne in the ribs. "Careful you don't get yourself a halo to go along with that sermon you're preaching, Mel."

"How do you mean?" Melbourne asked.

"Way you're carrying on, you'd think you're in the wrong line of work." Chait said. "What do you think the Comanches are doing with those guns Honest Bob sells them?"

"I dunno. I never gave it much thought before now," Melbourne said.

"Well, don't. Let it go, Mel. Let it go. This is just another job for us, a job of work. It don't bear too much thinking," Chait said.

"That's right. We came here to trade, not to fight," Sully agreed.

"Who asked you?" Chait said, turning on him.

Sully shut up.

More Comanches neared the gun wagon, gathering around. Dog Fat, an oily fellow with a big belly, brutish Spotted Calf, and lofty Tizane, almost a head taller than his fellows, Thieving Crow, Wolf Track, and others.

Shepherding the gun wagon as the Comanches grouped around it, Ricketts puffed away at his cigar. His closed fist was sweaty where he gripped the fuse cord attached to the gunpowder bomb.

"You know you can trust me, Eagle Feather," Honest Bob said with bluff heartiness, beginning his pitch.

"You no trust Comanche. You trust Dynamite Man," Eagle Feather said, indicating Ricketts perched on the gun wagon.

Unhappy at being singled out by Eagle Feather, Ricketts started, the cigar almost falling from his mouth. The result was to make him look even more guilty and self-conscious.

Honest Bob smiled, unabashed. "That's for safety's sake, Eagle Feather. Yours and mine. Any hothead tries to steal the guns gets them blown up in his face. A simple precaution, that's all."

In the blind above, Sam heard it all. "Ol' Bob's got the soul of a natural-born horse trader," he whispered.

Eagle Feather spat to show what he thought of Honest Bob's line of reasoning. He turned toward Ricketts. "You, Dynamite Man! Blow up wagon, you blow up, too!" Eagle Feather paused to let it sink in. "How you like that, eh? Damn you!"

Ricketts was dumbfounded, at a loss for words.

"He likes it fine," Honest Bob said airily, doing the talking. "He knows that everything's gonna go fine today with no trouble at all."

"You lie. Him scared," Eagle Feather insisted.

"Ricketts just ain't used to meeting a famous war chief of the Comanches like you, Eagle Feather. He's overcome by your greatness."

"You think you pretty damned smart, Honest Bob!"

"I can't deny it. But now to business."

"Honest Bob—businessman."

"That's me, Eagle Feather."

"Do not brag of it. All businessman liars," Eagle Feather said.

Such testing and taunting on the part of Comanche clients was nothing new or unexpected to Honest Bob. It came with the territory. It happened each and every time. They'd come on a lot more threatening and frightening than Eagle Feather. He just kept his eye on the main chance, pushing the deal through. That's why he was still alive, as well as being one of the best in his line.

"You bad friend," Eagle Feather said, going off on another tack. "We ride long, far. We Comanches thirsty, but you give us nothing to drink."

"Why, there's plenty of water all around!" Honest Bob said, pretending to misunderstand. "The creek's over there. Help yourself!"

"Water, *phaugh*!" Eagle Feather's expression of disgust was a cross between a choking cough and a throat-clearing. "Honest Bob funny man," he said, unamused. "Eagle Feather want whiskey—whiskey! What you drink!"

"No firewater here, Chief. No redeye hooch or whiskey. It's for your own good, for my good, for the good of us all. I ain't like them other fellows, crooks I call them, who pose as a friend of the Comanche. Honest Bob is a *real* friend. I don't get you all liquored up drunk with bad whiskey so's I can cheat you. You keep a clear head, you know what you're buying."

Some gunrunners did give the braves liquor to sweeten them up, Honest Bob knew. There was a word for such traders—*dead*. When a Comanche got liquored up, he went crazy drunk, indulging every mad murderous whim or notion he got in his head. Once he got a skinful of redeye, there was no stopping him . . . short of killing him.

"Remember, you know what you're buying from Honest Bob," he reminded Eagle Feather.

"You cheap crook and bad friend. That's why you no give whiskey to Eagle Feather."

"Wasn't there something about guns, Eagle Feather?" Honest Bob prompted, trying to get the deal back on track. "You want guns, don't you? That's why you're here. You want guns and Honest Bob's got them. Good guns!"

"Show me," Eagle Feather said, arrogant and demanding—his usual mode of address to white and red men alike.

"Show me the gold," Honest Bob said.

Eagle Feather nodded to Han-Tay. The warrior untied a pouch hanging from his neck by a rawhide thong. He gave the pouch to Eagle Feather, who opened it, pouring some of its contents into an open palm.

Fragments of yellow metal glinted in the blue-shadowed gloom below the cliffs. The glint of gold was sharp and bright even to Sam up in his perch on the cliff top.

The take represented a heap of scavenging. Mexican and American gold coins, gold pocket watches, wedding bands, chains, lockets, and bracelets—all of them gold. There were even a few raw golden nuggets in the mix.

Gold was in short supply for the vast majority of settlers and emigrants on the frontier. Most of those who actually had gold stayed the hell off the frontier. Sam wondered, *How many wagon trains were waylaid, stagecoaches robbed and plundered, and ranches and farms raided and pillaged to collect the take?*

Honest Bob breathed hard, his heartbeat quickening. His face lit up at the sight, underlit by golden highlights reflected off the handful of loot. "I think we can do business," he allowed, sounding out of breath.

"Gold—white man's firewater," Eagle Feather said, sneering. "You loco for yellow stone."

For once Honest Bob had no reply. He turned to face the outlaw gang. "Bring the crate with the star on the lid!"

The starred crate stood at the rear of the wagon's flatbed hopper, edging the extended tailgate. It looked the same as the others except for a palm-sized red star hand-painted on the upper right corner of the lid.

Fitch had his gun back but was still in the doghouse for killing Lank. He had a hangdog look. He was still pretty well hungover. He kept his head down, walked soft, and did what he was told without complaint. He and Sully hauled the crate across the wagon tailgate, wrestling with it.

"It's heavy!" Sully hissed through gritted teeth.

"Help 'em out, Half-Shot," Hump Colway said.

"Why me? Why do I have to do it?"

"Because I said so and I'm ramrodding this chore."

Half-Shot pitched in, joining the other two. Huffing and puffing, the three of them managed to manhandle the crate off the wagon and across the ground to Honest

Bob and Eagle Feather. The haulers set the crate down on the ground with a crash.

"Open it," Honest Bob said.

Hump handed Fitch a crowbar, and he went to work, wedging the prying end of the bar between the lid and the top of the crate. Squeals and screeches sounded as he levered up the cover and nails gave way.

The lid splintered, cracked, and broke. Fitch pried the pieces loose. Inside the crate were new guns—rifles.

Eagle Feather was no fool. Before he was done, he'd have every crate opened to ensure that they held the guns and ammunition he wanted and weren't filled with rocks. But the first crate had his full attention.

His mask of aloof indifference slipped. The unveiling of the armaments interested him intensely and he showed it. He crowded in, looming over the crate. Han-Tay stood close beside him. Wild-eyed and stony-faced, Maldito moved in alongside them for a better look.

More braves gathered round, dark eyes glittering in leathery faces.

Honest Bob pulled a rifle out of the crate, holding it in his arms, cradling it. "Winchester Model 1866, just like the pony soldiers have at Fort Pardee. My gift to the mighty war chief Eagle Feather!" He handed the rifle to Eagle Feather, who snatched it up greedily in both hands.

"The redskin's sure loving that piece," Melbourne snickered, low-voiced.

"He looks about as happy as he's ever gonna be," Chait agreed.

Eagle Feather frowned fiercely, a study in furious concentration as he hefted the rifle, weighing it first in one hand, then the other, then with both hands. Lovingly he ran caressing fingers along the machined cold metal barrel and the fine-grained wooden stock.

A thoughtful look flickered across his face as he worked the lever, then turned the rifle so that it was leveled on Honest Bob.

"It's not loaded," the gunrunner said.

Eagle Feather bared stained yellow teeth in a snarl. He shouldered the rifle, pointing it at a distant vulture flying high overhead. A metallic click sounded as he pulled the trigger and the hammer came down on an empty chamber. "Empty gun no good," he said, scowling. "Maybe shoot straight, maybe not. Who knows?"

Honest Bob was ready for that one. He handed Eagle Feather one bullet. Just one.

"Bob's taking a long chance," Half-Shot said, worried.

"Not so long," Hump Colway said. "If Eagle Feather cuts up, he'll be cut down fast. Look at Melbourne and Chait itching to throw down on him."

"Fat lot of good that'll do Bob."

"Bigger shares for the rest of us."

"Always looking on the bright side, ain't you? Shares depend on who's left standing, Hump."

"I'll be there," the hunchback said. "Hell, the Comanches ain't so dumb as to start a fight they can't win. They like living just like we do.

"But if something jumps off, don't forget to duck."

"Thanks. That's a big help," Half-Shot said. "But a shoot-out's like a prairie fire. Once it gets started, it eats up everything fast."

Eagle Feather fed the long bullet into the breech and changed his grip on the rifle.

A shot sounded.

Honest Bob lurched as if hit by a hammer. He was violently thrown down to the ground. He lay there inert, unmoving, showing not so much as a twitch of motion.

A breathless pause hung shimmering in the air as everyone held their breath, not knowing what would happen next, yet knowing the inevitable consequences of the fatal shot.

No one looked more surprised than Eagle Feather, who stood stupidly staring at the rifle, turning it over in his hands. He hadn't fired it. It hadn't shot, but a man was dead.

"You killed him," Sefton said to Eagle Feather, drawing his gun.

Again, a shot sounded.

It tagged Eagle Feather with a *thwack*. Like a wooden mallet slamming into a side of beef. He crumpled in the middle and went down.

Blood splattered on Han-Tay and Maldito, who were standing on either side of Eagle Feather, striking their faces and necks with stinging force, speckling them with ruby-red dots like scarlet teardrops.

It was Sefton's turn to look surprised. The gun in his hand was leveled and pointing at Eagle Feather, and yet he knew he hadn't fired it. No gunpowder smell, no smoke was curling from the barrel.

Both shots had come from Sam Heller's Winchester 66. His move put a thumb on the scales and tipped the balance back to hate—hate and fear. He paused to watch the party start. He did not have long to wait.

Sefton's gun had cleared the holster when the second shot struck, making it look like he'd shot the Comanche war chief. Maldito was the first to react, stepping inside Sefton's guard and clamping one hand down on the wrist of the outlaw's gun hand. His grip of iron immobilized Sefton's arm, numbing it where those thick strangler's fingers clutched it.

Maldito's free hand pulled a knife from a belt sheath at his hip. He thrust the blade deep in Sefton's belly, ripping it open, disemboweling him.

Maldito jumped back to get out of the way as gray loops of viscera spilled from Sefton's split belly.

The fight was on!

That's all the belligerents knew. For critical instants, both sides had been taken aback, neither side believing that the other would make a dumb play so disastrous, so fatal to the hopes and lives of all.

So of course it happened, or so they understood it.

After the heart-stopping pause, they got to it with no holds barred.

Fitch drew and shot two braves standing opposite him on the other side of the crate. Dog Fat was next in line but proved slippery and elusive as his namesake. He threw himself to the side, ducking behind a rock. He dove, came up rolling, and ran to his horse, jumping up on its back.

Fitch ran after him, chasing and shooting. Dog Fat kept zigging when Fitch thought he was going to zag, causing Fitch to keep missing. He pegged another round, missing the Indian but creasing the horse's rump. With a shriek, it upreared on its hind legs.

Dog Fat grabbed his rifle from where it was tied to the saddle, taking it with him as he fell off the horse. He lay prone on the ground, shooting at Fitch, whose gun was empty. He hit Fitch in the middle, mortally wounding him.

Fitch staggered but kept on going, mechanically working the trigger of his empty gun.

Dog Fat shot again and Fitch fell down.

On hands and knees, the brave started to get up, but his fear-crazed horse stepped on him, trampling him under. Dog Fat screamed, trying to get out from under flailing razor-edged hooves.

Frightened all the more, the horse began dancing on him, pounding him flat. Finally breaking loose, it ran away. Dog Fat lay in place, writhing like a half-squashed bug.

Still standing by the crate, Maldito was next on Sam's list. He was a bad one. Sam knew his history, knew the world would be well improved by his removal from it. But Sefton, though dead, was blocking Sam's clear shot on the dwarfish brave.

Sam shifted gears, swinging the rifle in line with another target—one of the outlaws guarding the corral. Sam's shot slammed him to the ground.

Thinking his partner had been downed by Comanches, the other guard cut loose at the nearest knot of braves, levering his rifle as he pumped lead. Shrieks rang out as braves went down.

Similar scenes were being enacted all over the place. Comanches and gun sellers were blasting at each other. Blood, noise, and death were everywhere.

Horses in the corral panicked. They crowded near the gate, pressing against it, shying, sidling, and shouldering. The gate flew open, slamming back against the fence, tearing loose from the rope hinges. The animals bolted from the corral, fanning out, racing for open spaces. Woe to anyone luckless enough to be in their way!

They ran down white and red men alike, plowing them under. Trampling was not necessarily fatal but it didn't help. When the last horse had escaped the mangled victims were in pretty bad shape. They wouldn't be getting up in a hurry.

The fugitive horses kicked up a lot of dust, further obscuring the scene.

Ricketts's jaw had dropped in open-mouthed astonishment when the shooting started, causing the lit cigar to fall. It dropped into the trough of the boot beneath the box seat. He ducked down and fumbled for the cigar, dropping it several times before getting a good grip on it.

He had a mission to carry out—blow up the wagon if the Comanches tried to take it. Well, if they didn't take it, it wouldn't be for lack of trying. They were sure enough on the warpath.

With trembling hands, Ricketts pressed the lit end of the cigar to the tip of the fuse, whose curling cordlike length terminated in a wooden keg filled with black gunpowder. The fuse sputtered into life, burning like a Fourth of July sparkler.

A bullet tore into his upper body, knocking him off balance. It threw him for a loop, and he let go of the fuse. A canny Comanche had shot him to forestall lighting the fuse, but he was too late. The fuse was lit and burning.

Ricketts pitched forward and to the side, falling in front of the wagon. He rose to his knees. A shot drilled him through the chest. He went down again, not getting up.

A Comanche brave rushed the wagon, knife in hand, intending to cut the fuse before it touched off the gunpowder. He clambered up the front seat of the wagon just in time to catch a bullet from Chait's gun. He pitched backward into the dirt.

The sputtering fuse burned lower, way low. Maldito started toward the wagon but shifted course fast when he saw the brave who was climbing the wagon get cut down. He flung himself to one side, saving himself from the bullet Sam pegged at him. Sam wanted Maldito dead and that gunpowder bomb blowing the gun wagon to kingdom come.

Maldito scrambled behind some rocks, crawling on hands and knees, too low for Sam to hit.

Sam breathed a silent curse. *Maldito is lucky, damn him!*

He stayed out of Sam's line of fire, preventing Sam from taking him down with a follow-up shot.

A couple of braves leveled rifles to cut loose on Melbourne and Chait. Rifles traded fire with six-guns. Chait dodged for cover, catching a bullet for his trouble. Melbourne swung his gun around to cover Chait. A Comanche rifle tagged him, spilling him into the dust.

Grounded, they were prime targets for Comanche bullets, which riddled them. They writhed and spasmed as each fresh slug ripped them, but soon they lay still and unresponsive. They were dead.

Sam had fewer opportunities for clear shots, but he managed to pick off one or two shapes amid the dust and smoke. Comanches and gunrunners were doing a pretty good job of picking each other off without his help.

Bison Creek was aswirl with gun smoke and dust. Men became dim outlined forms, stumbling and staggering. Gunfire lanced the murk with bright red and yellow lines seeking targets. Outcries sounded when a shot speared a man.

Time had run out on the fast-burning fuse. Its last fractional length sparked and sizzled its way into the big keg of black powder. There was a chuffing sound, like the heavy outrush of breath of some great beast, as the gunpowder ignited. Detonating.

The wagon and its contents vanished in a flash of light. A glare bright as the sun filled the space where the wagon had been. The explosion was a vortex of blazing forces—heat, light, and noise.

Sam ducked down, curling up in the hollow of the shooter's nest. He flattened himself as best he could, keeping his head down, clutching his rifle, and hugging it to him.

The ground shook. A brief thought flashed through him. It would be a hell of a note if the blast tore loose the rim of the cliff top where he was perched, sending him crashing down amid tons of rubble to add his remains to the boneyard.

A pillar of smoke and fire thrust skyward from the flat below. A vortex sucked up wreckage, hurling it aloft. The blast was followed by a rain of debris.

Sam was temporarily deafened by the explosion. The earth had been hammered like a gong, making his ears ring. Sam was in none too much of a hurry to stick his head up, not with all the debris pelting down. Some of it was big enough to knock a man's brains out. The cliff top was peppered with the stuff.

The downfall lessened, playing out. Sam uncurled himself, sitting up. His body ached from head to toe, the result of the concussive blast. He felt beat up, like he'd been hammered with iron fists and feet.

Beaten up? A thought struck him, making him grin. "Think this is bad? You should see the other fellow!"

Things had worked out better than he'd expected thanks to the keg of black powder Honest Bob had rigged as a last-ditch defense against being plundered by Comanches. It might not have made a clean sweep below, but Sam reckoned there wouldn't be many survivors.

Standing up on shaky legs, he brushed himself off.

Finding out if dirt had gotten into the rifle barrel and inner workings was a top priority. He didn't dare fire the rifle until he'd given it a clean bill of health. At least the cliff side hadn't come tumbling down, taking him with it. He grinned again. *A lucky break!*

Sam peered through the brush at the flat below. There wasn't much to see—dirty air, dirty sky, all paled by dust and smoke, like a low-level sandstorm. Yellow-brown billows slowly rolled across the plains, stately as sailing ships. Strands of black smoke coiled serpent-like through earthbound yellow-brown clouds.

Sounds? All he could hear mostly was the ringing in his ears.

He didn't want to break cover yet in case there were any survivors below to see him. That wouldn't fit in with his long-range plans.

Let gunrunners and Comanches alike think that the other side had betrayed them. Let the word go out to the bucket-of-blood saloons and deadfall dives, up into Comancheria, and south down the Comanche Trail deep into Mexico. Rumors of treachery would sow suspicion, causing discord and mistrust between gunrunners and Comanches and poisoning relations between the two.

Time passed. Dust settled though the yellow-brown haze that remained, deepened by long shadows of gathering dusk.

Bison Creek looked like it was, a battlefield. Bodies of men and horses littered the flat. The gun wagon was gone, pulverized. A wide shallow crater still smoldered, marking where the wagon had stood. The crater walls were streaked by veins and rays of dark brown earth heaved up to the surface. A heavy gunpowder smell hung over all.

Stray horses that had fled the corral roamed the prairie. Of the two-legged survivors of the battle and blast, there were only a few. A handful of riders raced south. Another small group hurried north. Neither bunch had the heart to keep fighting. They were getting out while they could.

Easy enough to figure what had happened. The Comanches who'd come out alive were the ones riding south, while the last gunrunners ran north.

The ordinarily horse-mad Comanches must've been pretty hard hit to pass up the chance to round up some of the many strays roaming the range. If they wanted to return to the Quesada homeland in the Llano, they'd have to get clear of the cliffs before striking west.

Sam had a pretty good idea where the gunrunners were bound. Their goal most likely was home base at the Hog Ranch near Fort Pardee. There they could lick their wounds while working up fresh new devilments.

Something must be done about the Hog Ranch soon, Sam resolved. *Something massive.* He grinned, satisfied. "Still, in all, a good day's work!"